SAVING SOPHIE

SAM CARRINGTON

avon

AVON

A division of HarperCollins*Publishers*
1 London Bridge Street,
London SE1 9GF

www.harpercollins.co.uk

A Paperback Original 2016
1

Copyright © Sam Carrington 2016

Sam Carrington asserts the moral right to
be identified as the author of this work

A catalogue record for this book is
available from the British Library

ISBN 978-0-00-824422-4

Set in Minion by Palimpsest Book Production Limited,
Falkirk, Stirlingshire

Printed and bound in the United States of America

Find out more about HarperCollins and the environment at
www.harpercollins.co.uk/green

SAVING SOPHIE

Sam Carrington lives in Devon with her husband and three children. She worked for the NHS for fifteen years, during which time she qualified as a nurse. Following the completion of a psychology degree she went to work for the prison service as an Offending Behaviour Programme Facilitator. Her experiences within this field inspired her writing. She left the service to spend time with her family and to follow her dream of being a novelist. *Saving Sophie* is her debut psychological thriller novel.

Readers can find out more at http://www.samcarrington.blogspot.co.uk and follow Sam on Twitter @sam_carrington1

In memory of my dad, Norman, and my mum, Mary.
Missed every day.

Prologue

Saturday

'Shh . . . Don't speak.' He releases the strap of the rubber ball gag with his left hand. His right grips a chunk of long, curly hair. Pulling it, twisting it, so she can't move her head. So tight, she can't move away from him. So tight, strands of black hair extensions break and tear from her real hair, tiny popping noises oddly loud in her ear.

The gag makes a soft thud on the concrete floor, an innocent sound, incongruent with the function it has just served.

'Stay quiet now. Still. It'll be over soon.'

He pushes his head up against her temple, hard. The slick tackiness of his sweat covers her forehead as he presses against her, rubbing his head from side to side. The putrid odour invades her nostrils. She tries not to breathe. Fear takes over; a whimper escapes from her dry mouth.

'No. No noise. *I told you.*' His voice is raspy, menacing.

Her eyes are wide and swollen, wet with fresh tears – her face stained with old ones. She opens her mouth, just a little, daring to utter the words screaming inside her head: *Please don't kill me.* He notices the slight movement of her lips and immediately presses his fingers against them, suppressing the words before they can be formed. Only her breath manages to leak through the gaps of his soft fingers; a stifled exhalation.

Her last.

CHAPTER ONE

Karen

The dog's barking alerted her to the late-night visitors before the doorbell sounded.

Muffled voices drifted in as Mike opened the front door. Then another voice boomed out. Karen jumped up from the sofa, grabbed the dog and ran out into the hallway. She wasn't expecting the sight that greeted her.

Wedged between two police officers was a bedraggled mess of a girl.

Sophie.

'What's happened?' She rushed forward, dropping Bailey to the floor. The barking turned to growling; she ignored it, her attention fully on her daughter. Tears had left tracks down her over-made-up face, her lipstick had bled and feathered, spreading red beyond her mouth.

'She's not in any trouble, we had a duty of care to bring her home.' Talking continued, but now in full panic mode, Karen switched off. *What on earth has happened to her?*

Sophie suddenly looked younger than her seventeen years; her little girl, barely able to stand, leaning against the porch wall as she attempted to move her mouth and produce coherent words. She failed.

Karen heard snippets of what the officers were saying as she fussed over Sophie – '. . . found wandering on her own along the main road in town . . .' She dabbed at Sophie's damp face with the cuff of her sleeve, '. . . all dressed in black . . . not safe . . .' She took Sophie by the arms and looked into her black, wide-pupilled eyes. *How much has she drunk?*

The three of them remained standing in the porch, the door flung open – the police officers, tall, official, on the threshold. The neighbours' curtains twitched. With shaking hands, Karen attempted to steady Sophie, whose black patent high heels slipped on the tiled floor. She didn't look at Mike, only vaguely aware of him thanking the officers.

'Why were you on your own?' Karen shouted. 'Have they left you again?' She didn't care about the police officers, the neighbours, or Mike's warning words coming at her from her left; they were a blur.

Sophie stared blankly ahead, her eyes unfamiliar. The bright blue, lively eyes Karen knew so well were dark; void of emotion. Empty of anything. But a mother could see the scared young girl behind them.

This wasn't the fallout of too much alcohol.

With the police officers gone, shocked voices erupted in the privacy of the living room.

'What do you think you were doing, Sophie?' Mike shouted, inches from her pale face. 'You stink of alcohol.' He recoiled.

'I don't know what she was doing . . .' Sophie looked up, her eyes fighting to focus.

'What who was doing, love?' Karen crouched beside Sophie, her words calmer now, softer than those spewing from Mike's mouth.

'I don't know who she is.' Her speech clumsy; the syllables tripping from her lips didn't appear to be linked with the form her mouth was taking. 'How do I know why Amy wanted to be Amy?'

'Have you taken something, Sophie?' Mike moved forwards again, grabbing her by the arm, forcing her into a sitting position on the sagging, cream sofa.

'No. No . . .'

'Mike! She's too drunk to know what you're even saying.' Karen searched his face for that hint of a memory, knowing they had both, in their time, been in a similar state. All teenagers got drunk, didn't they?

'So that makes it all right, does it? Karen – look at her. It's ten thirty, she's only been out of the house since six.' He stood and paced the room. Then he slumped on the two-seater sofa opposite, rubbing at his face, running both hands roughly through his greying hair. 'Anything could've happened to you, *anything*. Do you understand, Sophie?' His words spat out, his face contorted – an ugly expression, one Karen had observed before.

The laughter came out in short bursts. Unnatural. Not Sophie's light, contagious laugh: this one sinister, unnerving.

'You think this is funny?' Mike got to his feet, launching towards Sophie – half sitting, half hunching, her head lolled, practically on her chest, as if it were too heavy to keep upright. Perched on the edge of the sofa, it would only take one more forward motion and she'd be on the floor.

'Please.' Karen thrust the palm of her hand towards him. With her eyes narrowed, she willed him to leave the room; she wanted to deal with this in the way she thought best and his anger was a hindrance. She dragged her gaze from his. 'Sophie, love, were you with Amy?'

'What does it matter she wanted to be Amy?' More of the same spilled from her. It was pointless; getting any sense from her seemed unlikely.

Karen took deep breaths to try to control the anger germinating deep in her gut. Sophie's friends had clearly left her. It wasn't the first time either – only three months ago Mike had been dragged out of bed to pick Sophie up at midnight because she'd been stranded in Torquay with no money when her so-called friends had gone off. The usual 'it's just teenagers these days' didn't wash, it was plain selfish – left it wide open for things like this to happen.

'I need the loo.' Sophie propelled herself forwards. 'I need a wee,' she drawled.

'I'll take you.' Karen supported her, one arm around her waist, the other outstretched to aid her own balance as they made their way towards the downstairs cloakroom. They looked like a pair of children tied together, about to take part in the three-legged race. Mike, red-faced, strode the length of the lounge and back.

Karen waited outside the door with her head leant against it. This was going to be a long night. She heard the flush, then a clatter inside.

'You all right, Sophie?'

More giggling, then Sophie emerged, half sliding, half falling through the door. Together they made their way back to the lounge. Back to Mike, still pacing big angry strides.

'I need to get her to bed.'

'You don't say.' He averted his eyes from them.

Karen manoeuvred Sophie to face the stairs.

'Can you get her a glass of water, please?'

Mike huffed, before disappearing into the kitchen. Karen took Sophie up the stairs, struggling to keep control of the rubbery body; the laughing-one-minute, crying-the-next girl who, only a few hours ago, had left the house looking smart and beautiful in her new black dress. Karen scrunched up her eyes. She couldn't cry now. Not yet. This wasn't her Sophie. Not the Sophie who looked after her friends: picked them up when they fell, let them cry on her shoulder, took them home if they were drunk.

Why had they left her in this state? Or had Sophie left them? And she'd been rattling on about Amy; she'd seemed distressed about her. Karen's chest tightened.

Where *was* Amy?

CHAPTER TWO

Karen sat with her knees up and her back against the soft velvet-covered headboard, tapping the screen of her phone.

'What are you doing?' Mike asked, walking around to his side of the bed.

'Texting Liz.'

'For God's sake, Karen, it's midnight. Leave it.' He sat on the edge of the bed, peeling off his trousers. Small change from his pockets scattered on the wooden floor, clinking and rolling everywhere. 'Darn it!'

'I need to know if Amy's home safe.' Karen spoke the words quietly, thinking if she said them softly, he'd understand her need for reassurance.

'Sophie's so pissed up she wouldn't have a clue who she'd been out with. Anyway, she obviously got separated from them and now they'll be in the club until three. *Do not* worry Liz about it. Just go to sleep.' He was tired. Irritable. Karen knew he hated it when she couldn't let things go.

'Yeah, right, like sleep is possible now. I think it's more than just alcohol.'

'Relax.' He bounced up and down, settling himself and yanked the duvet up over his shoulder. He turned away from her.

'Mike,' she pleaded, adamant that the conversation should continue despite his warning tone. She had things playing on her mind: disturbing things. 'Don't you think she looked like she'd taken drugs? Or that someone had drugged her? The way she was talking . . .'

'Are you for real?' Mike flung the duvet back off, exposing his muscled torso, and sat up, eyes glaring. 'Don't you think the police would've been a bit more concerned if they suspected something untoward had happened? Just because you used to work with a bunch of screwed-up criminals, it doesn't mean every time Sophie goes out she's going to be targeted by would-be rapists.'

Karen smarted. 'You were the one who shouted at Sophie, said *anything* could've happened – weren't they your words?'

He rubbed his palms aggressively up and down his face, groaning.

'I meant she could have been knocked over, ended up in a ditch somewhere, and yes, it did cross my mind someone could have taken advantage of her. But that clearly didn't happen. What you're saying is that someone purposely drugged her. I've no idea what goes through your head. Now please let me sleep, we'll talk to her in the morning. It'll all be some pathetic teenage drama, some stupid fall-out with Amy, that's all.' He returned to his position, facing the window with his back towards her.

A tear rolled down Karen's cheek and hit the duvet cover. She stared at the mascara-stained drop for a moment, then ran her fingertip over it, smudging it. How could he be so insensitive? His irritation had pushed aside all he knew about her, her own traumatic experience: the attack, two years ago almost to the day. Had he forgotten why she was this way? She looked down absently. The cover would need washing now. She lifted her head, staring for a while at the back of her husband of twenty-three years. Then she continued the text.

> Hi Liz, sorry to text this late, was wondering if you've heard from Amy? Sophie has been brought back by the police in a right state – I don't know why she wasn't with the others! I hope the rest of the girls have fared better. Text me when you get this please.

She put the phone on vibrate and placed it under her pillow. Snatching her sertraline tablets from the bedside table, she popped two in her mouth and swallowed without water, then went to check on Sophie.

CHAPTER THREE

Sunday

The chinking of plates and jingling of cutlery infiltrated Karen's sleep. What time was it? The Sunday bells rang out from the church in the distance, the deep clanging tones coming and going as the wind carried them. She used to find the sound relaxing, reassuring even. Lately, though, it had become an irritation, a reminder of how long she'd lived in Ambrook. Moving from town ten years ago to gain the solitude that the tiny Devon village offered had seemed a good idea at the time. They hadn't been able to afford any of the idyllic chocolate-box cottages, having to settle for the more modern, less striking semi-detached house instead. But the views of Dartmoor had made up for that. Now, even that didn't interest her. She'd left it too late to move again, though, her current circumstances wouldn't allow it.

Beside her, tiny tapping noises on the floor made her open her eyes. A heavy weight landed on her legs. Bailey scrambled to her face and planted his good morning kisses. She gave his belly a half-hearted rub. Then she bolted up to a sitting position. She turned to Mike's side of the bed. Empty. He was the one crashing about in the kitchen. A glance at the alarm clock told her it was 8.45 a.m. Why hadn't he got her up?

Pushing Bailey aside, Karen shoved her feet into her slippers, grabbed the dressing gown and walked along the landing. Pausing outside Sophie's door, she listened for signs of movement, straining to hear breathing. Please let her be breathing. Don't let her have choked to death on her own vomit. Karen laid a trembling hand on the door knob. She'd checked a couple of times during her own unsettled night, but it'd been over three hours since her last. She took a deep breath and opened the door.

On her tummy. Light-brown hair messily spread over the pillow and part-covering her face. In the exact position she'd left her. Karen could only hear her own breathing: rapid, shallow bursts of air. Why wasn't Sophie making a sound? She reached a hand out, hovered it for a while before allowing it to lie gently on her daughter's back. Warmth touched her fingers. Karen's shoulders relaxed. Thank goodness.

'Sophie,' she whispered. Then more strongly, 'Sophie.'

Sophie's body wriggled under Karen's hand, her eyes opened. Still dark, still unfocused.

'What's the matter?' She wiped the wetness from her mouth with one hand, then turned over and sat up.

'How are you feeling?'

'Okay,' she yawned. 'Tired.' Her brow knitted as she ran her hand along the side of the bed, up and down the mattress edge against the wall. 'Have you seen my phone?'

Karen had left it in the kitchen, thrown down on the worktop following several failed attempts to access any messages that might shed some light on the situation.

'Yeah, it's downstairs.'

'Oh.' Sophie looked perplexed. Her phone never left her side.

'How did you get home last night?' Karen thought she'd play it cool. She wanted to hear it from Sophie's mouth, wanted her to feel bad about causing so much distress.

12

'Uh . . . Taxi?' She swung her legs around and sat on the edge of the bed, her eyes scanning the room. 'Where's my handbag?'

'Sophie.' Karen's voice, harsher now. 'It's downstairs as well. Look, you didn't come home by taxi. Don't you remember how you got back?'

Sophie looked straight ahead, and said nothing for a long time.

'Must've got a lift, then,' she said finally, looking at Karen. Her face appeared neutral; no sign of guilt, no indication of a sudden recalled memory of the police car.

'Bloody hell, Sophie.' Karen crossed her arms firmly.

'What? I can't remember, that's all. I'm home safe, aren't I?' Sophie lay down again, pulling the duvet back over her. 'I'm tired, I need more sleep.'

'Tough.' Karen's face flushed. She'd been gentle enough, now Sophie's matter-of-fact attitude bristled her. 'I'll tell you how you got home, shall I?'

'Urgh. Please can you leave me alone? I'll talk to you later.'

Karen stripped the duvet from her. 'No, Sophie, we'll talk about it right now.'

'Fucking hell, Mum.'

'I can't believe you don't remember.' She lowered her face level with Sophie's. 'The police brought you home, Sophie. The police.' She glared at her, waiting for a response, waiting for 'I'm sorry, Mum'. But no. She gave nothing. 'Are you going to say anything? Your dad went mental, you know.'

The smile spreading across Sophie's face was like a smack in Karen's. How dare she smile. Was Mike right? Did she think this was funny?

'Okay, Mum. Enough. I get it. I shouldn't have had so much to drink, I obviously annoyed you and Dad by coming home late, probably woke you up. I'm sorry. Joke over. But it's not like you've never got drunk, is it? Now can you leave me alone to sleep it off?' Sophie widened her eyes at Karen, 'Oh, and don't give me the tilted head crap, you always do that when you think someone's lying . . .'

13

Karen jerked her head back upright. 'Are you serious? Enough? I haven't even started. It's not a joke. And trust me, we were *not* laughing last night. You didn't wake us up in the early hours. You were brought home at ten bloody thirty. How the hell could you have got into such a state so quickly?' Before Sophie could retort, she added, 'Maybe that's why my head's doing this crap.' Karen cocked her head again, accentuating the move. She stopped talking, waiting for an explanation.

Despite Karen's anger, the shock on Sophie's face set her back. She really *didn't* remember the police ride. A knot developed deep inside her stomach. She nudged Sophie across the bed so she could sit on the edge. She took Sophie's hand in hers.

'Why were you on your own? Where were your friends?'

'I . . . I'm not sure. I don't remember.'

'Try. Please. It's important.'

'Why?'

'You have to ask? You were found wandering around on your own, in a drunken state near the roundabout on the main road going out of town. Then, when they brought you back, you rattled on and on about Amy, talking utter rubbish – kept saying something about how you didn't know she wanted to be Amy . . .'

'That's odd,' Sophie lowered her head. 'I don't understand—'

'No. Neither do I. Why had you left your friends? Or had they left you, like usual?'

'Oh, don't start, Mum,' she withdrew her hand from Karen's. 'Let me think about this. I can't . . .' She rubbed her hands over her face. 'I'm too tired, I need to sleep.'

Karen sat a while longer, staring at Sophie. She'd had the feeling last night there was more to this than being drunk.

Now she was sure of it.

CHAPTER FOUR

'Has the drunken mess surfaced?' Mike raised his eyes fleetingly from his iPad as Karen entered the kitchen, returning them immediately to whatever was more interesting. On his days off, if he wasn't watching TV or in the office, he had his head buried in his beloved iPad. Karen wished she'd never bought it for him.

'I went in and woke her.' Karen passed by him to get to the kettle. She touched its side, then flicked the switch. 'You want a coffee?'

No answer.

'Mike,' she shouted, 'you want a coffee?'

'Uh, no. Not long had one.' He placed the iPad on the breakfast bar. 'What did she have to say for herself? Any explanations?'

'She can't remember any of it—'

'Oh, of course not,' he rolled his eyes. 'Should've known she'd deny all knowledge.'

'No, I don't think it's like that, she really didn't seem to remember.'

'Don't be so damned gullible.' He snorted – an annoying habit he'd developed when belittling what Karen said. 'She knew she'd be in trouble, so she's taking the easy way out with this "I can't remember" bull.' He waved his arm dramatically. 'It doesn't wash with me.' He got up, pushing the bar stool back. The screeching made Karen wince.

'What are you doing?'

'I'm going to find out what exactly went on last night.' He was already at the kitchen door.

'No, don't. She's not up to it, you'll get nothing from her.'

He swung around to face Karen. 'I'll do what I see fit. She was out of order. She needs to know the trouble she caused, and what she put you through.'

'She didn't really put—'

'Enough.' He scowled. 'Stop sticking up for her. She was in the wrong, she has to learn there are consequences.' He disappeared up the stairs.

Standing, stirring her coffee, Karen considered how this was going to play out. He'd have a go at Sophie, she'd throw a strop, Mike would then blame Karen for Sophie's reaction; her short-comings were always laid at Karen's door, and then he'd be unbearable for about a week before he finally realised he'd over-reacted and apologise. She sighed and took a sip of the coffee, hoping it might quell the growing nausea. Mug in hand, she crept to the bottom of the stairs. No shouting. She raised her eyebrows. Unusual. She stayed there for a while, listening intently. Only muted voices.

Sophie's door opened. Karen scuttled back to the kitchen, spilling hot liquid as she went. Damn. Hearing his footing on the stairs, she quickly seated herself at the breakfast bar. 'Well?' She looked to him as he walked in.

'You're right.'

Karen almost dropped her mug. 'What do you mean?'

'She really has no clue about last night, Karen.' He plonked heavily on the stool opposite her. 'Why? I don't understand how she could get ratted to the degree she has no memory of anything past seven o'clock. That's not good. Not good at all.' He rubbed his forefinger along his bottom lip.

Karen's hairs prickled on her arms. The niggling worry in her gut grew into an intense knot. She hadn't checked her phone. Had Liz texted her back? She got up and ran to the bedroom. Retrieving the phone, she stabbed at the screen to access her messages. Her heart jolted. Liz had replied a few hours ago. **Amy didn't come home last night. She isn't answering her mobile, does Sophie know where she is? Liz xx**

Running back downstairs, Karen burst into the kitchen and thrust the phone in front of Mike's face.

'I told you not to text her, Karen.'

'Really? You're going to have a go about that now? Have you read it? Shit. Sophie was going on about Amy last night, and now Amy is missing.'

'She's not really missing, *is* she?' His tone was sarcastic, one reserved for the innocent ignorance of a child. 'She probably just stayed at a friend's last night and is sleeping off a hangover. Like Sophie!'

It was a valid point. He was probably right. But why did she have a nervous feeling, a worming thread of fear branching throughout her belly? How could she tell Liz that Sophie had no memory of the night, and had no idea where Amy was?

She re-read the message and then replied.

CHAPTER FIVE

Sophie

Why couldn't she piece the night together? Sophie sat cross-legged in the middle of her bed, eyes shut tightly, willing the memories to come to her. Pre-drinks at Amy's – she remembered that. There'd been six of them, the usual girl group: her, Amy, Erin, Becks, Alice and Rosie. Then some of the boys joined them – Dan, Jack and Tom – about half an hour before they planned on going into town. They'd done the shots, encouraged the girls, too. Sophie had at least three, but that was after the wine. She hadn't finished the bottle though; she remembered the wine had tasted off. It was still a lot to consume in a few hours, she guessed. But she'd drunk far more in the past and had never forgotten an entire evening. Hazy, maybe – but not a complete blank.

Her head hurt. A piercing staccato pain right behind her eyes. She rubbed at them, hoping to relieve it. It didn't work. Covering her head with the duvet, she sank back into the pillow and let her eyelids fall. They felt so heavy. Ugh. Why did she drink those shots? They'd clearly pushed her over the edge.

The morning's conversation she'd had with her parents played over in her mind. How can you be brought home by the police and not have any recollection of it? It didn't make sense that she was found, on her own, near the roundabout. It was within

19

walking distance of the nightclub. Had she been there? They never went to the club much before midnight, though. Her dad was going to question her for days. How could she tell him what she didn't know? Her only hope was that her friends could fill the gaps.

Her phone. She was bound to have a million texts by now. Where was it again? Oh, no. Downstairs. She raised herself into a sitting position and in what seemed like slow motion – her brain strangely disjointed from her body – made her way through the house. She didn't particularly want to face her parents, but she could hear their voices in the kitchen, so if she wanted her phone, she'd have to. It wasn't like she could sneak in without being seen, not the way she was moving.

Her mum flew from her seat as she walked in. 'Amy didn't return home last night.'

Her dad sighed, his head lolled back.

'I'm just going to check to see what messages I have. I'm sure she probably stayed at someone else's.' Sophie swiped at the mobile screen.

'That's what I've been telling her,' her dad said, shaking his head.

Sophie's pulse increased as she scanned the dozens of messages. Tom had sent four. **Are you OK, babe? Where's you at? I'm worried, can't find you.** And the final one – **Amy said Erin called you a taxi and they bundled you in it to go home, haha! Seriously tho, hope your feeling ok.** She scrolled through some others to see if Erin had messaged. She hadn't. She'd probably turned her phone off due to all the group message notifications driving her mad. Sophie looked up; her mum and dad were staring at her, waiting for her to give them answers. What should she tell them? She'd been put in a taxi to go home? Then how come she had been found on the other side of Coleton, the opposite direction to home? Great. More interrogation. She took some deep breaths. Her head throbbed: the characteristic post-drinking dehydration pain twisting together with a growing anxiety. She gave herself a moment before speaking.

'Tom's messages say that Amy and Erin put me in a taxi to come home.' The urge to retreat to her bedroom was huge, but she couldn't avoid her mother's eyes. They seemed dull, almost black, and below them dark circles made her look ill, haunted. Frowning, deep wrinkles were appearing in her forehead. Her mother looked older today, drawn. Her usual bouncy, curly hair hung about her shoulders in lank, lifeless chunks. She guessed her mother's worse-than-usual appearance was her fault. She must've been up all night worrying.

'So, why didn't the taxi bring you home?' Her mum's voice was shaky.

'I don't know. I really don't remember anything about a taxi. Well, anything about anything actually.' Sophie put her head in her hands.

'What about Amy? Any texts from her?'

'Just the one,' she lied, 'similar to Tom's. Hoping I'm okay and she'd talk to me tomorrow.' Why had she said that? Stupid, but she really wanted them off her back.

'Text her now, Sophie. Liz is worried.'

'If she isn't returning Liz's texts she isn't likely to reply to mine. She'll be sleeping it off. I'm sure she'll contact her after lunch.'

'It's pointless,' her dad offered, 'you know what they're like after a night out drinking, Karen. And don't even get me started on the fact you shouldn't be drinking at all, Sophie.'

The jingling caused them all to jump.

'Who's that?' her mum asked.

'Give me a chance.' Sophie fumbled with the phone. She could feel expectant eyes on her. She took her time reading it, then looked up. 'It's Maxi, from Anderson's. She wasn't even with us. She's just checking if it's my work or college week.' She felt the weight of their disappointment. 'Sorry.'

21

The room was still, the gentle swishing of water hitting against the dishwasher door a rhythmic comfort. Sophie wanted to escape the kitchen to her room. She edged towards the door.

'Where are you going?'

'Back to bed, Mum. I'm knackered.'

'Really? When you don't even know where your friend is? Aren't you bothered? I think you should look on Facebook, see if she's posted anything—'

'NO. Listen, will you? She'll be at someone's house—'

'Not just to see where she is, I want to know what taxi firm Erin used, I want to know what time they *supposedly* put you in it.'

'What's that meant to mean – supposedly?'

'Well, I find it very odd that they *said* they put you in a taxi but it never brought you home. Either they are lying or something happened in the taxi. I want to know which it is.'

'Why would they lie? Honestly, Mum, you're so annoying.' Sophie turned and went out the door.

'Oh, I don't know,' her mum shouted after her, 'because they are rubbish friends and are covering their backs.' She followed Sophie, continuing her one-sided rant. 'They left you and now, rather than take any flak, they've put together some cock-and-bull story, knowing you were so out of it you'd believe whatever they said.'

Sophie carried on into her bedroom without replying. She slammed the door and collapsed on the bed. The room spun. She closed her eyes. She didn't know what to think. Was her mum right? Had she been abandoned by her friends who had then concocted some story? She couldn't see it. Okay, so they'd got separated a few times during nights out in the past, but it was never as bad as her mum made out. It'd only been because they'd got drunk and wandered off to chat to other people and not been able to find each other again. Not answering their mobiles was

22

common, it *was* loud in pubs. Her mum didn't get that, and if Sophie had to hear another 'it wasn't like that in my day' story, she'd vomit.

No, she believed Erin had called a taxi, she'd always watched her back, even during their school days. It'd always been Erin who was the sensible one and Sophie trusted her completely. How had she ended up the other end of town, though? She replayed the evening again from the time she arrived at Amy's. It was useless. She could only recall up to the point where they'd left the house to walk into town. They were all together then, definitely.

Her phone vibrated. She grabbed it, praying it was Amy.

Dan. Bless him. He always looked out for her. A shame she didn't fancy him, everything else about him was perfect. Too perfect. Not bad-boy enough for her taste.

Morning gorgeous, how's your head? XX

Despite her banging brain and the stressful events that morning, she smiled. She tapped a reply.

Not great, hun. What happened last night?

She waited, watching the screen, praying for him to give an answer to end this mystery.

You were well wasted, love. You wanted to go home after just 2 pubs! Light weight ;-) xx

Okay, now she was getting somewhere. If she'd wanted to go home, then she must've felt terrible. She knew her limits, and when she surpassed them, she always left – went home. Always. So, she *had* got in a taxi, like Tom had said. This threw up new, more difficult questions. Questions she didn't want to face at the moment. Shit.

Her mum would have a field day. She'd be on to the police, making accusations about the taxi driver. It was inevitable; her job had made her believe the worst of everyone.

Did you stay for the duration then? Who was with you?

She tapped the side of the mobile, her long acrylic nails clicking against the plastic casing. It was ten minutes before the vibrating heralded an answer.

Ended up at Shafters, as usual. All the boys made it, but lost Amy and Erin way before the club.

That wasn't what she wanted to read. Shafters, the club's nickname, was the one Sophie was found near. Erin likely got fed up and went back to her dad's; she wasn't into clubbing like the others, she preferred the pubs. But the fact that Amy hadn't been with them was worrying. Where had she gone?

It was common for Amy to break from the group. Such a social butterfly, she loved being the centre of attention. And attention she got. Every night out, without fail, it was like she was the main act at Glastonbury: everyone crowding around her, bustling her, trying to get her to notice them. Her beautiful shiny, long dark hair, her flawless complexion, her vivaciousness; she had it all going for her. She was easily the most popular of the group. They'd met at work, Amy was on the beauty counter opposite the fashion concession Sophie worked for. They'd hit it off immediately, despite her being two years older.

Where was the last place you saw Amy?

Her acrylic nail lifted as she chewed at the skin on the side of her thumb. Why was it taking him so long to reply? All of her nails would need replacing at this rate. Maybe she'd have to do a group text. It might be a quicker way of getting the answers she so desperately needed.

Another ping. At last.

I saw her and Erin shove you into a taxi, outside the White Hart. I think she came into The Farmer with us, then. I can't remember seeing her again after. She'll have gone off with some bloke, you know what she's like. Xx

Yes. She knew what Amy was like. That's what worried her.

CHAPTER SIX

Tues 7.00 p.m.
Where've you been, my sweet? I hope you are going to reply by tonight. I'm fed up of sending texts and messages and getting no reply. I've missed talking to you, it's been 2 days! I want to know how the plans are coming along for our 'date', it seems like I've been waiting for ever! A guy can only be so patient, you know
   xxxxxx

Fri 11.57 p.m.
So sorry I haven't replied. I've been so busy. There's lots going on here, I'm not sure if I'm going to be able to meet up for our date tomorrow, something's come up. Looks like you may have to be patient for a bit longer!
   xxx

CHAPTER SEVEN

Karen

The Facebook notifications sent her phone into overdrive, each new alert sounding seconds after the next. Karen snatched up her mobile and pressed the Facebook app. Her shoulders slumped. The status she'd been dreading:

> Has anyone seen or heard from Amy? She didn't come home last night and her mobile is going straight to voicemail. Can you share this, please? Really worried.

It had started. Now the inevitable questions would follow.

'Sophie. SOPHIE.' Karen took two stairs at a time.

'What?' Sophie appeared at her door. She'd kept well out of the way for the entire day, only flitting downstairs to get food and then disappearing again before Mike detained her for further questioning. Karen had left her alone. There wasn't much to gain from continuing to ask her questions she didn't have an answer to. Her plan had been to try and approach Sophie's friends without her knowledge, social media was easy for this purpose: ask around, find out which taxi firm had been used and take it from there. The Facebook status from Liz had just changed those plans. This was getting serious.

'Liz is asking people to share her status on Facebook, Sophie. One saying Amy hasn't made contact yet, and whether anyone has seen or heard from her. Have you?'

Sophie's face scrunched. 'No. Nothing, I've sent like, twenty texts. And group messages. We all have.'

'All? Who is all?'

'Our group, nearly everyone that was out last night. No one has seen or heard from her.'

'What the hell happened last night? Something must have. Please, Sophie, you have to remember.'

'I can't. You going on about it and saying I MUST remember, doesn't help. I. Do. Not. Remember. Got it?' She stepped back inside her room and slammed the door.

Karen stayed, standing there stock-still. This was turning into a nightmare. Why wasn't Sophie as worried as she was? She'd be horrified if any of her friends had gone missing, she'd be going out of her way to help. She tried to calm down. Apart from sending texts and messages to the others, perhaps there wasn't much else Sophie could do at this stage.

She ran back downstairs into the dining room and fired up her laptop. Somehow, seeing it on the bigger screen made it scarier: thirty or so concerned comments from Liz's friends, and some from the group of teenagers Sophie mentioned they'd been out with, all saying the same. No one knew where she was. Karen started Googling *Missing Persons*. A few clicks later and she slammed it shut again. Maybe it was better not to look, better not to jump to conclusions.

How long do you give it before contacting the police?

Karen dialled Liz's number.

'Any developments?' Mike raised his eyes from his iPad as Karen walked in. He'd managed to make it to the lounge from the kitchen, a whole ten feet or so. He was now sitting, legs sprawled in front of him, back against the sofa, iPad balanced on his thigh.

'Liz is giving it another hour, then she's calling the police. I don't know how she's holding off. I would've done that already.'

'You don't want to spark a missing person's appeal then have Amy turn up, hungover and apologetic because she's been asleep all day. Too embarrassing.'

'I think I'd rather be embarrassed. Imagine holding off for an hour, and then finding out that hour had been vital. I'd never forgive myself.'

'Be grateful it's not your daughter, then.'

'Jesus, Mike.' She walked away. She should be doing something more constructive. The knowledge Sophie would become key if this got as far as the police played heavy on her mind.

'What about Erin? Has she told you which taxi she put Sophie in?' he shouted after her.

'No, I haven't got around to checking it out yet. Sophie hasn't heard from her, I don't think.'

'You do realise they are likely to be together, then?'

'That'd be good. I hope that's the case. I'll give Rach a call in a minute to check.' Karen wandered into the kitchen, her mind afloat with thoughts of what might have happened to Sophie. And what might have happened to Amy. She flicked the kettle back on. More coffee was required. 'I wonder if Liz has phoned the hospitals,' she said, more to herself than Mike. She leaned against the worktop, and while waiting for the kettle, checked the Facebook app on her mobile again. More comments offering 'hugs' and a couple of people had asked about hospitals. The reply from Liz was, yes, they'd checked already.

The police were clearly next.

Not much she could do right now. She'd keep tabs on Facebook and, with luck, there'd be some news soon. She sighed. There was still the washing in the machine – Mike's ranger uniform he needed for work tomorrow. She'd best dry that, he couldn't go up on Dartmoor with damp clothes. And they hadn't eaten – her mind had been too preoccupied to consider food.

Her chest tightened and the nervous feeling she was accustomed to squirmed in her stomach. There was so much to do tomorrow. She hated Mondays. On top of her daily household chores, she had the counselling. She put out both hands and spread them on the worktop to steady herself. She inhaled deeply through her nose, held it, then blew out of her mouth. Breathe. Repeat. The thought of facing the day with all the unanswered questions was daunting.

The ringing mobile stopped her thoughts. It was Rachel. At least a conversation with her oldest friend might lift her current mood *and* she could ask her to grill Erin about the taxi company. It'd be better if her own mother did it, rather than Karen stalking her on Facebook. It'd been a few weeks since she'd last spoken to Rachel properly, one thing or another preventing a call. They often went weeks, occasionally months, with only the odd text to check the other was fine. But it didn't matter; their bond was too strong for a lapse in time to break it. Rachel was Karen's rock and always had been. She wouldn't have got through the last two years without her.

Karen quickly pressed to accept the call.

'Hey, Rach. You beat me to it, I was about to call you.'

CHAPTER EIGHT

Sophie

Her head was still woozy. Almost an entire day of feeling like death – had it been worth it? Sophie sat in the same position she'd been in for hours, her limbs aching with inactivity. Her thumb swept across the screen of her mobile, scrolling through the feeds on Facebook, checking for any news.

The ding sounded unusually loud in her quiet room – it wasn't the noise for her usual notifications. She tapped the screen. A new email. She hadn't had an email for a while, not having used her account for months. Within the message from the unknown sender was a link. She should ignore it, delete immediately; it could be spam, a virus. Her thumb moved to the delete tab, then stopped. The words made her hesitate:

You're gonna want to see this. More will follow. Do you recognise her?

Without waiting to consider it any further, Sophie clicked on the link.

The picture was cropped. Faceless.

A black dress, hitched up, revealing bare legs. A small tattoo visible on one ankle.

She swallowed, the constriction of her throat making it painful.
She knew immediately who it was.

CHAPTER NINE

Karen

'Did you know Amy is missing?' Rachel's soft voice was edged with anxiety.

'Been keeping tabs on Facebook all day, do you know anything?'

'Was hoping you did. She was with Sophie, wasn't she?'

'Honestly I'm at my wits' end worrying about this. Well there's a story – you know me, Rach, there's always a story . . .'

There was a dry, nervous laugh, then: 'Go on, spill it.'

Karen retold the events of the evening: the police, Sophie's unfathomable ramblings about Amy, her complete lack of any memory of the night. Her eyes burned as new tears fell. Talking about it to Rachel brought it to life; seeing something unfold on social media was one thing, speaking about it was quite another. And now it was all too real; not distant, not happening to people she had never heard of. It was happening here, to those she loved and cared about.

'Look, don't get too worried. I haven't spoken to Erin yet, perhaps she knows more. It may not be what we're thinking.'

'How come you haven't spoken to Erin?' Surely that was the first thing she should've done.

'Mobile's switched off. And she's at Adam's . . . you know he's moved in with *her*, don't you?'

'No way! He only left yours four months ago. Oh, I'm really sorry, Rach, I've been a rubbish friend lately, you should've rung me . . .' Karen's free hand moved unconsciously to her face, running her thumb and forefinger along the bump on the bridge of her nose.

'Yeah, well, you've had enough on your mind. It's a story for another time – preferably over wine.'

'That's such a kick in the teeth. He's an absolute idiot.'

'You never did like him. Anyway, the thing is, the poxy house is right in the centre of Coleton, isn't it, so of course Erin thinks it's brilliant. Her dad's suddenly the best thing since the invention of the mobile because *he* has a house nearer to her friends *and* her job. Barely see her at weekends now, she goes out in town, goes clubbing, then staggers home to him. And *her.*'

'I guess it's an ideal situation, a teenager's dream,' Karen huffed. 'Sorry though, must hurt.'

'Like a knife straight through my very soul. You know how much I've put into this family, how much I adore Erin. It's killing me. He barely knew this woman before shacking up with her. But, let's focus on Amy . . .'

'Well, now you've told me this, I think it's fairly obvious. I bet Amy's with Erin at his. You'll have to phone.'

There was a long silence. 'Okay. If I have to.'

'Um, yeah, you have to. You're going to have to put all your resentment to one side, clear this up before the police get involved. If they haven't already.'

'I suppose I was hoping by phoning you first, you might already know where Amy was, stop me from having to humiliate myself.'

'It's just one quick call. Say what you have to, then go. Simple. Sorry I couldn't be more help – it's up to you, love.'

'Cheers, mate,' she laughed, 'I'll let you know the outcome.'

'Thanks, but please, for heaven's sake, let Liz know first, she's beside herself.'

'Of course. Right. Let's sort this out.'

Karen released a large lungful of air. *Another ten minutes or so and this will be over.* At least, the part about Amy being missing. The rest was only just starting: there was still the matter of Sophie's missing two and a half hours between being put in a taxi and being brought home by the police. She wasn't sure getting to the bottom of that would be so easy.

CHAPTER TEN

Sophie

The picture was of her.

Her, wearing the clothes she'd worn last night. And it was no selfie. Sophie threw the phone on her bed, as if it had sent an electric shock through her fingertips. She stared at it, then shook her head a few times, screwing up her eyes, trying to remember. But there was nothing. Who had taken this, and where? What were they intending to do with it, and what ones were to follow?

Standing, feet planted, paralysed in the centre of her messy room, Sophie clenched and unclenched her fists, then clicked her knuckles: pulling down one finger at a time with the thumb of each hand until they cracked.

What should she do? Forcing herself to move forwards, she reached to pick up the phone. Her hands trembled. The picture was still visible. She had to face this, figure it out. Zooming in, she navigated the background in an attempt to see if anything was familiar. It seemed she was in a chair of some sort, legs splayed, slouched back. She guessed from the angle of her body that her head was thrown back; her hair was out of sight. Sophie turned the phone sideways to see it from a different perspective. Apart from the black dress and the blurry dark image on the ankle, which she'd assumed to be her snake tattoo, this photo could be of anyone.

A warm sensation flushed through her. Perhaps it *wasn't* her. Any amount of girls had tattoos these days, you couldn't even see if it was a snake or not. And black dresses weren't exactly rare. This was someone's idea of a sick joke. Probably one of the boys taking the piss; could've even been Photoshopped. With new-found optimism that it was a prank, Sophie sat down on her rumpled bed and searched the original email for clues as to which of her so-called friends she could thank for frightening her half to death.

It didn't take long to realise she couldn't identify the sender. The email address wasn't a standard one. It looked ridiculously made up, certainly not one she recognised. It'd soon become obvious which of the boys had done it, though, they were incapable of keeping their mouths shut; they must be itching to send a text, Facebook message or tweet so everyone knew about their clever stunt. Oh, how funny they thought they were. Immature arseholes. It wasn't funny at all, given the fact that Amy still hadn't rocked up. It was getting worrying now; five thirty and still no sign. Even Amy would've slept off a hangover by now.

Sophie reluctantly accessed her Facebook page. Streams of status updates, but none from Amy; none from her friends saying 'Amy's back'. *For Christ's sake, Amy, where the hell are you?* Sophie got up, her legs leaden with fatigue, and ventured slowly downstairs. Perhaps her mother knew something by now.

'Have you heard?' Her mum's head snapped up the second she entered the room.

Sophie's mouth dried in an instant. 'No, what?' Her voice cracked. *Something bad has happened.*

'I meant, have you heard anything from Amy yet?'

'Crikey, Mum.' Sophie's hand pressed into her chest as she let out a sharp hiss of air. 'I thought you meant . . .'

'Oh, no. Sorry. I spoke to Rachel just now, and she said Erin had been staying at her dad's a lot at weekends – you didn't tell me about Erin's dad moving in with that woman by the way – how come?'

'Mum. Get to the point.' Sophie transferred her weight on to one leg and crossed her arms.

'Right, well, I'm assuming they're probably together – Erin and Amy – because Rachel said she hadn't heard from Erin.'

'Actually, that does make sense. Dan said everyone got to the club except Erin and Amy. Good. That will be it then.' But saying the words didn't reassure her. There seemed no logical reason why Amy would bother to walk to Erin's dad's when her own house was nearer to town. She wasn't even convinced they *would* go home together. They weren't the best of friends – Amy, being older, had come on to the scene later, after school, and had kind of replaced Erin; becoming Sophie's new best friend. That had never sat well with Erin. But for now, it was a theory which Sophie was willing to believe.

'That's what I'm hoping, Sophie, yes. Although it doesn't let you off the hook.'

No. She guessed as much. Her mother would be at her every day now, trying to get to the bottom of why she had no memory of the night, why she had ended up wandering the streets alone, what the taxi driver had done to her. It was going to be a night-mare. But, as long as they were all safe – her girls – she could take whatever hassle was headed her way. It could've been worse.

Bailey's deep growl at the window diverted their attention. His ear-grating bark filled the room. Sophie followed her mum to see what had upset him. For the second time in as many nights, there was a police car parked outside the house.

Now what?

CHAPTER ELEVEN

DI Wade

The brisk wind had whipped debris up, swirled it around and scattered the remains over a wide area. Even without the inclusion of the body, the scene looked as though a frenzied attack had taken place. DI Lindsay Wade surveyed the marshy land from behind the crime scene tape. The rash abandonment of burger boxes, paper, plastic bottles, leftover food; people's rubbish, discarded without a care. An ideal place to dump a body, and first appearances suggested the young woman, too, had been discarded without a second thought. She'd been left for someone else to clear up like the remnants of a meal enjoyed, but ultimately not worthy to be taken home – not even worthy of being disposed of with consideration.

When Lindsay had left for work nine hours ago, a murder wasn't on her list of possible cases. In a professional capacity it could be a good opportunity to show the DCI what she was capable of. And on a personal level it would mean she could divert all her time and effort into something other than her miserable home life. She stood still, hands in trouser pockets, biting the inside of her cheek. She wanted to take in the wider area before donning the white paper suit and going in. SOCO were busying themselves with securing the scene, protecting it and the evidence which lay there. Evidence that had the power to tell the story, and lead them to her killer.

The reports from those first on the scene, though, and the initial statement from the man who'd found her when his dog had strayed from the path, made it clear that this was the secondary crime scene. Lindsay knew the primary scene probably held the best clues – they needed to find it soon. With the vastness of this wasteland, which ran alongside the industrial park, and given the weather conditions, she had little confidence of the evidence here yielding much. As it stood, all hopes lay with the body itself.

The day was ending, the cloudy sky darkening rapidly.

There was at least hope of identifying the victim quickly. The description fit the missing person reported moments before she'd left for the scene. A family was soon to receive the worst news possible. When Lindsay joined the police service ten years ago she'd considered herself tough; not easily shaken – but she'd come to find that relaying news of a death was the hardest part of her job. Her stomach twisted.

She was going to hand this girl's family a life sentence.

CHAPTER TWELVE

Sophie

They sat, stiff, pillar-like in the lounge. Her mum wrung her hands together. Her dad stared straight ahead, face blanched, eyes wide. Sophie cracked her knuckles. The male detective, his legs long, awkward, scribbled in a pocket-sized book as Sophie gave him details of Saturday evening. Those she could remember. The other, a female, also wrote in a notebook, but stayed silent.

'I'm sorry . . . I'm not much use,' she stumbled, her face flushed. 'I can't . . . I can't really remember.' She hung her head, didn't make eye contact.

'You were the last person to see her, by all accounts,' the man who had introduced himself as Detective Sergeant Mack said. Her shoulders fell, folding in on themselves like collapsing cards. The last person to see her. The words hung, suspended like an accusation in the air.

'Um . . . actually I don't think I was.' Sophie fumbled with her mobile, then held it up towards the detective. 'Here, see.' The text from Dan saying they'd lost Amy and Erin way before the club. 'But that was after they'd put me in a taxi, so he must've seen her after me. And Tom. He said Amy put me in a taxi. There's another text from him . . . saying that she told him about it.' Sophie dropped her head again. Her words – practically finger-pointing, like a child not wanting to get the blame for something broken – her eagerness to ensure DS Mack didn't think she was the last one to see Amy shocked her. This was one of her best friends they were talking about. She was missing at best. Dead at worst. Why did she feel so numb; so distanced? Amy could be dead, but she didn't feel the horror, the devastation she imagined she should feel in this kind of situation. Why?

'Hmmm.' DS Mack's brow furrowed. He held the phone up briefly and locked eyes with Sophie. 'I'm going to have to take this.' He bagged it, placing it beside him – all without breaking his gaze.

Sophie's face coloured. She opened her mouth to protest, but knew it was pointless so shut it again.

'Could Amy have got into the taxi with you?'

'I don't know. I don't remember.' It's all she could say. All she'd been saying for the past twenty-four hours. The room fell silent, but the atmosphere was loud with tension. Sophie looked to her parents, her eyes pleading. She knew there was nothing either her mum or dad could say to help. They'd gone over the events of the night: the police bringing her home, the state she was in, her incoherent ramblings. They'd asked how come the police hadn't thought anything was wrong then. DS Mack said there was no evidence at the time that anything untoward had happened. She was a drunken girl who'd been parted from her friends. She didn't have any marks on her, no signs of any struggle. She didn't tell them there had been any problem. She just appeared drunk.

Now though, things had changed. This had developed into a serious situation. A body had been found in Coleton. One matching Amy's description. Questions needed to be asked, answers needed to be found.

'Does Liz know?' Sophie tried to break the silence, utter anything to move this on. 'Amy's mum?'

'She has been informed.' DS Mack shifted position on the sofa, which seemed to have swallowed his middle, making him look like he was all head and legs. 'Amy has yet to be formerly identi-fied. The parents are on their way to do that now.'

'Terrible . . . I can't imagine . . .' her dad mumbled, shaking his head. Sophie caught her mum shooting him an *I told you* look. She had obviously been right to be worried, right to think the worst. A chill ran through her. Murdered? How had this happened in the sleepy market town of Coleton? It wasn't like London, that kind of thing was expected there. She'd always thought of Devon as dull and full of old people. Yes, she'd heard her mum going on about those she dealt with at work: the criminals she'd supervised, men who'd committed some terrible offences – murder, even. But not committed here. Not her home town. She knew there were nasty people, her mum had been a victim herself, but despite her harping on to Sophie about her worries that something bad had happened Saturday night, even she hadn't uttered the word *murder*.

'I don't understand.' Her mum sat upright, suddenly animated. 'If the . . . body . . . if Amy, hasn't been identified, then it might not be her, so why—'

'Until we get confirmation, it's still a missing person case,' DS Mack jumped in, 'so we need to get statements from those who last saw Amy, regardless.'

'Right. Okay.' She slumped back. Sophie watched as the hope drained from her mother's face.

But, there *was* still hope. Sophie had to cling to that. It might not be Amy. She'd hold on to the optimism for as long as possible. Because the alternative was too horrific to contemplate.

The shrill tone of Sophie's mobile message notification cut through the room. DS Mack turned his head and picked up the plastic bag containing the phone. His eyebrows raised as he spoke: 'You've got a text.' He tilted his head, 'From a *Dan*.' He flipped through his notebook. 'Would that be Dan Pearce by chance?'

'Yes. Why?' Her words came out sharply. Sophie noted a look passing between DS Mack and her mum. Her mum had cocked her head to one side. Sophie looked away.

'His name is on our list . . . and he is the Dan you said may have been last to see Amy. Yes?'

'Uh, yes, that's him.' A rushing sensation filled her ears.

'Shall we take a look then, see what he has to say?' He was already undoing the bag, slipping the phone out.

'Clearly you're going to anyway.'

'Sophie!' Her dad leant forwards. 'Watch your tone.' He flashed Sophie his angry stare.

DS Mack struggled to stand, the sofa not ready to give him up, then handed Sophie the phone. He stood over her while she opened the text.

Come outside.

This wasn't good timing. She held it up to the detective so he could see.

'We'll need to speak with him, so perhaps you could text him, tell him to come *inside*.' He smiled, but stood firm. He watched as she texted.

A few minutes passed, Dan didn't reply. He didn't come to the door.

DS Mack retook the mobile from her. 'I'll let you go out and find him, then.' He peered out of the front window into the duskiness beyond, then perched on the edge of the sofa. Sophie took her cue and jumped up before DS Mack changed his mind and went outside to get Dan himself.

CHAPTER THIRTEEN

She'd escaped. A temporary reprieve. Her mum had begun crying, her dad pacing; she was numb. The claustrophobia had been almost too much to bear, she'd felt herself on the edge of breaking down. Outside, the coldness of the early evening air acted as a refresher, triggering a reaction, making her thighs shake, and hands tremble. She drew some deep lungfuls of breath. In . . . out, in . . . out. She'd seen her mother do this a lot for the past two years to quell her panic attacks. Was this what it felt like for her?

Sophie sat heavily on the dwarf red-brick wall partitioning their house from the neighbour's, waiting for Dan to show. Her street only had five other houses: two directly opposite, one either side of theirs and one at the end of the road on the corner. But, she could guarantee that each occupant was currently ogling out of their windows, trying to figure out what was going on. She was surprised that Bill, the nosey bugger from number twenty, hadn't come across to ask – as the self-appointed Neighbourhood Watch lead he liked to know the ins and outs so he could inform the rest of Ambrook. He was going to have a field day with this.

'Hey, Soph, you all right?' Dan appeared from behind her car.

'How long have you been there?' Sophie raised herself up and went towards him.

'Saw the police car. What's going on?' Dan's angular face showed patchy red blotches, the way it always did when he was nervous. A flash of suspicion shot through her mind: he lived in Torquay, didn't drive – how had he got here? And why was he hanging around outside her house?

'They're here about Amy.' Her voice, flat.

Dan shifted from one foot to the other, staring down at the ground. 'She hasn't been found then.' It wasn't a question.

What should she say? That they thought they'd found her, or rather her body? Oh, and by the way, I told the copper you might have been the last one to see her alive?

Instead, she managed: 'The detective wants to speak to you.'

Dan's head snapped up. 'Me? Why me?'

'Well, you were one of the last people to see her, he wants to ask you some questions, like he's just asked me.'

'What did you tell him?' His chest rose and fell quicker than was normal. What did he have to be concerned about? At least he had memories of Saturday night.

'Nothing.' She sighed. 'I can't actually remember anything. My last clear memory is at Amy's house with everyone, drinking.'

'You aren't serious?'

'Deadly.'

'Are you sure? It seems . . . well, unlikely.' He avoided eye contact, the tone of his voice implied he didn't believe her.

'Yes, I'm sure, Dan. But *you* do, so that's all right, isn't it.' She shook her head. 'Best get inside.'

'I'm not coming in.'

'You have to. He's seen your text saying you wanted me to come outside, plus, he can see you through the window.' She flung her arm up in indication. 'I've already been far too long – he'll probably be suspicious now, thinking we're trying to get our stories straight.'

'What the actual fuck, Sophie? Stories straight, why?' He grabbed hold of both her forearms tightly.

'Ow. Let go. What's your problem? You're acting weird.' She spoke the words through gritted teeth. He released her and let his arms hang by his side.

'I don't like where this is going, that's all.' His voice was shaky.

He *was* acting strangely, out of character. But then, wasn't she? She had to admit, none of it was truly sinking in; her own reactions weren't what she expected. It wasn't even the worst of it yet, he was going to hate it when he found out there was a body, and they thought it was Amy. Bile burned the back of her throat. She couldn't be the one to break that news.

'Come on.' She tilted her head towards the front door. 'We have to do this. They'll be talking to everyone from Saturday night, not just us.'

Dan let out a short, sharp breath, then followed Sophie inside.

CHAPTER FOURTEEN

DI Wade

DI Wade slid back the curtain, slowly, as if it could make a difference. Prevent the inevitable for a moment longer, give this couple a few more precious seconds before their lives plunged into the black hole of grief. She'd been here before. Only once during her time as DI, thankfully, but it'd burned a cavity in her consciousness, which had never been fully refilled. She could still see the small body – battered, discoloured, the skin beginning to deteriorate; the image branded on to her retinas. His killer hadn't been found, the case now a cold one. Lindsay Wade wasn't prepared to let it happen again.

Standing inches away from Liz Howard, Lindsay could *feel* her shaking. Not a tremble, but a full-body tremor. Her husband held on to her, to stop her collapsing. A few hours ago, her daughter was merely missing. A terrible thing: the fear of what might be, the not knowing, the constant eyes peeled in the hopes of catching a glimpse. Some people went through it for years, never finding their loved ones. Did it make these parents lucky that their daughter had at least been found? They might gain an element of closure. But then, the next stage: who did this to their beautiful girl? And what if the perpetrator was never brought to justice – what kind of closure was that?

Lindsay placed a hand on Liz's shoulder. 'Are you ready?' The words seemed ridiculous even as she spoke them. How can anyone ever be ready to view a dead body – a body they are expecting to be their child? The woman and man took hold of each other's hands, took deep breaths, and stepped closer to the window.

Lindsay closed her eyes, not able to watch their pain. She waited for the scream she knew was coming.

A brief, sharp wail emitted from Liz's open mouth before the man lost his grip and she slumped to the floor.

CHAPTER FIFTEEN

Karen

Dan's story may have come across as solid to DS Mack – Karen, though, was unconvinced. The whole taxi episode sounded weak, far too vague, as if he were speaking lines by rote. The same story the others had stuck to: Amy and Erin put Sophie in a taxi outside the White Hart. The exact same words. But had any of them actually seen this? Or were they only going on what Amy had supposedly told them? Conveniently, there was no CCTV covering that area, a fact DS Mack had reiterated as he scribbled notes in his pad.

But, perhaps she shouldn't be thinking about that right now. Her thoughts should be with Amy – and poor Liz. Her own gut-wrenching reaction to seeing Sophie in such a state, thinking something bad had happened to her, paled into insignificance compared to what Liz must be experiencing at this moment. She'd sounded relatively calm when Karen'd first spoken to her, convinced Amy would show up and that they'd all laugh about it afterwards. Now it was nothing to laugh about. Karen had only known Liz as long as Sophie'd known Amy, hadn't even met her in person – all communication had been via phone calls and texting. She'd no idea how she and Nathan would cope, or what support they had to help them through this.

When DS Mack left, he handed Karen a card, said to contact

him should she or Sophie have anything to add. Now, standing in the kitchen, she absently flipped the card over and over. It was unlikely they'd require it. What more could they say? Sophie hadn't been able to recall any more of Saturday evening, and Dan had offered no more than what had already been noted from his texts to Sophie. She held the card on to the cork message board and jammed a bright red pin through its centre. How were the police going to piece any of this together – to make sense of Amy's last known movements?

Last known movements. Karen's skin tingled as it turned to gooseflesh. She ran her hand up and down her arm to brush away the bumps. Her eyes stung as fresh tears threatened.

'You okay?' Mike came up behind her and laid a hand on her shoulder.

'What do you think?' She shrugged his hand off.

'I'll make a coffee.'

'Not for me. Don't need any extra reasons to stay awake tonight.'

'Tablets not helping?' This was the first time he'd referred to her medication. He'd never asked a single question about them before.

'They aren't sleeping tablets,' Karen shouted. 'They're to help with bloody anxiety. Anxiety, Mike. Not murder.' She retreated out of the kitchen, leaving Mike with a stunned expression on his face.

Idiot. Two years she'd been taking them, and he didn't even know what they were for? Why did she bother? Karen lay on the bed, staring at the darkening sky through the skylight. She hated the skylight. His idea to have it put in – to make the room more airy, seem bigger than its actual ten by ten foot size. In reality, all it did was annoy her: letting the sun spill in too early in the morning, which woke her up, and the moonlight send in shards of ghostly white at night when she wanted to sleep. She'd asked for a blind. It still hadn't materialised.

Distant whispers penetrated her thoughts. After DS Mack had

left, Sophie and Dan shut themselves away in Sophie's bedroom, much to Mike's displeasure. She wondered what they were saying. Were they trying to recap the events leading up to Amy's disappearance? Was Dan consoling Sophie, offering a friendly shoulder as she might have just lost her best friend? Karen couldn't, *didn't*, want to contemplate it. If this were Rachel missing, or dead, how would she be coping? Rachel was a permanent fixture in Karen's life, had been since they were three years old, when their mothers, themselves inseparable friends, had walked them to playschool together. They'd had times of separation, both going to different secondary schools, colleges, but they'd always gravitated back to one another. And then they both fell pregnant at the same time, having Sophie and Erin just weeks apart – the same as their mothers. Three generations. Now, even if they didn't talk for weeks, they knew they were always there for each other when it counted.

A pang of guilt shot through her. She hadn't been there for Rachel when her ex moved in with the new woman though, had she? She'd allowed that one to go right on past her, not noticing, not *feeling* the latest traumatic event in Rachel's life. She'd have to try to make up for that slip. Rachel had been there for Karen in the past. Particularly after the attack.

A shriek ripped through the room, causing acid to rise immediately into her mouth. She shot up. Her heart bashed an erratic rhythm, filling her ears as she ran to Sophie's room and whacked the door open, crashing it into the wall behind.

'What? What the hell is it?'

CHAPTER SIXTEEN

DI Wade

'It's. Not. Her . . . It's not her.' The words, spoken between shallow gasps. Tears rolled freely. Tears of relief?

'Are you sure?' DI Wade turned to Mr Howard for confirmation. He nodded his head, a thin smile evident as he helped Liz to her feet.

'I'm sorry to have put you through this . . . The description was so close to your daughter.' She offered up her arm, assisted her to the low seats in the viewing area. 'Are you okay?'

Liz pulled another tissue from her coat pocket and wiped at her nose. 'Yes. Yeah, I'll be all right.' Her face crumpled again. She looked up into her husband's face. 'Where is Amy?' She grasped hold of his sleeve. 'Where's our Amy, Nathan?'

'Mr and Mrs Howard, the police are conducting a missing person investigation. I'll inform them straight away and the search will continue, now an ID hasn't been made. We'll find her.' As soon as the words left her mouth, she regretted them. It was as good as a promise, one she couldn't be sure she'd keep. The look on Liz's face stopped DI Wade in her tracks. Despite the relief, there remained a pained expression: sad, upset.

Liz's eyes settled slowly on hers. 'It's not Amy—'

'I know, that's good, Mrs Howard—'

'No. It's not Amy.' She used the tissue to swipe away fresh tears. 'But I do know who it is.'

CHAPTER SEVENTEEN

Karen

Karen searched their faces. They were smiling.

'What? What's happened?' Her throat was tight, her voice squeezed through.

'It's okay, it's all okay now.' Sophie and Dan hugged each other, then Sophie pulled away from him, looking up to Karen. 'It's not her, Mum. The body they found, it's not Amy.'

'How do you know?'

'She's just texted. Show her, Dan.' Dan held up his mobile in a shaky hand. Karen snatched it and read the group text: **Sorry about all the fuss. Bumped into Jonathan and ended up at an all-night party. Been sleeping all day. AM SAFE!**

'How can you be sure it's her? Ring her. Ring her now, Sophie, please.'

'Of course it's her,' Sophie scrunched her face into a *don't be so stupid* look Karen didn't appreciate.

'What if the murderer has her phone and it's him texting?'

Sophie looked at her witheringly. 'It's not a film, *Mum*.'

Karen wasn't reassured. A body had been found. Murdered. A film was exactly what this felt like.

'Just do as I ask, please.' She held out the mobile to Dan.

Dan took it, and pressed the screen. 'Sure, Mrs Finch, I'll give her a call.'

A few moments of heart-in-the-mouth tension passed before Dan spoke. To Amy.

Karen put her hand to her forehead. Her relief came in the form of an instant headache.

'Good, I'm so pleased this is over. I'm going for a lie-down.'

Sophie and Dan, already in conversation about the events, didn't even notice Karen leave the room. She went downstairs first, to inform Mike of Amy's contact. He seemed as relieved as she did. Perhaps now things could get back to normal. Her kind of normal at least. She climbed the stairs, heavy legs making the fourteen steps seem more, then collapsed back on the bed. The anxiety of the weekend had taken its toll; she felt exhausted, mentally and physically.

Apart from the time of her own attack, this had been the longest weekend she could remember. The edges of the room blurred, so she closed her eyes. She wasn't particularly religious, but now, lying on her back with her eyes shut, she put her hands together in silent prayer and thanked God for Amy being safe. She also prayed for the parents of the girl who had been murdered.

Although one family was now released from the grip of anguish, another was about to be condemned to it. They shouldn't forget that.

CHAPTER EIGHTEEN

My Beautiful,
I simply can't wait to meet you, I'm craving you beyond measure! How can I be so lucky as to have you – although not in the physical sense – I have you in mind and soul, I guess the body part will have to wait? But not too long I hope. Please can it be soon? I want to be able to hold you in my arms, breathe in your delicious smell, be with you. Inside you. That moment when our bodies become one, I cannot tell you how much I want you. I feel as though we've known each other for years.

I know you feel the same. Email back as soon as you can, I'm here. Waiting.
xxxxxxxxxxxxx

CHAPTER NINETEEN

Karen

Monday

'Erin is dead.'

The cry had shredded her eardrums. The words replayed on a loop. It's all Karen had thought about during the night. The relief of Amy being found: brief, temporary, now replaced with a new horror. The victim wasn't Sophie's best friend; it was Karen's best friend's daughter. Sophie's friend since birth.

The call, late last night, traumatic in its entirety, had left Karen numb. Rachel's response following the outspill of those agonising words: *It was Erin*, had been one of shocked silence. Karen had been unable to think of a single comforting phrase to fill the void, had only repeated the words *I'm so sorry*. Lame, useless words meaning nothing; offering no support. But no words could fit this situation.

Karen replayed the heart-wrenching call, Rachel's desperation, the way her words had rushed out of her once the silence had been breached.

'I don't understand . . .' Sobs, gasping, gulps of air. 'The description . . . it was like Amy, not Erin. I hadn't seen her. Oh, Karen. She'd dyed her hair, had extensions put in at the weekend . . . I had no idea.'

'Oh Rach, Rach, love—' Karen's contribution to the conversation.

'Help me, Karen, I can't do this.' Wracking sobs, interspersed with more gasping, the sound harrowing, tearing at Karen's heart.

A deep pain gripped her. How was this happening? Why? And how could she help?

Now, after a few hours of disrupted sleep, she leant awkwardly against the kitchen worktop, while Mike stared at her. Karen cried. Her friend needed her. How was she going to support her when she struggled to even make it outside her own front door?

'You have to go to her.' Mike pulled her close, wrapped his arms around her. She allowed the closeness, the comfort, for a few seconds before pushing him away.

'How can I?'

'I'll drive you over there after your counselling session. You'll be fine.'

Sounded simple. Obvious. The reality was far more complicated.

'I don't think I can . . .' She took some deep breaths, trying to stop the rising panic.

'Oh come on, Karen, you've been having therapy, or whatever it is, for ever. Surely you can make it out of the house for this?'

The words cut, but there was an uncomfortable truth there. She really *should* be able to push herself to go to her friend. She looked down, unable to bear to meet the look of disapproval in Mike's eyes.

'She'd be here in a flash for you, you know that.'

'Rach understands how difficult—'

'She may understand why you can't make a coffee morning. I hardly think she's going to understand you failing to be by her side at a time like this.'

Karen could see he'd lost any remaining sympathy he might've had for her condition. He'd never understood it, not really. He'd been supportive for the first year, doing everything that required venturing outside, talking to her for hours, making allowances for her erratic behaviour – but he'd lost the ability to be compassionate

66

when she hadn't recovered as quickly as expected. Everyone had their limits, she guessed, and he'd found his.

'I said I'd call her again at nine-ish.' Her breathing shallowed.

Mike shook his head, turned away from her. 'I'm going to work then. Let me know if you get your shit together, and I'll take you to your best friend.' He slammed the kitchen door.

Karen clawed at the top buttons of her cotton shirt, popping a few as she attempted to reduce the restriction around her neck. Her breathing was out of control already, shallow breaths in rapid succession. She was going to choke. Her lips tingled as the carbon dioxide in her blood reduced. She had to act now or she'd faint. With trembling hands and a darkness in front of her eyes, she grappled in the cupboard under the sink.

She put her hand on the bag, withdrew it and began breathing in and out of it, the crinkling of the paper offering its usual reassuring sound.

CHAPTER TWENTY

Sophie

The memory was fleeting – a sudden image striking her while she was washing her hair in the shower. Black hair extensions. A chair. Erin. The words: *What does it matter she wanted to be Amy?* Her own words, uttered in what everyone assumed to be a drunken stupor, repeating continually in her head. Was it a real memory? Or some horrible vision her mind had constructed, knowing now the body – the dead, murdered body – was Erin's? It disappeared as quickly as it came to her. As hard as she tried to go back to it, make sense of it, it had gone. Despite the hot water hammering her body, Sophie shivered. Something was there, nudging right at the edge of her consciousness. Fear wrapped itself around her, crushing her – how had she conjured a memory like this? For now, the flashback, if that's what it was, was out of reach, she'd lost her grasp on it.

She'd decided to go to work, regardless of the developments, regardless of her lack of sleep. She needed to be around others and keep active to stop the thoughts. Last night's news had spread through every social network, the majority of her night taken up with messaging, shocked reactions, never-ending questions. The biggest, most asked question: who last saw Erin?

She'd see Amy at work. She craved contact with her. If she arranged her lunch break for the same time, she could go over

Saturday night with her, try to unlock some memories. Real, helpful ones.

Avoiding both her parents so far this morning had been a challenge; a deep sigh of relief escaped her upon hearing the door slam as her dad exited. So, only her mother to face before she left. She'd prolong leaving her room until the last minute.

Sophie's shoulders dipped. What an awful daughter she was. She should really be offering comfort to her mum. It'd been her best friend's daughter – her godchild – who had been brutally murdered. The news was bound to be full of it today and her mum was going to be alone in the house for most of it. Sophie knew Mondays were bad for her mum. Counselling. Every weekend the build-up began to affect her. It started around Saturday afternoon, like she was tensing up for it; her moods would flare, she'd be unpredictable. The inevitable accumulation of fear usually erupted by Sunday evening. Of course, her mind had been occupied this weekend; the usual effects hadn't been observable. This morning, though, she'd be in full panic mode. Sophie wondered whether she'd even make this morning's session. Maybe she would attempt to venture to Rachel's instead, to be with her?

Sophie's stomach roiled. Thoughts of how this was going to progress, this awful situation, whizzed through her head. So many people were going to be pulled into it. This was just the beginning, the immediate aftermath of the shock. What was to come was unknown. This sort of thing had never happened before. It was a first. A first no one had seen coming, an unexpected blackness that hadn't been forecast. The fallout was going to be huge.

A ping. A notification on her laptop. A cold sensation shot through her. A new email. Sophie knew, even before picking it up, what it was. She hesitated. Her breathing uneven. Swallowing rapidly, she opened the mail.

Another one.

No doubt remained now. It *was* her.

Who was sending these?

CHAPTER TWENTY-ONE

DI Wade

The smell was like nothing she knew. Lindsay Wade had arrived at the hospital morgue early – an unfortunate trait at times like this, as now she was being treated to an extra post-mortem, the one prior to her murder victim. She knew she was unlikely ever to get used to them, despite having been present at a fair few. It wasn't merely the stench. It was the way they manoeuvred the body on the cold, metal gurney. The way the head of the deceased slammed up and down on the block, while they hacked at the chest wall, pulled the tongue out from within, a sickening thud reverberating around the white sterile room with each action.

She shuddered. It was barbaric. A flash of her dad came to her. How she wished she didn't know about these procedures. Ignorance was preferable to knowledge sometimes. Images of his face the last time she'd seen him alive, his greying skin screaming out for oxygenated blood as his shallow breaths failed to circulate it – her own pale hand holding his as she sat by his chair, waiting for an ambulance to arrive. Her begging the doctor not to have her dad cut up, but knowing she'd lose that battle. She blinked them away, trying to bring herself back to the present. Another thud as the heart landed in the weighing scale. In a while, the majority of this man's insides would be shoved in a black bin liner, stuffed back into the cavity, and he would be roughly sewn up. Lindsay bit the inside of her cheek and turned from the scene.

Erin Malone was next up.

The preliminary examination of the body prior to post-mortem indicated asphyxiation as the likely cause of death; the puncture wounds evident in her abdomen appeared superficial, not deep enough to cause sufficient bleeding to cease respiration or stop the heart. This particular detail, left out of public knowledge, would, in all likelihood, be needed later in order to whittle out those cranks who crawl out of the woodwork in these cases to claim this girl's murder for themselves.

She watched a man wheel the trolley bearing Erin's body into the room, then turned her attention to the doorway. She could leave. Get someone else to relay the required information later. She wasn't sure she could stomach it.

But then, the family's hope was her responsibility now. She couldn't start ducking out at this early stage.

She was the one whose job it was to catch Erin's killer and bring justice and closure to them.

She had to stay.

CHAPTER TWENTY-TWO

Karen

She hadn't made it to the bathroom. The vomit burst from her, barely missing Bailey as he chased along beside her, thinking it was a game. The poor dog had been completely neglected over the weekend. He sniffed at it. Karen shooed him away, rushing to the cupboard to get kitchen roll to mop it up. Out the corner of her eye, she caught sight of Sophie, who stood watching her.

'You could help.'

'Sorry, Mum.' Sophie walked in and pulled a plastic bag from the container of carrier bags hanging from the tall cupboard door handle. Karen deposited the damp roll inside, retching as she did so. She noticed Sophie turn her head away, her face screwed up.

'Sorry. Not pleasant first thing on a Monday, eh?'

'Not surprised though.' She smiled thinly, her eyes glossy with tears.

Karen took the bag from her. 'I'll clean myself up, don't go to work yet, wait a bit, will you?' It was a plea. Sophie nodded.

Karen allowed the coldness to refresh her; the water splashed over her face, droplets ran down her neck. It felt good. She grabbed her toothbrush and brushed her teeth, spitting out the remaining acid-sickly taste, then ran downstairs, hoping Sophie was still there.

She was.

'How're you doing?' Sophie asked.

'Honestly?' Karen put her hand to her chest, taking in ragged breaths. 'Not great.' She fought to keep the tears at bay, knowing once she started there'd be an outpouring of all the emotion which had built up overnight. Sophie stepped forward, put her hand on her mother's shoulder. Karen pulled her in, hugging her tight. When she released her grip, still close up to Sophie's face, she saw puffy, red eyes.

'What about you? How are you feeling about it all? Must be a massive shock, Erin's always been in your life.'

Sophie opened and closed her mouth, shook her head and blew out a puff of breath. 'Do you know, I don't even know what to feel. That's weird, isn't it? Wrong?'

'No, love, no.' Karen touched Sophie's cheek, brushed her thumb over it, taking away a fat tear. 'I'm not sure how anyone is *meant* to feel. We'll all go through it differently. The important thing is to keep talking. Keep sharing.' Karen's head cocked to one side. 'Is there anything you need to share, love?'

Sophie pushed backwards. 'No. Why do you ask?'

'Sorry, it's just you seem . . . I don't know . . . distant, somehow. Like you have something on your mind.'

'Yeah, I do. Erin is dead. *She* is on my mind.'

'That's not what I meant—'

'I've gotta go. I'm late for work now.' Sophie turned to leave, but Karen grabbed her arm.

'Wait.'

'What for, Mum? I'm fine, there's nothing to worry about.'

Karen squinted at her. 'The fact you've said that makes me think there *is* something to worry about.'

'No. Really not.' The words sharp. Sophie's eyes avoided hers. 'Now you'd best get yourself sorted for your counselling, hadn't you? Or are you going over to Rachel's instead?'

Karen's pulse skipped. Good ploy to take the attention off herself for sure.

74

'I . . . I can't go there. I'm not even sure I can make the session today. Your dad isn't going to take me. I can't . . .' The usual dragging inside her stomach, the tightness in her chest, tingling lips.

Sophie sighed. 'Where's your bag?'

Karen pointed. Sophie picked up the paper bag from the worktop and handed it to her.

'I'm sorry, Mum, I've got to get going. Sit and relax for a bit, then phone Dad. Go to one of them, either the counsellor or Rachel.' She offered a sympathetic but firm smile. 'You must go to one of them.'

Sophie's heels clicked on the floor as she made her retreat, leaving Karen hunched, breathing in and out of the bag, eyes wide, pupils following her daughter's journey out of the house.

Karen sat at the breakfast bar, slowly recovering her breathing, letting the natural rhythm of her heartbeat return. Her mind worked over it: Saturday night, Sophie's behaviour, her words. As incoherent as she'd thought them at the time, her ramblings had continued to play over and over since the news about Erin. *What does it matter she wanted to be Amy?*

Rachel had been so shocked to find out Erin had dyed her hair over the weekend, had hair extensions put in. She'd resembled Amy, that's why there had been the confusion over the identification of the body. The body of Erin. Found metres inside the wasteland near the industrial park. Also in close proximity to the nightclub. And the roundabout where the police had found Sophie.

She liked to think they had no secrets. They were close. Weren't they? Sophie would confide in her if there *was* something to confide. Karen swallowed hard. But the uncomfortable lump of doubt had lodged itself.

CHAPTER TWENTY-THREE

Sophie

Mondays were generally sluggish to start, but so far, the store might as well have been closed; the footfall was pitiful. With tired eyes, Sophie gazed at the other assistants on the ground floor of the department: each had a similar unfocused, thousand-yard stare on their perfectly made-up faces. As if this Monday wasn't going to go slowly enough. She allowed her head to loll back, then she shifted her weight from one leg to another and fidgeted with her gold-effect chunky necklace before letting out a loud sigh. It was only ten fifteen. Not only that, but Amy hadn't shown up yet, her beauty counter was still unoccupied. Surely she'd be in, her message on Facebook last night had said as much. Sophie needed her to be here. Please let her just have overslept.

Irina was heading in Sophie's direction, her thin frame carrying the latest dress from the clothes concession she worked on, located a few down from Sophie's. On days like today they'd pass the time with idle chit-chat, and normally Sophie was glad to oblige, but she wasn't in the mood now. Any talking she planned on doing was in order to find out what had happened on Saturday night. Meaningless chat was simply a waste of breath and precious time.

'You lost, Sophie? You look to distance in daze.' Irina's once thick East European accent was diluting by the day to Sophie's ears. 'No Amy?' She spread her hands, pushed her mouth down at the corners.

Sophie shook her head. 'It's not looking good for her turning up now, is it?' She turned her attention to Irina. Half of her wanted to tell her about Saturday, get her thoughts. The other half didn't want to go into it with her; it was Amy she needed to speak with.

'She ill?'

'Possibly. She did send a Facebook message though, said she'd be in.' Sophie fidgeted with her fingers, Irina wincing at the sound of cracking knuckles.

'Come now. Tell Irina all about it. Something not right with you today.' Her dark eyes looked into Sophie's, searching. Ten years Sophie's senior, Irina had good instincts when it came to deciphering Sophie's feelings.

Sophie smiled and put her hand on Irina's forearm. 'Thanks, but I can't. If I start talking about it now, I'll just cry and then I'm *bound* to get a customer immediately.'

'Ha. Have you seen it?' Irina swept her arm in front of her. 'Place dead today.' She accentuated the word 'dead'. Sophie shuddered, closing her eyes tight.

'What the matter?'

'Really, Irina, it's been a dreadful weekend.' Her voice caught, her eyes blurred. She blinked rapidly.

'Oh no, sorry, Sophie. What happened?'

'A friend was . . . my friend . . .' Sophie wiped at her nose with the back of her hand.

Irina pulled out a tissue from the sleeve of her dress, handed it to Sophie. 'It clean.'

'She was killed, Irina. Murdered.'

Irina's hand flew to her mouth, then to her chest. 'No way. How? Where?'

'Here. Coleton. She was found . . .' Sophie swallowed hard. 'In the wasteland, you know, just off the roundabout before Shafters.'

'No. Way,' Irina repeated, her face blanched. 'Which friend?'

'It . . . it was Erin.' A small sob burst from her, setting off the inevitable chain reaction. Irina moved in, enveloping Sophie in a tight hug, containing her shuddering body within her wiry arms.

A breezy, casual voice interrupted the embrace. 'Perhaps you shouldn't have come in.'

Sophie's head snapped up, she pulled away from Irina. 'Amy.' Her voice cracked, her face crumpling again. Seeing her friend now, the first time since she'd believed her to be dead, resulted in the response she'd expected when she'd first been told about the discovery of the body. Delayed reaction was a bitch, she concluded.

A trickle of customers made their way towards them. Sophie hurried to the customer changing cubicles, checked her face in the full-length mirror, then returned to the counter with a wide, fake smile. The potential customers thankfully walked on by Sophie's department, heading for Irina's.

'I'll check back on you as soon as I can.' She rubbed Sophie's forearm, then rushed back to her concession, leaving Amy standing facing Sophie.

'I'm so glad you're okay,' Sophie placed the palm of her hand on her chest, 'I thought . . . everyone thought it was you, Amy.'

'I know, I know.' Amy made no move to reach out to Sophie, no hug, no trademark air kiss. 'I had no idea of all the drama, you know how it is.' She smiled. 'I bumped into Jonathan after you left and one thing led to another.'

'Jonathan from the dating site? I haven't even met this guy yet.' Sophie searched Amy's eyes.

'Yes, him. And you will, I'm sure.' She gave a coy smile. 'Anyway, best get to my counter before *Boss Man* lays into me. I'll catch you later, at lunch.' Before Sophie could continue, Amy swanned off. She noted her friend's appearance was less than the usual perfect today, so, despite the perceived lack of interest or concern, it had obviously affected her. Erin and Amy weren't – hadn't been – the closest of friends, certainly not like Sophie and Amy, and there had been tension between the two, but surely she was feeling just as gutted as her about this.

Erin. Murdered. Sophie still couldn't get her head around that. Being here felt surreal, Erin being dead just not credible. And now Amy was distant, behaving oddly. Nothing made any sense any more. Nothing added up.

CHAPTER TWENTY-FOUR

DI Wade

Erin Malone had been on Lindsay's mind since the post-mortem. She would be now until the case was successfully closed, the murderer safely locked up. Even then she'd remain a permanent echo, her face one of a number that would be lodged within her long-term memory. Having studied the photographs her mother had provided, Lindsay could see that Erin had been pretty in life. But now, in death, the mask of fear had transformed her features, the array of post-mortem photos depicting a different Erin. Lindsay was drawn repeatedly to the girl's bloodshot eyes. They held the image of her killer, the last thing she'd seen in this life.

Lindsay skipped breakfast, always did, she needed only coffee to kickstart her day – a large cafetiere of the stuff. She drained the last of it from her mug and slouched back, sinking into her oversized comfy armchair. The one item of her dad's she'd managed to save from that woman he'd married during his last year of life. The cow had taken every other thing he owned: possessions, money, his house. The lot. Money-grabbing old bag.

She leant forward, re-spreading the photos on the coffee table. There really wasn't much to go on. The post-mortem confirmed the cause of death as asphyxiation: the bloodshot eyes; the split skin at the corners of the mouth where an item, as yet unknown, had been forced inside; the purplish colour to her skin. Because of the weather conditions and the crime scene itself – Erin's body stripped naked and left in the marshy land – the discovery of latent prints or DNA had been doubtful. To make matters worse, the pathologist had found traces of bleach. The killer had been careful, organised. Despite Lindsay being glad there was no sign of a sexual attack, this too meant there was no DNA evidence.

The only silver lining had been the fibres taken from under Erin's fingernails. There was an outside chance they could be from material she was wrapped in to transport her body from the murder scene to the dumping ground, or from the boot of a car or the killer's clothes. All three would be a bonus, give them something helpful to go on. Lindsay prayed the fibres weren't merely from Erin's own clothes, which hadn't been recovered. There had been no skin – it seemed she hadn't put up a fight against her abductor. Maybe she'd been drugged, or rendered unconscious. The toxicology report might give them a fuller picture when it came back.

Lindsay was due to make a public appeal later. She had confidence *someone* would come forward with information. Plus, there was the group of teenagers that were out with Erin on Saturday night. They must know something of significance, either from the night itself, or in relation to Erin's background – they needed to be reinterviewed.

Currently, these two avenues were their best hope. And with the killer still at large, she needed to act quickly.

CHAPTER TWENTY-FIVE

Karen

Karen sipped the coffee, her hands wrapped around the mug, the warmth comforting her. Anxiety attack number one of the day had subsided, but more were likely. The very thought of facing the day alone was enough to bring on another. How must Rachel be feeling? An errant husband, her only child dead, her best friend a useless agoraphobic who couldn't even make it to her side. She tried to recall the coping strategies she'd learned with her counsellor, but somehow, this morning, she hit a blank, not successfully remembering a single one. Ridiculous. Two years of therapy and she couldn't summon anything? A new wave of panic flooded her mind. *Think, think.* She took some deep breaths, closed her eyes and envisaged her happy place. There. That was one of the strategies. *Come on, Karen, you can do this.*

With trembling fingers, Karen picked up her mobile. Rachel's went straight to voicemail. Ashamed of the relief she felt, she tried the landline. A groggy voice responded.

'Yeah.'

'Rach, it's me.' There was an audible exhale of breath on the other end. Karen's free hand clenched and unclenched, waiting for a response. The silence stretched. 'Rach?'

'Yeah, I'm here.' Her voice thick, monotone.

'How are you doing?' Stupid question, but Karen was lost. Lost for words, the right words – for the first time in twenty-odd years, she didn't know what to say, how to say it. She bit on her lower lip, waiting for Rachel to shout at her, to tell her what a dumb question she'd uttered.

'I need you.' A low, guttural moan travelled through the earpiece. Then tears. Karen tried to swallow the hard lump in her throat. Tears of her own now tracked hot paths down her cheeks. Her whole body shook.

'I know, babe, I know.' She fought with her own inner voice, the one repeating: *I can't do this, I can't do this.* Then she asked Rachel if she wanted to come over. *Coward.* Expecting Rachel to come to her was downright weak, unforgivable.

'I can't drive. I'm in no state . . . had so many sleeping pills last night . . . to try and block it out.'

Of course. Karen could relate to that: the need to sleep versus the inability to close your eyes. The desire to slip into unconsciousness, the wish never to reawaken into the nightmare. Would suggesting that Rachel could get a taxi anger her, upset her even more?

The phone slid in Karen's hand, her palm slippery with sweat. She swapped hands, wiping the dampness on her jeans. 'I . . . I don't know what to do, Rach. I want to be with you, I really do—'

'I'm on my own here,' Rachel's voice, pleading.

'What about Adam? Surely he's . . .' She couldn't finish what she'd begun. The memory of her previous call with Rachel returning like a kick to her head: he'd moved in with *her*. Whoever 'her' was.

'Adam's been and gone, just did what he thought was his duty to me, then went back to her.' The bitterness was evident. 'Karen, this is awful. I'm here alone and the emptiness is crushing me. Please come, Karen . . . you're all I have.' A choking noise, followed by a heaving, distressing cry: her suffering poured into a single animal-like howl.

Karen jerked the phone away from the source of the noise and closed her eyes tight, the horror of the situation threatening to overwhelm her. She tentatively returned the phone to her ear. 'Rachel, come on, love . . . I'm here, you know I'm here.'

The quick, staccato dialogue bursting from Rachel's mouth was difficult to interpret due to the erratic sobs, but one punctuated phrase hit home: 'What . . . if it . . . was Sophie?'

Yes, what if it *had* been Sophie? Karen's reaction to her being brought home by the police, the long hours of the night spent worrying about what had happened to her during the missing hours, were fresh memories, but unlikely to diminish over time. But at least she *had* come home. At least she *was* safe. Not dead, not gone. Poor Rachel, the memories of this time, this awful, unimaginable event, forever carved in her mind. No new, wonderful memories of Erin to replace them. Ever. What could be worse?

'I'm so sorry, Rach, I know you'd be here straight away . . . I'm trying, I'm really trying to get to you . . .' She let the insincere words trail, knowing they weren't entirely truthful.

'Couldn't Sophie bring you? You could close your eyes the whole way here.'

Before she stopped to consider her response, she was already speaking: 'It's her work week, she can't bring me.'

The '*Oh. Right,*' which followed were two words saturated with disbelief. 'She went to work . . .' Rachel echoed.

Karen realised how painful that must be for Rachel. Surely everyone should be too struck with grief to carry on their usual routines? She was sure she'd feel the same. After her attack *she* had questioned others' ability to get on with life – why didn't it stop because her world had tipped on its axis? How could people simply not drop everything and sit with her, help her through her traumatic event? Now, looking back, it had been a small thing in comparison to Rachel's trauma. She hadn't ever expected to think that.

What on earth was she doing, sitting here, asking Rachel to

come to her? What sort of friend was she? Mike was right to have been angry with her this morning, right to be disappointed. She was a failure.

Her thoughts were brought back to the moment; Rachel's crying had started up again after her brief reprieve, her words thick with grief:

'She was my little girl, my beautiful shining light. What am I going to do without her?' Then anger, a white heat of rage: 'What *monster* could kill my baby?'

And, Karen thought, where was this monster right now?

CHAPTER TWENTY-SIX

Karen's Monday had already veered off course and it wasn't even midday. The call with Rachel left her shaky, anxious and guilt-ridden. Of all the times to miss counselling. She hadn't missed a session in over a year, her routine now disrupted. It was usual for her agoraphobia to determine her schedule, along with Mike and Sophie – a lot depended on them offering their time to help. But now all three factors had dictated her day.

She tipped the dregs of coffee down the kitchen sink and contemplated the view from the large window overlooking the back garden. The grass needed cutting. Bailey would get lost in the undergrowth when he went outside to do his business. It was too wet to cut today, not that she could do it anyway. It would wait for Mike, he could do it at the weekend. Every now and then she braved going out the back, but only if it was quick – pegging out washing was the longest task she could manage without panicking. There was something about the houses either side that made her wary – too many windows, too many places someone could watch her undetected. And the six-foot fencing around the perimeter of the house might prevent someone climbing over easily, but they could hide behind it. Watching. Waiting.

No. Inside was best. She had more control over her environment inside.

As she was skipping counselling today, she ought to do something constructive. She needed to take her mind off things, avoid the horrible, dark thoughts about Erin's death, about poor Rachel. Shopping. Yes, that would work – log on to the Tesco website and sort this week's food shop. She wouldn't usually do it until Mike got home on a Monday evening, but under the circumstances bringing it forward seemed a good move.

Karen opened her laptop. It was positioned on the glass, rectangular dining room table where she always sat to trawl the internet. She chose the black leather and chrome chair facing the wall, closest to the patio doors leading to the back garden. The front window was at the far end of the open-plan lounge to her left. It was good to get the overall feeling of light, of an outside world, but not too much of it. If she positioned herself in a certain way she could achieve the right balance of enclosure *and* an illusion of space. Safe space.

Having completed the shop in record time, Karen selected the delivery slot for an evening. Mike or Sophie would be around then to open the door and take the shopping from the driver. She stretched back, clicking her neck from side to side. Her days were a far cry from those she'd spent working in probation. She'd never had time to pee then, let alone sit around trawling the internet and playing *Bejewelled* on Facebook. Part of her missed the job, the service users, her colleagues – but mostly she'd forgotten it, forgotten the woman who'd once inhabited that role. How quickly things had changed.

The dark cloud began its descent. Thinking back always had the same effect; a physical reaction creating a heaviness in her limbs, a black cloak dropping over her head. *Breathe in . . . and out. In . . . and out.* Karen reached for the keyboard, navigating to the desktop, and clicked on the icon that might stop the progression of another attack. The virtual lounge appeared on her screen. She quickly typed in the name of her online friend in the self-help clinic and waited. Hopefully she'd be logged in and see her 'red flag', indicating she needed someone to talk to urgently.

CHAPTER TWENTY-SEVEN

'Did you go?' Mike emerged through the kitchen door. He banged his rucksack on the counter then bent to untie the laces of his walking boots.

'I'm guessing you already know the answer to that, so why don't you cut the crap and say what you really want to say about me letting Rachel down. Get it over with.' Karen crossed her arms and hugged her chest. She turned her head away from him, waiting for the critical analysis of her obvious lack of loyalty. She'd heard it all before, albeit in a different guise.

'Don't jump down my throat the second I walk through the door.' He kicked off his boots, propelling them under the break-fast bar, flakes of dried mud leaving a trail. Karen tutted.

'Then don't attack me with nasty questions as soon as you set eyes on me.'

They both fell silent, the bitterness settling for a moment. This was how it had been for a long time, before Erin's murder, before Karen's attack. The two of them on stand-by, waiting for a single reason to strike, or go on the defensive – waiting to inhabit the roles they had each given themselves in this marriage. The hostility seeped through the cracks every now and then, when they couldn't be bothered, or didn't have the energy to fill them temporarily with tactful, carefully chosen words.

'It wasn't a nasty question. It *was* a question, because I wondered, if you hadn't yet made it over to Rachel's, whether you'd like me to take you this evening.'

Evidently, he was in the 'we'll paper over the cracks and be nice to each other' mode. Karen's arms loosened and slipped to her sides.

'Um, well . . .' She darted to the cupboards, clattering the tins around. 'I've got dinner to start . . . um, and then . . .' There was no *and then*, but she continued to flit from drawer to fridge, rummaging for the items for a dinner she hadn't even given thought to until now, hoping he wouldn't push the matter further.

'Karen.'

She ignored him as she went about choosing the right pan size for the unidentified meal.

'Karen, stop.' He came to her side, took the pan from her hand and forced her around to face him. 'Look at me.' He tipped her chin up with two fingers.

'What?' She faced him, but averted her eyes.

'I'll take you.' Softly spoken, compassionate, almost caring – the way he'd been a lifetime ago.

'I should wait for Sophie to come home.'

'Sophie's old enough to take care of herself, she doesn't need you.'

'She doesn't *need* me? What's that supposed to mean?' She pulled away.

'Christ. Just that she can cook for herself, she doesn't need you to worry about it for her.' He'd swapped the compassion for irritation like a flicked switch but she'd been the one to do the flicking.

'I know that. But she's vulnerable at the moment, and she *does* need me. She needs me here.' Karen stood firm. Mike's eyes travelled to the pan she'd picked back up. He took a step away from her.

'She will need you for support, yes, but at the moment I think Rachel's needs are greater, don't you?'

'Look, I've spoken to Rach today, she understands that I can't be with her in person, she knows I'm only a phone call away.'

'And that's good enough, is it? When you were attacked, how would you have felt if Rachel hadn't *physically* been there for you?'

'That was different—'

'Too right it was.' He moved towards Karen again, his finger jabbing in the air in front of her. 'You were a wreck, she drove straight over as soon as she heard, she stayed all night with you, sat with you, comforted you. And you hadn't lost your daughter, you'd just been a victim.' Mike's face was too close to hers, a fine spray of spittle overlaying her skin. He looked right into her eyes, then whispered: 'But, I guess you always are the victim.'

Karen's mouth fell open. No words came to her. Thrusting the pan into his stomach, she turned and walked into the lounge.

The television was muted, but the images jumped from the screen. Karen rushed to the controls and turned it up. Erin's face was in the background, the newsreader's voice low, serious. It was the first time Karen had seen anything official about the murder; she gagged on a mouthful of sick but managed to swallow it down, acid burning her throat. She paused the telly, not ready to hear more yet.

'Mike,' she shouted, his horrible dig at her temporarily forgotten. 'Come here . . . it's on the news.' Her voice faltered; she took some deep breaths, sat down on the sofa.

Mike strolled in, but didn't make eye contact with Karen. She restarted the news. Briefly, they were joined in their horror, their anguish, and both watched in silence as the story unfolded. Footage of the scene where Erin's body had been found, the detective inspector – a red-headed wispy-looking woman with a strong, firm voice – telling the bare facts, some fuzzy CCTV footage depicting Erin walking down the main street of Coleton. Karen gasped. Even though she knew Sophie had been with her, now

93

seeing her familiar form tripping along beside Erin brought a jolt; her daughter, together with a number of other girls who weren't easily distinguishable in the grainy image, walking side by side with a murdered girl. *How can this be happening?*

An appeal followed. DI Wade spoke in her firm monotone again, this time asking for help: an appeal to the public for information and witnesses from Saturday night, from anyone who may have seen Erin, so they could chart her last known movements. She stated they had some CCTV from the early evening, but none after Erin left the White Hart pub.

The pub from which Sophie's friends supposedly put her in a taxi to go home.

DI Wade ended with, 'I urge anyone with information that could help this enquiry to contact us. No matter how trivial you think the information might be, please let us be the ones to decide what is significant. Thank you.'

An incident line had been set up; the number appeared on the bottom of the screen. Mike finally turned and faced Karen. 'Wow. This is truly terrible.' And then he added something that made Karen's blood chill in her veins. 'What if he does it again?'

For some reason it hadn't occurred to her. She wrung her hands in her lap, staring blankly ahead. She didn't want to think about that possibility.

'Pray they get the bastard quickly, then,' she managed.

The sound of her ringing mobile tore into her thoughts. She reached to the sofa arm to get it. Rachel. A shiver ran down the length of her back and crawled across her skin.

This was going to be a tough conversation.

CHAPTER TWENTY-EIGHT

Sophie

Sophie's morning had dragged; she'd lost count of how many times she'd gazed at the clock on the till, keen to spend her lunch break with Amy. She'd hoped that together they could assemble some kind of timeline, recover some memories of the moments leading to her getting in the taxi, share their anguish and anxiety. But, despite Sophie leaping straight to the point and firing rapid questions at Amy the second they closed themselves in the staffroom, Amy told her the same lines, the same story the rest of her group had already given her. As Sophie listened to Amy's answers any hope she'd had of connecting with her ebbed away, pushed back by Amy's strangely detached tone as she recounted how she and Erin had put her in the taxi.

Sophie slumped further down in the chair, sighing loudly. It seemed less and less likely anyone was going to help her piece together the events of Saturday night. If the police had this much trouble, they would never catch Erin's killer. How would anyone gain closure or a sense of justice then?

'So, after you both bundled me in the taxi, where did you go?' Not content with letting it go, she pushed the conversation on.

'I don't remember.' Amy shrugged her shoulders, then stuffed her sandwich in her mouth.

'Really? Well, did you go back inside the White Hart, or go to the next pub?'

Amy chewed noisily. Apart from this, the room was silent. Sophie waited for her to finish her mouthful and answer the question. Her own food, a shop-bought salad bowl, remained untouched on the small table between them. The moment stretched. Sophie cracked her knuckles.

'Ew! Sophie, don't, you'll put me off my food.' Amy put the sandwich back up to her mouth, about to take another bite.

'Amy, did you hear what I asked?' Sophie's irritation was growing; she wanted answers.

'Yes,' she snapped, 'but we only get half an hour y'know . . . sorry if I have to eat.' She sounded like a sulky teenager.

'I'm worried, Amy. This is really scary. Aren't you scared? Don't you want to figure out where she went, who may have killed her? Don't you care? How can you be so calm? The killer is still out there!' Her breath ran out; she gulped in some air. Amy stared at her, eyes wide. She was still chewing. 'I can't take this.' Sophie propelled herself out of the plastic chair, snatched her salad and strode across the room to put it back in the fridge.

'Look,' Amy wiped her mouth with the back of her hand, 'if you think it would help, let's get together tomorrow after work – go for a drink. See if we can answer some of those questions – two heads are better than one, eh?'

It was the last thing Sophie felt like doing, but as she was making no headway, she didn't see she had much choice.

'Fine.' She left the staffroom and the unhelpful Amy behind. She'd have to think of another way of recalling Saturday night more precisely. She had to, not just for Erin, but for herself. Someone was playing with her, sending pictures, taunting her. It might just be a stupid joke, but it could be serious. Before mentioning it to her mum, or the police, she needed to remember more. She wanted to know where he took the photos, who he was and why it was her he was targeting. She hoped she didn't receive any more, she really didn't want to have to tell anyone, the embarrassment would be crippling, she'd never live it down.

As predicted, it *had* been the slowest day ever. Sophie grabbed her things from the locker, sliding a hand inside her bag to retrieve her mobile. Dammit. It was habit. The police did say they'd be able to give it back to her soon. She was bereft without her lifeline nearby. If they didn't hurry up, she'd have to buy a pay-as-you-go one.

As she stepped outside the staff door, a gust of wind snatched her breath from her. She paused, took in some deep lungfuls of the cold air, and looked up and down the main street of Coleton. Anderson's store was situated in the middle of the pedestrianised street. A street that hadn't changed very much in the last five years: a few cheap pound shops had come and gone, a grocery store had been replaced by a mobile phone shop, the walkway to the indoor market had received a facelift – an attempt at modernisation – but that was about it. A shudder wracked her body. This was a small, quiet market town – and her friend had been murdered here. Unbelievable.

She'd always felt safe in Coleton, safe out at night. Yes, there'd been trouble: a few brawls, arguments spilling from the pubs to the streets, drug issues. Somehow, they didn't seem significant enough to cause her to question her safety. Standing alone now, buffeted by the wind, Sophie did question it. Perhaps she'd been lucky. Now that luck had run out. An uneasy sensation filled her belly. A prickle began at the base of her neck, rose upwards, her whole head feeling tingly.

It's just the cold wind.

She turned, started walking the route to the car park; every few steps turning around, head over one shoulder, checking behind her. For what? She quickened her step. There were a few people milling about, some she recognised as employees leaving the other stores, their bright uniforms giving away their places of work.

Outside the pub on the corner, some of the usuals stood under the large, less-than-stable umbrella, shielding their cigarettes from the wind. A hurricane wouldn't keep those people from their habit. She carried on, crossed the road, passing the brown-bricked symmetrical building of the magistrates' court before she got to the pedestrian entrance to the car park, commonly known as 'the police car park' due to its proximity to the town's station. It was less than two minutes from Anderson's, but felt longer this evening.

Her breathing shallowed, she fumbled in her bag for the ticket, her purse. She always had the correct change for the machine, and with an unsteady hand, deposited the coins in the slot. Fidgeting, waiting for it to spew the ticket back out, Sophie scanned the area again. She couldn't see anything untoward, so why was she shaking? Why did she feel so uneasy? Snatching the ticket, she hurried to her car, pleased now she always parked it close to the machine. Once inside, she hit the central locking button.

What the hell was that all about? She was becoming her mother: a paranoid bag of nerves. She had to get a grip. It was only a day ago she'd found out about the murder of her friend, though, so she should expect some anxiety. What she didn't expect was to feel as scared as she did right now. After taking a few minutes to calm herself, to stop shaking, Sophie started her car and exited the car park. Once on the road with all the other 5.30 p.m. traffic, her unease reduced.

Safety in numbers.

But the question was still rattling around inside her brain: what, or who, was there to be afraid of?

CHAPTER TWENTY-NINE

Karen

'Did you see it? Did you watch the news?' Rachel asked, her voice wavering.

'We did, Rach. It's so unbelievable.'

'When I used to hear people say they expect them . . . their dead loved ones, to walk in through the door at any second, I thought, what a cliché.' She let out a short burst of laughter. 'Well, I am now that cliché. I'm constantly waiting for her to walk through the door, turning my head towards it every five minutes. If there's any noise, I'm up, at the door thinking she's home.' The tears started again. 'I just want my girl to come home. I do *not* want to see her face splashed on the telly, hear people talking about her, listen to the police say how he . . .' Karen heard Rachel draw in a big, ragged breath. 'How that murdering bastard hurt her. Oh, Karen, what he did . . .'

Karen's eyes stung with tears; she tried blinking them away. She sniffed, wiped her running nose with her sleeve. Mike passed her a box of tissues, mouthing *I'll take you there*. Karen shook her head, mouthed back, *I can't*. He walked off, heading towards the kitchen.

'They took everything,' Rachel continued, her voice barely a whisper.

For a moment Karen questioned her use of 'they', surely there

99

was only a single killer suspected. Then she realised she wasn't talking about the murderer, it was the police.

'Her laptop, items from her room, even clothes, which I don't understand . . . why do they need those things? They've ruined her bedroom, they've been to Adam's too, taken more from her room there.'

'Oh, darling, I know that must hurt. They're only doing it so they can figure things out, find out who she may have been talking to, seeing. *Any* bit of information they can glean from her things is a step closer to catching the bastard.'

'I can't bear it. I've lost her, now her possessions . . .'

'They will return them, you haven't lost them.' Karen flinched as she spoke, realising too late the sentence had sounded flippant. Rachel *had* lost her daughter, and no doubt the items in Erin's room had suddenly gained new meaning – a deeper appreciation, each holding a different memory of her. Having them taken away, even if she knew they'd be brought back, must feel like another part of Erin being ripped away from her.

Neither Rachel nor Karen spoke then, the expanse between them increasing in the silence. Karen knew she should at least try to be at her side. It was expected. Rachel *should* expect it as a bare minimum from her lifelong friend. She was letting her down, she knew it, and Mike certainly knew it too. Would Rachel end up hating her for it?

Rachel then uttered the question Karen had been dreading.

'You said before that Sophie didn't remember any of Saturday night, surely she does now? She *must* do, she must remember something, something that can help.'

Karen paused. She had to be careful in her approach to this. Knowing Sophie was one of the last to see Erin was a huge responsibility to bear. For Sophie and for herself. People, especially Rachel, would presume Sophie would be the one to unlock the mystery surrounding the events of those last few hours. She'd expect Karen to push her into remembering, force the issue to enable Rachel to thread together her murdered daughter's last hours of life. Karen didn't want Sophie to be the pivotal piece of the jigsaw, the focus of attention from police, hounded into recalling a night she'd already tried to remember on numerous occasions. She'd be made to feel guilty. Karen was afraid of the effects on Sophie, how it would affect them all. Their small family unit was already in a precarious position; this kind of stress wouldn't help. Karen had been trying so hard to keep the family together, but this threatened to tear it apart again, cause the cracks to reappear, run deeper. Become irreparable.

'Did you hear me, Karen?'

'Sorry, yes. Um . . . she hasn't actually remembered anything, I'm afraid.' She took a quick draw of breath, then continued before Rachel could jump in, 'She's tried really hard, spoken to the police, her friends . . . you know, everyone from their group, and basically she's no further forward . . . there's nothing new. I'm so sorry.' She paused, listening for Rachel's reaction.

'Oh.' Disappointment oozed through the line. Karen couldn't imagine how terrible it was, not knowing what happened to Erin, yet being aware someone else did. Someone must hold the key to the events: know where Erin went, what happened, how and who killed her. Personally, Karen hoped there was only one person with knowledge of all these details: the killer himself.

But, a niggling concern, a disquieting uneasiness over Sophie's claim not to have remembered a thing from Saturday night, together with where she'd been found, meant she wasn't so sure. She could trust her daughter, couldn't she? Of course in the past there'd been teenage cover-ups, things Sophie clearly didn't want to tell her parents about; parties, what she and her friends got up to. Usual things. But surely, when it came to something as serious as this, she wouldn't hide the truth. Would she?

CHAPTER THIRTY

The phone call with Rachel ended with more apologies from Karen. That was it. She had to pull out all the stops, she couldn't bear to hear herself spluttering another apology down the phone. She had to try and get to Rachel, she owed it to her. Tomorrow she'd get up and prep straightaway for the journey. Dig out her journal, her countless leaflets and self-help books, and work out the strategies she'd need to get to her. If she had a plan, she might be able to make it. She'd managed to get to her counsellor almost weekly, albeit with someone else driving her. Why was this task so difficult, verging on impossible? It really wasn't much further away from the counsellor's Torquay office, heading out of Torquay itself and along the rugged coast for a few miles. She used to love visiting Rachel, always trying to arrange the coffee meet-ups at hers because her house had a sea view which she found calming.

This wouldn't be a casual meet-up or a counselling session, though. Karen guessed the difficulty lay with the added apprehension related to the *reason* she needed to go. It was a level of anxiety she hadn't dealt with since her attack, and even then, that had been *her* experience, her own personal issues to deal with. Not someone else's. So, how could she be expected to cope? It wasn't merely an appointment where she sat for an hour and talked about herself, how her experience had left her fearful of venturing beyond her own four walls. This was going to be time spent where *she* was the one doing the listening, the comforting. It sounded easy, really. But in reality it felt like climbing Everest – the air thinning as she went, the oxygen being sucked from her lungs. Karen wasn't ready to be in the chair opposite the couch, as it were. Her role was to be *on* the couch. She exhaled loudly. Mike was right. She always played the victim.

Maybe it was time to change that. Rachel deserved it.

The slamming of the front door interrupted her thoughts. Sophie. Rachel's words came to her: *I'm constantly waiting for her to walk through the door*. Karen put her hands to her face, pressed her fingers to her eyes to stop tears escaping. How would she feel if she never again heard Sophie bursting through their door, slamming it so irritatingly hard as she always did?

'Mum? Where are you?'

Karen wiped at her face, stood up. 'I'm in here, love.'

'Dad's cooking,' Sophie said, making a face as she came in, throwing her bag down on the sofa. 'Why? He never cooks.'

'Hi, Mum, good day?' Karen said in a sarcastic tone, raising her eyebrows. Sophie stared back, narrowing her eyes, saying nothing. 'Never mind then,' Karen muttered. 'Don't be harsh, Sophie. I was on the phone so he made a start on it or we wouldn't be eating till nine.'

'On the phone to who?'

Karen didn't feel like a re-run of the conversation, or the news story. 'Rachel.' She said, quickly moving towards Sophie to give her a hug. 'How was your day?'

'Weird. Don't want to go into it if I'm honest,' Sophie lifted her shoulders up, gave a fleeting smile. 'I'm going up for a shower.' And she turned and left.

Karen thought Sophie looked pale, tired. Which was to be expected. But there was something else. Like a detachment, a numbness draining her usual liveliness from her. She seemed edgy and keen to avoid talking. But then she didn't want to talk herself right now, so perhaps it was the same for Sophie. She shouldn't read too much into her behaviour, she was in shock still, grieving for her lost friend. How *should* you act in those circumstances?

With all the drama of the unfolding events, Karen's focus had been on Rachel, on Erin. She needed to concentrate on her own daughter. Though she'd always felt they were fundamentally close, their relationship was strained. Her fault, she'd pushed Sophie to the back of the queue when it came to attention. The attack, her phobia, dominated the household. Her ability to be a good parent, a supporting one, diminished because she'd placed her own selfish needs first. She knew that.

If Sophie couldn't remember Saturday night, the unrecalled hours in which anything could've happened, then she'd have to help her. Karen'd known immediately, when the police brought Sophie back, that something was amiss. The stories from her friends were so unconvincing – if she'd been put in a taxi home, then why didn't she *get* home? The police, too, would realise this and come back, ask more questions – they had to be prepared for that. Have some answers ready.

Where should she start? The obvious people, the ones who had apparently put her in the taxi, were Erin and Amy. Then there were those who either might have seen that, or were told about it – Dan and, who was it, Tom? Yes, Tom. Karen hurried to the dining room and switched her laptop on.

She was friends with Amy on Facebook; she'd start with her.

CHAPTER THIRTY-ONE

Sunday 8.00 a.m.

Hey Beautiful, how are you this morning? I hope you have woken with me in your heart and mind! I dreamt of you, as usual. My night was full of visions of holding you. I awoke believing I knew what it was like to touch you, the echo of you remained on my fingertips for a few blissful moments, the memory of the texture of your skin, your body against mine, still fresh. It was amazing, and I can't wait for this to become reality. It's all I can think of, it dominates my every waking moment, my every unconscious thought.

It's been months now. I was really hoping you might feel ready to meet. We should be together, we would have an incredible future. I know it. You are my soul mate.

We are meant to be.

Xxxxxxxxxxxxxxxx

CHAPTER THIRTY-TWO

Sophie

With the towel loosely draped around her, Sophie sat on the bed, her laptop open beside her. The two pictures displayed on the screen mocked her. It was almost as though she was looking at pictures of a random girl, in a scene she'd never observed through her own eyes. Yet, she must have, the second picture clearly showed her face. Had she seen her surroundings, seen who was there with her – perceived everything – but chosen not to attend to it? Memory could only encode and store information for later retrieval *if* it was perceived *and* attended to. She remembered that from her psychology course – she'd found bits of it interesting, even though she'd dropped out early to do her NVQ in retail skills.

Was that why she was struggling to recall anything from Saturday night? It seemed unlikely her mind hadn't attended to even a small amount of information though. She could understand some missing memories, even a few significant ones – but the entire evening? There had to be another reason for her inability to remember. Apart from the obvious: alcohol.

Zooming in again, for the umpteenth time, Sophie moved the cursor around the picture: dark, concrete floor; a chair, wooden from what she could gather, only the bottom of two legs were visible, the rest of the chair obscured by her own body and black dress. Sophie gulped as she continued to scan, the hairs on her arms became erect, a coldness spread over her skin. There was something on the ground of the first picture. She moved the laptop closer to her face, squinted at the screen. Beside the chair lay an object, rounded in the middle like a ball, longer thinner bits protruding from it.

An image, sharp, quick like a flash from a camera, hit her: a gag, a man shoving it roughly in Erin's mouth. Tying it tight.

Sophie pushed the laptop away; her hand flew to her mouth to suppress the scream.

No way, no way, it isn't possible. She'd been there. She'd seen the man who murdered Erin.

Had she witnessed her friend's death?

Suddenly, Sophie wanted nothing more than to forget what she'd remembered. Her mind just couldn't process what it was telling her. It was too much to think about. She hoped no more of her memory returned. Ever. She could dismiss it completely then, go back to the blankness. But that *thing* was there on her laptop, blurry, like her memory, but there. What the hell was she going to do?

The noise of the hairdryer in her ears momentarily drowned out the horrifying thoughts. She took her time, dragging the process out. Usually she'd kneel in front of the long mirror to dry her hair; tonight though, she couldn't tolerate looking at herself. After blasting it until it resembled straw, Sophie flicked the off switch. She couldn't be bothered to straighten it. She unplugged the dryer and sank to the carpeted floor, pushing items of rubbish forward with her outstretched legs.

Her room was a mess. A bare-chested Justin Bieber looked down from the wardrobe door, his eyes seeming to chastise her for the lack of tidiness. Her attention turned to the framed montage of photos hanging above the dressing table. Erin smiled out at her from the group of faces. Sophie remembered how they'd bickered about who was the best artist, or the hottest – Justin or One Direction. It'd been childish. Fun.

No more.

She shook her head, wiping the tears away, and pulled herself up. She should get dressed; dinner must be soon. That was going to be a fun-filled half-hour, sat at the table in silence with her parents. Actually, she hoped it *would* be in silence, she didn't want them talking about Erin, or asking her more questions. Perhaps she'd bring her dinner up to her room, avoid the possibility altogether.

Or, perhaps she should tell them about the pictures.

Her mouth filled with excess saliva. No. That was a terrible idea, they'd freak right out. The scene played out in her mind's eye: a call to the police by her mum, being interrogated by the detectives in a stuffy room with her on one side of the table, them on the other, the pictures put in their hands to analyse. She shuddered, blinked the vision away. No. She couldn't say anything yet, the pictures wouldn't be helpful to the investigation anyway, they were of her, not Erin. And besides the gag, the chair and some concrete, there were no other clues as to where the pictures were taken. She couldn't even trust the source, her recollection, anything.

There was no point throwing this into the pot, not when there was nothing to gain, bar a load of hassle from her parents, particularly her mother. She'd go into overdrive, her panic attacks would rocket out of control, her phobia increase to the point where Sophie herself might be forced to stay in the house to be with her. She just couldn't stand the thought of that. And she had no idea how her dad would react. Didn't bear thinking about. This really was a nightmare. Just when she'd thought it couldn't get worse.

But what if this was merely the beginning? The person who sent these pictures to her said there'd be more. Questions suddenly swamped her mind: why was he sending them? If she'd been there, with Erin, why hadn't he killed her too? How did he know her email address? What else did he know about her?

The hollering of her name escalating the stairwell signalled dinner was ready.

But Sophie's appetite had gone.

CHAPTER THIRTY-THREE

Tuesday

Her stomach grumbled from lack of food. She'd been unable to eat breakfast either, a growing sickness preventing even the idea of eating. Sophie stepped outside into a much calmer atmosphere than the night before, the keen wind having surrendered to the light breeze which now whispered against her cheek. A shame her mind wasn't as submissive. She slumped into her car, turned the CD player on, pressed the forward button on the car's steering wheel to change to a more uplifting song, then whacked the car into gear as Katy Perry's voice attempted to fill her head.

Dark dreams had disrupted her sleep. She'd awoken that morning with a heavy feeling, an awareness she'd had more to do with Saturday night's events than she'd first thought. Snippets of the dreams remained with her, disturbing remnants; fragmented, like shards of glass from a broken mirror. Each time she remembered a splinter, it gave her a jolt of pain, as if it had pierced her skin.

Somehow, the overall sensation left her with the belief that stabbing had been involved in Erin's death. It was like her brain was attempting to show her what happened, revealing it bit by bit to protect her, knowing she'd be unable to handle all the memories at once. She'd avoided the news stories, the attention-grabbing headlines, choosing not to learn the details of Erin's death. It appeared the memories might come to her anyway, given time. As would the police. How long before they came knocking on her door again?

As Sophie drove into the car park, she came out of her thoughts, shocked to see where she was. She'd arrived on autopilot. Shaking her head, she pulled into her usual space. She sat still for a while, to gather herself. Across the road, a group of school kids shouted and pushed each other. She watched them with a mixture of annoyance and jealousy. She hated that they were so stupid, careless in their actions. One shove into the road could see a passing car plough into them – something similar had actually happened not long ago, the girl suffering devastating, life-changing injuries.

More than that, though, she was envious of their carefree attitude, their naïvety. She'd been one of those kids only a year or so ago. Now, already, she wished she could go back to that time: no responsibilities, the only thing to worry about whether she had on-trend clothes, the right make-up, the best mobile phone. The excitement, the longing to leave school, get out there. The big-wide world was not all it was cracked up to be.

Sophie checked her face in the visor mirror. Too pale. Grabbing her bag, she retrieved her foundation, deftly adding another layer. Orange was preferable to white. A quick glance at the clock informed her she was late. Dammit. She didn't need hassle from Anderson's store manager, he was always quick to jump on anyone who was late. In a sleep-deprived daze, she made her way into the store. As she walked, head down, oblivious to anyone around her, all she could think about was whether she should confide in Amy. She was still the only other person who might throw light on the situation, but given her attitude yesterday, Sophie wondered just how much help she'd be.

Before entering the staff door, Sophie turned to look behind her, the uneasiness she'd felt last night returning. Squinting against the sun snaking its way between the gap of the clock tower and adjacent building, Sophie could make out a few early morning shoppers milling about: a teenager struggling with a screaming toddler, an old woman dragging a tartan trolley bag behind her, a young couple who looked as though they were headed for Costa Coffee. But no one Sophie recognised. Her heartbeat pulsated in her neck. She continued scanning the pedestrianised walkway, not able to shift the sensation that something was wrong. Someone was watching her. She scrunched up her eyes. No, her dreams, memories, had unsettled her; she was on edge, that was all. No one was even looking in her direction; she was being silly. Still, she wanted to get inside quickly, to the safety of the brightly lit store.

Amy was already in place behind her make-up counter, smiling broadly. Her fake one, reserved for customers. She looked up, saw Sophie and put a hand up by way of acknowledgement. Sophie returned the gesture before carrying on to her concession. She took the rota from behind the till. On her own until lunchtime. Typical. She needed the company now, the prospect of being alone with her unpredictable thoughts was unbearable. She looked up to Irina's end of the store. A new girl stood at the till, talking to a customer. Pity. No Irina to take her mind off things. Returning the clipboard, she surveyed her concession area – whoever had last been working had left it untidy. She'd normally be annoyed, but today she was glad. She took a deep breath and set about busying herself.

Standing at a rail rammed full of sale clothes, Sophie absently flicked through the hangers, periodically taking one out, swizzling the hook of the hanger around before replacing it, ensuring uniformity with the others. It was a thankless task, but about the only one she felt capable of carrying out correctly today. Despite the people around her, Sophie had never felt so isolated, so alone. Her welling tears went unnoticed.

'Why's your mum contacting me on Facebook?' The voice came from behind her.

Sophie swung around, her hand on her chest. 'You scared me.'

'In a world of your own there, weren't you. Sorry.' Amy's smile didn't reach her eyes. 'Really though, I know I'm friends with her, but I didn't expect a grilling.'

Bloody hell, Mum. 'What do you mean, a grilling?' She was afraid of the answer.

'Going on at me last night, questioning me about the taxi firm. I don't remember which firm it was. It was a taxi. It had a sign on it. I shoved you in it. End of.'

'Sorry, Amy. She'd been worried about it when I got home that night, you can imagine how much more she's stressing about it now, after, you know, what's happened to Erin.' She offered Amy a smile, hoping her mother hadn't gone further.

'Well, it's not on, really. It's not as if the police didn't have enough questions.' Amy's hands went to her hips; she took another step closer. Clearly there was more to come.

'I know. Again, I'm sorry. But she's my mum, she worries.'

'Yeah, I suppose she hasn't got much else to occupy her, has she, being a prisoner in her own home.'

Sophie took a step back. 'Well, perhaps she has reason to worry, Amy.' Her tone revealed the offence she'd taken.

'Why? What the hell does she think happened?' The heads of several shoppers turned their way, the shrillness of Amy's voice drawing attention.

'Shh.' Sophie looked around her. 'We should discuss this at lunch.'

Amy didn't make a move, standing square on, hands remaining on her hips. Sophie hadn't seen her like this in all the time she'd known her. She was at a loss as to how to handle the situation. *Good one, Mum. Thanks for making this even more difficult for me.*

'I'm out for lunch,' Amy said eventually. She cast her eyes downwards to her diamante watch, an expensive gift from her boyfriend. 'I'm off in a minute actually, got an appointment first, I only came in to set up for Maxi, so now will have to do.' She crossed her arms, waiting.

Sophie's brow creased. Out for lunch? Was she trying to avoid her?

'She's just concerned that . . .' Sophie paused. How could she tell Amy her mum doubted her friends' honesty, how she suspected them of concocting a story to ensure they didn't look bad? 'She thinks it's . . . odd, that I was found going out of Coleton, when as far as everyone else was concerned a taxi took me home.' That sounded subtle, not accusatory. Amy stared in silence. Sophie, compelled to fill the gap, continued. 'She suspects something bad happened in the taxi,' her posture slumped, 'like I was drugged or something.' She whispered the last bit, aware their conversation could be overheard.

'What, some random taxi driver decided to take advantage of you, you mean?' Amy's voice softer now.

'Yeah, something like that. Look, I really hoped you'd be able to talk through the night with me, see if you can help me remember?'

Amy shook her head. 'You know, it probably isn't a good idea to remember. Once remembered, you can't erase it. Some things are best left well alone, Sophie.' With that, Amy turned to walk away.

'We're still up for tonight, though, aren't we?' she called after her.

'Yeah, yeah.' Amy waved an arm without looking back.

There was a truth to Amy's words. But deep down Sophie couldn't leave it alone, it wasn't an issue she could simply walk away from, as her friend had just walked away from her. She couldn't ignore the emails and pictures; it was imperative to recall as many details as possible. Somewhere tucked away in her brain the memories of her friend's murder could be stored, locked away, possibly for her own self-preservation.

The man who murdered Erin needed catching before he could harm anyone else. Perhaps the police already knew who he was. She prayed that was so, that they didn't need whatever she could dredge up – then she could bury whatever it was that'd happened Saturday night.

CHAPTER THIRTY-FOUR

DI Wade

Yesterday's televised appeal had already generated a lot of information: sightings of Erin at different pubs, reports of people acting suspiciously on Saturday evening, unusual activity at the industrial units, even names of possible suspects. It would take some wading through, some careful filtering to figure out what was significant and required further investigation immediately, what could be delegated to another inquiry team and what could be discarded.

Her team, headed up by the Senior Investigating Officer, DCI Bainbridge, had been set up in an incident room at Coleton police station. It was a fairly small station, but there were a couple of rooms dedicated to them: a backroom big enough for the majority of the required tasks to be performed comfortably, plus another smaller one. Lindsay loved the energy in the room, fed off it. Sitting on the edge of a table now, coffee in one hand, a briefing sheet in the other, she took it all in. The buzz, together with the caffeine hit, literally made her heart beat faster – a burst of adrenaline. It's what she lived for.

The briefing was quick. There wasn't a lot to say at this point. Everyone had their tasks – the next few days were going to be mental.

'We're going to need to get that group of teenagers in, you got the list?' Lindsay directed her question at DS Mack who, at an impressive six foot five, could never quite avoid her line of vision.

'Yeah, they've all been spoken to once, and I'm afraid not one of them was that helpful.'

'It's been a few days,' Lindsay shrugged, grabbing hold of her ponytail and sweeping it over her shoulder. 'It's worth another shot, they might have remembered something of relevance by now.'

'Although,' Mack tilted his head to one side and flicked to a page in his notebook, 'Sophie Finch was a bit of an odd one.'

'Oh, odd how?' Lindsay bolted up from the table and moved closer to Mack.

'Really didn't recall a thing from Saturday night, she said she'd been told by her friends that she'd left the pub, the White Hart, early on in the evening, and got in a taxi. But a couple of our PCSOs picked her up later at the roundabout, near the nightclub, pissed out of her head.'

'Interesting. The nightclub is near the murder scene, isn't it?'

'Pretty close, yes. She didn't remember being there, though. She claimed to have no idea how she'd become separated from her friends at the pub, let alone how she ended up on the other side of town. From my observations, Sophie's mum and dad seemed a bit uptight, not just because of the situation, I mean like controlling; straight-laced. They were shocked by the whole thing. I'd hazard a guess they have quite a short leash on the girl, weren't happy about her being out and about at seventeen.'

'Right, thanks Mack. But looks can be deceiving.' Lindsay began to weave her way back to her desk. 'Speak to the relevant officers, will you? See if they can remember more detail about her behaviour when they picked her up.'

'Sure. I've also got her mobile phone, was going through her texts to see if I could glean anything useful.'

'Great. Keep me updated.'

CHAPTER THIRTY-FIVE

Karen

Clearly, she wasn't going to gain much from Amy. Last night's curt reply to her questions may as well have read *bog off and leave me alone*. Karen, elbows on the table, propped her head up in her hands. She stared vacantly at the screen. Sophie had left without a word that morning. The kitchen remained clutter free: no remnants of cornflakes, no splashes of milk, no dirty bowl discarded on the worktop, which Karen berated her for daily. She hadn't eaten – the curry Mike had made last night had barely been touched. How was she going to last the day?

Right, she had to think. She had to attempt to gather some facts. The keys on her laptop clicked away as she typed a response. Another question. She hoped she wouldn't get Amy's back up to the degree she felt compelled to block her.

What time did you put her in the taxi? Did you tell the driver where to take her?

Karen waited. Five minutes passed, and no return message from Amy. She was probably at work by now. She drummed her fingers on the keyboard. Bailey looked up from his bed in the corner of the dining room, fleetingly interested in the noise, then snorted and let his head fall back down on to his paws. He looked bored. Mike normally walked him before he left for work. This morning he'd left to respond to some emergency on the moors before light broke, with Bailey still flat out. So, no walk today. His despondent little face pointed to the fact he somehow knew this. She'd asked Mike to take him to work with him on numerous occasions – the benefits of being a park ranger, surely. He was yet to oblige.

While she waited for a reply that might not come, Karen searched through Amy's friends list. She clicked on the profile of every name she recognised as one from the Saturday night group. Selfies flooded the screen. These teenagers were so full of themselves, bursting with their own self-importance. Didn't they realise most of these images were available for anyone to see? Rosie's profile picture was a shocker, verging on pornographic. Did she have any self-respect? Karen tutted.

She conceded it was the way of the current generation, in this age of technology, of social media. People's lives were lived online; if they didn't have a page full of selfies, group pictures, images of themselves or friends in compromising positions, it meant they led dull and uninteresting lives. If you didn't have tons of 'likes' attached to each photo, you were a no one.

Due to their security settings, the content of each profile page she found was limited to friends. Only Alice's and Dan's were public. She could trail through those, see what they'd put as status updates within the last forty-eight hours or so. Alice, a freakishly tall, slender girl, hadn't been to the house for ages. Sophie said she was training to be a nurse and because of her shift work she rarely socialised now. Saturday night had been her first night out with the group for months. Scanning Alice's page, Karen noted that she hadn't updated it in the last few weeks. A dead end, then.

Disappointing. On to the next.

Dan's made for interesting reading. His version of events as told to DS Mack in her very own lounge had been disquieting, his statuses from the last few days even more so. However, she was most interested in Saturday night's. She worked through them in chronological order:

March 7, 6.32 p.m. 'Getting on it with the girls'

The attached picture featured a line-up of multi-coloured shots, at least twelve, and four girls about to drink them: Sophie, Amy, Erin and one tagged as 'Becks' who Karen didn't recognise. Two girls were in the background, one must be Alice, the other she couldn't make out. She was shocked to see how Erin looked. She'd had shoulder-length, muddy brown hair the last time she'd seen her, only ever wore minimal make-up. In this picture, she looked very different, not the girl Karen knew. She resembled Amy – long, dark, fake hair extensions tumbled over her shoulders, her eyes heavy with eyeshadow and mascara, making her appear older. Just as Rachel had said. She unpeeled her eyes from the image and moved on to the next status.

March 7, 7.01 p.m. 'My boyz. Gonna be a good night!'

Karen knew the three of them in the line-up: Dan with an arm hung loosely over Tom, whose tongue appeared to be in Dan's ear, then Jack, T-shirt pulled up to reveal a nipple. Empty shot glasses and lager cans were strewn on the table behind them. Just gone 7.00 p.m. and already they were tanked. Their assertions that they couldn't remember the specifics of the night were beginning to look plausible. Still, Karen wasn't convinced. Something had happened, someone must know. The next status, the last one from Saturday night, had a photo attached. Karen thrust her face forward, closer to the screen.

March 7, 8.13 p.m. '2 down . . . 3 to go!'

The subjects of the photo, Jack and Tom, standing outside a pub, weren't the interesting part. Behind them, in the background on

123

the opposite side of the road, was a car. She couldn't make it out, it was pretty dark, blurry, but it didn't look like a taxi – there was no sign visible above the car, or on its side. Bent over, by the window on the driver's side, Karen recognised Amy. Stood beside her were Erin and Sophie, arms around each other – Erin holding Sophie up? Karen squinted. Admittedly, the figures were distorted, but if she had to place a bet, she'd put it on it being them. She checked the time stamp again. This must be when Sophie got in the car.

Maybe it hadn't been a taxi after all.

Did Sophie get in a random man's car? Surely, the girls must've known him to allow that to happen. Two and a quarter hours until the police brought Sophie home. What on earth went on in those hours? And why did her friends all say she was put in a taxi home? Didn't they realise it wasn't a bona fide taxi?

She had to tell the police.

Karen pushed the chair back, rushed to the pin board and snatched the card DS Mack had left. She started to dial the number, then stopped. Should she be calling the police at this point? She reflected on what information she had. A photo of an indistinguishable car in the background, too dark to make out. Not much to shout about. But, there'd be experts who'd be able to enhance it, they might pull something helpful. After all, the detective woman on the news said to let them be the judge of what was significant. She should let them know, leave it to them. She began tapping out the digits again. Her fingertip hovered over the fifth number. Stupid. They'd obviously be checking out the social sites of Erin's friends themselves. They probably had this information. Plus, no doubt Rachel must've done the same thing she was doing right now.

Shit. Rach.

A heat spread to her cheeks. Karen checked the clock. It was nearing midday; the plan to work through her coping diary and self-help books to prepare herself to get to Rachel's now well overdue. Engrossed in her fact-finding mission, it'd gone clean out of her mind. What was the best way forward now? Discarding DS Mack's card with one hand, disconnecting the call with the other, Karen headed to the bookcase.

The middle of the three shelves housed an array of self-help books: *How to Manage Your Anxiety*, *Overcome Your Obstacles*, *I Can Make You Confident*, plus at least another fifteen of them in a regimented line. Orderly. Unlike her head. All that guidance, advice, helpful strategies, and here she was, still stuck within the confines of this house. Karen's eyes scanned back and forth, finally settling on *Agoraphobia: Practical Solutions*. Settling cross-legged on the floor, she began flicking through the chapter headings.

A ping sounded from the dining room. A message. It took some effort to stand back up. Old bones. A reply from Amy. She clicked on it:

I'm not sure what you want from me, I told you I can't remember the details. Sophie seems to be getting away with that excuse. Look, I'd love to help, I really would. I know it's important, but it wasn't at the time, so I didn't think to write down the company or the taxi's number plate. As far as I was concerned, I was doing a good deed, getting Sophie, who was beyond drunk, home safe. Yeah, maybe I should've got in with her, made sure she got to her destination. I'm sorry now that I didn't, seeing as it's caused so much trouble.

Hmmm. Stroppy teenager, but point taken.

Undeterred, Karen wrote:

Ok, thanks anyway Amy. I'll try Dan.

Even though she wasn't friends with him, Facebook allowed messages to be sent. It'd probably go in the 'other' messages folder. Dan might not see it, but compelled to try, Karen hammered out her questions, hit send, then went back to her book.

CHAPTER THIRTY-SIX

Oh my God, oh my God . . . chest is tight . . . breathe, think of warm, soft sand . . . *rapid breaths, can't get air to my lungs . . .* the gentle lapping of waves . . . *I'm going to be sick . . . heart's going to burst . . .* relax your muscles, listen to the waves . . . *sweating now, shaking is worsening . . .* what are you meant to be thinking? Change internal dialogue . . . *head woozy . . . going to faint.*

Karen was at the porch door.

One hand gripped the handle, the other arm was outstretched, palm flat against the glass side, preventing her from falling. *Sit down, you have to sit, you're going to faint.* Sliding down to the cold tile floor, legs to one side, Karen gasped for breath – jagged intakes of air desperately attempted to get to her lungs. Tucking her legs behind her, she manoeuvred herself on to all fours and crawled through the inner door to the lounge. The self-help book lay open over the arm of the sofa. She swiped at it, knocking it across the floor.

'*Stupid bitch.*' Her throat was tight, but she forced the self-reproaching abuse through her vocal cords, the distress squeezing out. Flipping herself over, she collapsed, her back against the sofa. She balled her hands into fists and pounded her thighs until they numbed.

Minutes later, still propped up, Karen's breathing slowed. The other symptoms gradually subsided now she'd removed the source of the anxiety. Or, rather, removed herself from it. How was she ever going to remove the cause of her anxiety? Therapy, copious amounts of money spent on books, and she was still hopelessly imprisoned, captive in her own home, her own mind.

The safe zone.

This was her sentence: a life sentence. And it was self-inflicted. Moreover, she'd inflicted it upon her family.

Rachel would've given up on her coming by now. She'd failed her. Another phone call to say sorry? How many times could she apologise? The silence of the house scorned her. Straining to hear some ounce of noise, concrete proof she wasn't totally alone, Karen tilted her head. The hum of electricity running the fridge-freezer, the soft, snuffling noises coming from Bailey, the distant sounds of birds, all reassured her. It was okay. Life was going on.

Not for Erin. Not for Rachel.

Her mind wasn't forgiving, wasn't going to allow her to brush over her helplessness, let her get away with excuses.

Would anyone else?

Her hand still held a tremor. She watched the twitching fingers, wondering why they were the last thing to recover. Oh, of course, she hadn't eaten. That wouldn't be helping. Typical of her, chastising Sophie for it, and then being as bad herself. Sophie was a worry. She hadn't been the same since Saturday night, there was something running deeper – under the surface: a fear. A secret? Was there more to uncover? It was a horrible prospect, maybe one she'd ignore for now, not willing – or able – to cope with more anxiety at present.

Finally stable enough to stand, Karen moved to the kitchen. She looked outside as she passed the patio doors. It was a sunny day, a bit breezy though – leaves from the neighbours' trees danced along the patio. Her eyes travelled to the moorland in the distance. Black smudges appeared like a patchwork quilt – cast by the smattering of clouds; a glint of light flashed as a sunray caught the mirror of a car driving over the moor. There was a clear view to the granite rocks of Haytor; they appeared closer than usual. Did that mean rain? Wasn't that one of the old wives' tales her mother used to tell her? She used to love visiting Haytor, climbing the rocks with Mike, hiking to the top. That seemed such a long time ago now.

She moved away, turning her back on the view to the outside world.

Dropping two slices of bread in the toaster, she sat on the bar stool, waiting for the pop. So much to think about. The possibility of there being more to come didn't want to be ignored. It'd forced its way in now, and was refusing to leave her muddled head. Useless trying to push it aside. With no other human company to distract her thoughts, her actions, she knew she'd have to continue her Facebook investigation with the likelihood that Sophie was holding something back and perhaps had recalled some memories. Her own daughter. Keeping secrets from her. Desperately important secrets. Was she mad, thinking that?

Toast jumped from the slots. Karen jumped too. *Why am I so nervy?*

Karen considered her next move while buttering the toast. She tilted her head back, checked the wall clock. Two hours before Sophie got back. Okay, then it was safe to have a little look in Sophie's room, see if there was anything on her laptop. But wasn't that wrong, obtrusive? It'd be password-protected anyway. Still, it was worth a try, wasn't it? For her own peace of mind. Karen wrestled with the idea until she swallowed the last mouthful of cold toast. Then headed upstairs.

It was messy. Far worse than usual, as if a hunt had taken place for a misplaced item and everything that wasn't it had been scattered across the floor. Seventeen, yet her bedroom resembled a much younger teenager's shit-tip. Karen shook her head. One thing in her favour, she guessed, at least Sophie wouldn't realise she'd been in there snooping. Her eyes scanned the floor: clothes – probably dirty; a plate; three glasses; DVD cases – open and missing their discs; handbags; cotton wool balls – used; make-up; coursework, and there – peeking out from underneath a towel – her laptop. Karen picked a path through the chaos and snatched up the towel. Damp. *Nice one, Sophie.*

Resisting the urge to straighten the duvet, Karen sat on the bed, laptop balanced on her thighs. She set about gaining access, knocking the pangs of guilt from her with each hit of the keys. *Damn.* The screen flashed up the words 'Incorrect login information. Try again'. Three attempts later, still the same error message. It could be anything. No way of guessing beyond the words she'd already tried. Today was not a productive one, she sighed.

What else would be helpful? Did Sophie keep a journal? Doubtful – everything was encased in her mobile phone. Her life was in it, as she'd informed Karen on countless occasions when she'd gone on at her for constantly being attached to it. Mind you, she was probably really missing it now the police had it. Her laptop wasn't as portable; it must be frustrating to have to wait to come home to catch up with her friends' daily activities. Probably one of the reasons she appeared so moody at the moment.

What was Karen doing in here? Really? She didn't even know what she was searching for. *A delaying tactic* – the voice of her therapist cut through. She pushed the annoying voice back inside its compartmentalised box. It wasn't delaying, it was important; she had to find out what had happened to her daughter. Carefully placing the laptop back in the exact same location, then reluctantly draping the same damp towel over it, Karen backtracked to the door. Her eyes returned to the towel. Perhaps she could exchange it for a dry one, Sophie wouldn't notice. She'd have to, it'd play on her mind otherwise, it could damage the laptop.

As she bent to swap towels, something caught her eye.

A black bin liner – a visible bulge signifying something inside – squashed under her bed. Could be rubbish, but judging by the rest of her room, why had she bothered bagging a small bit of it? Ducking down, Karen reached an arm into the space and slowly retrieved it. Felt like one item. Squidgy. The liner was folded and taped – something she had parcelled up to sell on eBay? But why shoved under the bed, then, rather than leaving it out to take to the post office?

Only one thing to do. Open it, then reseal with fresh tape. She'd never know.

CHAPTER THIRTY-SEVEN

Sophie

The cardboard coaster curled up on one edge. Sophie fiddled with it more, folding it back and forth until it broke off. She flicked it with her thumb and forefinger, sending it shooting across the table. Reaching forward, she grabbed another, began the process again, lifting her eyes every few seconds towards the pub door. Amy had finally got back to work at two. Hell of a long lunch. Then she'd shot off after work to get some more money from the hole-in-the-wall outside Asda, saying she'd meet Sophie inside in five.

That was ten minutes ago.

The pub, dimly lit, oozed seediness. They occasionally popped in after work, though, as it was convenient. Sophie sat in the usual corner, the table furthest away from the bar. Yet she still attracted the attention of several men sat on the stools there, could feel their eyes giving her the once over.

Hurry up, Amy.

Sophie took another sip of her Diet Coke. Sitting alone, she couldn't ward off the images, the dark thoughts swimming around her mind. Erin, the chair, the pictures . . . the knowledge she could have been there. She felt sick again and pushed the Coke away. The pub door swung open. Finally, Amy.

'Sorry, got chatting.' She sat down opposite Sophie. 'Mine's a vodka and Coke.'

Sophie rolled her eyes. 'Er . . . Right.' Unbelievable. Late so she could get money, then expects her to buy. Rifling through her bag, she found a fiver, and her fake ID, got up and headed towards the bar surrounded by smarmy men.

Amy was engrossed in texting when she returned with her drink. Why did Sophie get the impression she was going to be of no help at all?

'Here you go.'

No response. Head down – both thumbs fiercely tapping away at the keypad. After another minute or so, Sophie huffed loudly. 'Are we going to chat then, or what?'

Amy giggled, raising her eyes fleetingly. 'Yep, two secs.' She dramatically hit the send button, then placed the phone face down on the table. 'Right. You have my full attention.' She smiled.

Don't do me any favours. 'Good. Okay, you said you'd help me try and figure out what happened Saturday night, so let's start with when we left your house.' Sophie sat forward, leaning in closer to Amy.

'Well, I suppose we left just after seven, the boys wanted to get on it early. They were so up for it, were pretty ratted before we even left, actually.'

'I remember that bit. Still don't know why they were eager to go into town so early. It's their fault I got so drunk so damned quickly.'

'First pub, Spoons,' Amy continued. 'Didn't stay there long, then the White Hart.'

'So when we left Spoons, we were all together?'

'Yep. Didn't you see the CCTV footage on the news?'

'No, missed it, couldn't stomach watching any re-runs either.' Sophie let out a long breath.

'Anyway,' Amy was on a roll now, her voice animated, 'we all headed down South Street to the White Hart, you'd already had

134

enough, we practically dragged you. We stayed in there for, ooh, about half an hour, maybe more, I'm not sure, it's not like I was clock-watching. Remember any of that?'

'I feel there's something there, some vague recollection of being at the bar . . .' Sophie rubbed her forehead. 'Oh, I don't know.' A headache was starting.

'You said you wanted to leave. I thought you meant to another pub, but when I suggested the next one, you told me, no, you had to go home.'

'And where was Erin at this point?'

'With me and you. The others were chatting outside, I believe, smoking – you know Becks, always hauling us outside with her, then ditching us to get into deep and meaningful chats with fellow smokers.'

'And Erin phoned for a taxi?'

'Yep, said she agreed you should go home, didn't want you making a complete tit of yourself, as usual—'

'Hey!'

'Sorry, but do you not *remember* projectile vomiting while performing Lady Gaga on the karaoke in the Locomotive a few months back?'

'Oh, blimey, yeah, okay, point taken.' Sophie couldn't help but smile at the memory. But why could she remember that, even though she'd been wasted, but not an event as important as this? 'Did you hear Erin on the phone, did she say who she called?'

'No, Sophie. You're sounding like your mother now. And on that note, like I said earlier, I really don't appreciate being made the scapegoat for this.'

Sophie bridled. 'Oh, Amy, she's not suggesting you're responsible for any of this, honestly. She's doing what any mum would do. Trying to find out what happened. It's not only for me, you know. Erin *is* her best friend's daughter.' She caught herself. 'Was.' Every now and then, the gravity of it smacked her full-force, sending a judder through her insides. She lowered her head and fiddled with an acrylic nail.

'I know. Sorry,' Amy said, her tone softer. 'I have this constant sick ball in my stomach, can't get rid of it. I've been avoiding thinking about Erin, how it must've felt, how scared she was . . .'

Sophie had the urge to tell Amy about the pictures she'd been sent, to share the visions haunting her, and her biggest worry: that there was a very real possibility she'd been with Erin that night. And seen her killer. She regurgitated a mouthful of Coke, clasped her hand over her mouth, swallowing hard.

'You all right?'

Sophie managed a nod. They sat quietly for a moment, neither looking at the other.

'I wish I'd been a better friend,' Amy said, the tears sparkling in her eyes, their greenness sharpened.

Sophie reached a hand across and laid it on top of hers. 'You can't think like that, hun. It'll tear you apart.'

'Difficult not to, Soph, isn't it?' Her eyes penetrated Sophie's. Could she see the guilt in them? The pain, which must be evident, knowing she had probably witnessed more than Amy could ever imagine – had maybe even been there when her friend died – and had done nothing to help? And she reckoned *she* should've been a better friend. No one had let Erin down as much as she obviously had. Continued to do now.

Suddenly Sophie wanted to change the subject, talk about things like they used to. Mundane, everyday things: the weird customers they'd had during the day, the teachers on her college course, the antics of the boys, plans for nights out, nights in. Safe topics. But she couldn't tear herself away from the conversation, she needed more information. That was the reality. She had to push on.

'At the taxi, then, who was there?'

Amy heaved a sigh. 'I've been over this a million times, Soph.'

'I know, I know. But it's important.'

'Me. Erin. You. That's it.'

'Did you see the driver, get a good look at his face? Would you recognise him if you saw him again?'

'No. No and no. You finished your interrogation now?' Her eyebrows lifted, disappearing into her fringe.

'Nearly. Which direction did the taxi go? And where did you and Erin go next?'

'I don't really remember. Once you were in, I kinda turned away, went back in the pub.'

'You said earlier that we only stayed in the White Hart for about half an hour, so are you sure you went back inside, not on to another pub?'

Amy scrunched her eyes up, placed her fingertips at her temples. 'Um . . . I think I just nipped back inside to gather up the others, before heading to the next one.'

'Right. And Erin?'

'Well, I assume she was still with me when you left, standing beside me on the pavement.' She paused, eyes narrowing, then looked up to the right, like she was searching a memory. 'But, I could've left her standing there when I crossed over to go back inside to get the others, I suppose. I'm not sure I remember her being with me.'

'Yes. I bet that's it.' Sophie sat upright, a glimmer of hope glistening at the edge of the darkness of her despair – a possible breakthrough in this whole mess. 'That's when she went off, or was taken, or whatever.'

'Maybe. The TV said there was no further CCTV footage of her afterwards. So it would make sense.'

'She definitely didn't get inside the taxi with me, did she?'

'Why would she have?'

'I don't know, perhaps wanted me to get home safely? Didn't like the look of the driver, thought there was safety in numbers?'

Amy drew herself up indignantly. 'Oh, okay. So what you're saying is she was a good friend, I'm a useless one. Basically what your mum is thinking. In fact, I'm sure she's *accusing* me of letting you down, letting Erin down. So it's all my fault. Yep.' Amy jumped up. 'Blame me.' Her anger escalated quickly, unexpectedly.

'I am not blaming you, Amy. I'm just saying what might have happened. I don't even know—'

'Whatever. Look, perhaps you and your mother should give me a wide berth for a while, anyway, eh? And do me a favour, tell her to quit her stupid *hit list*. Dan's apparently next, or so she threatened, but he doesn't know any more than me. Leave him alone.' Without a backwards glance, she left.

The pub door shut with a resounding thud.

Great. Not how Sophie had wanted that to go. But, she'd gained something. It was entirely possible that Amy didn't wait for the taxi to drive off before she went back into the pub, leaving a brief moment when Erin could've climbed into the taxi as well. A tingling spread to her fingertips. Had Erin been as drunk as Sophie? Is that why the driver took advantage? Or had he been waiting for such a situation to arise? And is that how they'd ended up together, maybe, if that flash of memory she'd had told the truth?

Too many questions. And for now, she'd hit a wall, with no conceivable way over it without more help. But not from her mum. Her interference had caused enough problems.

CHAPTER THIRTY-EIGHT

Karen

'Why are you trying to make my life so difficult?' Sophie burst through the lounge door, strode up to where Karen was sitting.

Karen moved forward. 'Er . . . hello would've been nice.' A frown crinkled her forehead.

'Ruining my friendship with Amy is *so* the right way to go. Thanks a lot. Not like my friends are dropping like flies or anything.'

'I only asked her a few questions, Sophie. And don't say that, that's an awful thing to say.' A prickly sensation, a warning of tears.

'Sorry, but it's how I feel.' Sophie slumped on to the two-seater sofa, her rant seemingly over.

'Yeah. I know.' Karen got up and moved across to sit next to her, placing her hand on Sophie's knee. 'Let me show you this picture I found, Sophie—'

'No, Mum. Enough.'

'Please.' Karen jumped up and walked towards her laptop. 'You need to see what I mean . . .'

Sophie let out a low groan, pushed up from the sofa and turned towards the door. 'I'm not interested in your stupid theories.' She paused, eyes narrowed. 'Get a life.'

That stung – pushing Karen backwards as if a physical object had made contact with her body. Her mouth opened, closed again, muted.

'Are you going to let her talk to you like that?' Mike barged his way through the ajar door, knocking into Sophie. She glared at him, her mouth set in a straight line.

'Great, so you're joining in too, are you?' Sophie made to push past him.

'Sophie, love, don't . . .' Karen, alert to the change in atmosphere, tried to intervene to prevent a blow-up.

'You should listen to your mother.' Mike's expression was contorted, and his face was too close to Sophie's.

'Like you do, you mean?' She turned back sharply, her face reddened. 'Listen to yourself . . .' Her voice, harsh. She gave a short, sharp, sarcastic laugh.

It *was* going to blow up. Karen stepped back from them, her breath catching, a stabbing pain seizing and paralysing her lungs. And she'd started this. Her hands went to her middle. She pushed her fingers into her sides, bent over, gasping for air.

'I . . . need,' shallow breaths, 'my . . . bag.'

'Right, of course you do. Get her stupid bag, Sophie.'

'*You* get it.'

'I asked you.' Like bickering children. Mike then turned to Karen, 'It's a ploy, have a panic attack, stop me from telling Sophie off . . . you always do this.' His anger, spilling, spreading from Sophie to Karen.

Sophie wasn't backing down. 'There you go again, *Dad*, you tell me off for the way *I* speak to her, then *you* treat her like she's worthless.'

'I . . . am . . . here,' Karen managed, clasping at her chest. This was too much in one day, she was going to have a heart attack.

'For pity's sake. Look at her.' He shook his head and pushed past both of them, heading for the kitchen. He took his time returning with the bag and gave it to Karen without looking at her.

'You should grow up, really, Sophie. Your mother's only trying to find out what happened to you because you were too irresponsible, and now you claim not to remember anything. You brought this all on yourself.'

Karen listened as best she could while blowing in and out of her bag.

'Yes, that's right, Dad, because you never did anything irresponsible in your entire life, did you?'

'Don't turn this around! Face it, you screwed up Saturday night. Don't blame me for your mistakes. I'm not bailing you out.'

The sobbing came immediately; like a flick of a switch the tears turned on.

'I wouldn't expect you to.' Her streaming nose mixed with the tears, both running into her mouth. Sophie swept a sleeved arm across it then ran from the room.

Karen, shocked and not fully recovered, could only stare at the empty space where Sophie had stood. She shouldn't have mentioned the picture. Not yet. Not until she had a firm idea of its significance. Added to her finding earlier, the two things *were* connected, she was sure of it. But how they were linked she had no idea. Now it would have to wait for another day.

Mike's expression remained fixed – his clenched teeth tightening his jaw muscles, creating hard lines. It would be a while now before he relaxed, and she needed him to be calm so that she could be. She'd give it ten minutes, then begin the process of softening over the edges to make the hours before bedtime bearable.

Hands, rough, tight around her neck. A knee to her lower back, her body squashed hard against the driver's seat – shards of white light detonating like fireworks in her head as her face smashed against the headrest. His breath in her ear, his voice deep, a whisper: *I'm going to have fun fucking you.*

Karen bolted upright, clasped one hand to her throat. *Can't swallow, can't breathe.*

'Hey. Shh . . . you're dreaming.' Mike's hand touched her arm.

'Get off, leave me alone!'

'It's okay, Karen, it's me, it's Mike. Shh.'

The man continued to whisper hushed threats while holding her tight with one strong arm, chest pressed into her back. *You better not go to the cops. It was your idea remember; you wanted this. . .* His other hand was in her hair, twisting the curls around his fingers, pulling gently at first, then snapping her head back. Pain. The smell. Constricted. Enclosed. *I can't breathe.*

'Karen. *Karen.*' There was an explosion of light.

'What's the matter, what's happening?' Karen blinked, the brightness of the main bedroom light stinging her tired eyes.

'You were having a nightmare,' Mike's soothing voice. 'You haven't had one like that for ages. You okay?' He sat on the edge of the bed, concerned eyes searching hers.

'I was reliving it . . . It was awful.' Karen relaxed her shoulders; tear-filled eyes met Mike's. 'Sorry. I'm really sorry.'

'Nothing to be sorry for.' He touched her arm, gently circling his thumb on her bare skin.

'There is.' Karen pushed the duvet off her legs, scrunching it up towards Mike, swung out of bed and walked unsteadily to the en suite. She wouldn't usually close the door, but now she did. She wanted to hide the tears from Mike. Her legs were shaky; she shut the toilet seat, sat on the cool lid. It had been a while since she'd dreamt of him. Of it. The remnants of the fear remained in her bloodstream, the adrenaline causing the shakes. In reality the attack had only lasted minutes; seemed a lot longer, though. At one point, she'd thought her life was over. The feeling of hope slipping away with each forced breath. But she'd fought back at the last moment, grabbing her fallen shoe and shoving its six-inch heel hard into his groin. She'd escaped from her car, her temporary prison, before he could finish whatever he'd intended. She hadn't been seriously harmed. Not physically, like Erin had. How had Erin felt in those last moments of her life? Knowing it really was game over. *Don't think about it, clear your mind.*

It was inevitable the nightmares would start up again now. The counsellor had assured her that the dreams would eventually lessen, but might cluster in times of stress, or if she was bottling up her emotions. Tick. And tick. Great. She'd have to start her sleeping medication again. She thought she'd progressed from those.

'You coming back to bed?' Mike's voice interrupted the one inside her head.

'Yep, just coming.' Karen tore off a piece of toilet roll, wiped her nose.

'Turn the light off again, will you?'

She flicked the switch.

CHAPTER THIRTY-NINE

Hey Gorgeous,
Hope you've had a good day, and didn't work too hard. I've missed you.

I love that I can always talk to you, like, properly – in-depth, sharing my deepest thoughts. Weird that we have so much in common given the age gap. Apart from our music tastes – you're on your own with some of those groups!

I've had a tough day today, thinking about Dad. I've been re-reading his letters, you know how I get -- it makes me angry, yet I still have to do it, still put myself through the torture.

Having you helps, though. Thoughts of being with you keep me going, bring me through the darkness to a better place. You are my shining light, guiding me to my future. Our future.

There's only one barrier to get over, before we can be together, forever.

But, you love me, so that's not going to be a problem.

Message back – I need you tonight.

xxxxxx

CHAPTER FORTY

Sophie

Wednesday

She was there on her own. Her dad was at work, her mother incapable of making the journey. Francesca, her concession manager, hadn't been impressed that she'd asked for time off. She'd explained the reason and all she got was, 'Couldn't you arrange it on one of your days off, or during your college week?' The cheek. You couldn't exactly say no to the police.

Sitting in a plastic chair, like the ones in schools, she fidgeted, shifting her weight to relieve the discomfort of the hard edges sticking into the backs of her thighs. Sophie cracked her knuckles one by one, causing the decrepit-looking officer behind the desk to give her sideways glances of disapproval. Why were they making her wait? They were the ones who'd wanted her to come here. To make a statement; question her further. Her stomach flipped. At least last time when she'd been asked questions she was able to truthfully say she couldn't remember anything. How was she going to play this now? She wasn't ready to tell them what she thought she might've seen. Not yet.

The officer turned to face her square on, peering over the top of his bifocals. Her face flushed; she lowered it quickly, in an attempt to escape his stare. The heat made her skin prickle. *Great. I look guilty before they ask me a single question.* In her peripheral vision, she saw him go around the desk. He was coming to get her.

'If you could follow me please, Miss Finch.' He motioned for her to get up. Her whole body pulsated; she could feel it moving, rocking gently forward and back. What if her legs gave way when she stood? 'Okay?' His tone, firm. He was staring again.

'Yes. Sorry.'

She followed him down a narrow corridor. Stopping abruptly, he rapped the knuckle of his forefinger on a closed door. Sophie noted the sign: a sliding one that read 'Interview Room – Engaged'. Presumably, if you slid it across it would say 'Vacant'. Definitely more apt in her case, although, not quite as vacant as she'd been when she'd previously met DS Mack. How was she going to cope inside this room? How could she avoid telling them about the pictures? A muffled voice indicated that they should enter.

'Hello, Sophie isn't it?' The woman smiled as she stood and pulled a chair out for Sophie.

'Yes.' She sat, scanning the small room. It wasn't like the interview rooms she'd seen in police shows on the telly, where there was a single table with two plastic chairs either side of it, no natural light and one of those two-way mirrors. This one had soft chairs, a small window and, thankfully, no mirror. Sophie's shoulders relaxed.

'Okay, Sophie, I'm Detective Inspector Wade, you've met Detective Sergeant Mack already.' She directed a hand towards the man who'd taken her mobile phone. 'We asked you here to make a formal statement regarding the night of Saturday March seventh, the night Erin Malone was murdered.'

Sophie flinched.

'I know you gave an initial statement to DS Mack; we want to now formalise it, plus, see if you've remembered anything further. We've interviewed other people who were with Erin that night.'

148

She offered what looked to be a reassuring smile. She didn't add '*so, no need to worry, then*', which would've reassured her more. 'And now I would like to hear from you. Can I make sure you're happy to continue without a parent here?'

'Yes, I'm fine with that.' No choice even if she wasn't.

DS Mack reached across the table to the recording device, which sat like an elephant in the room, while DI Wade went through the formalities.

Sophie sucked in a breath and watched the recording light flash as it awaited her statement.

The interview lasted less than thirty minutes. She had stuck rigidly to her story, that she couldn't remember much past seven in the evening. The flashbacks, the horrifying awareness of being there, with Erin, the emailed pictures – all left undisclosed. The thought of verbalising it, of showing the humiliating pictures, was far too much to contemplate. She needed to bury it deep inside her mind so she didn't have to deal with it, what the photos could mean.

She'd be in so much trouble if she told the police and they realised she'd known about the pictures since Sunday. Withholding evidence. She had good reason though, didn't she? He wouldn't be stupid enough to send them from an email that could be traced to him. So there was no point in showing them, they wouldn't be of much help. She rubbed her stomach in an attempt to relieve the sick feeling.

So, why did she feel so guilty for not telling them?

She'd been surprised at the direction the interview had taken. Once they hadn't gleaned much from her, they'd moved on, talking about how unusual stranger attacks were, and saying the perpetrator was generally someone known to the victim. Then DI Wade rattled off the names of everyone from her group of friends and gave a short bio, like they were up for the same job at an interview. She and DS Mack asked her questions about who Erin may have been seeing, if she knew of her past boyfriends, if any of the guys out that night had ever been involved with her. Any arguments.

Weird. They were obviously suggesting that one of her friends had something to do with Erin's murder.

Sophie's mind strayed back to the time of her mum's attack. The police had believed the attacker to be someone known to her too. Her mum had been adamant she'd never set eyes on him before, but Sophie distinctly remembered them pushing her, asking for a list of men she'd supervised, past and present – thinking someone with a criminal history was the most likely candidate. It was the start of her mum's problems. The family's problems. Things hadn't been the same since.

If they thought it was someone Erin knew, and the police had also said this to her friends when they'd been interviewed, who was going to be the first person they suspected?

The last person who saw Erin.

Which, in Sophie's mind at least, was looking more and more likely to be her.

As she walked towards her car, Sophie turned. The feeling of being watched set her skin crawling. She'd had the same feeling since Monday. A few police officers walked towards the station door, a woman and child crossed the path behind her. No one else was visible. Maybe they were concealing themselves, ducked behind a parked car, hidden behind one of the walls. *I'm over-reacting.* She quickened her pace, the fight-or-flight adrenaline response kicking in. She reached the car, gave one more furtive glance around before jumping in. Her shaky hand dropped the keys as she tried to push it into the ignition. They fell into the footwell. She bent to retrieve them, then righted herself.

A face pressed up against her window. Pale, wide-eyed and staring.

An involuntary scream escaped.

CHAPTER FORTY-ONE

DI Wade

'What did you make of that then, Mack?' Lindsay handed him a coffee and sat on the edge of her desk with hers in both hands. She rarely sat in a chair, preferring the elevated position of the desk, or standing, so that she could see all around the incident room.

Mack sat back in his chair, stretching his legs out. He looked up at Lindsay, his eyebrows drawn. 'Well, she was fidgety, avoided eye contact, nervy. But, I don't know whether I'd put that down to her being in a police station on her own, her friend having been murdered, you know – it's a lot for a seventeen-year-old to cope with. Don't you think?'

'It is. But . . .' Lindsay pulled her shoulders up towards her ears. 'I don't know, something was *off*, I could sense she wasn't telling us something.'

'Ah, well. If you can *sense* it, you must be right. You could sniff out a cod in a fish shop.' Mack snorted, coffee spilling over the side of the cup as he laughed at his own joke.

'I think that's a compliment,' Lindsay said, raising herself from the desk. 'Right, come on, let's go through the other interview transcripts from the Saturday night group, see if we can spot any inconsistencies now we have Sophie's statement. I'm still thinking that Daniel Pearce was jumpy, too, and he was sticking *so* closely to the story that Amy Howard gave. Like they'd rehearsed it.'

'Yes, Boss.' Mack pulled his legs back and sat up straight. He grabbed the file.

CHAPTER FORTY-TWO

Sophie

'Shit!' Sophie swung the car door open, smashing into Dan. 'What the hell?'

'Did I frighten you?' Dan rubbed his hip.

'What do you think?'

'Sorry, just wanted to catch you before you drove off.'

'Well, now you have my attention.' Sophie got out, shut the driver's door, then leant back against it. 'What are you doing here?'

'I was going to ask you the same.'

Sophie narrowed her eyes. His face was ashen; dark skin beneath his eyes gave the impression he'd been beaten up. Perhaps he had.

'I was asked to give a statement. You?'

'What did you tell them?' He ignored her question.

'Why do you want to know?'

'Don't screw around with me, Soph. Just tell me.' His lips tightly closed, his eyebrows drawn so close they almost touched. He leaned in closer.

Sophie put both hands up, palms facing him. 'Hey, back off. Get out of my personal space.' She gave a laugh, her attempt at being light-hearted. But she didn't feel it. The laugh sounded nervous, even to her.

He shook his head and turned away, but stood his ground. 'I need to know what you told them. What they asked you.' His tone, mellower now. Calmer. 'They're pointing the finger at me, aren't they?'

'What makes you say that?' A stupid question, given what they'd implied during her interview.

'They questioned me like I was a criminal, Soph.' He took a step back, pushing his hands into his jeans pockets. 'Went on about it being likely that Erin's killer was known to her—'

'Yeah, they were saying the same to me, too,' Sophie admitted.

'They think it was one of us.'

'Uh, I don't know they were necessarily suggesting that. Maybe just that *we* could know who it was if Erin had?'

'Did you tell them, you know . . . about me and Erin?'

'No, Dan. That was ages ago, I think they were concerned about the more recent boyfriends Erin had, not some drunken one-night stand she had with you.'

The deep creases in his forehead softened. 'Thanks.'

'No need to thank me, it's not like I was keeping it from them to protect you, only I didn't think it was necessary, that's all. You two have been – sorry, were – fine with each other. We often laughed about it, actually.'

'Oh, cheers.'

'Anyway, what you doing following me around?'

'Not following.' Indignation showed in his eyes. 'I saw you drive this way, knew you were obviously headed for the station, so walked up to see if I could catch you.'

'Grill me, you mean.'

'Sorry. This whole thing's making me all edgy.' A shudder shook his body, confirming the truth of what he'd just said.

'You should be careful. Makes you look like you've got something to hide.' Sophie fixed her eyes on his. He kept the contact, not blinking. The moment stretched. It was like they were both afraid to be the first to blink, or look away.

'I've got to go.' Sophie broke his stare and, defeated in that round, turned to get back in her car.

'What are we going to do?' Dan held the door, preventing her from shutting it.

Sophie huffed. 'About what, Dan?' Her tone displayed her irritation.

'About all of this shit! Are we going to all get together . . . talk it through?'

'I don't know, I guess so. I've only seen Amy. And you, obviously. Do a group message, see what you can arrange. Well, actually, you'll have to Facebook me. They've still got my mobile.' She indicated back towards the police station with a wave of her hand, then pulled on the inside of the door. Dan let go.

In her rear-view mirror, she watched him, his figure silhouetted against the backdrop of darkening clouds. Even when she drove away, he remained there, standing still, arms at his side, staring after her car. At the traffic lights she turned left, and out of his field of vision. Only then did she relax. DI Wade had planted the seed of doubt. Had it been her intention? Turn them against each other? This was an awful situation. Not trusting her own friends.

But, she realised, she didn't even trust herself.

Sophie pulled up outside the house, having to park on the road as her dad's Land Rover was blocking the driveway. Oh, so he couldn't go to the police station with her because he was working, but he'd managed to pay a visit back home. She really had angered him last night; clearly, he wanted nothing to do with her.

She was on her own in this mess.

Not wanting to go inside and find out why he was home, Sophie remained in the car. What was she going to do about all of this? Maybe Dan was right, they should all get together, the group from Saturday – thrash it out, see what they could come up with. But what if one of them *was* involved; did kill Erin, and was now sending her the pictures? She couldn't imagine what they'd be trying to gain by doing that, though. No. It seemed impossible it could be one of them. She knew them, had known them for years, gone to school with them. Apart from Amy, who she'd later met at work, and Dan, who she'd met through Amy. But they were sound. Surely, none of them could be doing this.

It might've been an accident? An argument gone wrong, a scuffle, Erin fell – smacked her head, died. Sophie rubbed her face. Pointless. Of course, it wasn't an accident. Her flashbacks didn't match with an accidental killing. It'd been purposeful. Planned, even. It couldn't possibly be one of her friends. For one, they weren't that clever. And more to the point, they weren't that sadistic, cruel. They weren't psychopaths.

A movement at the front door caught her attention. Her dad was leaving, his face set, unsmiling. *Perhaps Mum's had another panic attack.* Head lowered, he made his way to the Land Rover. He didn't even indicate whether he'd seen Sophie, just climbed in, started the engine and drove off. Now she *really* didn't want to go inside. Whatever the reason for his being home, it didn't look too much like it'd reached a satisfactory outcome. She craned her neck to see inside the front window of the house, but couldn't see her mum. Good. Hopefully she hadn't seen her either.

The rest of the day was hers now, she realised; they weren't expecting her back at work. Turning the key in the ignition, Sophie checked her mirror and moved off.

She knew where she should go.

If her mum couldn't go and see Rachel, then she would.

CHAPTER FORTY-THREE

A chill consumed her insides, gripped her intestines, squeezed her heart.

Erin's bedroom was quiet. Empty.

Sophie ran her fingertips gently over a photograph on the dressing table. A picture of the girls. Smiling. Blissfully happy. Erin's lips were puckered, placed on the side of Amy's cheek. Sophie, with her arms around Becks. Four of them together before a night out, always the most fun part of the evening. The laughs, the gossiping – getting ready with her girls was the best. Sophie bit hard on her lower lip until she tasted the metallic tang of blood, but it didn't head off the tears.

'Thanks for coming, Sophie.' Rachel stood at the threshold of the room. Sophie turned, her face crumpled; a choking moan emanated from her. Rachel moved in and threw her arms around her. They stood, embraced; joined in a grief that was only just beginning its passage through them.

Not able to stay longer within the sadness of the abandoned room, Sophie asked if they could talk downstairs. They sat opposite each other at the large wooden table in the kitchen and had coffee. The same table Sophie had sat at a hundred times with Erin. Rachel talked about her memories of Erin and Sophie as children: how they'd once wandered off when they were four, picking berries from the hedgerow, and had walked too far and got lost. How they'd played for hours with the big leaves from the front garden bush, pretending they were money, using the wrought iron gate as a bank counter and pushing the leaves underneath, counting them out like a cashier would. They laughed at the memory of the Sylvanian family house with all its contents, the one Sophie had always been jealous of. 'I've still got the lot.' Rachel smiled.

Innocence. Only seemed a few years ago, really. Who would've known those memories of her childhood would be so poignant, so fragile?

'I haven't been able to share any of this with anyone. The only person who's been here really is the family liaison officer, and she knows nothing about Erin. Not Erin when she was alive, anyway.' Rachel looked down, fiddling with her hands in her lap.

'I know. I'm sorry that Mum . . . that she hasn't made it here.' The guilt she felt wasn't hers to own, yet she felt responsible, somehow. She should've been more supportive, helped her mum get here. 'I'm sure she'll get it together soon, she's not staying away on purpose.'

'Oh, I know that, love. Just wish . . .' Her voice became high-pitched. 'I wish she could be here . . . I need her so much, Sophie.' The tears started over. Bigger tears, heavier crying; a sobbing which tore through Sophie's chest. She got up, moved around the table and held Rachel tight.

'I'm sorry. I'm so sorry, Rachel.'

Their bodies rocked together, a comforting movement; a slow dance to a silent song.

'They took things from Erin's rooms, here and at her dad's, you know.' Her voice was muffled by Sophie's cardigan.

Sophie pulled away slightly, so she could understand what Rachel was saying.

'What things?'

'Her laptop, for one. Some things from her dressing table, her bedside table. A journal. Although I thought it was empty, she was given it one year by Adam's sister, she'd only just taken it from its cellophane.'

'Will you get them back?'

'Apparently. It's the thought of people, police, touching it though, reading her personal stuff. It's a violation.'

'It must feel that way, but if it helps them catch whoever did this . . .'

'Yeah. I know. That's what your mum said. And Adam. It hurts that I'm going through this alone. Erin is Adam's and mine, yet, he's there with *her*. I'm trying to cope with all this without the father of my child. Our dead child.'

Sophie winced. 'I'm so sorry, that's lousy.'

'And she had the nerve to talk to me about Erin, too. Bitch. Said Erin had been having issues. Had confided she was unhappy. What right does she have having heart-to-hearts with *my* Erin?'

'It must be difficult, but maybe she was trying to be nice, get Erin on her side as it were?'

Rachel shrugged hopelessly. 'Whatever. What really sticks the knife in is that Erin didn't feel able to talk to me about it. She hadn't mentioned a thing about any problems. Nothing.'

'Did *she* bother to tell you what the problem was?'

'Eventually, after I threatened her . . .'

'Oh.' Sophie raised an eyebrow.

'I know. I'm not proud; she rubs me up the wrong way, taking my husband of twenty years after only knowing him a few months. Anyway, she said Erin had been talking about wanting a boyfriend, someone who treated her, made her feel special. Mentioned her thoughts about going online to meet this man of her dreams.'

'Really? She never said any of this to me. Are you sure?'

'*I'm* not sure. *She* was. Also went on about how Erin was jealous of some of her friends, wanted to be more like them . . .' Rachel broke down again. When she regained her composure, she added,

'Wanted to be as popular, as pretty. Said she never got the attention they did.'

Sophie's chest tightened. Surely, she couldn't have meant her. She didn't have a boyfriend. Amy? It must be Amy she'd referred to. The popular, pretty one with a seemingly wealthy boyfriend, one that showered gifts on her. So, she'd wanted to be like Amy, that's why she'd dyed her hair, had extensions put in. *How do I know why Amy wanted to be Amy?* Her own, confused words came back to her. They were beginning to make more sense. Maybe Erin had also wanted the life Amy had. Was seeking it out.

And Amy met her boyfriend online.

At least some pieces were beginning to slot together.

'Did Erin go online, then, like on a dating site or something?'

'It's possible, yes.'

'Then, someone online may have . . .'

The sentence didn't require finishing. They both knew where she was heading.

'It's a line of enquiry the police were keen to follow, yes. I assume they're hoping to find something on Erin's laptop, a trail, some solid evidence of who she'd been chatting to.'

'Why didn't Erin tell me?' Sophie's shoulders slumped. Erin usually confided in her. Why not about this?

'That's the question I've been asking myself for the last three days. I'm her mum, and we've been through so much. Why in God's name did she talk to that woman, and not me?'

'I guess she was keeping us both in the dark, then. The question is, why? And who else, apart from Adam's girlfriend, did she tell?'

CHAPTER FORTY-FOUR

Karen

'I've never heard of anyone's phobia actually worsening with treatment. But, congratulations, you've managed it.'

Back inside the house, Karen sat on the sofa breathing in and out of the bag, while Mike stood over her. The attempt at getting to Rachel's had failed before Mike had even turned the first corner of the road leading out of theirs. Pathetic. Or so he'd said.

'It's not a phobia . . . as such,' Karen struggled to speak. 'It's a condition. Brought on by anxiety. As the anxiety increased . . . so did my symptoms.'

'I don't get it. Seriously. I mean, you started off afraid to be in the car on your own. Understandable. Then it progressed to not liking the car at all. Then afraid to go outside on your own, and now you're afraid to leave the house, period.'

'Yeah, thanks for the rundown.' She put the bag down. 'It's not like I don't remember my decline. Thanks.'

'But why so bad? What am I paying that counsellor for? Are you sure she's even qualified?'

Karen's chest tightened. 'Why don't . . . you go back . . . to work.' She squeezed the words out, hoping the tone came across as harsh as she'd intended.

'Better had, *someone* needs to bring some money into the household.'

Oh, that's right, bring that up now. Haven't heard it in a while.

Karen watched through narrowed eyes as Mike turned and slammed the door on his way out.

Once the roar of the car disappeared, Karen went to the dining room, to her laptop. Now that he'd increased her anxiety further, a distraction was required. Five emails. Mostly spam.

Delete, delete . . . delete.

The two remaining ones looked important. She'd deal with them later.

Her finger hovered over the documents icon. Why did Mike have to make her feel so useless?

She moved the cursor across the screen.

He must hate her, to continually remind her of the fact that she let them down.

She clicked the icon and selected the file.

It was her penance; when she felt this bad about herself, the situation she'd forced on to her family, she revisited the diary she'd started after the attack. This was the first time in eight months, though. She'd done well. How had she been so stupid, so naïve? You'd think someone in her job role would think of the consequences, weigh up the pros and cons of agreeing to meet up with a man she'd only seen at work a few times. He came across so charming, selling his snacks to the staff at a lunchtime – full of compliments and cheeky winks. Aimed at Karen. He would linger at her desk, keen to engage her in chit-chat. He made her laugh. Made her feel good. Staring now at her words from two years ago, they reinforced the fact this was all her own fault. Her mess.

Aside from the need to punish herself, she'd kept the entries in a separate file just in case.

In case she ever told the truth. In case she was ever brave enough to talk to her counsellor about what really happened – that she'd

162

agreed to meet her attacker, that he wasn't a stranger. That she'd been the first victim of the man known now as the Carey Park rapist. It would aid her recovery, she knew that, but how could she come clean? What would the fallout of that be?

Her throat tensed as she read the first lines of the entry, visions of that night forcing themselves into her mind. *His fingers tight around her neck.* Her stomach contracted as she read another passage, her words on the screen bringing back the sounds of that night, the smells; the pain. *The struggle to escape his grip tearing at every muscle.* Reading the last line, her breathing shallowed, each breath an attempt to get air deep within her lungs. *His hands restricting her oxygen, slowly strangling the life from her.*

The door slammed.

Karen jumped, shut the laptop. Shut out the memories again. For now.

'You okay? Oh no, Mum, where's your bag?'

'I'm fine, I'm fine.'

'You don't look it, you're practically blue.'

Sophie ran around to the kitchen. 'It's not here, where is it?' The rise in her voice gave away her panic.

'In the lounge. It's okay. I don't need it.' It was true; her anxiety hadn't reached the stage where the bag was required again. Had Sophie not turned up when she did, putting a stop to her self-loathing mission, well, *then* she may have been in trouble.

'Sure?' Sophie held the bag out, a single raised eyebrow indicating disbelief.

'Really.' Karen moved past Sophie to the lounge. 'How did it go at the station? All done?'

'I guess so.' Sophie perched on the arm of the opposite sofa. 'They were going on about it being likely Erin knew her killer, like they said to you when you were attacked, that you must've known him.'

Karen stiffened and drew in a ragged breath through her nose.

'Right, well, we know that's not always the case, don't we?' She

163

avoided eye contact with Sophie. 'What about the taxi driver, did they mention whether they're looking into him?'

'No. No, they didn't say.'

'Well, that's stupid, surely he is the main suspect at this time?'

'I don't know, Mum. Perhaps he is. They aren't going to tell me, are they? And anyway, they've got Erin's laptop; maybe they're investigating her online activities.'

'What for? And how do you know that?'

'I went to Rachel's.'

'Oh. Right. That's good. Well done.' Her daughter was clearly a better friend than her. 'How did she seem?' Guilt soaked her words.

'She seemed sad, Mum. Alone. Devastated. Every word you can think of to describe someone whose daughter has just been murdered.' Sophie wiped a tear away. 'Anyway, Rachel said Erin had told *whatsherface* she wanted to be more like her friend, I'm guessing Amy, and to have a boyfriend who treated her. Like Amy's. And Amy met her boyfriend through a dating site, the one they keep advertising on telly.'

Karen's shoulders dropped. An icy chill bit at her spine. 'Do you think it's someone she met, then? Did *you* meet him?'

'It's possible. More likely than it being anything to do with one of us. And no, I didn't even know she was thinking about going on a dating site, we met enough guys when we were out, she never even hinted she'd try it.'

'What do you mean, more likely than one of you?'

'Oh, I got the feeling they, the detectives, were suggesting one of our group could be responsible due to their theory of it being someone Erin knew. Which is ludicrous.'

'Is it?'

Sophie got up. Her mouth dropped open. 'Are you serious? Of course it is. None of us are capable of hurting anyone, let alone killing them. How can you even—'

'Sorry, sorry. I know. Calm down. It's just, well, that Dan is a bit . . . *off*, don't you think?' The look washing over Sophie's face caused Karen to retract quickly. 'No, no of course you don't think that, wouldn't be possible. Although, I really believe he's hiding something . . .'

'Whatever.' She shrugged. There was a detachment in her voice.

'You think so too, don't you?' Karen studied Sophie's face, watched for a reaction. She seemed to be struggling, a tug of war with her conscience; her loyalty split? She finally looked up.

'He is acting a bit . . . odd.' The words seemed hesitant, as if they were difficult to get out. 'He keeps kinda showing up, like he's been following me.' The last words rushed out, as if saying them quickly would lessen the impact.

'You should tell the police, let them know, he could have something to do with it. I knew he wasn't right, not telling the whole story when he was here.' Adrenaline kicked in, she was rambling. 'He turned up here, texted you, made you go out to him, didn't he? Checking up on you?'

'Mum, please.' Sophie's hands went to her head and rubbed at her temples. 'I can't think straight.'

Karen got up, strode to the dining room, unplugged the laptop and sat back down on the sofa with it. After quickly minimising her diary document, she swung it around so Sophie could view the screen. And the photos of Dan on Saturday night.

'Really, Mum? You're *stalking* my friends, what are you playing at?'

'I'm not *playing* at anything, and I'm not stalking.' Karen lowered her chin, eyes pinned on Sophie's. 'I'm trying to find out what on earth happened to you.' She willed herself to keep calm. 'Anyway, look. Look at the picture, behind the boys, do you see?'

Sophie shook her head. 'Is this the picture you were going on about last night?'

Her 'mm-hmm' response vibrated through her closed lips. Sophie tutted, but approached the screen, bending in close.

'Looks like me, Amy and Erin. So what?'

'Precisely. But, what do you notice?'

'We're standing by the car.' She squinted. 'Looks like we're chatting.'

'And the time the picture was taken?'

'Eight thirteen.' Sophie straightened. 'So, you think this is the taxi I got in?'

'I think it's the *car* you got in, yes. But I don't think it was a taxi. Look. There are no usual markings on it.' She waited for it to sink in. Readying herself for the backlash of indignation, the counter argument. The accusation of Karen being paranoid.

There was none.

'But Amy said . . . she said I was put in a taxi, that it had a sign on it. There has to be a simple explanation.' Sophie's brow furrowed.

She didn't expand on what that explanation might be. Karen feared it was because she didn't have one.

'I have the feeling it's far from simple. One thing *is* clear, mind. There is a killer out there. And you might well know him, Sophie.'

Her face, the colour washed out despite the make-up, turned up towards Karen's.

'Mum . . .'

'What is it? What's the matter?' Karen put her hand across and touched her cheek. It was the way she'd said *Mum*, like something big was going to follow.

'I . . . well. Nothing really, I'm just scared I suppose.' Her eyes fell downwards again, focused on her lap. 'I want the police to catch him, and soon.'

That wasn't it. Not what she really wanted to say. Karen could sense it, but didn't want to force the issue.

There was definitely more, something she was hiding. Something more about the events of Saturday night, and the content of the bin liner.

CHAPTER FORTY-FIVE

Sophie

She'd wanted to tell her mum, she really had. But something had stopped her. It was like she'd lost the ability to talk, suddenly drying up, unable to communicate. Why couldn't she just get it out in the open, tell her about the emails, and now this latest development?

The small brown envelope had been tucked longways under her windscreen wiper, barely visible from inside the car. She hadn't noticed it until she reached home, what with the scene outside the police station with Dan having taken her attention, then the trauma of visiting Rachel. She wished it had rained, the vile thing would've shot off her windscreen then and she'd never have had to see it.

Inside the envelope was a note, and a picture – a photograph, folded neatly in four. It was similar to the others: her dress above her waist, exposing her knickers – but there was one terrible difference – she was smiling. Why was she smiling? She tried to focus on the words of the note instead:

I'm glad we've made a connection, I know we did the very first time we met, but now I can feel it strengthening, as we get closer. I think we're kindred spirits, you and I, I could

*tell by the way you looked at me when I had your friend. I
sensed your enjoyment. You could've stopped me, but you didn't.
You smiled.*

You liked it, didn't you?

Connection? What was this weirdo on about? She prayed for this
to still be a sick joke. The fleeting images she'd had could have
come from nightmares which were now coming back during her
waking hours. Not memories of reality, memories of her dreams.
Yes, that made sense. Why would she smile if she'd watched Erin
being hurt? That was ridiculous.

But, there was the sensation she'd been having of someone
watching her, following her. Perhaps whoever was sending the
emails, the pictures, *did* have it in for her, wanted to harm her even.
He might be using the knowledge of Erin's death as a way of getting
to her, messing with her mind. It had to be someone she knew.
Had Dan put this on her car? He'd had the opportunity. Or maybe
it'd been put there when she'd been inside Rachel's house.

A throbbing pain pressed against her temples. This was messed
up and she couldn't get the pieces to add up. Maybe this person
sending emails and pictures was separate from Erin's murderer,
not the same guy. But was Dan involved in some way?

And was *she*?

CHAPTER FORTY-SIX

Karen

Thursday

Karen awoke with a groggy thickness in her head – a direct result of the lack of decent sleep; the little she'd managed interspersed with visions, whispered threats and dark corners. Danger lying in wait. She forced her legs to move, to drag her body to the bathroom – every muscle heavy, weighted down by guilt. The unwelcoming tiles sent a cold shock through her feet, setting her nerves on edge. Flipping the wall cabinet door, she rifled through its contents and found some paracetamol. She really should eat first, but she'd rather put up with nausea over a headache. She didn't want to let the darkness win.

Although, it was doing a good job of winning in every other area of her life.

A gentle creaking of the house, the sounds of movement, suggested the other occupants were up and readying themselves for the day ahead. Pushing the mirrored door closed, Karen paused, contemplating the woman in front of her. She pinched at the loosening skin on her cheeks, her chin. With a hand on each side of her face, she pulled back towards her ears, until the skin was taut. *There you are, Peter.* Karen smiled despite her mood, the memory of one of Sophie's favourite childhood movie moments springing to mind. Peter Pan in *Hook*. How many times had she watched that?

The old Karen had disappeared, lost in the folds of age, and the responsibilities that came with it. Subsumed in a relationship that had stolen her identity, bit by bit. The single wish she'd made to regain some part of her – who she was – now a glaring mistake. One she'd been punished for. A momentary slip of her moral code had turned into more of a landslide. Would it have happened if she'd had her mum to turn to, to ask for advice? Losing her when she was twenty-five had been devastating. Going through pregnancy, childbirth, a difficult first year, all without her mother's support, had left her mourning her loss even more. She'd been left parentless.

Would she really have confided in her mum, though? After all, she'd never even mentioned it to Rachel, afraid of her reaction. It would go against everything Rachel stood for. Karen ran her fingertip across the bump on her nose and looked at it from different angles. A permanent reminder. She had to be honest to herself, if not with anyone else. She hadn't confided in anyone, and she wouldn't have either, even if she had the opportunity. She didn't want others to think badly of her. Still didn't. No one needed to know, now. It was all over. The only remnants of her mistake a broken nose and her worsening psychological state.

And the repercussions of her decisions.

The conversation with Sophie last night, about Erin meeting someone online, had set off warning alarms. Karen shivered. It was so easy to get carried away with the messaging, agree to meet too soon, thinking you've found *the one*. While many couples met online these days and it all ended well, there were those who weren't so fortunate, met the wrong sort. Had Erin met with such a man? You never really know who you're talking to, it's only ever typed words, ones you can write, delete and rewrite until you come across in the right way, the way you know will sound best, most impressive – saying what you think the other person wants to hear. So easy.

'Mum?' Sophie's head appeared around the bathroom door.

'Yes, love.' Karen turned away from her reflection.

'I'm running late for work, just wanted to check you're all right before I go.'

Sophie's eyes lowered to the floor. Her voice was quiet. Shaky?

'Yeah, not too bad, thanks love. You?'

'Good. Yep, I'm fine thanks.' She ducked back out without another word, closing the door.

Karen's ears filled with her heart's panicking beats. Sophie was far from fine, that was obvious. When would she say what was bothering her? If she waited for Sophie to open up, she could be waiting ages. It could be too late to help. Tonight, when she returned from work, Karen would sit her down and confront this head-on. She'd let this go on for long enough. If Sophie wasn't going to willingly open up, she'd have to force the issue.

Mike had gone to work too by the time Karen got downstairs, leaving the house eerily silent. Peculiar. It was as always, but now the house's peace was nearly as suffocating as her attempts at leaving it. She crept through to the kitchen, as if trying not to disturb anyone. The shiver ran the length of her spine, as if someone had walked over her grave. She shook it off. *What's the matter with you?*

The uneasy feeling sat like a lump of undigested food in her belly. Coffee. Need coffee. A note propped up against the kettle reminded her to phone the doctors for her repeat prescription. Sophie's writing. Bless her. She'd also have to ask for more sleeping pills while she was on the phone. There was a PS added in Mike's scrawl, stating, *Phone and get new appointment with counsellor.* She flicked the kettle switch and rummaged in the cupboard for the coffee jar. One minute he was having a go, asking what he was paying the counsellor for, then he was reminding her to rebook her missed appointment. Talk about mixed signals. Then again, that was his forte.

Sitting at the breakfast bar, coffee mug in hand, Karen wondered what she'd do with her day. It was only ten past nine. She sighed. A morning of phone calls looked likely. Doctors, counsellor. Rachel. A shooting pain at her temples warned of a stressful day ahead. She swallowed the rising panic. *Only a few phone calls, come on, that's easy. You can manage. Start with the easy one, work your way to the difficult one.* Wasn't that what she'd repeated again and again to the offenders she'd worked with when discussing problem solving?

But what more was there to say to Rachel? Her words of comfort felt hollow, her attempt at conveying understanding futile: how could she possibly understand? She could only *imagine* what she was going through, and without offering the physical comfort, Karen didn't have much to give. If she thought this house seemed eerily quiet, what must Rachel's feel like? Thank goodness Sophie went to see her yesterday. At least one of them could show their support.

The vibration made the phone jerk across the worktop. Karen jumped up. A text message, the number not recognisable at first glance. It was from Sophie's new pay-as-you-go phone, the temporary one she'd bought as a fall back because the police had yet to return her iPhone.

Can you ask Dad to meet me from work tonight, please?

Karen chewed at the inside of her cheek. Why? She'd never asked anyone to meet her from work before. She'd driven. How could Mike meet her? Karen tapped a reply.

I'll ask him. But why?

A few minutes passed, then another vibration.

Tell him to meet me outside the staff door at 5.30. See you later.

No explanation. What was she going to say to Mike when he asked why Sophie needed him, as he was bound to?

What was going on with her?

CHAPTER FORTY-SEVEN

Sophie

It was no longer a feeling. She was sure.

Whoever put the note under her wiper was still watching her.

The second she got out of her car at the car park, she could feel him as undeniable as the bitter chill of the dropping temperature. The days of questioning her gut feelings culminated now in an absolute knowledge *he* was here. The one sending the pictures. The connection he'd talked about in the note must be related to him seeing her when she was going to and from work; the eerie sensations were him following her. Could he be the one who'd murdered Erin? Had her visions been right – had she been there, watched her die? His intentions might have been to let her go, make her believe she'd been the lucky one, then stalk her, frighten her. Make the chase more exciting until he made his final move.

The horrible suggestion she'd enjoyed watching him hurt Erin made her sick. *He* was sick. She could no longer pretend to herself that this was someone's joke. It *was* real.

She'd been so close to telling her mum that morning, again. But seeing how stressed she'd looked – how old – had stopped her. Her dad was right: she'd screwed up. Big time. This was her fault. Telling her mum would only complicate things, make the situation worse. Wouldn't it?

175

What a mess.

Instead of getting straight back in the car and driving back home to safety, Sophie locked it and looked around her. She felt suddenly angry. No way was she letting him win. A game had a winner and a loser. So far, she'd been on the back foot – her fault for not taking the emails seriously. He was one step ahead. She looked up towards the police station; it was only fifty metres or so up the road, could she make it there?

Where was the psycho hiding?

He could actually be near the station, hiding behind a wall, waiting to jump her. Risky, though. Surely, he wouldn't do anything there. Where else could he be? She couldn't see anyone directly in her path; she could make it to the magistrates' court, to the crossing. But there was no way of telling if he was inside the canopied entrance and she'd have to pass by there to get to the crossing.

She couldn't stand here contemplating. She'd have to make her move soon. A car was pulling into the car park, stopping at the top end. She could wait for the occupant to get out, see which way they went, follow their path. It might mean a detour to work, skirting the town instead of the direct route, but better that than walking her usual way and risking being the only person around. Her heart ferociously pumped, readying itself and her muscles to take action. For an awful moment, Sophie thought the woozy, rushing noise in her head meant she was going to faint. She forced herself to take deep, steadying breaths. The man that had climbed from the car walked towards the exit at the other end of the car park. If she timed it right, she could covertly slip in behind him, follow in his footsteps.

But what if it was *him*?

She let him pass, then wrapped her white coat around her tightly. She began walking, her legs wobbling, casting her eyes around to see if there was anyone else. A builder pulled his van up on the opposite side of the road, the wheels snagging on the loose gravel in the pull-in.

176

Was that him?

Where were the girls from Anderson's, the other shops? She darted her eyes this way and that, searching for a glimpse of the bright red tops of the employees of the store. There. A couple of women had come into sight on the corner. Quick. *Run, Sophie. Run.* Tears tracked across her temples as she rushed across the road; she blinked against the cold air and threw her head back over her shoulder, checking if anyone was following.

A figure moved out of the shadow of the magistrates' court doorway.

She'd been right, he was waiting there for her.

Her throat tightened, each fast intake and exhalation of frosting breath sent a shooting pain to her lungs. Not waiting for the pedestrian crossing lights to go red, she flew across the road. The women had disappeared around the corner.

He was behind her, hurried footsteps nearing.

Scream, draw attention. Surely he'd back off then. Wouldn't he?

The store loomed in front of her.

Nearly there. Keep going.

Last corner before the staff door.

She risked a look behind.

A man, medium height and build, a dark hoody. That's all Sophie took in, fear snatching the ability to focus.

At the door. Punching the keypad, clumsy fingers hitting the wrong numbers.

'Dammit. *Come on!*' The voice unrecognisable as her own.

Finally, a beeping indicated the right code. *Hurry up, door. Open.*

Propelling herself through it, Sophie turned and pushed it, all of her body weight forcing it shut against its will. It squealed: shrill, like a scream.

It shut. The clank of the lock, reassuring. She was panting, still leaning against the door.

The man stood on the opposite side of the glass. Smiling, his open mouth producing foggy clouds of rapidly appearing and disappearing breath.

She backed off, eyes still on his, unable to tear them away – the green of his irises sharp, penetrating. Almost hypnotic.

She finally turned towards the stairs, took two steps at a time and ran into the locker room. She collapsed on a bench, all her strength gone.

There was no way she was leaving here tonight on her own.

CHAPTER FORTY-EIGHT

DI Wade

A million things were swamping her brain. Wednesday's interview with Sophie Finch in particular continued to niggle at her. Sophie's tendency to avoid eye contact with either her or Mack threw doubt on her assertion of not remembering anything from Saturday night. But when they'd gone through all of the interview transcripts they'd found nothing of use. Perhaps her behaviour really was because she was scared, still in shock, like Mack had thought. But Lindsay couldn't let go of the feeling that it was because she knew something, was holding back. Not telling them something. Could it be she didn't want to implicate someone? A friend. Daniel Pearce, for example. Now, that was one cocky lad, rubbed Lindsay up the wrong way straight off. But they *were* just teenagers. And their friend was lying in the morgue. Would any of them act in a normal way? Were teenagers ever normal?

Sophie's text messages hadn't brought anything new to the table. Clearly as far as her friends were concerned she'd got in the taxi and was going home. No one openly admitted otherwise via text. But, if one of them did know something they could be in danger. There was no way of telling at this stage whether Erin had been the intended target, or if she'd been chosen at random. Either way the killer was highly organised. And there was no way of knowing if she was going to be the only victim, or merely the first.

One thing was certain. They were going to have to keep an eye on the group of them.

CHAPTER FORTY-NINE

Karen

'Mike, it's me. Look, Sophie has asked if you'll meet her after work, five thirty. I don't really know why . . . I think something's wrong. Can you do that? Right, see you both tonight. Bye.' Typical it going to answerphone when she needed him, he must be in a dip in the moor. She hoped he'd listen to his voicemail. Karen looked at the note from Sophie and Mike's hurried scribble tagged on at the end.

'OK. Continue making the calls, Karen.'

Two down. One to go.

Another answerphone. She left a message for Rachel, a brief 'how are you?' Her words were predictable, the same as any other well-wisher would say. Not the words of a best friend. She was useless.

What now?

Another cup of coffee, her third. Then back to her laptop, and the Facebook search.

Just seen your message, Amy said you'd probably ask. I can't tell you anything different to what you already know. I've no idea about the taxi, which firm, who was driving it. Sorry. Wish I could be more help, but I can't. Dan.

So, Amy had tipped him off.

Karen re-read the message. Definitely sounded like those two were in it together. *Can you hear yourself?* She rubbed at her eyes. Mike and Sophie were probably right, she was looking for something that wasn't there, grasping at meaningless snippets of information, any hope of getting closer to the truth of what happened. Maybe there was no conspiracy; they did put Sophie in a taxi, but hadn't taken notice of, or remembered, the taxi firm. Just as they both asserted. She was trying to force the pieces of the puzzle, ones that didn't fit, to make this whole situation better. Right. To stop anything else from happening.

Somehow, Sophie's and Erin's stories were linked, she knew it, was afraid of it. And there *was* something there, some clue, a connection staring her in the face, she was sure. Being too close, invested emotionally, might be why she couldn't see it. If she took a step back, it could reveal itself.

She pushed back in the chair, raised her arms and put them behind her head. Bailey watched her, his brown, doe eyes filled with unconditional love. A rare thing indeed. Dogs were so trusting. She reached down, gave his head a rub. 'I know, boy, I'm losing it, aren't I?' His tail gave a wag, which she took to be a sign of his agreement.

Erin's Facebook page. She hadn't even looked at it. She sprung forward, searched *Erin Malone*. Her page filled the screen like a memorial. Why hadn't she thought about it before? Killers loved to be part of the aftermath of their deeds; the thrill of reliving the crime was such a draw. Seeing the outpouring of grief as the direct result of their actions made them feel good. Powerful.

He may have even left his own message of sympathy.

Karen started at the bottom. There were hundreds of comments to trail through. It was going to take some time. She had plenty.

The small print began to blur. Hours of reading each and every post strained her eyes. A pain pulsated in her forehead. She'd have to give it up for the day, start making the tea; Mike and Sophie would be home soon.

The laptop clock changed to 17.52. As she reached to pull down the laptop screen, one message came into sharper focus.

With each word, her stomach tightened, a nervous ball pressing against her ribs. She struggled to swallow, her mouth drying. The name attached to the comment was unfamiliar. But the wording was not. The style, the use of elaborate language, all had a certain feel about it. No. She was tired, reading between lines again in the desperate attempt to discover something, anything which would keep the trail alive. She wanted to find something solid, evidence of foul play, and her search had tipped her over the edge. She'd gone way past normal behaviour now. If she thought there was something untoward, she should call the police. But she hadn't found anything untoward, had she? Not really. A condolence message on Facebook using long words was hardly a significant clue.

She had to stop this nonsense. *Karen, stop this and do something constructive.* The tea. Must start tea. She took some onions from the vegetable rack and dropped them on to the chopping board. She slid a knife from the wooden block. Whatever she was going to cook, onion was going to have to be an ingredient. Karen stared at the knife in her hand; it shook with the intensity of her grip. All her muscles rigid. The door slammed reassuringly and Karen relaxed a little.

'Hi guys, sorry, tea's going to be late.' She turned to greet Mike and Sophie.

Only, Sophie wasn't there.

CHAPTER FIFTY

'Where's Sophie?' Karen dropped the knife back on to the chopping board.

'What do you mean?' Mike shoved his rucksack on the worktop. 'Not back from work yet?'

A coldness spread through her. 'Didn't you get the message?'

'Er . . . no. Guess not.' Mike pulled his phone from the inside of his pocket.

'No good checking it now, is there? Sophie wanted you to meet her from work.' Her tone raised an octave.

'Why?'

'I don't know, she texted me and asked, so I called you to tell you.'

'Well, I'm sorry. It was really busy today, I was out on the moor for most of it—'

'You check your stupid phone every thirty seconds when you're home.'

'No point checking my phone when I know I never get a signal. Don't stress, I'll call her now.' He pressed a button on his mobile, put it to his ear. The pause stretched, his brow furrowed. 'Gone straight to voicemail.'

Karen put her arm out and found the surface of the worktop to steady herself. Her heart wouldn't steady though; it was hammering so hard she could hear it. A fear grasped hold of her throat, squeezing, tightening, suffocating her. Mike's voice came and went – close, far away, close, far away. What was he saying?

'Karen. She's probably driving. Why are you getting yourself in a panic over this?'

All she knew was that her body was reacting to this in the only way it knew how.

'We have to call the police, Mike.' Her breathing ragged. 'She should've been home by now.'

'She's what – half an hour late? I really don't think they'll be quick in sending out the search party.'

'Don't joke around. It's not something to take lightly . . . not after Erin. The killer *is* still out there, you know!'

'Okay, okay. Look, take it easy. I'll jump in the car, drive her route, you keep trying her mobile.' Mike snatched up his keys. 'She may have broken down.'

'I don't like the timing, she asked for you to meet her, she's never done that before. And now she's not come home. Something's definitely up.'

'Try and relax, let me know if you hear from her in the meantime, will you?'

'Yeah, okay. Please find her.'

After the noise of the door slamming, the house fell silent. Karen could only hear the whooshing of her blood, like an unborn baby's heartbeat on a Doppler ultrasound. A pull in her stomach, the memory of being pregnant with Sophie, that bond only a mother can know. The umbilical cord may have been cut, but the love, the instinct to protect, never severed. Karen clenched her arms around her middle.

What if Mike couldn't see her anywhere?

Carry on with the tea, take your mind off the time.

Not that she felt hungry now. She finished chopping an onion, then got the mince out the fridge and grabbed the other ingredients. Sophie would be hungry when she got home; she'd enjoy her favourite meal, cottage pie.

A scratching at the back door. Damn. Bailey. She'd let him out ages ago. She slid the patio door open; he ambled past her, paying her no attention. Payback. She stood and, for once, allowed the evening air to blow against her face. Usually it would set her anxiety off, but now it felt cool, refreshing. She looked out over the moor in the distance. The sun was setting, dipping behind the church, the splash of oranges and yellows streaked across the sky, transforming into a pinky haze as it reached Haytor, the rocks now appearing black and foreboding against the beautiful backdrop. At least it wasn't dark yet. Mike should be able to spot Sophie's bright red Yaris if it *was* along the route. There were still a few hours before complete darkness. If she wasn't home, or hadn't been in contact by then, well, then she'd really panic.

CHAPTER FIFTY-ONE

Thurs 11.53 p.m.
Why haven't you been in contact? I've sent loads of texts and emails. Are you OK?

You aren't avoiding me are you?

Please can you message, because, you know – if you can't come to me, I'll have to come to you.

I miss you.

xxxx

CHAPTER FIFTY-TWO

Sophie

Where the hell is he?

Five thirty. She'd specifically asked for her dad to be here to meet her. Having sensed her jumpiness and shooting her concerned looks all day from the beauty counter, Amy had offered to walk her to her car. She'd declined, because as far as she knew her dad was coming. He felt a safer bet than another female, given the circumstances. Clearly the bastard had already managed to take both her and Erin, so there was no comfort in Amy's offer. Now, though, as she stood in the cold internal corridor of the staff entrance with hopes of her dad turning up, fading, it seemed preferable to having *no one* escort her.

Stupid, piece-of-shit phone. No signal. She hit it against the wall, lifted it high above her head, moved it around. Not a single bar. She stared through the glass door again. No sign of him. On the plus side, there was no sign of her stalker either. Perhaps she could make it to the car easily, without trouble.

Five forty.

She might have to chance it; her dad obviously wasn't coming. *Give him a bit longer.* Sophie rubbed her hands together, jiggled her legs, tried to get the blood flowing around her body to provide her with some warmth.

The security guard. He'd still be in the store. Find Dave. He'd gladly walk her to her car. She turned to walk back up the stairs. A knock on the door, a gentle tapping. She froze. Whose face was going to be there when she turned around? *Please be Dad.*

She took a few more stairs up, so she was closer to the top, before craning her head around.

Her jaw shook, knocking her bottom teeth against her upper ones; the chattering echoing in her ears. She slumped down on the middle stair, composing herself before descending the rest. She released the door.

'What are you doing here?' She poked her head outside, checked up and down the street, then pulled Dan inside.

'What's the matter?' He frowned, but allowed Sophie to drag him in.

'Some weirdo bloke hanging about, that's all.' Did that sound nonchalant enough?

'Really? Where?' Dan went to move back outside.

'No, not now. Earlier. I'm not sure where he went, didn't want to chance walking to the car on my own.' She stared at him. 'So?'

'So, what?'

'What are you doing here, Dan?'

'I've come to take you out.'

'I'm about to go home, have tea, go to bed.'

'I thought we could have fish and chips along the seafront—'

'It's freezing, why on earth would I want to go by the sea?' She folded her arms.

'You've got a coat, haven't you? Anyway we can keep each other warm . . .' He winked.

'Good try.'

'Come on, it'll be good to blow away the cobwebs after a long day. My treat.'

'Ha! Some treat. Cheap fish and chips, and I get to do the driving.'

'Yeah, well, can't have it all, my dynamic company's worth it, isn't it?'

Sophie shrugged. Was this the best idea? After this morning's event, she figured the day couldn't get worse.

'Okay, *Dynamic Dan*. Deal. Remind me to text my dad when I finally get a signal though, he was meant to be meeting me.' She looked up and down the road one last time before leaving the safety of the store. Still no sign of her dad. 'Clearly he couldn't be bothered. Come on.'

Still wary of being followed, Sophie kept alert, checking behind her every few steps as they made their way to the car park. He was here somewhere, hiding, watching, waiting. She hoped having Dan with her would be deterrent enough; that he wouldn't merely see it as a challenge. Dan might put up a fight to protect her, but he wasn't exactly big or tough, and something told her he wouldn't win.

Teignbay was only a five-minute drive down the dual carriageway; it was always the group's beach of choice because of its proximity. They parked up on the road nearest the pier, the keen wind buffeting Sophie as she got out of the car.

'I could be safe and warm at home right now.'

'Yeah, but look at that, Soph.' Dan pointed to the side of the pier where the dark, choppy water met with the orange tones of the sky. It was stunning.

'I see fab sunsets outside my back door, over Haytor is just as beautiful.'

Dan shook his head. 'You are *so* hard to please.'

A smile pulled at her lips. Then the thought: *You don't deserve to be smiling* stopped her. Alive and smiling. Two things Erin wasn't. No more sunsets for her.

'Penny for them.' Dan stood watching her.

'Sorry.' She tore her eyes away from the glowing sky.

'You can smile, you know. Your life isn't over, and Erin wouldn't want you to be miserable.'

Her face burned. Had he completely read her mind? She opened her mouth, though no words came.

'Let's walk, shall we?' He put out his hand and went to take hers.

'It's okay. I'm fine.' Awkward. She put her hands in her coat pockets, not wanting to give him any ideas.

'Sorry. Thought it'd keep you warm.' He pulled his coat zip up, tucked his chin inside it and walked a few paces ahead of her. As she hurried to catch up with him, he quickened his pace, the space between them lengthening. He was headed for the pier.

'Hey, wait up.' The wind caught her voice, carrying it off. Dan strode on regardless. 'Oi!' She broke into a jog, manoeuvred past some kids on skateboards, brushed past a couple walking hand-in-hand, and was out of breath when she finally reached him. He was laughing.

'Did *that* warm you up?'

'Oh, very funny.' She knocked her shoulder against his. For a moment, life was back to normal: the usual banter with Dan, friends out together having a laugh. They wandered past the motionless, empty rides and she shivered. There was still the tinge of sadness, loss, and guilt. They slowed as they reached the end of the pier. Keeping her eyes forward, locked on the darkness of the sea, Sophie thrust her hand into Dan's. Neither of them spoke. What seemed like leading him on minutes before, now felt the right thing.

For the moment, she felt safe.

After walking along the pier, they headed for the fish and chip shop. The food in the paper balancing on their thighs, they sat on the edge of the concrete fountain in the centre of the walkway.

'Pretty good . . . for cheap fish and chips.' Sophie rolled the empty paper, got up and threw it in the bin.

'I know how to show a girl a good time.' He winked. Again.

'Jeez, Dan, what's with all the winking tonight? You trying it on with me?'

His eyes lowered. 'Ah, gotta give it a go, eh?'

'No. No, Dan, you don't. We're friends. That's all we're going to be. You know that, right?'

'What's with holding my hand then?'

'Oh, come on. Holding hands doesn't mean anything.' She walked off, back towards the car park. Taking his hand had clearly been a misjudgement. What had been a comforting gesture on her part had obviously been taken to mean more on his. Dammit. She turned around. He was following. This was going to make for an awkward journey.

Sophie got to the car, waited inside, the engine running, heater turned up full. Where was he? He hadn't been that far behind her, but now there was no sign. *Hurry up. I want to get home.* She smacked her palm on the horn, the beeping gaining the attention of the skater boys. Still no Dan. If she had to get out of this car . . .

A dark figure emerged from the alleyway between the buildings. Her muscles stiffened. She held her breath. The figure weaved through the parked cars, making its way to hers. *It's not Dan. It's him.* He'd followed them here. She reached across to lock the passenger door. Too late. The door swung open. She screamed.

'What the hell, Sophie?' Dan stood back from the door, fingers in ears.

'You scared the shit out of me.'

'Are you for real?' He climbed in, staring at her, 'Um . . . you knew I was coming . . .'

'I couldn't see you, you disappeared. Then all I could see was a dark figure. Didn't look like you.' Her breathing was rapid, her words staccato.

'You're so twitchy. That bloke got you rattled, huh?'

She didn't want to get into a conversation about him. 'You made me jump, that's all.' She started driving. 'Now, put your seatbelt on. I guess I have to drive you back to Torquay.'

'Unless you want me to come back to yours?'

'I would still have to drive you home at some point tonight, so no, it's fine. I want an early night, thanks.'

'Sure. Whatever you like.' He clunked the seatbelt into place. 'But, Sophie?'

'Yes?'

'I am always here for you, if you need me. As a friend.'

Sophie's stomach contracted. He knew there was something else. Why didn't she tell him? She needed to confide in someone, this whole situation was becoming seriously scary. *Tell him.*

'Thanks, that means a lot.' She turned her head to the road in front and pushed the car into first gear.

CHAPTER FIFTY-THREE

Karen

She could see him hesitating at the front door of the porch. He was alone, afraid to come in, knowing she would freak out because Sophie wasn't with him. He hadn't found her. Karen opened the door for him, every muscle in her body trembling.

'No sign?'

'Nope, sorry.' Mike walked into the hallway and began to untie his boots. 'Look, don't get in a state, she may have gone out with Amy after work, she does that sometimes, doesn't she?' The waver in his voice gave away his own uncertainty.

'Yes, but she asked for you to meet her, why would she then go off with Amy?'

'Because I didn't show up?'

'Why didn't she ring then, in that case?'

'I don't know, Karen. No signal? Did you try Amy though, just in case?' He ushered her into the lounge.

'No.' Karen lowered her eyes. 'Didn't think she'd answer me.'

'Why not?'

'Oh, no matter now, it's fine. I'll try her.' She looked around the room. 'Or I would, if I knew where my phone was.'

'I've no idea how you manage to lose it time and time again, you're only in the house all day.'

197

'I know, I know. I walk around, put it down, and forget where. Ring it for me, please.'

A muffled ring. Kitchen? 'Thanks.'

'That's not me.'

Karen flew from the room, ear tilted to the direction of the noise. Under the tea towel. She snatched it up, accepted the call.

'Where are you?' she screamed into the phone. The anger, not meant, was the form her relief took.

Mike came by her side, his hands splayed and eyebrows raised, mouthing, 'Where is she?'

Karen took the phone away from her ear, 'With *Dan*. It's him, she's driving.' She shook her head before returning the phone to her ear. Mike tutted and went back towards the lounge.

'Tell her she gave me a heart attack. How much more does she think I can take?'

Karen heard apologies, she was on speaker. 'Just get yourself home.' She ended the call and went back to Mike.

'Can you believe that, I mean, I know you didn't show, but what was she thinking going off with him, not bothering to even text?'

'At least she's safe.' Mike looked up from his iPad. 'Is she on her way home?'

'She's dropping Dan off first. I feel sick.' She collapsed on to the sofa.

'She's so selfish, what she's putting you through.'

'Yeah, well I guess we've all been there . . . you know, putting ourselves first.' The sarcasm would be lost on Mike. She doubted it would even register.

'You say that now, now you know she's safe. But what if she hadn't been? Would you be so forgiving then?'

She couldn't really say anything to that. Yes, it was only the relief that Sophie was okay that made her soft and more able to forgive her actions, her lack of consideration. She'd be livid if she were still sitting here now with no knowledge of where Sophie was. If her selfishness had put her in danger.

But her behaviour still underlined the fact that something was going on with Sophie. There was a reason she'd wanted Mike to meet her. A reason why she'd been acting strangely and why she'd hidden the black bin liner under her bed. She couldn't avoid it any longer.

It was time for a serious mother–daughter chat.

CHAPTER FIFTY-FOUR

Sophie

She was a few minutes from home and fretting about how she could get around this. When she got through the door, the questions would rain down on her. The first being: 'Why did you ask Dad to meet you?'

Be honest, Soph.

The thought sickened her. Be honest. *Yep, tell your anxiety-ridden mother you think you were with Erin when she was murdered, that you've been receiving disgusting pictures of yourself in compromising positions . . . and, by the way, Mum . . . I'm being stalked.*

Okay, then a variation of the truth. A massive variation. She could say that Dan had been hassling her. That was a fact, at least, though probably not fair to Dan. Her mum would believe it, though, she didn't seem to like him much. But then she'd ask why she went out with him, in that case, and had driven with him to the beach. *Cross that bridge if I get to it.*

The house came into view as she turned the last corner, the lounge light casting an eerie glow on to the street through the closed curtains. They were both in there waiting for her. She parked the car, sat and cracked each knuckle, taking a deep breath before going in.

'Sorry for stressing you out.' Her opening line – get in with a quick apology, an attempt to defuse what was likely to be a shit-storm.

Just her mum in the lounge. Sitting at one end of the sofa, legs tucked up and to one side. Her face flat, expressionless, turned up towards her as she spoke.

'Yes, I was stressed. Am still.' She patted the sofa, indicating for Sophie to sit beside her. 'Sorry, though, that Dad didn't get to you. He didn't get the message.'

'I thought he was still mad at me, decided to teach me a lesson.'

'He wouldn't do that.' There was a shocked tone to her voice, which Sophie didn't understand. He'd done plenty of things to teach her lessons, why was leaving Sophie to stew so remarkable?

'Really? You don't reckon?'

'I admit, he may do some things that seem a little mean some-times, but not with you, Sophie. He'd never purposely not be there for you if you really needed him. Despite how he comes across, he adores you. He'd do anything for you.'

'Talking of him, where is he? Not cooking again, surely?' The smell of food wafted through the house.

'Upstairs in the office. We ate already, I've put some cottage pie back for you.'

'Thanks, but I'm not hungry now, had some fish and chips with Dan.'

'Hmm . . . yes. What was all that about?'

Now. Do it now. Tell her.

'He came by Anderson's, wanted to go out, that's all.'

'So, how come you wanted Dad to meet you if you were going out with Dan?'

'I didn't *know* he was going to be there.'

'So, he's still stalking you, then?'

This is where she'd usually argue, put up a fight, tell her mum not to be so stupid. Now though, it was an opportunity to either say, yes, he was stalking her, or tell her the truth.

'He is acting a bit weird, I give you that.' She waited, gathering herself before continuing. 'But it's not him who's the problem.'

Right, here we go.

She stared at her mum, trying to gauge her mood, predict her likely reaction. She was silent though, waiting for Sophie to speak.

Just say it, Sophie, for Christ's sake.

'I think, well, I'm not sure, but there's a possibility I really may have a stalker.'

There. Not so hard. She squeezed her eyes shut.

'Right. Okay, so what's been happening?'

Sophie let out a puff of breath and opened her eyes. Her mum had sat forward, frowning, but actually seemed quite calm – no panic breathing. Yet.

'It's a long story—'

'I've got plenty of time, start at the beginning.'

She couldn't. Not the beginning, not Saturday night. That would be too much.

'Well, I'd been getting odd sensations, like I was being watched, since Monday really. I thought it was just because of what'd happened to Erin, playing on my mind, you know?' Her mum nodded, but said nothing, waiting for her to continue. 'So, anyway, I kept alert, in case my feelings proved to be right. And then I saw him.' Her own breathing shallowed, heart fluttered hard, like a trapped butterfly in her chest. 'He followed me to work, I got inside the staff door quickly, but he stood outside, body pressed against the glass, staring in at me.' She stopped, couldn't continue.

'Are you sure, Sophie? It could've just been some weird bloke messing around, couldn't it? I mean, maybe a one-off, rather than someone *stalking* you.'

'It seemed personal to me, not just a joke, or a one-off.'

Her mum looked to be considering this, her eyes narrowing in concentration. Then, 'Sophie?'

'Yes?' What was coming? What had she thought of?

'What's in the bin liner under your bed?'

She's been in there. She already knows.

'My dress.' A lump in her throat, tears threatening. It was all going to come out.

'Why did you shove it in a bag?' Her mum's voice, calm, but now with a hint of concern.

The calmness wouldn't last long if she told her.

'It was the Topshop one I was wearing on Saturday. I thought it may be important to keep it.'

'But why would you need to? Unless—'

'Can we discuss this later? Tomorrow, when Dad's at work. Please.' She bottled it.

Her mum put both her hands to her face, rubbing at her cheeks. 'As long as we do have this talk, Sophie. I think it's overdue, don't you?'

Why was she so composed? She'd been shouting, giving it her all, having panic attacks and everything before. Why wasn't she now? 'Yes, Mum. It is. And we will. I promise.'

It wasn't how she'd envisaged spending her day off work, but she had to talk about it now, confide in someone. It'd gotten serious. And suddenly she was afraid. Really afraid.

CHAPTER FIFTY-FIVE

DI Wade

Friday

As predicted, a lot of the information gained since the appeal had resulted in dead ends. The one piece which had initially set Lindsay's pulse galloping – a woman reporting late-night activity at the industrial units adjacent to where the body was found – turned out to be a group of lads smoking dope at the back of one of the empty units. CCTV picked them up, they'd been there for twenty minutes, then left the way they'd come. Careful monitoring of the rest of the CCTV gave them nothing, the angles were all wrong. The perpetrator could've driven so far, and then dragged the body to the marshy part of the wasteland without detection.

The incident room was uncharacteristically quiet following this latest disappointing news. Lindsay felt the air of tension, and a degree of melancholy. She sat at her desk, her knee bouncing, knocking the solid heel of her shoe rhythmically on the floor.

'That's not annoying at all.' Mack, sitting at the next desk, didn't take his eyes from his monitor.

'I know, can you believe it, it's like he's a ghost, not showing up on any CCTV, no sightings . . .'

'No. I meant you doing that is annoying.' He took the pen out of his mouth and pointed it at her feet.

'Oh. Sorry. It's just frustrating.'

'Yep. It surely is.' Mack slipped the end of the pen back in his mouth, returning his attention to the computer screen.

'Any luck from the footprints?' Lindsay flicked through her notes.

'Nope. The ones recovered weren't useable, ground was too wet, no clear markings or distinct foot size.'

She blew her cheeks out, expelling the air in a loud hiss. Then she looked up. 'Ah-ha. So the perpetrator's shoes must be mud-encrusted. If we *had* a suspect and could find his footwear we might get a match for soil at least.'

'Yeah, possibly. So, now we just need a suspect.' Mack raised his eyebrows, gave a weak smile.

Yes. Yes they did. The media and public were beginning to get impatient. They were keen to see someone placed in custody for the murder of their local teenage girl. They wanted answers: why hasn't anyone been caught? Why haven't you got suspects? And the biggest, worst question: do you think they will strike again? So far, they'd not given them anything near satisfying results. They had to change that. And fast.

'Anything from the taxi firms?' Lindsay continued in what she hoped was an upbeat, encouraging tone. She had to keep her team's enthusiasm up.

'Clarke and Webster are on that, Boss. But there's nothing as yet.'

'No positive IDs of either Sophie or Erin,' Lindsay said to herself. She got up and walked in a circle, hand up at her mouth chewing a thumbnail. Then she turned to face the team. 'Okay everyone,' each face turned her way, 'we need to get motivated, get thinking. He's not cleverer than us, he must've made a mistake somewhere along the line. *We* must be missing something.' Lindsay paced, all eyes were on her. 'Where's the next CCTV along from that pub, the White Hart? We have a timeframe – someone check the taxis and cars that went by in that window.'

A low groan emanated from the room.

Lindsay stopped pacing and stood, hands on her hips, staring at the team. The entire room became still.

'I'll get on that,' DC Sewell shouted from the back.

'Good. Glad to hear it. Come on, let's try and get something concrete by the end of today.' She turned and headed back to her desk. 'Because this is seriously beginning to piss me off.'

CHAPTER FIFTY-SIX

Karen

Dark images punctuated her sleep: a man hiding in the shadows, a girl, tied and bound being slowly strangled by a faceless man; a creature. Sophie, dragged into an alleyway, her screams muffled by big hands, her legs kicking, not connecting with anything. Sophie, limp.

Still.

Lifeless.

The light of the morning hadn't come soon enough. Seagulls incessantly tapped their beaks on the light tunnel, the sound piercing holes in her skull. The subsequent throbbing pain didn't allow the dreams to dissipate. The nightmares stayed sharp, in full focus.

Didn't Sophie realise how the information she divulged last night would affect her? Karen rolled on to her back, staring up at the circle of light. Yes. Of course she knew – that's why she hadn't mentioned it before, she knew exactly how Karen would react, how it would affect her condition. Poor Sophie. What else had she held back from telling her, afraid of the repercussions?

There was a full day, now, in which to find the underlying cause of all of this. No Mike. Just her and Sophie. She had to handle this in the right way: not too many questions, let her speak without interruption. Keep calm. That was the biggest problem. Whatever Sophie was going to tell her, remaining calm was key. If she panicked, had an anxiety attack, then Sophie would stop talking, wouldn't share. She'd be back to square one.

No paper bag, then.

She hadn't spoken to Rachel since Monday; Rachel hadn't returned the voicemail Karen'd left on Thursday, but that was hardly surprising. She needed to make amends somehow for her lack of support. Perhaps once Sophie had told her what was going on, she'd give her a call, find out how she was doing. She'd no idea of the timescale for Erin's funeral or anything: if the coroner was releasing her body soon, or whether they had to wait. She should know these things, as Rachel's best friend. Karen sat on the edge of the bed, her head in her hands, squeezing her skull from both sides, hoping to expel the pain from within it.

Bailey whimpered at her feet. He stared up at her, hopefully. She reached down and gave his head a rub. He started pawing at her arm. He was hungry. She got up, beginning the routine as usual, the same as every other day. Monotonous. But, if monotonous meant safe, she was all for it. Was Sophie about to upset the routine? Yes, she'd wanted to find out what really happened Saturday, and yes, she'd been 'investigating' everyone she could online. But, did she really want answers, or had it just been something to do to occupy her mind, prevent her from going mad?

But now she knew answers could be on their way, she wasn't so sure she wanted to know.

'Have you had breakfast?' Karen looked on as Sophie paced the kitchen.

'Can't. Feel sick.'

'I think you should try. Come on, I'll make us a bacon sarnie.' Karen turned the grill on, got the bacon from the fridge. Sophie's hand shot in front of hers.

'No. Really, I don't want to eat. I'll puke. You go ahead though if you want one.'

Karen backed away from the fridge. 'Nah. Can't face it either. Let's go sit in the lounge, shall we? Then you can tell me what's been going on.'

It was like sitting waiting for bad news, waiting for Sophie to start the conversation she knew was going to change things. Was she mentally prepared for this?

'Okay, look, Mum, I don't want you to freak out over this.'

Already Karen's palms were wet with sweat, her pulse at a ridiculous speed, as though she'd been running. Her chest was painfully tight. *Deep breaths. Stay calm.* She wanted to say 'I can't promise that', but knew she shouldn't. She watched Sophie, saw the tension in her face, and recognised the frightened look in her eyes – the same as Saturday night. She had to be strong now. Sophie needed her to be composed and strong. Karen nodded to encourage her daughter to go on.

'After Saturday night, I was emailed some pictures.' Sophie paused; she was wringing her hands and cracking her knuckles, the habit Karen hated.

Karen closed her eyes, waited for Sophie to carry on. 'Well, actually, I was sent one to start with, wasn't even sure the picture was of me. Thought it was a joke, one of the boys trying to be funny,' she gave a short laugh, 'you know how they are . . . twats really.'

'But it wasn't one of the boys.'

'No, I'm almost sure of that now. The next one he sent made it clearer. It was definitely me and I was wearing . . . I was wearing—'

'The dress you'd worn on Saturday night,' Karen finished.

'Yeah. I gathered you'd done some snooping.'

'I'm sorry. I was worried about you, about your behaviour. I knew something wasn't right. I found the bin liner, your dress inside. Sorry. You'd have done the same if you were in my position.'

211

It didn't really excuse it, but it was the best she had at this point. 'Anyway, go on.'

'Yeah, well, we'll save the privacy conversation for another time. So anyway, the message with the pictures said there were more. Then I was getting those creepy sensations that I was being watched when I went to and from work. And yesterday, I saw him.'

Karen couldn't refrain any longer. 'Hang on, let's get this straight. You were sent pictures of yourself from Saturday night. Where were you? Had he taken them from the pub you were in? Were you with your friends at the time? What were you doing? I don't understand.'

'Mum. Slow down. Look, it doesn't matter about that for the minute, it's the fact he's following me that's scaring me. Can we concentrate on that please?'

'Okay, so we have to call the police.'

'I knew you'd say that. I don't want to—'

'Why the hell not, Sophie? How am I meant to protect you from a stalker?' Karen knew her breathing had shallowed, was becoming more rapid.

Don't lose it.

'I don't know,' Sophie shouted. She jumped up from the sofa and began pacing again.

Sophie and her father were more alike than she'd ever admit to Karen: the pacing, that same quick temper, the inability to contain it. It was the reason they clashed repeatedly.

'They'll look into it, find out who he is. Stop him from doing it!'

'I want it to just go away, this whole thing.' She collapsed on the floor and sat hugging her knees, fat tears rolling down her pale cheeks.

Karen moved behind her, putting her arms around Sophie's shoulders. She laid her head against her daughter's and rocked her gently. She breathed in the sweet smell of shampoo, her own tears now dampening Sophie's hair.

'I know, darling, I know.' She stroked Sophie's head. 'I'm afraid it's not going to, though. We have to deal with it.'

Sophie pulled away, turned and faced her. 'And that's coming from you.'

The words, softly spoken, not in malice; it was a straightforward statement. A valid point. Who was she to spout about dealing with stuff?

'Together. We can face this together. I realise I'm not a good role model, but I am your mum. I will do whatever it takes to help you. Protect you.'

'In that case, can we leave the police out of it, for now? If I ignore the messages, have someone with me at all times, I'll be safe. Right?'

Karen considered this for a moment. 'How is he sending you messages? On Facebook?'

Sophie looked away.

'Sophie. How is he sending the pictures, the messages?'

'Email.'

'So, he's someone you know? He must be, to have your email.'

'I don't know.'

'Love. You can't get through this by giving the "I don't know" answer to everything. You *have* to know some things.' She tried not to let the frustration show in her voice. She was failing. 'Come on. It's time to tell me what you do remember, what you know. Because you do remember some things. Don't you?'

'Oh, Mum.' Sophie covered her face with her hands.

'Darling, what?'

'The pictures. The ones he sent. They weren't . . .'

Karen swallowed the fear and waited for Sophie to go on. She willed her heart to continue to beat.

'Weren't what, love?' she encouraged.

'I can't tell, exactly . . . but it looks like . . . I'm . . . *Shit.*' Sophie shut her eyes. 'My dress. It's been pulled up.' She didn't continue, her sobbing too much to be able to form coherent sentences.

'You have to show me.'

Sophie shook her head. 'No. No. No.' She withdrew from Karen and ran from the room. Leaving Karen, hand clutching at her chest, hyperventilating.

CHAPTER FIFTY-SEVEN

Sophie

She slammed face down on the bed, her crying muffled by the pillow. She couldn't show her mum. Couldn't show anyone. She'd allowed it to happen, for that monster to do God knows what to her. The pictures were disgusting.

She should delete them.

Yes. Of course. If she deleted them, no one would ever see them. No one would know she'd been there. With Erin. The thought of keeping them to try to figure out where they'd been taken was pointless. She wasn't going to show the police either, so there was no reason to save them. She could plausibly deny everything if they were no longer stored on her laptop.

She launched off the bed, grabbed her laptop and fired it up. *Hurry up.*

Footsteps on the stairs. *Mum's coming.* She'd be forced to show them. *No way. Come on!* The screen flashed up, her fingertips stabbing the keys, entering the password.

Her mum was at the door. The handle squeaked.

She ticked the boxes beside each picture message.

Her mum burst in. 'Sophie. Don't.'

'Sorry.' Sophie hit delete. Then quickly clicked on the recycle bin and emptied that too, before her mum could stop her.

'You silly girl. You silly, silly girl.' Her arms dropped to her sides, her shoulders slumped.

'Really? What makes you an expert?'

'They were evidence, Sophie. Evidence that might help the police get him.'

'And you'd give the police evidence which made you look bad, would you? Made you out to be a total slag. Dirty, disgusting pictures of your bare flesh for them all to see. You'd give them to the police?'

Her mum said nothing.

'Well, would you?'

'If it helped catch this man, yes. I would.'

'I'm sorry I'm not like you, then. Sorry to disappoint.'

'You could never disappoint me.' She clambered across some clothes and sat beside Sophie on the bed.

'Not even if . . .' She couldn't finish the sentence, didn't want to hear herself saying it.

'Whatever it is, we will help you through it. Me and Dad.'

'You don't understand. I don't want people knowing. Anyone. Not even you. *Especially* not Dad.'

'Right.' She recoiled from Sophie. 'I see. Okay, fine.' She got up, and without glancing back, she left, with the parting words: 'You know where I am if you change your mind.'

Yes. She knew where she was. In the same place she'd been for two years. Secluded. Imprisoned. Removed from the real world. How could she possibly help? How could she have a single clue as to how Sophie was feeling? She knew nothing.

Confiding in her had made things worse. Imagine if she'd told her the rest. That her stalker must be Erin's killer. There was no way she'd be able to talk her out of calling the police.

She'd have to keep it to herself after all. She would just have to take steps to protect herself. Make sure that from now on she wasn't alone walking to and from work or college. She was sure Amy would walk with her to her car after work most nights. But would that be enough protection? Dan. He, too, would be happy to escort her. Again, though, enough to deter the stalker? Her dad was the only likely person who would offer solid protection. Or the security guard.

All of the options had two flaws, though. One: they weren't all going to be available at the times she needed them; everyone worked different hours, particularly her start hours. And, two: all of them would immediately alert the police.

College could offer more protection; a stalker wouldn't chance alerting the teachers of his presence or risk the police being called. That seemed a minor plus in the scheme of things – every other week she *might* be okay. Maybe she had to face facts. There wasn't a way around it; the police had to become involved. But, what if they linked the stalker to Erin's murder? What if they caught him and he implicated her? How could she prove she wasn't involved? And what else did the killer have in store? More pictures? She shuddered. Perhaps she'd go off sick. Stay at home. Like her mum. Two reclusive fuck-ups together. What a truly depressing thought.

He'd get bored though. If he couldn't see her, get to her, he'd soon tire of internet stalking. Move on. But move on to who? Someone else from her group. Amy?

And if he did, it would be her fault.

CHAPTER FIFTY-EIGHT

September 2014

Weds 11.45 p.m.
I'm sorry, I know you feel let down, but that's no excuse for the emails you've been sending. Your anger has shocked me. You've been this amazing, kind and loving man for the last 12 months, please let's not end it on a bad note.

I have explained my situation and why I can't continue this any more, but I wish you every happiness for your future. You'll find the right person, every bit as wonderful as you say I am, and you will be happy. I'm sure of it.

It just can't be with me.

CHAPTER FIFTY-NINE

Karen

Was it a coincidence that Sophie believed someone was stalking her? If it hadn't been for the disclosure of the photos, Karen might have thought Sophie was overreacting. A direct response to Erin's murder could be heightening her senses, stimulating her mind to create a drama where there wasn't one. When you were on edge, everything seemed like a threat; a noise, a shadow, a person in the wrong place at the right time – all added to the intensity of emotions, fed the fear – adding to the perceived danger. Karen knew this all too well.

But the photos threw a different light on it. Could they be someone's idea of a joke, as Sophie had thought? One of the boys thinking they were funny? Pretty sick joke, but she wouldn't put it past them, especially Dan. If only she'd seen them, been able to evaluate them, assessed if they were the real deal. Mind you, Sophie obviously thought they were, or she wouldn't have been so horrified, deleting them without letting her see. How could they be that bad? She'd been in a pub, what's the worst state he could've captured her in? She'd said her dress was pulled up. Had she been so drunk she'd collapsed on the floor, dress hitched up for all to see? Or had he got her on her own, in the toilets, or outside?

Her stomach grumbled. She might not *feel* hungry, but her body still demanded nourishment, something other than coffee. It was only ten fifteen, nowhere near lunchtime, but she'd skipped breakfast again. She rummaged in the cupboards. Nothing took her fancy, so she slammed them shut again. Perhaps Sophie would drive up the shop, buy them something ready-made they could have for lunch. She yelled up the stairs.

Sophie sauntered down, stopped midway and plonked herself down on the step.

'You fancy going up the shop for me, get us both something nice for lunch?' Karen held out a twenty-pound note.

'Yeah. Might be a bagful of chocolate though.' She leant forward, and with an outstretched hand, took the twenty from her mum.

Karen grinned, 'I'll accept your choice, whatever it might be.'

'I'm sorry, Mum. You know it's not because I don't trust you . . .'

'Okay. Why, then?' Karen sat down on the bottom stair, back against the wall.

'I'm stupid. Dad was right. It's my mess. I shouldn't involve anyone else in this. Least of all you—'

'*Me*? Least of all me?' Her sharp intake of breath prevented more words.

'You know, after all you went through. Why you're like this. How can I drag you into it?'

Karen screwed her face up, tightened her lips, willed the tears not to come. 'Oh, Sophie. My darling girl.' She crawled up the steps to get to Sophie and held her tight in her arms. 'I'm your mum. It doesn't matter what I went through . . . you are my priority. I know it may not seem like it sometimes, but *least of all me*? I'm the one person you should absolutely involve.' She shook Sophie's shoulders. 'Do you understand?'

Sophie nodded, giving a half-hearted smile through the tears. 'Yes. Okay. Sorry I deleted the pictures.'

'It might've helped to have them, to identify this stalker guy. Were you definitely the subject of the photo? He couldn't have been meaning to capture someone else in the pub?'

'It was me. Just me.'

'How did he get you on your own, where were your friends?'

Sophie sighed, her shoulders dropped. 'The pictures weren't taken at the pub, Mum. At least not in the main part. A basement maybe . . .'

'A basement? Oh, I thought . . .'

'I know. I didn't want to freak you out. And possibly I didn't want you to be right.'

'About what?'

'Something *did* happen in the hours between leaving the pub and the police bringing me home. Like you thought.'

'Oh, Sophie.' Karen massaged her temples with the forefingers of both hands. 'Do you remember, now?'

'Not really, no. Snippets. Odd bursts of memory, in no real order.'

'I know you've deleted the pictures, but tell me what exactly they depicted. Everything. And if they were sent via email, what address were they coming from?'

'The email is a dead end, some ridiculous-sounding address, not like Gmail, or Yahoo or anything. I will tell you about the photos, but let's have something to eat first.'

'Hang on. When you say a ridiculous email address, like what?'

'Something along the lines of "Big man at I have the power dot com". It's why I thought it was a joke.'

'Oh, yeah, that's strange.' Karen let her breath out in a rush. She'd been holding it, waiting. She got up and turned to descend the stairs.

'Although, the last one was different.' Sophie's voice, coming from behind her.

Karen turned back. 'Yeah, what was it?'

'"Ideal man at your place or mine dot com."'

The words echoed, hit against the inside of her skull. She shook her head, the woozy sensation spreading. The stairway rose to meet her face.

'Mum!' Sophie's hands grabbed at her beneath her armpits. 'Mum, you okay? Can you hear me?'

The voice, far away, cotton wool in her head dulling the sounds. A river of thoughts flooded it, washing the cotton wool away, her hearing suddenly acute.

'Mum. Did you faint?'

'I'm okay, I'm okay. Sorry. My blood sugar's low.'

'No. That's not it.' A worried look stealing the sparkle from her eyes. 'When I said the email address, you drained of colour instantly. Why?'

Excess saliva spilled into her mouth, she swallowed again and again. *How? Why?*

'Seriously Mum, you're frightening me now. What is it?'

'I've heard of that email address. I know it. Unless there's another person with the same one.'

'You can't have the same as someone else, it doesn't allow you to choose it if it's already taken. How have you heard it? I mean, who do you know with it?'

'It's a long story. I don't get it, though. Why?' Every pulse point pounded against her skin, the blood rushing to her vital organs. Sophie stared at her, her brow creased deeply, waiting for an explanation.

She must be wrong. There she was, internally accusing Sophie of overreacting, seeing something that wasn't there, and now she'd done the same. Jumped to a ridiculous conclusion, fuelled through fear. Easily done. There was no way on earth it was the same email account. Couldn't be.

Karen whipped her head around at the sound of the letterbox smashing against its metal surrounding. It sounded like a gunshot. Her hand flew to her chest. The thud of something landing on the mat reassured her it was just Val, the post woman. She knew

224

Karen well now, was patient when there was a delivery, waiting with a smile as Karen took her time to get to the front door. Obviously nothing to be signed for today. She patted Sophie's leg. 'We need to have a long chat.' Bailey's barking filled the hallway.

'Yes. Sounds as though we do,' Sophie shouted above his noise. She helped Karen up; made sure she was steady. 'Bailey! Enough.' She picked him up, soothed him. 'I'll go put the kettle on.'

Karen stood in the hallway, recovering her composure. Through the glass inner door, a shadow remained. Val must have something requiring a signature after all. She hadn't heard the doorbell ring over the barking. She was good, waiting for Karen the way she did. Sophie was in the kitchen, she could shout her, get her to sign.

Grow up. Do it yourself.

The inner door was easiest; it was the one opening to the outside world which troubled her. She'd made a hash of it more than once.

It's only Val.

Once at the outer door, she took a deep breath, opened her eyes, reached for the door handle. She stopped.

It wasn't Val.

That was close, almost opened the door to a stranger.

The man, huddled over a rucksack, appeared to be packing catalogues into it. Karen glanced down, noticed the catalogue on the mat. She released a heavy sigh, relaxed her shoulders. The man suddenly stood upright. She backed away. He turned.

Their eyes met.

He smiled at her. She returned the gesture, then retreated into her safe zone. She wasn't up to pleasantries with the people responsible for the deluge of junk coming through her letterbox daily. If she'd felt braver, she would've thrown his stupid catalogue back at him.

'You okay, Mum?'

'Yep, just coming.' She discarded the catalogue, an out-of-date Betterware one, on the hallway table.

'Who was it?'

'Damn Betterware man. I swear it's a different one every month. I don't like seeing all those different faces.' Karen took the mug from Sophie. 'A quick coffee, then go get that lunch treat, will you? I'm in need of calories.'

'Me too. Thanks Mum.'

'Don't thank me yet. After our chat you may not want to speak to me again.'

CHAPTER SIXTY

DI Wade

DC Sewell thrust a tin of biscuits, together with a piece of paper, under Lindsay's nose.

'Here you go, Ma'am, thought you could do with a sugar hit. They're chocolate ones.' Sewell rattled the tin in encouragement. 'And the analysis came back on the fibres.'

She'd said it as if it were an afterthought, like the biscuits were the important thing. Lindsay bypassed the tin and snatched the report, a little more aggressively than she intended.

'Thanks.' Lindsay scanned the printed report. She heard the rattle of the tin again.

'You should have a snack, keep your energy levels up.' Sewell – one of the older DCs on the team who always called her 'Ma'am' despite her preferring the less formal 'Guv', or 'Boss' – was clearly attempting to mother her.

Lindsay took a biscuit without looking. Sewell moved off, obviously satisfied she'd done her duty.

She read the report through several times, then called for hush. The incident room fell quickly into silence.

'Okay. We knew there were no skin cells under Erin's nails, but we were hopeful the analysis of the fibres might bring us some joy.' She looked up, scanning the faces in the room. Expectant eyes. Ones waiting for a break. 'Which they would, if we had any items of clothes to match them with. Anyway, there is a total of three different kinds of material, so if we can get a move on and recover the victim's clothes to eliminate them, then we might have the killer's fibres right here.' Lindsay waved the report in the air.

'He's probably burned her clothes. He's been very careful with everything else, ' DC Clarke offered. 'The entire area surrounding the industrial units and marshland have been swept. None of the units appear to be the primary scene. Until we have a suspect . . .' He hung his head. No one else spoke.

'Okay.' Lindsay tried another avenue. 'What about the laptops? Any online activity that could lead us to someone she might have agreed to meet? What about the dating site?'

'Laptops have nothing of significance,' Webster said, breaking the quiet frustration that Lindsay physically felt.

'That's weird. Surely there'd be a trail if she'd been on a dating site?' She was aware of Sewell on the phone, watched as her hand waved in the air to gain everyone's attention. Lindsay drew in a breath and held it. *Please be something good.*

'What is it?' Lindsay asked when Sewell replaced the receiver.

Sewell looked to Mack. 'You were checking Sophie Finch's mobile for texts, Mack.'

'Yep, but didn't find anything of interest, so, although strictly speaking I probably shouldn't have, I gave it to the tech team to access other files on her phone that might be helpful. So?'

Sewell grinned. 'Well . . . looks like that was a good move.'

Lindsay wasn't one for suspense, or unnecessary dragging out of leads. 'Well, spit it out, Sewell!'

'Young Sophie Finch has some interesting emails and pictures she didn't tell us about, Ma'am.'

CHAPTER SIXTY-ONE

Karen

Sophie hadn't bothered with having coffee, more intent on going to get them a treat instead. Karen had about ten minutes before she returned from the shop. She opened her laptop, navigated to emails and clicked on the file named *J&K*.

A warm sensation spread inside her. Her face flushed. Hundreds of messages immediately filled the screen. She shouldn't look at them, should really have deleted them long ago. But during the low points, the particularly hard days, they offered comfort. They were difficult to let go of, deleting them meant deleting him. And she wasn't ready for that. Reading them gave her hope. The recalled memories managed to drag her through her darkest moments. Kept her going.

If she'd gone to him, things might have been very different. She'd have been free. In every sense of the meaning.

But, she hadn't. He was gone, the memories of what might have been forever kept alive in her imagination. Sometimes, she lived out her fantasies in her daydreams, pretending, like a child with an invisible friend, that he was with her, by her side. They would chat for hours on end, everything perfect: he touched her in just the right way, spoke to her with a kindness; an old-fashioned courteous way, which endeared him to her. He listened; he enjoyed the same things she did.

Then reality washed the daydreams away. She wasn't ever going to meet him.

He was not coming back.

Or was he?

Manoeuvring the mouse over one of the emails, Karen studied the address.

Idealman@yourplaceormine.com.

Could it be? If Sophie was right, then it had to be, didn't it.

So, the big question was, *why?* Why go out of his way to contact Sophie? Maybe because Karen had snubbed him, ignored his many attempts at emailing, removed all his contact details, and this was his only way of getting her attention. A bit dramatic. They'd not parted on the best terms; it had been her decision to end it, despite wanting more. How could she leave Mike to start a new life with him when she had such a debilitating condition? He'd asked repeatedly to meet her during the twelve months they'd been in contact, but she'd put him off, stalling his every request. She hadn't dared take another chance, not after the attack. It was safer to keep this one merely as an internet connection. There was little choice anyway, she couldn't leave the house to meet him and she wasn't going to invite him over. She'd never told him her reasons, though, afraid he'd stop communication if he didn't think there was a real chance of them meeting. And, she might even recover one day, eventually feel it was safe to see him. She'd wanted to keep him around, keep her options open.

Sophie entered the kitchen; the clatter of items tipping from a carrier bag brought her back to the present.

'I've spent the lot, hope that's okay,' Sophie called.

'Sounds like it.' Karen poked her head around the corner. 'You weren't kidding about the chocolate.'

Sophie smiled. 'In times of crisis, there's always chocolate and wine.'

It was the most natural smile Karen had witnessed all week.

'Oh, you've bought wine too?'

'Yep. For tonight. Obviously not for lunch.'

'I say, *why not?*' Karen put on a fake posh accent. 'Come on, let's do it. Might make my task a whole lot easier.' She took the wine, unwrapped the foil and began twisting the cork.

'Your task?' Sophie narrowed her eyes to a slit. 'Sounds ominous.'

'Oh, it is.' The cork popped, fizzy liquid bursting from the neck of the bottle. Karen placed her mouth over the end, Sophie laughed; grabbing some glasses, she tilted one up so Karen could quickly pour the wine.

'Dad would have a fit if he came home and we were drinking.'

'Let's hope he's stuck on the moors then and won't pop in for lunch.'

'Ha! Cheers.'

They sat on the stools at the breakfast bar and clinked glasses. A lovely, rare moment. One Karen couldn't remember happening for a long time. And she was about to ruin it with her revelation. Her deceit laid bare. She could sugarcoat it, leave parts out. Sophie need know only the minimum. If it was him following her, she deserved to know the reason. The only good thing, if it *was* him, was knowing it could be sorted easily, without police involvement. It was Karen he was trying to gain the attention of; he wasn't after Sophie. She would stop this herself, all she had to do was contact him again.

That held some comfort.

The trouble with secrets is that they seldom stay that way. It all comes out in the end. *You can't bury your past indefinitely, something always catches you up.* Advice she'd imparted many times to the men she'd supervised, yet failed to heed herself. She deserved for Sophie to think badly of her. She deserved to suffer. But she had to try to face up to this, for Sophie's sake.

Right. Where to begin.

'I'm sorry, Sophie, for all of this.' An apology to start.

'How is this your fault?'

'Because, I think I am the root of your current situation, the reason your stalker is targeting you.' Karen took a large gulp of wine.

'And how do you get to that conclusion?' Sophie's intense eyes searched Karen's.

The clock on the wall beside them ticked loudly, like a steady heartbeat: tick . . . tick . . . tick.

A daughter. Not the person who should hear a mother's secret. Her daughter. Her only child.

Once spoken aloud, the words were out there. A secret no longer.

Tick . . . tick . . . tick.

'His name is Jay.'

CHAPTER SIXTY-TWO

The doorbell prevented further disclosure.

'I'll get rid.' Sophie placed her glass down and jumped up from her stool.

Karen hung her head. She'd spoken his name. A release, of sorts – the green light to continue. Now she had to give Sophie a summary of her indiscretion.

Would Sophie judge her?

She swallowed more wine, the effects already apparent, her head fuzzy.

How do I tell her I wanted to leave her father? She fiddled with her wedding band, twisting it around on her finger until her skin burned. *Hurry up, Sophie; get rid of whoever it is, quickly.*

The kitchen door opened. Rachel followed Sophie in.

Shit.

She shuffled like an old woman towards Karen, eyes pinned on the wine glasses.

'Something to celebrate?'

'Rach.' She rose from the stool. 'So good to see you.'

This didn't look good. Rachel barely responded to Karen's greeting, refusing to make eye contact.

'Yeah, well, as you weren't attempting to come to me, thought I'd best make the effort.'

Karen reached out and hugged her. Rachel's body stiffened, her arms fell limply over Karen's shoulders. Karen moved away. 'Come, sit down.' She drew out another stool from beneath the breakfast bar. 'Want a coffee?'

'No offer of wine for me, then.' She took the stool, positioning it beside Sophie's.

'Um, well . . . sure. Didn't you drive, though?'

'Please, Karen, you know I wouldn't drink and drive. Or you *should* know. Being my *best friend*.'

Karen opened her mouth, but didn't know how to respond.

Rachel pursed her lips together, gently shaking her head. 'Don't worry, Karen, my family liaison officer brought me, she's waiting in the car, so I can't stay long.'

'Oh, okay.' Karen's posture relaxed. 'Right, Sophie, pour Rach a wine please.'

Sophie raised her eyebrows, but did as she was asked.

'What's this in aid of then?' Rachel held the glass up, 'Drinking to Erin, are we?' Her tone, cold, matched the look in her eyes: in them pooled a mixture of detachment and bitterness. Both were to be expected in a way, but came as a shock nonetheless. Was this what Karen had been so anxious to avoid? The reason for her failure to leave the house to visit Rachel? Seeing the result of murder, the hurt and pain left with the living. Watching someone suffer wasn't easy. It was far easier to avoid all manifestations of it. Run from it, hide yourself away from it.

Karen was an expert.

'More a case of drowning out reality, an attempt to feel better. Granted, not the best way . . .' She lowered her eyes.

'Only works for short periods.' Rachel downed the wine in a few mouthfuls. 'Top me up, love.' She held her glass up to Sophie, who remained standing, poised as though deciding whether to stay, or take flight.

'What's the family liaison officer like, then?' Karen ignored the fact Rachel had drained the glass Sophie had just refilled.

Rachel wiped her mouth with the back of her hand. 'Fan-bloody-tastic.'

Karen shifted her position. She deserved this hostility; she had to ride it out.

'Does she stay with you all the time?'

'Nope. I don't want her hovering over me, fussing. She pops over, gives me updates. Not that there've been many. She's okay, I guess. Let's me talk, rant, whatever. When I've had enough, I tell her so.'

'I'm glad you have someone, who, you know—'

'Is there for me? Yep, good job someone is.'

'I'm sorry.' Karen dropped her head. Her fingers found the stem of the wine glass, twiddling it, turning it round and round. The two words weren't nearly enough. She looked back up at Rachel. 'I'm so sorry I've been a crap friend. The agoraphobia . . . it's so bad . . .'

'Only so many times you can get away with that excuse, Karen.'

Out the corner of her eye, Karen caught the expression on Sophie's face. *Touché.*

Rachel always told it straight, had done all through their childhood, their teenage years. If Karen wanted an honest opinion, a truthful appraisal of a situation, Rachel was the one to go to. Maybe that's why she hadn't confided in her about Jay. Some things didn't require honesty, merely understanding.

'I know, it's a reason, though. I'm really trying to force myself—'

'*Force* yourself?'

'I know that sounds bad. I mean force myself out of the safety of this house. Regardless of the reason, Rach, it's still hard . . .'

'I'm struggling with that, I have to be honest. After everything we've been through, all the years of watching each other's backs, rushing to each other's aid when the shit hits the fan. Remember when Phillip Jessop from Year Five dumped you, said you were frigid, and you called me, in floods of tears?'

Karen smiled, 'Er . . . how could I forget? I was devastated.'

'Yeah, and after a ten-minute conversation with me, where you cried and said your life was over, you finally asked "What does frigid mean anyway?". I think we wet ourselves laughing, we didn't even know if the term was derogatory or a compliment.'

'So many examples, Rach.'

'Yes, there are. But, do you know, there are no examples that are as huge as this. This situation, this shit-hitting-fan moment is the biggest, worst . . . And I feel like you've abandoned me.'

Devastation didn't come close. She'd let Rachel down. She hadn't attempted to justify it in her own mind, but now, with Rachel verbalising the words from her head, it hit her properly. Hard.

Where did she go from here? Was their relationship irreparable? The only possible solution to make amends would require leaving the house, visiting Rachel regularly, being there beside her.

Tell her you'll visit. She needs to hear you'll visit.

'I realise how it looks, I am here for you, I would never abandon you.'

'But you won't come over, help me with Erin's room, talk to me, and share memories. In person?'

Where's my paper bag?

Both sets of eyes were on her. Expectant, hopeful.

'I want to . . .' She had to do better than that. 'I'll . . .' The words evaporated on her tongue.

'Thanks for the wine.' Rachel stood, wobbled, then righted herself.

'Don't go yet, Rach.'

'I've said what I came for. Asked for your support. I have to go, Carol's waiting.'

'Pop over any time.' Karen pulled at her hair. *What a stupid thing to say.*

Rachel's head whipped round. She made a snorting noise through her nose. 'Sure. See you, Sophie. You're welcome at ours . . . mine . . . any time. You know that, don't you?'

236

'Yeah, and I will, I promise, Rach.' She moved in to give Rachel a hug. As she did, she widened her eyes at Karen, shaking her head. 'I'll see you out.'

Now they both hated her. Perfect. Just as she was about to tell Sophie about Jay. Talk about the final nail in the coffin.

'Right, well, that was awkward.' Sophie returned and plonked down on her stool.

'Life is complicated, Sophie. Grief is a process, it goes through stages, Rach is hurting, lashing out at the moment . . .'

'Oh, I know that, I was meaning *you* made it awkward, not her.'

'Oh, I see. Thanks.' *Here we go.* 'Again, life is complicated. My condition isn't something I can choose to have one day and not the next.'

'Can't you see how much she needs you? She's destroyed, Mum. I hate it, seeing her like this.'

'Don't you think I do, too? Why does everyone place so much emphasis on me *physically* being with her? I can support her over the phone, email, text, she can come here.'

'That's so selfish.'

'I don't have to explain myself to you.' Karen slid off the stool and walked towards the lounge.

'Isn't that exactly what you were about to do, before the doorbell?' Sophie followed.

'I've changed my mind.'

'Excellent, so now you're abandoning me as well as your best friend.'

'Don't be so ridiculous.'

'If you don't tell me about this *Jay*, who you think is my stalker, you're putting me in danger. You can't just tell me he exists and then refuse to say anything else about him! Not telling me amounts to abandoning me, placing me at his mercy.'

'That's a bit dramatic. He isn't going to hurt you.'

'How can you be sure of that?'

237

'Because all he wants is for you to tell me that he's following you, to force my hand, make me get back in contact with him again.'

'Are you telling me that you and Jay had an affair?' Sophie's face crumpled.

Karen opened her mouth, but stumbled on her words. 'Soph—'

'Don't *Soph* me,' she said, her lips twisted. 'So, are you two seeing each other behind Dad's back still?'

'Still? No, I never actually *saw* him, not in person, only in photos he sent. Our contact was only ever online, texts, a few phone calls . . .' Karen watched Sophie's face for a clue to her thoughts.

'Why?'

'I couldn't agree to meet him, not after the attack, I didn't think it would be safe to meet someone else after that.'

'No, Mum. Not why didn't you meet him. Why did you do it? Cheat on Dad?'

She'd started this now. To be able to finish it, she'd have to tell Sophie how she'd fallen out of love with her dad, how she'd sought excitement from a dating site.

CHAPTER SIXTY-THREE

'MAILER-DAEMON' Failed delivery.
I can't believe you're such a bitch. How can you leave me hanging like this? All the months of talking to me, leading me on, making me think we have a future together.

You lying whore. Can't even be bothered to answer my emails, texts OR calls. Changed your number, have you? Why have you completely cut me out?

Don't think I can't find you. We were meant to be together. You're all I have. You are my future – despite what you did I forgave you. I wasn't meant to fall in love with you, but I did. I love you and I know you love me.

I do know how to put this right, how we can be together. It might take time, but I'll make the time for you.

CHAPTER SIXTY-FOUR

Sophie

She couldn't believe what she was hearing. Her mum. Her forty-seven-year-old agoraphobic mother, a cheat. How dare she do this to them? As if she hadn't pulled the family in opposing directions enough. Now, here she was trying to defend her indiscretion. Saying it wasn't really cheating, as she never met him. Didn't sleep with him. Did that make it all right?

They sat on the sofa nearest the window; the curtains drawn. Together, but with enough distance between them so she didn't have to touch her. Sophie turned her body to the side, an attempt to create a barrier to the words that were about to follow. Perhaps her mum felt more at ease telling her the shameful details while sat on a comfy sofa, but Sophie did not.

'How long did this . . . affair, this . . . *thing*, go on for?'

'It wasn't an affair, Sophie. I told you, we messaged, emailed . . . it was nothing, really.'

'What did you write, in these emails and messages? What the weather was like, what you had for tea?'

'It doesn't matter what was in them—'

'It does to me. And I'm damn sure it will to Dad.'

'Please, Soph.' She cocked her head on one side.

Bloody hell. All the times she'd done that to Sophie, stuck her head to one side, implied she was lying. And all along, it was her.

She was the liar.

'Please, what? Don't tell Dad?' She chewed on her bottom lip. Her eyes locked on her mother's.

She didn't offer an answer.

'Okay.' Sophie closed her eyes, shutting out the image of her deceitful mother. 'I'll give you a chance to explain. Before I tell him.'

'Sophie! You don't understand—'

'Oh, but I—'

'NO,' she shouted, put her hands up in front of Sophie's face. 'You don't. And that's fine, you shouldn't have to. None of it's your fault. It's mine *and* your dad's, an accumulation of laziness, not willing to work on the marriage, putting up with each other's bad behaviour. Selfishness. No time for each other. It's many things. Things which can't be put right overnight.'

'That's why you wanted someone else?'

'I guess I wanted a quick fix. Something to make me feel good about myself.'

'A new haircut and some retail therapy couldn't have done that?'

'Superficially, yes. I did loads of things to paper over the cracks. They were always a temporary solution, though. Nothing I did, *we* did, ever began mending the underlying problem. Our foundation crumbled, Sophie. All we've ended up with in common is you. It's become an unspoken understanding—'

'What? That you're only together because of me?' She paused. Silence. *Wow, is she for real?* 'That's ridiculous. I'm seventeen, not a child.'

'I know. You're still our little girl though. You need our protection. Our *joint* protection.'

'Oh, right. Yeah, because that's exactly how it feels in this house, like you're both working together to protect me. You two are at each other's throats half the time. In front of me. How is that being protective? In fact, if this is your idea of joint protection, I'd much rather you didn't bother. Just get a divorce and have done with it.' Her outburst extinguished itself. It came as a release, the bubble of resentment which had built up over the last few years, suddenly over-inflating beyond its capacity and bursting. It seemed as though everyone had stuff to get off their chests today. A quietness settled between them. Perhaps they were both exhausted from this day of revelations. Bailey put his nose under Sophie's elbow, nudging it so he could rest his head on her lap.

'Poor dog. He's so stressed, Mum, with the constant arguments, the horrible atmosphere.'

'I know. It's not fair. Not fair on anyone.'

'This has come as such a shock. I know it may seem as though I'm overreacting . . .' Sophie twisted Bailey's fur in her fingers.

'No. You have every right to feel as you do. I made a mistake.' Karen sat forward and moved closer to Sophie. 'A few actually. Now it's come back to bite me . . . as did the last mistake I made . . . Huh. I really don't learn, do I?' She raised her eyes, trying to meet Sophie's. The smile, unsure, feeble – an attempt at gaining her sympathy?

'I don't think I want to know about any other mistakes, thanks.' She tutted and pushed Bailey off her. He skulked over to his basket.

'Fine by me. Can we get back to the current situation, now, please?'

'Yes. I guess we should. You'd best tell me why you believe it's *your* Jay who's following me. Because I find it hard to believe, if I'm honest.' Her mum must be jumping to conclusions. Surely she was wrong, her scrambled brain not working right.

Because if Jay really was her stalker, that meant he was also Erin's murderer.

Was that even possible?

And how was she supposed to tell her mum that? She obviously felt she knew this guy, thought he was amazing, had even considered leaving her dad for him. She believed he was following Sophie merely as an attempt to get her attention, that he was only a harmless stalker, a disgruntled lover attempting to get to her through her daughter. Sophie was sure her mum didn't suspect for one second her online lover was actually capable of murder. She hadn't made the connection because she hadn't seen the photos. Because Sophie couldn't bring herself to tell her what they were of, or the fact she thought she'd been there with Erin.

If she told her what she really feared it would push her over the edge; send her anxiety levels higher than ever before. She'd need more than a paper bag to recover from this one.

Sophie lay on her bed staring up at the ceiling, the shade on her bedside lamp casting wispy shadows. She traced them with her eyes, making the abstract shapes into familiar objects. She'd tried the same with her abstract family, attempting to make it into a familiar one that fit with her ideals; was the same as many of her friends' families. That illusion was well and truly shattered now.

What a weird day.

Her mum had put up a convincing case about Jay being her stalker. Eventually, following some emotional blackmail – which had to be done – she'd shown Sophie some emails. All fairly tame thankfully, but they did come across as quite desperate. Telling her he loved her, how he wanted to be with her. Every one ended with him begging to meet. Each of hers in return made excuses why she couldn't. He'd got needy, fed up.

It made sense he would seek a different avenue. A way around the block, a diversionary tactic.

Her. She was the only route to her mother.

The next step was to be sure. Sophie groaned as she considered the supposed 'plan'. She didn't know why her mum had even suggested it. It was so far beyond achievable, she'd almost laughed. She was adamant though. She wanted to see for herself – identify Jay as the stalker. Of course, it wasn't really going to happen. Apparently, she was going to ride in with Sophie to work in the morning, let Sophie walk on and hang back a bit, to watch to see if he was there. See if he followed. Once she was one hundred per cent sure he matched the pictures she'd printed off the computer – sure it was Jay – they were going to consider their next move. Or so she'd said.

When she'd first spoken about this plan, Sophie had panicked. If it turned out that she was right, that it *was* Jay, her mum might hold off calling the police. She wouldn't want her lies to surface. But, if it wasn't Jay, which was by far the likelier outcome, then her mum would call the police and the rest of the stuff would come out. Sophie would look guilty, be humiliated. Ridiculed. Blamed.

Her panic had subsided after a while, though. It was never going to happen. One – her mum would struggle to make it past the front door. Two – if she managed that stage, she'd end up stranded in Coleton, as she'd never cope with driving herself home again. And the idea of a taxi . . . well. So, basically Sophie was back to square one. She'd no one to walk to and from work with. *But*, at least the police weren't going to get involved – she definitely didn't want to go back for another grilling at the station.

Sitting at the dining room table for dinner had been an uncomfortable half-hour. She ate as quickly as possible, eyes on her plate, avoiding her dad's. If she looked at him, into his eyes, he'd see the guilt. It might not be her fault, as her mum had repeated a dozen times, but she now felt guilty by association. She knew now. She held the information, the knowledge of her mum's betrayal. By keeping it inside of her, not telling him, she was helping to hide the secret. She was an accessory. It seemed like she was an accessory to every bad thing at the moment. Murder. Adultery. What else could she add to the list?

Her phone buzzed.

Only a handful of people had the number of the temporary phone. She assumed it would be Dan. It was.

Amy's having a meltdown. We all need to get together.

Sophie sat upright. Amy? Having a meltdown? Didn't sound like her.

What about? Where and when do you want to meet? And who is 'all'?

Dan replied within seconds.

She's had too much to drink. Is going on about letting Erin down, being the worst friend, etc. Drama Queen ;-) Both of you come to mine after work tomorrow? The others will make their way here too. The Saturday gang.

It was the last thing she wanted. Certainly didn't need it now.

Does Amy know about this?

Dan's reply surprised her: **It was her idea. See you tomorrow. Sweet dreams.**

Was he having a laugh?

Tomorrow. Saturday. A week since Erin's murder. And Amy wanted to meet then? *Why?* It'd be like some macabre anniversary. What were they going to do, sit around and each say how thankful they were that it hadn't been them? She didn't fancy being out at all, especially at Dan's. If it was Amy's idea, then why weren't they meeting at hers?

She didn't like this one bit.

Although, it would mean that for one night she would be 'covered', not left alone to walk back to her car. Saturday, then, was sorted. Her mum would be with her in the morning, Amy in the evening.

But what about the rest of the time – when she was on her own? Those were the moments she was most concerned about.

Those were the times when something bad could happen.

CHAPTER SIXTY-FIVE

Karen

Saturday

Karen stood in the doorway of the en suite, a cotton pad in one hand sweeping across her cheekbone. 'Sophie's taking me into town this morning.'

'Really? That's good.' Mike didn't lift his head, continuing instead to thread his belt through the trouser loops. 'Are you meeting Rachel?'

He had to ruin it, didn't he? Couldn't he praise her for attempting to get outside the house? 'No. I'm trying small steps first. If that's okay with you?' Had she managed to keep the sarcasm from her tone?

'Absolutely. Once you've done that successfully, you'll be able to go a bit further, won't you?' He looked at her briefly, before pulling the fleece over his head. It left his hair ruffled. At one time, she would've gone over to him, brushed it down again with her hand, kissed him. Now, she simply turned away and went back into the en suite.

'Like I said, small steps.' She raised her voice so he could hear her. 'I wondered where you'd be today, you know, if there's a problem.'

'You mean how far away will I be when you get stuck and can't make it back home?'

It sounded as if he were smiling.

She wasn't having that. She pulled the flush hard, watched the cotton pads swirl in the toilet bowl and disappear, held her head up and went back in to face Mike.

'No. I won't need you to come save me, don't worry. I'll do this.'

'Fine. That's good. Because I'm on the other side of Haytor. Not only is the signal bad there, it's a good twenty miles away, so I wouldn't be any use to you anyway.'

Nothing new there, then.

'At least I know not to try.'

'Seriously though, what if you can't drive back?' *Now* there was a hint of concern.

'Bus?' What a terrible thought. *I have to be okay to drive home. I have to be.*

'It's a plan.' He shrugged a shoulder, came around to her and took her hands in his. 'You can do it. I have every faith in you.' He kissed the top of her head. 'I'll look forward to hearing all about it tonight. Shouldn't be a late one today, it's not even my Saturday really. Maybe around four. Okay?' He dropped her hands and walked out before she could respond.

One minute he was mocking her ability to go outside, next he was telling her he had *faith* in her. How was she meant to decipher him? Anyway, whatever. Basically, if she was going to do this, after Sophie left her, she was on her own. The only person she'd be letting down if she failed was Sophie. And as this was her mess, her fault Sophie had got involved, she had no intention of letting her down again.

In an hour from now, she hoped she'd know for sure if Jay was Sophie's stalker. The prospect both comforted and terrified her. On the one hand, if it was him, she knew no harm would come to Sophie, she could deal with it herself and it would be over. On the other hand, if it wasn't Jay, an unknown male threatened the safety of her daughter. And Erin's killer was still out there. She shook that thought from her head.

Karen picked out a plain white, baggy T-shirt to wear – loose enough to prevent her getting too sweaty during the inevitable panic stage, where any tight clothes added to the feelings of restriction and claustrophobia. She sighed and sat on the edge of her bed. What a mess she was. What else could she do to prepare for this? Cold drink. That might help; perhaps she should take some extra tablets too. *Paper bag. Must remember the bag.*

'You doing okay, Mum?'

'Yes. Yes. Fine.'

'You are sure about this, aren't you?' Sophie continued into the bedroom and sat beside Karen. 'I mean, I could try and take a photo of the weirdo, save you coming in.'

'No. I want to see him in the flesh.'

'All right. Up to you.' She patted her on the arm and got up to leave. 'Oh, but, I need the car for later. Dan texted last night, Amy is apparently in need of a group get-together and wants to meet at Dan's. So . . .'

'Oh. Um . . .' *Bollocks.* Although the thought of driving worried her, the thought of a bus was terrifying. At least in the car she was alone, could freak out a bit, give positive reinforcement statements aloud to herself: manage the situation, keep everything under her control. On a bus, full of strangers who would stare, judge her, and ridicule her – that was a really frightening prospect.

'Okay,' she closed her eyes for a second, inhaling deeply, 'I'll get the bus home. Probably a better idea anyway. Don't want to be a danger to other drivers.' She attempted a laugh, but the tightness in her throat caused it to come out as a squeal. Her armpits tingled with the beginnings of perspiration.

It was starting.

She needed to go now, before it took hold.

* * *

At the door. The residue of a thin mist clung to the sides of the porch windows. Sophie was in front of her, leading her through. Out.

'Don't drag me.'

'I'm not, Mum, it's okay, you're doing great.'

The air, fresh and damp, touched her face. She kept her head down. Focused on the ground. One step. Sophie's car was in the drive. She'd driven it in, passenger side closest to Karen. Two steps. A clunk, as a door opened. Three steps.

'Sit in, now.' A gentle, guiding push.

She was in. The door slammed. Safe inside the car.

'Excellent, Mum, you're doing really well.' The soft whoosh of the wipers swept the film of moisture across the windscreen as Sophie started the engine.

She'd got this far on Wednesday. This wasn't a success yet.

Her breathing shallowed.

Like it had on Wednesday.

An unbearable heat enveloped her skin, her face on fire.

Like it'd been on Wednesday.

'Stop the car!'

'Why? Mum, we haven't even got out of our road.'

'I can't do it. I'm sorry. Go back.'

'What was your point in coming with me?'

'I know, I'm sorry, I—'

'No. Tell me. What was your aim, why did you want to come?'

'To see him. Find out. Stop him.'

'Right. Say it again.'

'Eh?'

'Say it,' Sophie shouted.

'I want to see him. Need to find out if it's Jay.'

'Again.'

'I need to see him for myself, find out if it's Jay.' More conviction this time. She repeated it again. And again. Head down, she stated her aim, like a mantra.

Sophie pulled out on to the main road leading to town. Ten more minutes and they'd reach the car park. She didn't speak any more, no further words of encouragement. Karen's voice and deep breathing were the only noises in the car.

'We're here, Mum.' Sophie thrust her arm through the open window, pressed for the ticket. The barrier lifted.

'Really? Are we?'

'That's good, isn't it? You've done it. Mum, this is the farthest you've been for ages, you know, apart from the counsellor's.'

'Yes. Yes, it is. I feel sick.'

'You're fine. Come on, the worst is over.'

'It's absolutely *not*.' How could she say that? This was the easy part.

'I'm trying to be supportive?' Sophie shook her head. 'Come on then. Let's do this.'

CHAPTER SIXTY-SIX

Karen willed her muscles to move her legs, to get her out of the relative safety of the car. They resisted. She opened the door and grabbed her thigh with both hands, moving one leg free of the vehicle. Then the other. She was out. She leant back against the closed door, hunched over, eyes down. If she lifted them, she'd see the vast expanse of open space. Panic.

'Are you going to be okay, Mum?' Sophie bent over her and swept a chunk of hair away from her face. She shut her eyes tight. 'Mum?'

She could hear the nerves in Sophie's voice.

She had to look up. Get a grip.

Come on, you need to see him. Look up.

She straightened, opening her eyes, keeping them on Sophie.

'Right. Good. We can do this, Mum.'

Hearing Sophie's sudden confidence buoyed her. She was here now. She *could* do it. She held on to Sophie's upper arms and risked a quick glance around the car park. There was no sign of mist in Coleton. Instead there was a darkness, an oppression of low cloud. Seemed apt.

'If he's been following you regularly, he'll have already seen you drive in and know I'm with you. I've probably frightened him off and all this will be for nothing.'

'Nooo. If you've frightened him off you've done your job, protected me. So, it won't have been for nothing, will it?' Sophie was mothering her, talking to her as if she were coaxing a child.

'Protected you for one day only? That's not good enough. If I don't see him, I won't know if it's Jay. I have to know.'

'Are you ready for me to walk off?'

Karen glanced at the image held tightly in her trembling hand and nodded. As ready as she was ever going to be.

Sophie kissed her on the cheek, whispered 'I love you', and turned to leave.

'Take care, Soph.'

'You too, Mum.'

Okay. Concentrate. Keep focused. Who's looking Sophie's way, who's following?

Sophie reached the courthouse, walked slowly towards the crossing. Karen moved forwards too. She wanted to be far enough behind to make the stalker think he could follow Sophie unnoticed, yet close enough to make a positive identification. An old bloke pushing a bike stood beside Sophie at the crossing. Was that him? They crossed. He walked in the opposite direction. No.

Karen carried on walking. Sophie turned, caught Karen's eye, shook her head gently. She'd put him off, he must've seen she was there and disappeared. *Damn.* Karen was level with the courthouse, Sophie nearing the corner. It was now, or not at all; she was almost at her work entrance. That's where Sophie said she'd seen him last. Could she have missed him? He may have sneaked around the corner as they were taking their time in the car park.

Karen hurried; no time to panic now. Sophie had disappeared out of sight. She rounded the corner.

A man stood flattened up against the glass door of Sophie's work entrance. She stopped. Only a few metres away.

Was this the stalker?

A dark hoody, a beanie hat, blue jeans. It's all she could take in.

Turn around, you bastard.

She took a step closer.

Both his hands pressed on the door. His tongue protruded, licking the pane. He groaned.

Karen wanted to throw up. Disgusting man. Could this really be the man she'd fallen in love with?

He turned.

Karen jolted backwards.

His eyes met hers.

He smiled, tilted his head up in acknowledgement. Then he walked towards her.

Karen stumbled backwards. He brushed past her, their arms touching.

A shock raced up her arm. She held her breath.

After he'd gone, she remained standing in the middle of the pedestrianised walkway, the picture crumpled in her hand. Shock giving way to the inevitable panic.

Paper. Bag. In. Car. Don't lose it here. Not now.

A hand landed on Karen's shoulder. She screamed. People turned to look in her direction, but seeing nothing untoward, moved on.

'Mum, are you okay? Do you want to come in and sit down? Shall I call Dad?'

'I'm . . . no. I'll be all right. Really.' She stumbled towards the metal bench in the centre of the walkway and sat down heavily. *Breathe in . . . and out . . . in . . . and out.*

'You saw him, then?'

'Yeah, he's a real piece of work.' Karen opened her hand and unfurled the picture, looking at it briefly before meeting Sophie's imploring eyes. 'But, it's not him.'

'Are you sure? I mean, did you get a proper look at him?'

'I saw him up close, Sophie. I got a good look. And it's definitely not him. Not if this is anything to go by.' She held out the picture for Sophie to see. 'I'm afraid Jay is *not* your stalker.'

CHAPTER SIXTY-SEVEN

DI Wade

Lindsay sat in her car in the police car park. She pulled the visor down, sliding the cover to the mirror across so she could check her appearance before going in. She'd barely slept since Sunday, her face now showing the strain – its grey, weary complexion screaming lack of sleep. Whether that was to do with the case, her empty bed or a mixture of the two, she didn't know. She still slept on her side, habit as well as a part of her that couldn't let go of the hope. Although, possibly, it was time to admit defeat, given that she'd received divorce papers that morning. She didn't suppose there was any coming back from that. He'd already moved on according to her source – he'd been seen, hand-in-hand with a busty blonde wandering around Plymouth Hoe. She'd tried to refrain from making the obvious joke when her friend, Fi, had imparted this information. But failed.

The commute to the station from Lindsay's house in Plymouth was a tedious one and added a good hour on to her journey, as well as contributing to her tiredness. She slammed the visor back up and grabbed her cardboard cup of coffee from the holder. She'd be in work before the others on her shift – she enjoyed the early morning peace of the incident room, the opportunity to get her head together before her team arrived.

She spent more time in there than she did at home, she liked it that way. It came with the job; she'd always put in the hours to her work, even before Tony had left. Another sticking point. He'd suggested marriage guidance, as if she was going to pay to sit and spill her guts for some pompous, know-it-all, high-and-mighty tosser to judge her. Besides, when would she have the time for that? Probably why he'd suggested it in the first place, knowing full well she couldn't spare the time. Or, wouldn't spare it – that's what he'd said. Another black cross to add to the many she had against her. She should've married a copper, at least there'd have been an understanding that her job came first. Or, perhaps she shouldn't have married at all. She wouldn't make the same mistake again.

'Oh, hey, Mack.' Her heart dipped as she swung open the door to find Mack already in the room. He was leaning back on two wheels of an office chair, feet up on the table. His brown wiry-looking hair was stuck up at the back as usual. Lindsay was always tempted to flatten it down, but had managed to refrain. One day. 'Don't mind me.' She gave him a friendly nudge as she walked past him.

'Hey!' He flung his legs back down and hung on to the desk with both hands to prevent the chair slipping from under him. 'And a good morning to you too, Boss. Thought I'd get on it early on this fine Saturday morning. Can feel the pressure, can't you?'

That went without saying. It was a week after the murder, the pressure was on to get someone in custody, or at least look as though they had a credible suspect. Apart from anything else her career would take a bashing if this dragged on. And heaven help her if another dead girl turned up. As with all things, you got squeezed from the one above you. She pushed her team, and she felt the crack of the whip from SIO Bainbridge. Their only real lead had been Sophie's emails, the unearthing of those had been a real buzz – pictures that appeared to be of Sophie, taken by someone who threatened to send her more. But, as yet, it was just that – a lead. They'd yet to question her about them, or find the source of them, and until they did, all they could do was hope the culprit came good with his promise of sending more, perhaps revealing something solid they could act on. Delaying questioning Sophie had been Lindsay's call. She had a gut feeling that Sophie would be more useful to them covertly. Confronting her directly might cause her to clam up – and the person responsible for the pictures go underground.

She chose to leave Mack's question open. 'You sure you haven't spent the night here, Mack?'

'May as well have done, fat lot of use my two hours of kip were. Feel wrecked.' He rubbed at his eyes, the skin beneath them crinkling like tissue paper.

'Ah. Pretty as a picture, you are. Almost as lively looking as me today.' Lindsay knew she might *look* strained, but she'd never verbalise it to the rest of the team; only Mack was privy to her confessions of tiredness or stress. She trusted him not to consider it a weakness in her, or talk behind her back. She wasn't weak. Far from it.

But she had the feeling this investigation was going to test her strength to the extreme.

CHAPTER SIXTY-EIGHT

Karen

Each body was a potential attacker. Each face, a threat. Each corner, a hiding place. She wanted to be back in her safe zone. Now. The town hadn't fully awoken, shop fronts only just beginning to open, people hurrying on their way to work. It didn't stop her from seeing danger at every step. When had been the last time she'd ventured here? Had to be a good fourteen months ago: she'd attempted to meet Mike's sister for a coffee, quash Mike's concerns about her becoming a recluse and snubbing his family. That particular outing hadn't ended well, a full-blown anxiety attack the second she'd set eyes on her poor sister-in-law. How would this one conclude?

'Keep head down. Keep feet moving. Each step is one closer to home.'

She repeated this over and over.

What if she bumped into Rach? How would it look? Can't make it to her house, but can go into town?

'Keep feet moving. Don't think about it.'

Where was she? She had to look up, check the direction. People stared at her. She looked like a mad woman, muttering to herself, shuffling along staring at the ground. At this point, it didn't matter. They could think what they liked.

261

Okay, good, she was at the indoor market entrance. The bus stop was close. Head down again. Don't look. Don't stop.

A strip of blue blocked her path. White above. Thank the Lord. The bus.

Karen climbed the steps, thrust the coins at the driver without making eye contact, grabbed her ticket and sat on the first seat, nearest the door. She'd done it. The first part, at least.

Relax. Half an hour and she'd be home.

Her mind conjured Jay's image: short, black hair, coarse texture. Dark eyes, a little too close together, a strong, square jaw line. A crooked smile, a small scar visible under his bottom lip. A clean-cut face, olive complexion. She had a dozen pictures. One of him on holiday, lying by the pool, bare chest, a sprinkling of hairs on his sternum, otherwise smooth. Another, taken on his thirty-seventh birthday this year, posing in front of a pub, arm around a life-size inflatable doll, a joke gift from his best mate. He appeared tall against it. He'd told her he was six foot four.

Everything about Jay was different from Sophie's stalker. She'd been wrong. Had fear made her jump to the wrong conclusion? It niggled her, her mind not ready to let go of the belief that it was him. She remembered the moment when she'd finally messaged him saying she wanted to cool things. He'd reacted badly, sending a nasty email in return. He'd been quick to flare, his words harsh, a sharp contrast to every other loving email he'd written. She'd been shocked at the sudden change, how rapidly it'd then escalated into threats of telling Mike if she didn't carry on their relationship. It saddened her, to think this man, the one she'd confided in and shared her dreams, her deepest, darkest thoughts and feelings, could so easily turn on her. He'd said he loved her.

She'd been sure when Sophie mentioned the email address that it was him. Did he have someone else stalking Sophie? It would explain the disparity. Maybe he'd roped someone else in, was paying them to do his dirty work, and even though it wasn't Jay, there was something about him she couldn't place. She closed her eyes and conjured the face she'd just seen. Those unusual piercing green eyes, that in any other circumstances she'd find attractive, were familiar. Did she know him? Karen shuddered. Jay might have more than one person involved in his vicious game.

There was only one way to find out. Give him what he was after.

When she got home, she would email him.

She'd never been so relieved to walk in her front door. Bailey greeted her with the most enthusiasm he'd mustered all week, jumping up, hitting against her shaky body. He must be so confused. Probably thought she'd abandoned him. Karen collapsed under his weight and sat with him, letting him lick her all over until he'd covered her in drool.

She was proud of her achievement, but had no time to revel in it now. She had work to do. She pushed Bailey off and headed to the kitchen to make a drink; her throat was parched. Whilst waiting for the kettle to boil, Karen retrieved the archived file on her laptop.

Jay's emails.

Familiar feelings returned instantly. New ones now added to the mix – apprehension and fear. She was about to start up something she'd been compelled to finish just six months ago. Only this time, she'd no idea what to expect.

If she was right, and Jay was involved somehow with Sophie's stalker, then she'd perhaps get answers from him, find out what he wanted from her. If she was wrong, well, then she would reopen old wounds, and who knew what the repercussions would be. She made a coffee, settled in front of the screen, fingers poised over the keys, about to compose an email that could open Pandora's Box.

She'd be vague, to start. Test the water. See if he replied.

Hey Jay,

I know it's been a while, and I'm messaging you despite saying I wouldn't contact you again. I'm sorry if this causes you distress, that's not my aim. Are you well? I hope you've managed to move on, and perhaps have a new relationship. I don't wish to open old wounds by emailing you, forgive me if I have. But, I had to try and contact you as I need to ask you a question. I would really appreciate it if you could please email me back. For old times' sake?

Thanks.

Karen x

Was it good enough? Friendly enough? Subtle? She read it, tweaked it.

If she knew him as she thought she did, he wouldn't be able to resist replying. She took a sip of coffee. Swallowing it was like trying to squeeze an inflated balloon through a cardboard tube. She put a hand to her throat, massaging it. She felt her pulse banging against her fingertips. Was she doing the right thing? Some things should stay buried. A heaviness lay in her stomach, a swirl of nausea snaking around her gut. She'd closed the door on Jay. She hoped she wasn't making a huge mistake by opening it again. She placed her hand back on the keyboard.

Five, four, three, two, one . . . SENT.

Perhaps soon, she'd know for sure.

CHAPTER SIXTY-NINE

DI Wade

'This could be relevant.' DC Clarke sounded on the verge of excitement as he headed towards Lindsay with a report sheet in hand.

'I don't want *could*, I want *is*.' Lindsay perched on the edge of a table, hopeful for good news whilst they awaited a breakthrough on the email account. 'Go on. Amaze me.' She gave a thin smile.

'Got a call from a woman claiming to have been followed by a man today, from the centre of Coleton to where the buses stop outside the market—'

'Really? Is that it?' Lindsay crossed her arms and sighed loudly, disappointed with this information. 'Some bloke was probably just walking in the same direction, getting a bus even. How shocking.'

'Hang on, hang on.' DC Clarke put up a hand. 'Give me a minute, Guv.'

'Sorry, go on.'

'She went on to say that once she got on the bus, heading for Torquay, she noticed he seemed to be following another female, not her as she'd first thought. So she continued to watch him until her bus left.'

'And?' Lindsay stood up, allowing an ounce of hope to develop.

'He followed this female closely, she didn't appear to be aware of him, and he put his hand out as if to touch her as she stood outside the bus waiting to get on. But instead he put his nose to her hair and looked like he was sniffing it, then she reckoned he took some.'

'Of her hair? Like a strand of it?'

'Yeah.'

'Okay, so that's odd behaviour. Did the woman he snatched it from notice?'

'According to the witness, no. Just boarded the bus without turning around. Perhaps she didn't feel anything. Anyway, we've asked the woman to come in and complete an E-FIT. I thought it was worth it in case we get any similar reports.'

'Good thinking. It's got to be worth a go. It's probably a long shot, but it *could* be our guy – perhaps he stalks his victims prior to killing them. Would the woman be able to identify the female he was following?'

'She was asked that at the time of reporting, and no. Said all she could say about the woman was that she had dark, mid-length hair. Her attention had been on him, and trying to remember his features so she could tell the police.'

'Fine. When we get the E-FIT check for any CCTV, see if we can follow *him*, see what he's been up to.'

CHAPTER SEVENTY

Sophie

Was it a good thing or a bad thing her mum didn't think her stalker was Jay? Apparently he hadn't matched the photos she'd seen of him. If she was right, at least that would mean Jay wasn't the killer; her mum hadn't been in love with a murderer, so all good for her. Sophie, however, was no nearer to finding out who the man really was. Had it been Jay, she'd have had support from her mum and help in getting rid of him without police involvement.

Better the devil you know.

Now she was back where she'd begun – with an unidentified psycho following and taunting her. Would her mum push her to go to the police now she herself had nothing to lose? Sophie wasn't looking forward to going home later. Thank goodness she was going to Dan's first, putting off *that* conversation had to be a good thing. The thought of being with the Saturday gang had played heavily on her mind throughout the day. Watching Amy at her make-up counter, all smiles and banter, grated. She certainly didn't look as if she was experiencing any kind of meltdown. *Drama Queen.*

The store cleared out. Sophie wielded the Hoover like a weapon, sweeping it fast and erratically across the ridged beige carpet, which had seen better days. She watched as Amy disappeared upstairs. She'd better not leave her here alone. She pulled the plug, wound the cord, threw the Hoover out the back and ran to the staffroom.

'Wait, Amy.'

Amy turned as she reached the external door. Sophie, out of breath, ran down the steps to her.

'Sorry, was I meant to be waiting for you?' Her face, innocent.

'Well, Dan said you asked for us all to meet up at his after work, so I assumed we'd go together?'

'Dan said that?' Her eyebrows met in the middle.

Sophie muttered under her breath. Her confusion mixing with irritation.

'What's the matter, Soph?' Amy pressed the digits on the security pad, the front door swished open.

'Dan texted last night. Said you were having a meltdown, wanted everyone to meet. At his.'

Amy stopped outside, spread her hands and shrugged her shoulders up. 'I said it would be good to get together, yes. I did *not* imply I was having any kind of meltdown, and *he* was the one who suggested tonight at his. Seriously, what's he playing at?'

'I did wonder why we'd be meeting at his if it was your idea. He's been pushing for this all week, though, so we shouldn't be surprised really.'

'I don't know what it's going to achieve. Can't change what's happened, no good will come of going over it. Personally, I feel bad enough about what happened. I don't need anyone else telling me what we could have done differently.'

Sophie linked arms with Amy and steered her towards the car park. She didn't resist, probably didn't even notice which direction she was walking now her rant was in full swing. Sophie looked cautiously behind them, casting her eyes in doorways. A figure, part obscured by an advertisement board, shifted and took a step out from the pub entrance.

She drove Amy on.

'What's the rush?' Amy tripped on the kerb, her heel catching. 'Blimey, Soph.' She looked up, aware now of her surroundings. 'You giving me a lift, then, I take it.'

'Yep. May as well.' Sophie sped up, dragging Amy with her. 'Come on.'

Once inside the car, Sophie hit the central locking button. The deep, resounding *clunk* was reassuring. She caught a bemused expression from Amy. She wasn't stupid; she could tell something was up. Now might be a good time to tell her.

She swung out of the car park. At the junction, she slammed on the brakes, flinging her and Amy forward.

'Jesus.' The contents of Amy's bag spewed on to the floor. She pulled at the seatbelt, attempting to loosen its hold.

Sophie stared dead ahead, her eyes transfixed on the figure. He'd walked in front of them. Stopped. Stared at her before moving on. Just as she'd feared – he wouldn't let the fact she had someone with her discourage his stalking.

A horn blared from behind them. Amy finally looked up from gathering her items from the footwell.

'What did you slam on your brakes for?' She rubbed at her neck. 'Shit, you gave me whiplash.'

'Didn't you see him? Walked right in front of the car.' Sophie set off again, gesticulating with one hand to the driver behind.

'No. Just as well I wasn't driving then.' Amy laughed.

So close. Somehow, now didn't seem the right time to tell Amy about him. Perhaps at Dan's. The thought produced a sinking feeling.

Who knew what was going to come out of this get-together. What was Dan playing at?

CHAPTER SEVENTY-ONE

'I've got some pizzas in the oven, should keep us going.' Dan flitted around, ushering them to the lounge, his jittery movements immediately setting Sophie on edge. Why had he been so keen for this to happen, why had he twisted things about, saying the get-together was Amy's idea, not his? She was irritated by his lack of honesty, after all that fuss he'd made about being her friend when they went out the other evening.

'I'm not staying long, Dan,' Sophie said as she took a glass of Coke from his outstretched hand.

'Oh, right.' He looked disappointed, but had no time to say anything else as the others all piled in and seemed to distract him.

Amy and Sophie exchanged quizzical glances. Soon the room was buzzing. It was odd. Wrong.

One of them was missing.

They didn't always manage to all be together at the same time, what with a couple of them working and a few at college, but that was fine. Knowing someone was absent due to work or college was a world apart from knowing that one of them was dead. Saturday night had been the first time for months the gang had been complete. It had been so short-lived.

Sophie drifted back into the conversation after hearing her name spoken. Becks was staring at her, wanting an answer.

'Sorry. Say again?'

'I said, do you remember anything yet? Whether you saw Erin after you left the pub. About the taxi drive, at all?'

Great. More interrogation. 'No. I've got nothing. Me and Amy have been over it, trying to unlock something concrete. It's a blank.' Her cheeks burned.

'Oh! Forgot,' Amy blurted. 'You'll never guess who came for a makeover today?' Her eyes widened. She paused for effect and Sophie, thankful for the diversion, asked, 'Who?'

'Okay, well it was a long shot you'd guess anyway. Only that tart, Maria.' She sat back, seemingly pleased with this declaration. Everyone remained silent. Amy slumped, tutted. 'You *know*, Adam's new girlfriend. Erin's *step-mum*?'

'Oh. Had no idea of her name, she's "whatsherface" in our house,' Sophie said. She didn't get the big deal anyway. 'So what?'

'A makeover though? Bit weird, isn't it, what's she getting glammed up for – Erin's funeral?' Becks piped up.

Amy flicked her hand under her hair. 'She had a go at me.'

'What?' Everyone sat forward, now interested in Amy's story.

'I know, right. The cheek of the woman. Who does she think she is? She reckoned Erin was miserable because of me. Because of how I look, how popular I am. Gave Erin low self-esteem, *apparently.*'

A difficult one. Sophie knew how hard Erin had tried to fit in; she'd never stated Amy was a problem, though. Not to her. But this was exactly what Rachel had been talking about, and that, too, had come from whatsherface – this *Maria*. Why had Erin spoken to Maria about her insecurities, but not any of the group?

'What did you say?' Jack said, with a mouthful of the pizza Dan had handed out.

'I was taken aback, actually. I know Erin and I had differences occasionally, knew she liked to copy me, didn't think it was a big deal. I told Maria that.'

'Do you think she's stirring it up for the rest of us?' Becks asked.

'She *and* the police. What's their game? Why is everyone pointing the finger at us?' Dan's issue was clearly not resolved from the day Sophie had seen him at the police station.

'Better than taking a good look at herself, if she can palm the blame on to me,' Amy said.

'What do you mean, why would she need to take a look at herself?' Sophie was beginning to wonder where this was heading.

'Well, it wouldn't surprise me if it was her who pushed Erin over the edge, made her feel insecure about her looks.' Amy's voice was animated now, playing to her crowd. 'She was the bitch who was vying for Adam's attention and hated Erin being there, even worse when Erin began staying over regularly, like it was a competition who could gain his attention for longer.'

'Really? Erin didn't mention anything like that.' Rosie, who'd remained silent up until now, obviously decided it was time to speak up.

'She hadn't seen you for ages, Rosie. She told me about it. On Saturday night in fact.'

Sophie's stomach lurched. 'You never told me that when I was asking you about Saturday. About Erin. Why not?'

'Sophie, you were being so weird about everything, I don't know, it didn't seem relevant at the time, too busy warding off yours and your mother's rain of questions. Now Maria's been in accusing me of being the problem, I remembered Erin's conversation.'

'Yeah, Soph, you've been a bit highly strung since all this.' Dan's helpful contribution.

'Is it any wonder? Aren't all of us? Anyway, you're a fine one to talk, Dan. You've been sneaking around, following me, losing the plot all week.'

'Now, now, *girls*. Put your handbags away.' Tom put up a hand, his attempt at calming the situation. The smirk betrayed his real thoughts.

'We shouldn't be having a go at each other.' The sensible, pragmatic Alice waded in. 'We should be sticking together. Now, let's get back to Adam's girlfriend. What do you know about her, Amy?'

'Not a lot. Erin said her dad moved in with Maria not long after they met. He'd said there was no point waiting, they knew how they felt about each other. Time was of the essence.'

'She's not up the duff, is she?' Jack laughed.

'I don't know. Doesn't look like it though, skinny as a rake,' Amy said.

'Why the rush then?'

'No idea.' Amy shifted position, relaxing back against the sofa. 'All I know is that they'd only known each other for a month or so. They'd met at the garage where he works. She'd brought her car in for a service—'

'And he gave her a full service instead.'

'Tom! Not really appropriate . . .'

'Well, whatever,' Tom went on, more serious now. 'So you're saying Adam didn't know Maria very well and within weeks he moved in with her?'

'Yes, and Erin was understandably put out. If you ask me, that's a recipe for disaster,' Amy said.

'Rachel didn't say much about the situation when I saw her,' Sophie added. 'Only about how she was upset that Erin confided in Maria, rather than her.'

'Oh my God.' Amy shot up. 'Something's just come to me.' Her face stony, serious. She looked at Sophie. 'It was her . . . Maria, who gave Erin the number for the taxi.'

'Are you sure? You couldn't remember a thing about the whole taxi episode before.' Sophie sat back, shocked at this sudden revelation.

'It's because we're talking about Maria, it's just hit me. Wham. Erin was at the bar with me, and you, Soph, and when we said about a taxi, she scrolled through the numbers on her mobile saying . . .' Amy paused, placing her hand on her forehead. 'Erin said Maria had recommended a taxi driver for the night, someone she knew who was reliable and trustworthy.'

None of the group spoke following Amy's unexpected recollection.

Dan broke the silence. 'You have to go to the police with this info, Amy. He might be the one who last saw Erin alive.'

'He might be the one who killed her,' Alice said. 'And he's still free to do it again!'

'The police must have Erin's mobile, though. They'd have investigated the last calls she made, followed them up. They probably already know about the taxi driver,' Tom suggested.

'True. We're bound to be ten steps behind the police,' Sophie said.

'Odd though. Dodgy. Perhaps Maria wanted something bad to happen to Erin. Get her out the way so she had a clear run with Adam.' Amy spoke quietly, as if it were only a thought she happened to say aloud.

As unlikely as it sounded at first, Sophie couldn't help but contemplate it. She thought about what Rachel had said, about how suddenly Maria had come on to the scene. Amy's theory might be plausible.

If it was, how did Sophie fit in? Why had she been involved in this?

All along she'd assumed Erin had got in the taxi with her to make sure she'd get home safely. But what if it was actually the other way around? Had Sophie inadvertently stumbled into some bizarre plot to get rid of Erin? That's why the man didn't kill her as well, because she'd never been the intended victim; she'd merely got in the way.

It seemed a stretch of the imagination, Adam's new girlfriend wanting his daughter dead.

But, the words of DI Wade echoed in her mind: *It's generally someone known to the victim.*

275

CHAPTER SEVENTY-TWO

Karen

Karen refreshed the screen again. A stubborn zero remained at the side of her inbox.

Mike said he'd be home early, so she had to be careful. Not that he'd notice, or question what she was doing. He hadn't all the time she'd been messaging Jay. No doubt he'd get home, throw his boots off, shower, then retreat into his bubble with the iPad. His 'downtime'. Because clearly wandering over the moors all day was so stressful. It hadn't always been that way. He'd had the trainee ranger job when they met, their first dates had involved numerous outings and picnics, Mike assuring her he knew the best places. He was the longest-standing member of the ranger team now, responsible for his own area of Dartmoor. He always took his duties very seriously – but lately he appeared to have taken this to the extreme and certainly acted as though he cared more about his working life than his home one. Karen tutted. Their daily environments couldn't be more disparate. His, a vast open space – freedom to roam; hers, small and enclosed – a self-imposed prison.

Karen came back to the moment, and opened the J&K file. She started at the bottom – the very first contact from him. That one thread ran to fifteen messages, the subject heading: *Could you be the one?* Corny. She'd seen the heading a hundred times on the dating site, but remembered laughing anyway. The next thread: *Glad I found you*, contained forty-six messages. He started the conversations, always first to make a new thread. He became wittier with his subject headings as the time went on, always producing a smile from her when she received a new one. They got to know each other better during the second exchange, each message within the thread became more personal, longer, more detailed. By the end of the third thread, Jay knew Karen's hopes, fears . . . and the beginnings of her desires.

Oh, no. The things she'd told him. It'd seemed innocuous at the time, the deep conversations, the sharing of each other's lives – past and present. Having worked with criminals, master manipulators, she should've been more cautious and not divulged so many personal details. But he'd found her when she was vulnerable from the attack, hurt both physically and emotionally. She simply hadn't recognised the danger. It was just talking, not meeting. What could possibly go wrong if she didn't agree to meet? It was harmless and filled a void. He made her feel better about herself. And he gained, too. Or so he told her.

Karen put her arms on the table. She held her chin in her hands, her fingers covering her mouth to stop the gasps from materialising.

Now she read the messages with a new perspective.

You stupid, stupid woman.

Over the course of a year, she'd given him everything he needed. Names, likes, dislikes, routines, insecurities, dreams. The names of Sophie's workplace and college. Everything. She'd equipped this man with all he needed to stalk her daughter. She pressed her closed eyelids with her fingertips to try to form a seal, but the tears leaked out anyway.

The way he'd seduced her with his words, giving her the most graceful compliments, admiring her strength, her love for Sophie. When he confided he had no parents or siblings, Karen genuinely

278

felt devastated for him. She knew what it was like to lose parents; she related to his pain, his suffering. She'd helped him through his darkest moments, talking well into the early hours. They shared a connection, a strong bond. Without ever having met. Her heart had swelled with love for a man she'd never seen. He'd given her a reason to keep going.

How could she even consider that he was behind the stalking? Surely, she'd instinctively know if he were dodgy. She *knew* him.

Or, she knew the side of him he'd allowed her to see.

She saw the stalker today. He didn't look the slightest bit like Jay.

Not the Jay in her pictures.

Karen's eyes flicked to the top left of her screen.

She stopped breathing.

Inbox (1)

The old feelings returned, now with an added punch of adrenaline.

It was him.

Her eyes moved across to the subject heading.

Subject: My angel returns

Palpitations. Getting a new message from Jay always produced them. This time, they weren't from excitement. She'd reconnected with him to satisfy her need to know. Now, she couldn't bring herself to open the email. Afraid of what it said. Scared to start this up again. He'd been pretty nasty before she'd broken all contact. This subject heading suggested the opposite lay within the electronic communication.

Only one way to find out. Karen breathed in deeply, and opened it.

My darling Karen,

Wow! I did not expect to see your name in my inbox again, what a genuinely wonderful surprise. I see you've changed your email account, well – I have it again now!

Am I well? Yes, not bad. Am I in a new relationship? How could you possibly ask this? Of course I'm not. How could I be? You were my one and only, my soul mate, my destination. Once you left me, there could be no other, Karen.

So, you have a question for me. Go on, ask of me what you will. I await your reply with great anticipation . . .

Jay xxx

Oh, hell. She read it again. She'd have to ask him about Sophie outright, he was coming across all lovey, clearly wasn't going to say anything of his own accord. What if it wasn't him? He'd be really angry at her for suggesting that he was menacing her daughter, assuming he didn't have anything to do with it. *Dammit.*

She typed out her question. Deleted it. Tried another angle. Scrapped that, too. Okay. She would go for an apologetic-sounding accusation. She shook the tension from her shoulders. And attempted it again.

Jay,

I know what I'm about to ask may sound awful. If I'm not right. And if I am wrong, feel free to be mad at me. But I have to ask. When I stopped our online relationship, you threatened a lot of things, got nasty. I had to block you, delete contact information, to stop the constant barrage of emails, texts and even calls. I guess that might have hurt you, made you even angrier. Perhaps you wanted to get back at me? Maybe even get back with me. I don't know.

Have you been contacting Sophie and having her followed?

No going back.

She sent it. Sat there, waiting. Wondering.

She imagined his face as he read it. Heard his voice, shouting aloud at her accusation. She saw him typing rapidly, full of rage that she could think such a thing of him.

She was wrong. It couldn't be him. He wouldn't get someone to follow her. Not the Jay she knew. How would she get out of this? Once he answered, denying any such thing, what then?

She was about to find out.

A new message.

Her mouth dried. She hesitated, wasn't one hundred per cent sure she wanted to know his reply. At first, her eyes scanned over the email. It didn't take long, his response only four short lines.

Ah. You got me. Won't bother messing about.

    Yes, Karen. I have been contacting Sophie. I don't have anyone following her though.

    That's all me.

She wanted to be sick.

How? She'd seen the stalker. It wasn't Jay.

Anger took over. Had he lied to her?

Bastard. How dare he do this? What was his game?

CHAPTER SEVENTY-THREE

Karen paced the dining room, unsure of what to do. Furious thoughts flowed through her mind as she hammered out a reply that didn't match her feelings. She'd hold back. For now.

I don't understand, Jay. How can it be you? I saw the man following Sophie, and it didn't look like you. Why are you contacting her, sending pictures? Is it to get to me? Do you hate me that much?

Have you been lying to me this whole time?

The wait for a reply stretched. How had she got him so wrong? It couldn't have all been a lie, there's no way she'd have fallen for it. Surely.

Karen,
My feelings for you were never a lie. Just the pictures.

It was me you saw, the real me. We touched. All those months of longing, being desperate to see you, feel you. And there it was, in that brief moment of contact you looked at me, and you touched my soul. As I knew you would. I need more of that.

I couldn't bear to think I'd never see you. You stopped all contact, suddenly. Cruelly. I've forgiven so much of what you've done. But you went beyond the boundary of my rules. I want to love you, forgive you again.

We will be together, Karen. Just you watch and see.

This wasn't happening. He was delusional. What, *who*, had she got involved with? She took a moment, attempted to gather her thoughts. She had to approach this carefully, think her responses through. How she dealt with this would directly affect what he did next with Sophie.

So, you aren't who you portrayed online. To me. The pictures of you are fake.

You aren't targeting Sophie after all. The trouble you're going to, following her, frightening her with those pictures, it's all a ruse to get to me, is that right?

Well, now you have what you want, I'm back in contact with you. We can work this out without Sophie's involvement. Without Mike's. Unless you want the police involved?

Best it's just you and me. Yes?

That might do it. Give him a hint that she was willing to involve the police.

You and me. Perfect. That's how this is ending, Karen. First, though, a score requires settling. You're currently ahead, and we can't have that. We have to be on a level footing, you and I. For our future to work.

284

CHAPTER SEVENTY-FOUR

Sophie

Monday

Sunday had been an awkward day of snatched whispers with her mum, and avoidance of her dad. Sophie had needed to tell her mum what Amy had said about Maria giving Erin the taxi driver's number, to see if there were any links between her and the events that night. There'd been no opportunity to tell her the full story, but she'd managed to impart snippets. Enough to set off her mum's antennae. She'd spent a number of hours on the computer afterwards, sat with her back to the dining room wall, her laptop screen shielded from their view. Sophie's curiosity was piqued.

She didn't have time to wait for her dad to leave for work this morning; she had to be in college for eight thirty to ensure she got a parking space close to the entrance, so the full conversation with her mum would have to wait until this afternoon. She only had three lessons today, so she could be home well before her dad. A vague recollection of her mum sneaking in very late last night, telling her it *was* Jay stalking her, played around the edge of her memory. Was she dreaming it, or had her mum actually told her Jay was the stalker? She couldn't be completely sure.

Sophie swung her car into the college. Only a few spaces remained right outside the building. Good call to come early. She twisted around in her seat, checking around the perimeter of the car park. Nothing. A dark car pulled up on the road outside of the college wall, too far away to make out the occupant. Was it him? He'd never been in a car as far as she knew, always on foot, so hopefully not.

Quick, get in the building now.

She sped up the pathway, swinging her arm around to lock the car door with the button on her key. She was in. Safe. So much easier than work. Perhaps this college week meant a reprieve from Jay's attention. He wouldn't get near enough here.

Once in the classroom, her apprehension dissolved. A few other early students gathered at one table, chatting about their weekend. All was normal. For now. Even the sun was making a rare appearance, sending tracks of yellow through the window, hitting her table and ricocheting off – making her skin glow with a pleasant warmth as it touched her face.

Sophie pulled out her folder, placed it on the desk and slumped into the chair. If her memory was right and her mum had come into her room, told her it was Jay – how was it going to play out now? Would he stop following her and sending pictures if he was back in touch with her mum? But then, what did he want with her? She'd have to warn her mum, somehow break the news to her about him being the one who'd murdered Erin. Otherwise, her mum was in danger too.

Could this get any worse?

As the classroom began filling up, two figures appeared at the door. They stood talking to her teacher. Sophie looked away, sinking lower in her chair. Really? Were they here for her? DI Wade and DS Mack moved back from the doorway. Mr Allen squeezed through, beckoning to Sophie.

She closed her eyes. Oh, please, not now.

But it wasn't like she could just ignore them.

'Sophie Finch.' The voice was loud enough for the whole class to shut up and look in her direction.

Great.

The room was silent as she walked out, hushed conversations starting up again as she shut the door.

CHAPTER SEVENTY-FIVE

DI Wade

'Hi, Sophie,' DI Wade said. 'Can we have a chat? We've got a room just down the corridor, shouldn't be disturbed there.' She put a hand on Sophie's shoulder, gently guiding her in that direction.

DS Mack held the door open for her and Sophie, then he followed them in.

'What is it?' Sophie's voice was shaky. She looked from her to Mack.

'Oh, nothing much really. I'm afraid there haven't been any significant leads. We were hoping you may have remembered something?' Lindsay raised one eyebrow.

Sophie sat on the arm of a low chair and fiddled with her fingers. She looked down at them, saying nothing for a long time. Lindsay was about to prompt her when she finally spoke.

'There *was* something that came up, actually. To do with Saturday night . . .' She seemed to take in a deep breath and hold it. Was she about to say something important?

'It's come to light that the number for the taxi driver Erin called was given to her by her dad's girlfriend, Maria—'

'Ah, yes, we've already been given that, but thank you.' Mack dismissed it with a wave of his hand. Sophie's mouth dropped.

She obviously hadn't been expecting that response. Lindsay wondered why.

'How are you doing, anyway, Sophie? Must be awful to lose a friend, especially under such terrible circumstances.' Lindsay used her soft voice, the one reserved for telling bad news or trying to be approachable. She was hoping it would encourage Sophie to open up.

'It's still so . . . unreal, really. I don't think it's hit me yet.' She fiddled with her fingers again, cracking the knuckles of one hand. Lindsay had noted this during the initial interview at the station, took it as a sign of nerves. But maybe there was more to it; anxiety, stress. Lies? Would Sophie finally break and mention the emails?

'Did you go to the site where she was found?' Lindsay asked.

Sophie's eyes widened. 'No! I couldn't . . . wouldn't want to see. Anyway, isn't it all cordoned off?'

'Not all of it now. And you might find it actually helps, you know, seeing all the flowers and tributes. It sounds odd, probably, but it can make it real, help commence the grief process. Because at the moment, I'm wondering if you're holding on to far too much.'

Sophie's face took on a stony expression. 'I don't think so. I can't face it, seeing the exact spot where that vile killer discarded her.' Her nose turned pink and she pressed her lips together tightly. Tears came. 'That bastard stabbed her, strangled her, and for what possible reason? When are you going to catch him? Why haven't you made progress?' The anger, abrupt in its expulsion, came as a shock. Lindsay turned sharply to Mack. Had he picked up on what she'd just said?

'We do have a number of avenues yet to investigate—'

'Well, why aren't you out there investigating? Instead of here? What use am I to you?'

Lindsay remained silent, letting the questions ride. She saw Mack put a hand inside his jacket pocket. He took a step towards Sophie.

'Here. I wanted to hand this back to you. We're done with it, thanks.' He held out Sophie's iPhone. 'Just thought, as we were here, we'd see if you had any further information, that's all.'

'Oh, right. Thanks.'

'We'll leave you to your college work then, Sophie.' Lindsay turned to leave. 'Just one more thing . . .'

Sophie sighed. 'Yes.'

'There've been reports of a man following women in the area. We're in the process of obtaining an E-FIT of the suspect. Have you noticed anything unusual, anyone taking more of an interest in you, Sophie?'

Sophie kept eye contact, but pursed her lips, shaking her head. 'No. Can't say I have.'

'Okay. Keep alert though, yes? And don't hesitate to call us if you're worried. Anything you see that's at all suspicious, call immediately.' Lindsay smiled, gave a curt nod of her head, then left with Mack.

'How come you didn't try and push her, get her to open up about receiving the emails? We might find out who they're from without having to wait.' Mack strode to the car, swung the door open and began folding himself inside.

'Gut feeling is she doesn't know who's sending them. But, if I frighten her now, force her to spill before she's ready, she might not lead us to anything important. I want to sit it out. Watch her. See what happens.' Lindsay tapped her fingers on the steering wheel, staring towards the college.

'What if nothing does? We can't afford to sit on this. We should confront her now.'

'Mack, Mack . . . patience. It doesn't *always* pay to be a rugby player at a ballet now, does it?'

Lindsay started the car, giving Mack a sideways glance before setting off for the next place on her hit list.

CHAPTER SEVENTY-SIX

Karen

What was Jay on about? A level footing? Evening the score?

Karen had gone over it all night long. There was nothing to get even for. They'd had an online relationship, she'd finished it. End of. Where's the score to settle there? He'd lost it. And he hadn't replied to her last email accusing him of such. Of course, he'd ignore her purposely now, make her wait. He clearly wanted the full effect of her desperation, knew leaving her hanging for a while would drive her crazy.

Why was this happening to her?

She'd crept into Sophie's room in the early hours, crouched down beside her bed, and, whispering so as not to alert Mike, told her briefly about the emails from Jay. Sophie's sleep-filled eyes had fought to focus. Had she taken in any of what she'd said? Sophie had left for college before Mike had gone to work, so Karen hadn't got another chance to speak to her alone. There was a certain comfort in knowing Sophie was at college this week. It was far less likely Jay would hang around her for fear of being spotted on CCTV and teachers notifying the police.

Mike's mood when he gave her a cursory kiss goodbye that morning seemed off, distant. Did he sense the tension? Or had he noticed when Sophie bundled her into the kitchen yesterday, out of his earshot, to tell her about Maria? There'd been no time for Karen to tell her about Jay then, with Mike creeping in behind them, supposedly to make a cup of coffee.

Yesterday afternoon's search of Adam's new girlfriend on the internet had generated few details. On every social media site, Karen found the same information. Maria Nickson, aged thirty-seven, self-employed bereavement counsellor. This was interesting, given the circumstances. Yet, no other facts were listed, no personal information found. Nothing before November 2014. Not on a single search engine. Peculiar. Practically everyone Karen knew had been on Facebook, Twitter, Instagram or Pinterest for a number of years. Not merely four months. Sophie said Maria and Adam had moved in together a month after meeting. So, she showed up, moved in with Rachel's husband and set about gaining Erin's trust, all within four months.

The most significant thing was that she didn't seem to have existed before then.

Investigating Maria had been yesterday's distraction technique. So far today, housework had been her ally, busying herself with chores in order to prevent the constant refreshing of emails. How much longer was he going to make her wait?

Her phone pinged.

Bolting up from loading the washing machine, Karen ran to the dining room. She flipped up the screen, unlocked it, and navigated to emails.

There. Finally.

Two words, Karen.
Andrew.
Watkins.

That's it? That's all he was giving her?

Watkins. Sounded familiar; nothing was coming to the forefront though.

She typed a reply: *Don't know what you're talking about.*
Less than thirty seconds later:

Really? You're fucking with me, aren't you?
   He's someone you used to know.
   Someone you royally screwed over.
   Ring a bell now?

A sliver of memory floated marginally out of her reach. *Someone I screwed over.* Could be to do with probation, referring to her recalling someone to prison for breaking their conditions. But, who? There'd been dozens in her time. *Andrew Watkins.* Why didn't she remember the name? Her mind raced back over the period of her attack. The police had gone on and on at her, pressing her for names of likely suspects, convinced her attacker was someone she supervised. Had she given them Andrew Watkins' name to put them off the real trail?

Surely she hadn't. She'd been a mess, didn't want Mike finding out about her secret meeting with the 'sandwich guy' from work who'd attacked her. But would she really implicate someone she knew to be innocent? Even if she had though, the real attacker had been caught and imprisoned just four months later following another attack, a more sustained and serious one than she'd been subjected to. It was a horrifying thought that someone else had suffered at his hands, and that she might have prevented it if she'd given more details to the police at the time.

She was beginning to hate herself. The person she'd become was unrecognisable, the old Karen merely someone she used to know.

Think, think.

There was no way she'd email back until she remembered. Without access to the probation database she couldn't search the name, and since she'd left the service, her options were limited. An ex-colleague might be able to help. How could she enquire without risking the inevitable question of why she wanted to know?

She'd give the office a call anyway; drop his name into the conversation, see what came of it.

'Oh, hi Kerry, glad you picked up.'

'Karen? It's been so long, how are you doing?'

'Well, not great, if I'm honest. Lots going on. How's the old place been since I left?'

'Apart from the fact it's missing the best probation officer we had, you mean? Huh. Same as ever really, my lovely.'

'Ahh, I miss it too . . . sometimes.'

'Now, now. I think we both know that's a lie.' Kerry treated Karen to her hearty laugh down the phone. 'What can I do for you anyway? Sure you didn't just ring to find out about this place.'

'I did wonder if you wouldn't mind wracking your brains for me, actually.'

'I can try; not much to wrack these days, might not be of any use.'

'No worse than mine, honestly. I've been asked about this bloke and I know I've heard his name, but can I place it? Probably isn't anything to do with work, but can't for the life of me figure out where else I'd have heard it.'

'Go on then spit it out, let's see.'

'Andrew Watkins.'

Karen could hear Kerry repeatedly muttering his name, obviously attempting to grapple some semblance of memory together, as she herself had been doing. Keys tapped in the background. *Bless her, she's looking him up.* She knew she could count on Kerry.

'He was one of yours,' she said finally.

Those weren't the words she wanted to hear.

'Oh. From when?'

'Way back, no wonder you didn't remember his name. Case notes from your sessions would've been handwritten and filed away, not much on the database apart from the dates.'

'Which are?'

'Nineteen ninety-eight he came out on licence. Three months later, he breached his conditions. You recalled him.'

Ninety-eight. The year Sophie was born.

She'd gone back to work within three months of having Sophie – they'd needed the money.

'We'd recently completed all our training, remember?' Kerry was saying. 'We were newbies together. Both floundering. You more so, what with your little Sophie being a nightmare at night. Poor thing, you were always knackered.'

She remembered it well. And now she remembered Andrew Watkins.

Known to most people as Drew. He'd always said, 'I'm not a bad person, you know. Just had some bad luck.' It used to make her laugh; she'd thought it ridiculous. Of course he was bad. He committed crime – aggravated burglary, in fact. How could he class that as bad luck?

When he'd got out on licence, she'd supervised him. And when he broke the terms of his conditions by visiting an off-licence, she recalled him. Her first recall.

So, what did Andrew Watkins have to do with Jay?

She thanked Kerry, said her farewell. Then emailed Jay to get some answers.

CHAPTER SEVENTY-SEVEN

'I think things may be getting a whole lot murkier.' Sophie flew in, dumped her bag and flopped on to the sofa.

'No shit, Sherlock.' Karen sat next to Sophie, twisting so she could face her.

'Oh no, what's that meant to mean? What's happened with you now?'

'Oh, please.' Karen held out a hand. 'You first.'

'Well, the police visited me at college today. DI Wade and her sidekick, Mack. Mentioned *other* women who are being followed, and I get the impression that not only do they think it's the same guy, but that he is going to target me too.'

'Others? Why? I don't get it. Yes, he's targeting you. But it's personal. He wants to get to me.' Karen rubbed at her eyes. 'Jay's been in contact.'

'Really? What did he say?' Sophie sat up sharp.

'It transpires that a long time ago, I recalled his dad to prison.'

'That's it? So what? You've recalled loads to prison; it's no big deal. And anyway, how did he know it was you? And isn't it a bit coincidental you two were in . . . a relationship, or whatever . . . and you happened to put away his dad?'

'Seems none of this is a coincidence, Sophie. I can't begin . . .'

She squeezed her eyes shut, took a moment. 'His emails seem full of anger. It's all wrong. All lies.' Her nose tingled, eyes filled. She was going to cry.

'Woah, hang on.' Sophie put her arm around her shoulders. 'Come on, Mum. I think we need to start at the beginning, don't we?'

The two of them slid off the sofa and sat on the floor with their backs against it. Where was the beginning? Karen wasn't even sure. She started with how she'd gone back to work, despite Sophie being a baby, how she hadn't coped: stress, tiredness, guilt, all adding to the daily tensions her job already held.

'Looking back, now, I was too harsh, Sophie. Too quick to make the judgement call to get Drew recalled. I could've helped him, given him another chance. He hadn't broken any of the main conditions, more a minor one. It'd been my first ever recall, I got caught up in it once I'd made the decision.' She looked down at her hands, then back up at Sophie, her lovely daughter who'd been an innocent baby when all this had happened. 'Who'd have thought a single choice seventeen years ago would have such an effect on our lives now?'

'It wasn't your fault. He knew the conditions, chose to break them. Only got himself to blame.'

'Yeah, but was sending him back to prison really the right course of action? I could've kept a closer eye on him, increased the frequency of his supervision appointments. I knew his son had only just turned twenty and didn't have a mother around. Why didn't I think of the knock-on effects on him?'

'You probably did. You had your reasons, *and* superiors who backed your decision. You can't change it now. Anyway, it's so long ago, why is Jay still hung up on it?'

'I don't know, but it seems that Jay has been holding a grudge ever since.'

'He's said this?'

'The emails have pointed to that, yes. I can't believe . . . the whole time . . . I'm so stupid.'

'Look, I am hurt that you went online to meet some random bloke, I'm not going to lie. But I am sorry it's turned out this way.'

Karen shook her head. 'Not so random, though. He searched for me, had been searching for years. Everything we talked about, all the amazing conversations I thought I was having, the bond, the closeness. We talked for hours about how we'd suffered when we lost our parents, and all along he knew everything he said was part of a bigger plan.'

'Do you know what the plan is?'

'To make me pay, Sophie. To get even.'

Sophie put her head in her hands. 'What does that mean, exactly?'

'I don't know. He said his aim is still to be with me, supposedly, which I don't get, if he's so angry with me. And his words *are* angry. In the email, he talked about "settling the score before our future can be perfect". Or words to that effect. I don't know what to do.'

'I have to tell you something.' Sophie brought her head back up and looked into Karen's eyes.

More revelations? She couldn't handle much more. *My chest is tight. I can't do this now.*

'I'll get your bag.' Sophie pushed up off the floor.

Karen took deep breaths. *What more is there? How much worse is it going to get?*

She took the bag, put it to her mouth.

'The photos Jay sent. I don't know where he had me . . .' Sophie stalled.

Karen nodded, widening her eyes, letting Sophie know it was okay to continue.

'We were all in some dark room, possibly a basement, I can't tell.'

'All?' Karen's voice was muffled inside the bag. She breathed deeper, trying to slow her respirations.

'Jay had me there. And Erin, too. The night she died. The night he killed her.'

301

Karen dropped the bag. Every muscle sagged under the weight of the shock disclosure.

'Jay? Jay killed Erin? Can't have done. You're mistaken, Sophie. You couldn't remember anything from Saturday night, why are you saying this?'

'Calm down, please, Mum.' She pushed the bag back in front of Karen's face. 'Keep breathing. In . . . out. In . . . out.' Karen did as instructed and watched as the tears flowed down Sophie's cheeks, hitting her cream top, spreading outwards as the material sucked in the moisture.

Karen removed the bag again. 'Why do you think that?'

'I've had bits of memory come back to me, fleeting images, smells. Feelings. I'm sure I was there. The photos, they were of me with my dress up, legs apart . . . some, you know, sexual stuff . . .'

Karen's breath caught. The paper bag crinkled as her fingers gripped it tighter. 'And you can see Erin in the pictures?'

'No. Just me. But the memories, they are of Erin. Tied to a chair, like the one I'm in. Gagged. And, I keep getting visions of him . . . cutting her, jabbing at her stomach with a knife.' Sophie put her hand up to her mouth as if preventing sick from expelling.

'Okay. I see how you may think you were there, with Erin, but your mind is an incredible place, can conjure up all sorts, not always actual memories. False memories. Heard of them?'

'Yes. Did it in psychology at school, but I don't think that's the case, Mum. I was there. I went in the supposed taxi, he took both me and Erin. He killed her, let me go. Then the police found me wandering feet away from where Erin's body was dumped. You knew all along something bad had happened . . .'

'Yes. Not this, though.'

It couldn't be right. Sophie's anxiety, her fear, had twisted the reality, made her remember things that hadn't happened. She hoped. Prayed.

Because if she was right, this had gone beyond anything she could possibly control.

CHAPTER SEVENTY-EIGHT

DI Wade

'Come on then, Sergeant Mack. Let's drop by on Ms Nickson, shall we?'

DS Mack and DI Wade made their way from the college. It was interesting that Sophie had mentioned Maria Nickson just after they'd received an anonymous tip-off which stated that the girl-friend of Erin's father, Adam, had information vital to the murder investigation. Of course, it could be nothing. It was possible the call was a hoax, even an act of revenge. It was a sad fact, one which Lindsay had seen before: a disgruntled ex-wife, outraged at a cheating husband, reports strange or illegal behaviour at the address in an attempt to get even. Rachel Malone immediately sprung to mind. The call could even have come from Sophie. She'd appeared keen to impart the same information that the caller had, and on top of her obvious reluctance to mention the emails she'd received, it meant she was fast moving to the top of Lindsay's 'persons of interest' list.

Anyway, a lead was a lead. And Lindsay prayed this was one.

Mack parked the Volvo at the end of the road, the only space where they wouldn't cause an obstruction, and they walked in the sunshine to the house's entrance. Maria Nickson, slim, blonde, with a perfectly made-up face, answered after the fourth ring of the doorbell. Lindsay couldn't help thinking she'd taken her time so that she could perfect her make-up first. She also couldn't help but think that Mr Malone had traded his wife in for a younger model.

'Detective Inspector Wade,' Lindsay flashed Maria her warrant badge, 'and Detective Sergeant Mack. Can we come in please?'

Lindsay thought she saw a wave of panic cross her face, before she stood back to allow them both to enter. Maria showed them into a small lounge, and sat heavily in an armchair. She hadn't spoken a word. Lindsay and Mack sat, squashed together uncomfortably, on the two-seater sofa.

'We need to talk about Erin's online activity, Ms Nickson.'

Maria wrung her hands in her lap and looked, eyes wide at Lindsay. Was she going to speak?

'It's . . .' She cleared her throat. 'It's Maria.'

Lindsay smiled at her. 'Okay, Maria – when police came here and took some of Erin's belongings you told them about Erin going on a dating site. Online. By all accounts you were the only person Erin confided in. Is that right?'

'Well. I mean, yes. As far as I knew she only told me. But I can't be sure of that.'

'Mrs Malone, Erin's mother, said you seemed very sure at the time.' Lindsay flicked to a page in her notebook. 'She said, I quote, "She was so smug, couldn't wait to tell me that Erin confided in her not me". Does that sound about right?'

Maria's skin flushed, she seemed to be finding it difficult to swallow. Why so edgy? Lindsay raised her eyebrows to Mack. He took the signal, and continued asking the questions. Lindsay got up from the sofa and paced the perimeter of the room. She stopped by the sideboard, picking up framed photos and replacing them. Out the corner of her eye she noted Maria's uneasiness. It was one of Lindsay's tactics, and Mack was used to it now.

'We've checked both laptops used by Erin and found no evidence of any internet dating sites, chat rooms, anything of that

304

sort. So, I wonder why you said that?' Mack's smooth, deep voice always gave an air of calm, whatever he was saying.

'Well, she would've deleted any evidence of it, wouldn't she?'

'Why? They were her personal laptops, nothing wrong in what she was doing, why delete it?'

'You know teenagers, secretive creatures.' Maria gave a nervous laugh.

'Anyway, her recycle bin hadn't been emptied for some time, and there was no evidence there either.' Mack didn't take his eyes from Maria's.

Lindsay retook her place next to Mack. 'Where were you, again, on Saturday night?'

'Here with Adam.'

'And he will verify that?'

'You know he will, you've asked us both already. What is this?' Maria's eyes darted from Lindsay to Mack, her pupils swallowing her green irises.

'Did you give Erin a mobile number for a taxi firm?' Lindsay dropped in the question which directly linked to the information left by the anonymous caller.

Maria's shoulders stiffened and her head moved backwards, giving her a double chin. Her mouth slackened in a look of surprise.

'Er . . . No. I don't think . . . no. I didn't give her any number.'

'Well, as you're aware, we haven't recovered Erin's mobile phone, but the phone company has provided us with an itemised list of calls made from it. Erin didn't make any calls on Saturday night, yet she was seen by a number of people using a mobile phone. Did you know she had another phone, Maria?'

'Um . . .' Maria's mouth twisted to one side, 'I think she did. Yes. A pay-as-you-go one. She used it when she was out around the town. She'd previously lost two contract phones. She mentioned getting a cheap one to take on nights out.'

'And you didn't think to mention this before?'

'I'd forgotten. Sorry.'

'Strange then, that we didn't find her main mobile, if she left it behind in favour of the cheap one,' Mack said.

Lindsay jumped in with the question that she really wanted answered. 'A few people have mentioned you had a strained relationship with Erin to begin with, when you first started dating her dad. What can you tell me about that?'

'I'm young, Detective Inspector Wade, and her dad moved in with me in a matter of months of leaving her mother. Yes, there was a bit of animosity.'

'I'm sure that couldn't have made your life easy then, eh?'

'It was something I had to work on, yes.'

Lindsay let the silence engulf the room for a few minutes as she tried to think how you'd work on something like that. Where would you start? Being nice, friendly – probably overly friendly to start with, in an attempt to win Erin's approval. Gifts? Possibly. And what if none of that worked and Erin began to make her life a misery? Two young women vying for a man's attention. Could get ugly. And Erin had the advantage of using her blood tie, and Adam's new status as an abandoning father, against Maria.

Lindsay's thoughts were interrupted by the front door flinging open. Adam burst in.

'Has there been a development?' His face was red, sweaty from exertion.

Lindsay stood. 'Morning, Mr Malone. Sorry, not as such, no. We're here just to ask a few more questions following an anonymous call.' It was the first time Lindsay had mentioned this fact. She watched for Maria's reaction. She just frowned, and then looked down at the floor. Avoiding their eyes?

'Oh. I see.' There was a defeatist tone to Adam's voice. Poor bloke, his world had collapsed in around him. 'What can we help you with?'

'As you know, we didn't find Erin's mobile phone, but we know she used one on Saturday night, a pay-as-you-go one.' Although

Lindsay was directing her eyes at Adam, she could see Maria in her peripheral vision. As she was speaking she saw Maria sit forward. Was she trying to get Adam's attention? Lindsay turned in time to catch Maria open her eyes wide at him, her facial muscles tightening. Then Adam said what Lindsay imagined Maria had been trying to stop him mentioning at all.

'Oh, yes. That'd be the phone Maria gave Erin,' he gave a thin smile, 'as a gift when she was trying to get Erin onside. She'd been, let's say, a bit awkward when Maria and I first got together. Maria had been kind enough to program in all the numbers she'd need when she was out pubbing it, or whatever.'

Lindsay and Mack both turned to face Maria, but it was Mack who got in first.

'So, Maria. *You* gave Erin the phone and *you* program important numbers in. I'll ask again. Did you program in a taxi firm's number?'

There was no colour to Maria's skin now, she looked as though she might faint. 'No. No, I didn't. I put ours, her mum's and her friend's ones in, took them from her main mobile. I really didn't put a taxi number in it.'

But, if that were the case, why had she lied about giving Erin the phone in the first place? Perhaps the anonymous caller wasn't a hoax after all. But Lindsay would need hard evidence – and without the phone and with Maria's denial, there was none.

CHAPTER SEVENTY-NINE

Sophie

Tuesday

No sign of him.

If only she could be at college every week. Jay clearly didn't feel as confident in this environment as he did in her work one. Having left early to park in the spot closest to the college entrance again, she decided to sit in her car for a while, rather than go in to class. She scrolled through her text messages. Dan hadn't replied to those she sent last night. Not like him. Was he sore at her? Their brief exchange at his yesterday – him accusing her of being highly strung, her accusing him of following her and losing the plot – wasn't the nicest. She still couldn't help but question his motives for getting them there: lying, saying it was Amy's idea when it was his. What was he playing at?

As she chucked the mobile into her bag, it pinged. Talk of the devil?

She got it back out. No. Not Dan.

Wondered how you doing? Worried about you. Pop in shop later, come see me.

Irina. It'd been over a week since they'd last had contact. She ought to see her, let her know she was all right. Not that she was. Her head was a mess, so much had happened; too much to fully comprehend.

She slammed the car door, scanning the perimeter of the grounds as she headed to the entrance. No lone figures, no shadows in corners. There was a car parked on the far side of the road adjacent to the college. It looked the same as the one yesterday: dark, possibly a Volvo. She squinted, trying to decipher the number plate, but could only see a W at the beginning and the number 3. Was Jay watching from a safe distance, keeping an eye on her movements even if he couldn't follow on foot? She made a mental note to check the road again when she broke between lessons.

Sophie stared at the walls, the ceiling. Her portfolio lay open at the same page as it had an hour previous. Luckily, her assessor was busy working through someone else's, not taking any notice of Sophie's inaction. Nausea tugged at her stomach as she replayed the last week's events: Saturday night, the revelations, the knowledge she and her mum were getting in deeper and deeper, drowning in the lies.

The thought of Jay wanting some kind of revenge worried her most. If this was in relation to her mum recalling Jay's dad, him blaming her, the fact remained that their family was now his target. Was his dad still in prison, or was he involved somehow too? And why had he killed Erin? A warm-up exercise? A warning of how far he was willing to go? Did he murder Erin with Sophie there so he could implicate her, ensure she was afraid of going to the police?

That way he could manipulate her, her mum, the situation – and get exactly what he wanted. Whatever that was.

'Sophie, are you feeling okay?' Gill, the NVQ assessor, finally realised Sophie hadn't done a thing.

310

'Sorry, I'm not feeling the best. Headache. It's difficult to focus on the work.'

'If you're not up to it, go on home. You're almost finished now anyway, aren't you?'

'Only have one more piece to write up.'

'Fine. Go get some rest, hope you feel better soon.'

Sophie packed her folder into her bag. She might take this opportunity to pop in and see Irina.

The car opposite had gone. Good. One less thing to concern herself with.

As she pulled out on to the road, her mobile began pinging. The signal inside the college building wasn't great, and now it seemed a succession of notifications were delivering all at once. She was popular this morning; she'd heard at least ten. Releasing one hand from the steering wheel, Sophie kept her eyes on the road while ferreting inside her bag to find her phone. Waiting at a traffic light gave her a moment to see who they were from.

Amy. All of them.

With no time to read any, Sophie placed the phone on the passenger seat. She'd park up in the centre of town and check then. What was so urgent? She tapped her nails on the steering wheel, cursing the slow traffic ahead. *Come on.* Amy rarely texted. And shouldn't she be at work? Sophie checked the car clock. Only 11.46 a.m. Amy didn't get lunch until after twelve. She must have taken a sickie.

Finally, she reached the central car park and found a space.

Apprehension filled her as she scrolled to the beginning of Amy's messages. The first was a simple **Text me back.** Then, **Where are you?** Next, **I need to talk to you.** Each one more desperate. The last, **Where the hell are you? I've tried your mum, she said you're at college. But I've rung them, and they said you were off sick. WTF is going on?**

Before she had chance to text back, Amy sent another.

> Dan's not answering any messages, his phone straight to voicemail. Worried.

What *was* going on? Sophie replied:

> I'm fine. Left college early as got headache. Haven't heard from Dan either. In town now, do you want to meet?

Sophie walked with her head lowered, looking at the screen, awaiting Amy's reply. She should phone her mum as well, let her know she was now in town. She ought to make sure that she always knew her whereabouts. Just in case.

Her bag, slung over one shoulder, bounced off people as she walked past them, her eyes not on the way ahead. A jolt, a collision with another pedestrian, sent her phone crashing to the ground. Sophie, her breath knocked from her, whispered an apology. The man chastised her for being inconsiderate. She muttered 'Sorry' again, then bent to pick up the phone.

Then she saw him. Dan, along the road, standing outside Costa Coffee.

Oh, good. She could tell Amy not to worry. Sophie raised her arm, opening her mouth to shout out to him. Her voice died in her throat.

Dan stood beside Jay.

Sophie backed into a shop doorway. Why were they together? She edged out, peeking around the corner. They were chatting. Dan looked up at Jay. They were smiling.

Sophie stared in disbelief.

They knew each other.

CHAPTER EIGHTY

A coincidence? It had to be. They went out all the time around town, Dan probably knew him in passing. What if it was more than that? Could they be in this together, somehow? Dan, involved in a murder, Erin's murder? It was unthinkable. Yet her mother had always felt uneasy about him.

Sophie darted out from the doorway and followed in step behind some people as they moved in the direction of Dan and Jay. *Please don't spot me.* A gathering of charity workers gave her enough cover so she could discreetly walk into the store. She headed straight for Irina.

Irina dropped the bundle of clothes she'd been carrying as soon as she spotted Sophie, and strode over, arms outstretched.

'Glad to see you, Sophie. I been so worried. You never reply to text.'

'I'm sorry.' She allowed herself to be wrapped in Irina's arms, thankful for the comfort of someone not directly involved in the situation. 'It's been a mad week.'

'But you okay?' Concern-filled eyes penetrated hers. It wasn't possible to lie to Irina.

Sophie pulled away, screwed her face up, and shook her head.

'Come,' Irina gripped Sophie's arm, 'I have break now. Let us talk in the staffroom.'

'Oh, it's fine, really. You'll get in trouble, you haven't got a break now, have you?'

'You more important than job, Sophie.'

Irina had a way of looking hard, scary. Rarely smiled. A 'don't mess with me' attitude.

Sophie had never been more grateful for it.

Even though an hour had passed, Sophie's curiosity got the better of her, and instead of leaving the store by the rear entrance, she peered out the front door, and cast her eyes up and down the street. They'd gone. She had a bit of a walk now to get back to her car. She shuddered, gooseflesh appearing on her arms.

They might *both* follow her.

Don't be stupid. She pushed the thought away.

She felt glad she'd gone to see Irina. Outpouring some of the week's events had helped. Irina remained quiet, still, while Sophie talked, her expression neutral. There was no sign of fear or shock – no outward judgement. Just a calm, reassuring demeanour. Mind you, if she'd told Irina *everything*, it might have been different. Irina would've told Sophie to go to the police. Anyway, for now, seeing Irina had lowered her level of anxiety which, given her new shock discovery, surprised her. If only Irina could be with her all the time.

Dammit. Amy.

She'd not checked her phone again. The vision of Dan with Jay had taken priority in her thoughts. When she reached her car safely, she looked to see if Amy had replied.

No, don't worry. I was spinning out a bit, but as long as you're okay, tomorrow will be fine. Was thinking of coming over to yours, if that's all right? When do you finish college?

Thankfully Amy didn't mention Dan again. She needed to digest the latest information before sharing it with her, or anyone else involved.

If she shared it at all.

Because with every day that passed, it seemed there was one less person to trust.

The conversation picked up almost where it'd left off the day before. Her mum sat at the breakfast bar, her hands around a mug of coffee, probably her twentieth of the day. Sophie faced her.

'We can't keep this to ourselves, Sophie. It's too big, now.'

This, coming after Sophie mentioned seeing Dan with Jay in town.

'But, it'll all come out. You and Jay, your infidelity. It'll kill Dad.'

Her mum shook her head. 'Doesn't matter about me, or your dad. I have to do something, stop him from hurting you.'

'You can't tell the police. Jay will tell them I'm involved, that I watched him, didn't stop him. I may have even helped him. He said I enjoyed it. There was a photo, of me . . . I was smiling, Mum. Smiling while watching him murder my friend. *Your* goddaughter. What else does he have on me? Other photos? Perhaps even video footage, I don't know, but shit. What'll happen to me?'

'What do you think is going to happen if you *don't* tell the police? That it's all going to go away? That Jay will disappear and leave us alone? Forget what he started? No chance, Soph.'

'The police will catch him,' she slammed her hands flat down on the breakfast bar, 'without us having to tell them a thing.' The tingling sensation, painful, shot up through her arms.

'They might.' Her mum shrugged. 'But he'll implicate you then anyway. Either way, he'll drag you into his messed-up world, shift some blame on to you. Me. Tell lies. It's clearly what he does. He does it really well. It'll look better for you if you go to the police first. If things come to light later, evidence you took a part in his sick actions, they'll be more lenient with you.'

'I can't. Not yet.'

'Why?' Her mum's breathing was erratic now. 'For heaven's sake, he's in this for revenge. He wants even. And I have a nasty suspicion you are the pawn in whatever deluded game he's playing . . . Eye for an eye.' She got up, snatching her paper bag from the drawer. 'We can't risk it. We know a murderer, Sophie. He killed your friend!'

Sophie threw her head down on the breakfast bar and banged it up and down a few times, the pain briefly dulling her senses. 'I don't know. It's all too much, all happening too fast. I need to think this through, get it straight in my head first.'

'What more is there to get straight? It's simple. You said Jay is a murderer. You could be his next victim.'

'There *is* more to consider, like, what has Maria got to do with this? How is she involved? DI Mack said they'd already been given her name by someone. Who? Then, there's Dan – now I've seen him talking to Jay I know he's involved in some way. It's a great big web of deceit, it's bigger than you and me, more complicated. And why should *we* be the ones to come out of this badly? If we wait it out, others may take the fall. Wouldn't you prefer it if Dad never had to find out about your sordid affair?'

'I've told you, it wasn't an affair.'

'Okay, so you're happy for this to all come out, are you? For it to be spread in the news, all across social media, that you're a cheat and your daughter helped a man kill her friend. Your best friend's daughter. How will Rachel ever forgive us?'

Sophie watched as the colour left her mum's face, the true horror of the situation dawning.

'No. Of course I don't want that. It'll destroy our family. Rachel. But—'

'There is no "but", Mum. Let's give it a few more days. See what pans out. Please. Before we ruin other people's lives. Let's try not to be selfish . . . for once.'

'Selfish? I think ensuring the man who murdered Erin is

caught and preventing further deaths is the opposite.' The colour returned to her face in a flash of anger. 'It's selfish to keep quiet.'

'For me,' Sophie pleaded. 'I'm scared. Wait it out for a bit longer, see if the police get him and the others without us wading in. *Please.*' She watched for a change in her mum's expression. The hard line of her jaw softened, her face slackened.

'I'll give it another couple of days, that's it.' Her mum's eyes narrowed. 'And you'd better hope nothing bad happens in that time, because you do *not* want someone else's blood on your hands, Sophie.'

'Like I've already got Erin's, you mean.' Sophie's shoulders slumped.

They stared at each other. For now, there was nothing more to say.

CHAPTER EIGHTY-ONE

Karen

'Eh-up, this looks serious. What's going on?'

They hadn't heard the front door, they were so busy arguing over the best thing to do.

Karen jumped up. 'Is that the time? Sorry, haven't even started tea.'

'You crying, Sophie? What've you two been arguing about now?' Mike raised an eyebrow towards Karen.

'Nothing. We were talking . . . about Erin.' Karen began her routine rummage through the fridge. Sophie shot her a look she assumed was a warning not to say a word.

'Oh, I see.' He walked to Sophie; put a hand on her shoulder. 'You okay, love?'

'Yeah, I'm fine. Well . . . I will be.'

'It'll take time, these things always do. Life will get back to normal, eventually.' He looked to Karen, then added, 'Won't it, Karen?'

Really? Was he trying to be funny? It hadn't returned to anywhere near normal after her attack, how was it going to after this? She refrained from commenting. Sophie made her excuses and left to go to her room. She knew she was wrong, not going to the police with the information she had. Despite not wanting her lies to be unearthed, ever, Karen knew it had to be done. There was no other way of stopping Jay.

'Had another emergency on the moor today.' Mike stood, leaning against the worktop, watching as Karen prepared the meal.

'Oh? What this time?' She tried to inject some enthusiasm, some interest into her voice, but wasn't sure that she had managed it.

'Burning car. Came across it early, thought someone was in it.'

'Was there?' Now she was interested.

'It really looked like it, but by the time the fire crew arrived it was so badly burned, I couldn't tell. They had a special unit there, forensics and all. I had to leave them to it. I'll check tomorrow, see what it was all about, probably just a stolen car. Hopefully.'

'That's terrible.'

'It happens more than people think. The moors are so vast, people tend to believe they can dump things there and it won't be found for ages. It certainly means they're more likely to get away with it. As for poor sods who want to end their lives, the remoteness almost guarantees no one will find them before they've done the deed. There have been a few over the past couple of years. I wouldn't be surprised if there are dead bodies up there that'll never be found.'

'Hmm . . . like the Moors Murders, they never found one of those poor kids. It's awful.' Karen looked out of the window, at the expanse of wilderness stretching across the entire view out the back. The scenery was beautiful, untamed, a reason they had bought the house.

Now, as she thought about Mike's words, she saw it differently.

'There are some horrible people out there. Can't imagine losing Sophie like that.' Mike's face took on a faraway expression. Karen looked away, daren't look him in the eye. What would he say if he knew what was going on now? More to the point, what would he *do*? He'd never forgive Karen if anything happened to Sophie. She was certain of that much.

She carried on chopping vegetables, trying to think of another topic of conversation, a safer one. It was unusual for Mike to talk about his job these days, even more so for him to hang around her in the kitchen; usually he'd have disappeared into the lounge and immersed himself in his iPad by now. He'd acted weird yesterday, had seemed distant, not in the way they'd both been generally in their relationship, but in a preoccupied way. And now he appeared dejected, lost – he seemed almost like he wanted to open up to her.

A pang of guilt shot through her. Who did he have to share the events of the last week with? Who was supporting him? His colleagues at work? Doubtful. For one, he worked independently a lot of the time, and two, she couldn't remember the last time he'd even mentioned a name. The last colleague she'd known of was from about three years ago, when she'd met 'Colin' at a rangers' activity weekend. He wouldn't want to lean on her either, afraid of her collapse if he did, and he couldn't disclose his true feelings, his worries, to Sophie. And he wasn't one to openly discuss his problems with his mates, he always had the 'hard man' image to keep up.

Karen laid the knife down, wiped her hands on a tea towel, and went to Mike.

'Sorry.' She opened her hands, tentatively moving closer. 'I've been so wrapped up in this, been worried about Sophie, you know?' She put her arms around his middle, placed her cheek against his chest.

'It's fine. That's how it should be. I can take care of myself.' His tone was flat, his arms felt limp around her, the indifference evident.

It's what she deserved.

The evening dragged. Mike had taken Bailey for a walk, he'd been gone two hours already. Perhaps it was his way of coping, taking time out from her, alone with his thoughts, rather than sharing them. She'd tried at least. Sophie stayed in her room, not taking the opportunity to talk to her while Mike was out of the house. She clearly didn't want to discuss the current situation further. Karen watched TV without actually seeing it, her body occupying the space in the room but detached from the reality of it.

Ten o'clock. Still no sign of Mike. Should she be worried? She peeped through the curtains. The street lamp illuminated the bushes opposite and the stretch of pavement that ran alongside the houses until the darkness converged with the corners at both ends of their street. No movement. She shivered and let the curtain drop back, aware that her breathing had quickened. She was safe inside, but the mere act of looking out into the darkness was enough to set off her anxiety. Pathetic.

The mattress creaked, then depressed, gently rocking her body. The duvet pulled tight over her shoulders. She loosened it from where it was tucked underneath one arm, as she felt it being dragged over to the other side. A warmth touched her skin. What time was it? It seemed as though she'd been in bed for hours – had Mike only just got back? She tried to lift her head from the pillow. Too heavy. Her tablets had kicked in.

Her mind closed down again, sinking into another dark dream.

CHAPTER EIGHTY-TWO

Sophie

Wednesday

Sophie sat on the edge of her bed, shaking. The remnants of another disturbing dream touched every nerve ending, causing an uncomfortable tingling; a stabbing sensation.

Stabbing. Screaming. Begging.

She squeezed her eyes shut.

Erin's stomach punctured. Blood. Laughing.

She clasped her arms around herself and gently rocked.

Blinking red light. Camera.

He'd recorded it all. She felt sure she remembered him pointing a camera in her face. Remembered his voice, telling her *do it, do it.*

What had she done?

Despite not wanting to leave her mother today, for fear of her contacting the police if she wasn't around to keep an eye on her, she was going to college. Having missed most of yesterday, she figured it'd be best to go for the morning session at least, to get her portfolio signed off by the assessor. She had to take her mind off this mess.

Creeping from her room, Sophie popped her head around her

parents' bedroom door. Only her mum in bed, on her back, a throaty rasping noise arising from her wide-open mouth. She wouldn't disturb her to say goodbye. The longer she slept, the better.

She pulled her coat-hood up – the drizzle would do nothing for her hair – and flung her bag on the passenger seat of the car. Then she sat and checked her messages. None from Dan. She'd ignored Amy's last text too, unsure of how to respond. Did she want Amy to come over? Her surprise recollection about Maria giving Erin the taxi's number still smarted. After all her attempts at getting Amy to help her remember, the sudden '*by the way*' revelation angered her. An audience of one didn't do it for Amy; she'd probably waited until she had a room full to ensure a greater shock factor.

Sophie sent her a text saying she was welcome over at four-ish. Perhaps she'd be able to do some digging, find out precisely what Dan was up to. If anyone knew something of interest, Amy would.

Crawling behind a tractor almost all the way into town, plus leaving later than she'd planned, meant there was no parking space next to the building for her today. Typical. But although she'd seen Jay yesterday, in town with Dan, there'd been no sightings of him at the college this week, so hopefully there was no need to worry. Even the dark car that'd been parked up opposite the college was absent.

Her mind wandered during the class. She knew she couldn't prevent her mum from contacting the police for much longer. She seemed resigned to the fact that her infidelity, her secrets, would surface and that life would take a downward turn. Even more so than it already had. Her mum's need to protect her would always be stronger than the desire to keep her secret.

Life really was about to get complicated. The thought of what her dad would do bothered her the most. They hadn't been getting on, not for a long time. But imagining how hurt he'd be, not only about his wife cheating on him, but about Sophie keeping the dirty secret, twisted her insides and fuelled her guilt.

If only there was a way to stop him ever finding out.

A vibration jolted her from her thoughts.

Dan. What did he want?

I have to talk to you. Just you, don't tell Amy. Shit, Soph, things have got out of hand. Meet me at the back of Stover Park. Has to be out of the way. I'm being followed.

Could this be for real? Dan being followed? Perhaps she'd been wrong to jump to the conclusion that he was involved with Jay. Could Jay be targeting him, too? She'd have to go, she'd never forgive herself if something happened to him. Her mum could be right – more blood on her hands. The situation was spiralling. She'd meet Dan, talk it out, and perhaps they'd go to the police together. There might still be a way of leaving her mum out of it, a way to keep the secret buried. Hers too. There was only one way to find out.

She texted back, agreeing to the meet.

As she'd been sick the previous day, her assessor accepted her excuse to leave again.

She ran across the car park, forgetting the puddles she'd deftly avoided earlier. Swinging her wet legs into the car, she quickly shoved the key in the ignition, whacked it into gear and sped off. Adrenaline made her hands shake. She gripped the wheel harder, but the sensation spread up her arms. Ten minutes later, she pulled into the park entrance. He'd said to go to the back of the park; she followed the track, keeping alert, her eyes intensely peering through the intermittent windscreen wipers. There were no vehicles. No people. Where was he?

'You better not be taking the piss, Dan.' She tutted, snatched up her phone and texted him: **Where are you then?**

A few seconds after she hit send, she heard a muffled bleeping coming from the back seat.

Odd.

She turned to the sound, as a hand reached towards her.

CHAPTER EIGHTY-THREE

DI Wade

Erin Malone's family set-up seemed a complex one. After interviewing Maria Nickson yesterday, Lindsay had more questions than answers. Would a visit to Rachel Malone's be useful at this point? They could try to untangle the family relationships, perhaps get Rachel's perspective on Adam and Maria. Although, she'd already given some information and seemed pretty angry about Maria's claim that Erin had confided in her about how unhappy she was. Would they gain an accurate picture from Rachel, or an emotional backlash against Adam?

They weren't much further on, but they were on their way to Rachel's anyway. It couldn't hurt.

'What are you thinking, Boss?' Mack's knees were wedged against the glove compartment of the Volvo, as if to stop himself being flung about by Lindsay's erratic driving.

'I'm thinking "What a complete wash-out. What exactly have we got?"' She threw the steering wheel around, taking the left corner hard. She tasted the metallic tang of blood. She'd bitten the inside of her cheek repeatedly over the last ten days; an uncomfortable habit left over from her teenage years. Now it was sore, and likely to turn into an ulcer.

'We'll get a break soon.' Mack's hand reached for the handle above the door. 'Any chance I can live to my big five-o please?'

'You're not that old, are you?'

'Um . . . I like to think I've reached an age of maturity . . . and another year closer to retirement. It's not old. It's privileged.'

Lindsay couldn't contain her burst of laughter. 'Brilliant, never heard it called that before. Oh dear, you make me laugh.' She wiped at the tears with the back of a hand. 'To get back to you saying we'll soon get a break – I admit, I'm losing hope. And patience. It just seems like a lot of chasing our tails, half-cocked leads that go nowhere, or surveillance that isn't getting results. People are giving us the run-around.'

'Yep, there are a few of those. I get the feeling more people are involved in Erin's abduction and murder than we first thought. Someone, or some people, are hiding significant details. And I don't mean just Sophie Finch.'

'Yes, I reckon you're spot on there. Don't they realise you can't bury secrets forever?'

'Ahh, but they always think they can. That's the point. But we'll get them, Boss. In the end we *will* get all of them.'

CHAPTER EIGHTY-FOUR

Karen

The queasy sensation infiltrated her dream. She opened her eyes, then closed them quickly, the light assaulting them. Her head swam. She hadn't been drunk last night, had she? She reached an arm across to Mike's side. Empty. *What day is it?* Had he left for work already, without waking her again? She propped up on one elbow, and reached for her phone, blinking her eyes repeatedly in a vain attempt to focus. *Weds 18 11.16 a.m.* She'd slept in late. The medication had worked too well, her body yet to acclimatise again, having been off it for so long. The tiny light on her mobile flashed, showing she had a notification. She'd have to check in a minute. A sharp pain in her stomach and the watering in her mouth told her she was going to be sick.

The retching produced only bile; the acid burned the back of her throat. She didn't remember having these side effects when she'd first been prescribed the tablets. She swilled her mouth with water, then brushed her teeth. A sudden thought – had Sophie gone to college? She hadn't come in to her to say goodbye.

She checked her room. Empty. She hollered her name down the stairs. Nothing. Great, so both Mike *and* Sophie were avoiding her. Or, maybe she had come in, but Karen'd been in too deep a sleep to rouse. Wrapping the dressing gown around her, Karen headed downstairs. She needed toast, coffee – anything to refill her stomach again, to stop the hollow ache. It wasn't until the kettle clicked off that she noticed the silence. Too silent. Something missing.

Bailey. Where was Bailey?

She called all through the house and checked his usual hiding places – nothing. Perhaps Mike had put him outside before he left. The back sliding door was unlocked, but shouting his name didn't bring him running from the garden. Mike must've taken him to work. Finally, he'd listened to her pleas. Karen closed the door, locked it.

Now she was completely alone.

The flashing on her phone reminded her that she hadn't read the notification. Probably just a Facebook one anyway. Phone in one hand, coffee mug in the other, Karen unlocked the screen. Text. From Mike.

So sorry about not coming home last night. After I dropped the dog back and knew you were in bed, I took off, drove around. I needed some time out, to think. Drove so far I ended up sleeping in the car, couldn't face coming home. Hope I didn't worry you. Can we talk tonight?

The splintering of china shattered the silence as Karen's mug hit the tiled floor. Hot liquid splashed up her legs. She jumped back, but too late to avoid it. She grabbed a dishcloth and held it under the cold tap, wrung it, and pressed it against her skin. The stinging brought tears to her eyes. *Shit.*

Mike brought Bailey home.

Mike then left and stayed out all night.

So, her memory of him getting into bed last night was a false one?

And, if he brought Bailey home, where was he?

CHAPTER EIGHTY-FIVE

Her call to Mike went straight to voicemail. *Bloody moors.* He'd never disappeared overnight like this before, even in the worst times of their marriage. *Needed time to think things through.* Why now? Did he feel that she and Sophie had been keeping him out of the loop, sense they were being secretive? And sleeping in the car, what was that about? He could've just slept on the sofa.

She shook her head. So many things she'd do differently, if only she could have another chance. Starting with Drew. Had she gone back to work later, following proper maternity leave, she might have approached everything without the stress and tiredness that had tinged everything she did: every judgement, every choice, every action. All of it clouded due to sleep deprivation and guilt.

It'd started with Sophie's birth.

What if it ended with Sophie's death? The cycle complete.

Is that what Jay wanted?

She needed Sophie home. She'd have her mobile on silent while in college, but she might pick up her texts.

Come straight home after college. Need to chat urgently.

Karen hoped Sophie would see it and leave immediately. She had to get Sophie home, in the safe zone, away from Jay. Away from Dan, too, if Sophie was right. Even Adam's girlfriend, Maria. Jay's poison had spread; he'd somehow injected it into others, created his own circle of evil, everyone within it having a role to play in his game. But only he seemed to be the one who knew all the players. There was one certainty as far as Karen could see.

It couldn't end well.

A cold dread prodded the length of her spine. Mike had definitely stayed out purposely last night, hadn't he? The text sent by him willingly? What if he hadn't returned from walking Bailey? There was no sign of the dog in the house.

Had Jay done something to them? She fled to the front window, drew back the curtains. No car.

She expelled the air from her lungs, her posture relaxing. He must've driven off then, like he said.

She hollered for Bailey. Still no sound. She went to the back door, unlocked it again and slid it back. She called Bailey a few times. Nothing.

The shed door was ajar, banging gently in the wind.

Mike always locked it. She ran her tongue over her dry lips, swallowing hard.

'Bailey!' Her voice wavered, sounded small, lost. She called again, more forcefully.

She strained to hear, hoped for some sound – any sign of her dog.

Her hand slipped on the door frame; she almost fell outside. She quickly retracted herself, shut the door. Staying there, hands pressed against the glass, she breathed deeply for what felt like an hour. She turned the key.

Did Jay know where she lived? Would he come here, to her house?

The memory of Mike getting into bed beside her flashed in her head.

The saliva in her mouth evaporated instantly – she tried to swallow, her attempt failing.

No way. It wasn't possible.

Her legs went numb. She moved to the kitchen using the work-tops to keep herself upright, knocking things from the surface as she dragged herself along. *Must get the bag.* Her knees buckled as she reached into the cupboard. She sat on the floor and blew in and out of the bag. What next? Email Jay? Ask him what was going on? Her eyes fell to the Betterware catalogue that'd fallen to the floor in her scramble to get the bag.

Oh my God.

The image of the man who'd delivered it flashed in front of her eyes. It was Jay, it was him on her driveway with the rucksack of catalogues, that's why his face had been familiar, how she knew those intense green eyes when she'd seen him outside Anderson's. He *did* know where they lived.

Karen flung her head back, and banged it against the cupboard door. A terrible thought barged its way into her mind. If Jay had managed to get inside the house last night, *did* get into her bed – could he still be here? It was enough to give a surge of adrenaline to her weak legs. She propelled herself off the floor and took the biggest knife from the block, gripping it tight.

This wasn't fair. This was her safe zone. *Outside is the scary place. Inside is safe.* She'd been telling herself that for two years. How could she be wrong now?

Breathe. Keep calm.

She struggled to listen for sounds of her intruder above the noise of her heartbeat. She stopped at the bottom stair, leaning against the wall. Where would he be hiding? Wardrobe? Hers or Sophie's? Bathroom, in the shower? The main one or her en suite?

Please don't be here. Let me be wrong.

Each stair creaked. He'd know she was coming. He would be ready for her.

In through the nose, out through the mouth. Slow. Steady.

Halfway.

A drip. She could hear a dripping noise.

Bathroom?

He was in the main bathroom.

She moved one leg up, next step reached. Near the top now. She extended her neck, couldn't see over the banister. The bathroom door was ajar.

Drip, drip.

Sophie probably had a shower before college and hadn't turned the water off fully, that was all it was. She crept further, on the landing now. No one behind the banister. A small sigh escaped her mouth.

Was she overreacting?

With the knife outstretched, she pushed the tip of it against the bathroom door.

What was she going to do if he was in there? Stab him?

Yes. Absolutely.

The door swung open fully, pushing up against the wall. No one could be behind it.

Her breath hissed from her pursed lips. *He's not in there, you're safe.*

She poked her head around the corner. The shower curtain stretched across the bath.

She stopped breathing.

With her left hand she reached for it, held the edge of the shiny fabric. Knife in her right hand, angled downwards. *Is this the best way to hold the knife?* Would she be quick enough to inflict harm, or would he disarm her easily? Should she point it up?

I don't know. Just do it.

With a swift movement, Karen ripped the shower curtain back, lunged with her right hand.

The scream hit off each of the four walls, vibrating, the echo filling the small space.

She dropped the knife, covering her ears as she fell to the floor.

CHAPTER EIGHTY-SIX

Sophie

The shock of having him come at her from behind stunned her into silence. Sophie couldn't even scream. His hand held something in it. A rag? It was wet against her mouth, her nose.

She fought against him, her hands scrabbling in the air, then pulling at his arms. They tightened more.

She gulped for air. He was whispering against her ear, 'Shhh, don't fight it. Relax, Sophie.'

He'd been in her car. Waiting. For how long? Why hadn't she noticed?

She was stupid. Why had she trusted that text? Her mum was going to go mad. She should've told her where she was going.

Too late.

Her heart was banging hard. Would it stop?

Was she going to die like Erin?

CHAPTER EIGHTY-SEVEN

Karen

'No, no, no, no.'

Karen lay still. All her strength drained. Her throat dry, scratchy. The scream still echoing, although she'd stopped.

He'd been here. In her house. In her bed.

He'd killed her dog. The bastard.

Bailey's lifeless body lay in the bath. Brown fur matted with dark blood.

Why?

How did one decision lead to this moment? Why should she be punished for doing her job? Was she the only person in Drew and Jay's lives who'd ever wronged them? Why her? And why had he gone to these lengths?

What was next? Karen had to do something, call DS Mack. Get this killer caught, put away. She heaved herself up using the side of the bath to aid her. She kept her eyes averted, not wanting to see him again. His dead, glassy eyes. Poor Bailey. She grabbed a towel from the rail and threw it over his little body.

What about the rest of the upstairs? He might still be here, watching, waiting to attack her next. She had to check before doing anything else. Raising the knife again, and with her back flat to the wall, Karen moved out of the bathroom. She'd check the farthest room first, leave her own until last. Sophie's room could be hiding a few people, let alone just one. She stabbed at clothes piles, the curtains, bedding. Each fresh jab left a mark, a tiny hole or tear in the material.

Room by room, she did the same. Jay wasn't here.

The shed. The door had been open.

She fled down the stairs, smacked the knife down on the breakfast bar and ran to the window. The shed door still thumped gently, the extended bolt catching the side. If Jay had hidden in there, she felt sure he'd gone now. Her doors and windows were locked. There was no way he could enter again. No point in him hanging around. He'd done what he came for.

Karen sank to the floor. Head in hands, she cried, the sobs wracking her body. She'd never been so alone. And who was the one person she wanted to turn to now, who she'd always turned to in any crisis?

Rachel.

What a total mess.

She'd asked the question – *why her?* Well, the answer was obvious, wasn't it?

Because she deserved every hateful thing coming to her.

A dinging. Faraway.

Karen strained her ears. Her phone? Where was it?

She moved to the lounge, searching the source. It wasn't a notification – it was ringing.

Please be Mike or Sophie.

She snatched up the phone.

Amy. Why was she calling?

'Hey, Amy. You okay?' She attempted to disguise the tears, the panic.

'Sorry to bother you, Karen.' Her voice, quiet.

'No, no problem. What's up?' She wiped the tears with her sleeve.

'I'm meant to be coming over to see Sophie later, after she finishes college.' A pause. 'But, I want to speak to you first. If you're free.'

Karen almost laughed. 'Of course, Amy. I think that's a good idea, actually. I wouldn't mind having a chat before Sophie comes home. A lot's been happening.'

'Oh? What do you mean? What stuff's been happening?'

'We'll talk when you get here. Come now, Amy, will you?'

'On my way.'

If Amy wanted to talk, she must know something.

She'd hold off calling the police until Amy had said her piece.

CHAPTER EIGHTY-EIGHT

Sophie

Pressure behind her eyes, a pulsating in her neck, blood rushing to her face. Her head ached. It took too long to lift it, to take in her surroundings. Inside a building. Abandoned? Lots of broken glass, a scattering of industrial-looking furniture. Some chairs. She was attached to one by a rope which looped around her middle. She still had her top and jeans on, but her coat had been removed. Her hands and feet were loose, her soggy-bottomed jeans flapped at her ankles as she wriggled her legs to make sure. She could get out of this. A bit of careful twisting to cause the rope to slacken at her waist, then use her hands to raise the rope above her head. Easy. Why hadn't he tied her properly? Was it a trap?

'What do you want?' Her voice, crackling, breaking the silence.

She squinted at a shadow; it grew larger, emerging from behind the door of a separate room. An office perhaps?

'Hello, Sophie.' The man stretched his thin lips to form an amused smile that reached his eyes, crinkling the skin at his temples. She knew that smile now. 'Nice to have you all to myself.'

'Why? What do you want with me?' Tears weren't far away. She screwed her eyes up, determined not to show him weakness.

Jay stared. Said nothing.

'Answer me,' she shouted. 'You son of a bitch, answer me.'

341

He stepped closer.

'How did you get me here? And where's Dan, what have you done to Dan?' The panic tipped in her voice, the fear audible.

'Oh, Sophie, Sophie. Dan's fine.' His laugh grated. 'Your *friend* has been extremely helpful in getting me this far. Getting you here.'

She knew it. Knew his behaviour had been odd. Her mum had been right. Again. How could he have done it to her, lured her away from college so this creep could get his hands on her?

'Where is he? Let me see him.' Sophie wriggled in the chair. 'Dan. *Dan!*' She wanted to look him in the eye. Tell him what a shit he was for helping this freak.

'Shh now.' Jay placed the fingertips of two of his fingers on her lips. 'Be quiet, or I'll hurt him too. He's close. But he's a little *tied up* right now.' He laughed.

Sophie snatched her head back, away from his touch. 'If he's been so helpful, why have you tied him up?'

'You and your pathetic friends all seem to require restraint. The poor sucker didn't know what he was doing – didn't realise he was playing into my hands until it was too late – then he lost the plot, threatening to hurt me.'

'Shame he didn't manage it.' She lowered her eyes. So Dan hadn't purposely led her to Jay as she'd believed. He'd been tricked.

'You were each so easy to manipulate. I slipped into your lives and, like a chameleon, I blended in. I found out about you all – knew where to be at the right times. All it took with Dan was a friendly chat outside a coffee shop. Someone older to advise him how to get in with the girl he fancied. Course, I didn't tell him he was stupid, wasting his time with you. I couldn't tell him then that you wouldn't be around for much longer.' He shook his head mockingly. 'You were all so gullible.'

Sophie's head pulsated; the pressure within it increasing with each word Jay uttered. Her body shook. What exactly was he planning?

'If your big plan is to get my mother here, you've screwed up.'

'Oh? You mean, she won't come to save you? Come on, Sophie. You're her life, she'd do anything for you.'

'How do you suppose she'll get here? You know, being that she's a total agoraphobic?'

His brow creased, he sneered.

'She can't possibly drive herself,' Sophie went on. 'The only times she's been out of the house, someone's had to counsel her through the trauma of it all and drive her. The police could bring her, I guess.'

His lips twitched, the muscles moving like a ripple effect across his face. Her words had touched a nerve. Didn't he know? She grabbed on to this, hoped it would make a difference. 'Ha! Plan foiled now?'

'Not at all.' He jerked towards her and put his hands either side of her face. Squeezed hard. 'Don't be naïve, *Soph*. Yes, it was my plan to have her here at the crucial point. I wanted to watch her, enjoy the look on her face as I killed you.' He licked her cheek. 'That same kind of expression you had when you watched me kill Erin.'

Sophie pulled her head away from him. Her muscles spasmed. She'd watched as Erin died. She kicked out, thrashing her arms and legs. Jay laughed as he jumped back, a safe distance away from her limbs.

'Anyway, if your mum isn't here to watch, it's not the end of the world. Don't think her absence will save you. It won't.' He threw his head back, laughing, showing off a mouth full of fillings. 'I'll do it anyway, you silly little girl. The end result will be the same. I'll have taken someone precious from her . . . like she did me. We'll be even. The future will start afresh. Our future will begin in that moment.'

'You're *pathetic*.' She spat at his feet. 'It wasn't my mum's fault your dad was a criminal who couldn't hack the outside world and had to be put back in prison. He got what he deserved.'

The slap knocked her sideways, her head whipped to the right

343

as his hand crashed against her cheek. Tears ran down it, stinging as they rolled over the raw flesh.

'Shut up,' he shouted, spittle flying from his mouth. 'Don't even speak about my dad. You know nothing. Your mother ruined him. Ruined me. She's the one who should be punished.' He paced, erratic angry strides, his hands up, gripping his own hair.

'Why kill Erin then? If it's her who should be punished, why kill an innocent girl?'

'Ah, well . . .' He licked his lips. 'Erin was a favour for a friend. But then I saw the potential.' He moved to her side, grabbed her hair and pulled down, forcing her face up to look at his. 'I knew it would give *her* something to think about, show her how far I was willing to go. She'd know when I got hold of you that I was serious. About wanting to be with her.'

He was enjoying this, she could see the excitement sparkling in his eyes.

'You can't scare someone into being with you.'

'No, she won't be *scared* into being with me. Don't you get it? She'll *want* to be with me. I'll be the only one who truly understands her pain. The only one she can turn to.'

'You're so stupid. What about my dad? He'll understand . . . he'll know her pain.'

'But, Sophie,' his voice high-pitched, condescending. 'She doesn't love your father. She loves me. How else do you think she came to me? She was looking for me. Searching.'

Sophie shook her head vehemently. 'No. She was looking for a bit of excitement. That's all you were to her. She loves my dad.'

'You're a kid. You don't understand, I can see that. It's okay. You'll see. When Karen comes to me, you'll understand then how deep her love is. For you. And for me.'

Sophie closed her eyes. Nausea was taking over.

She made a silent prayer, hoping her mum had gone against her wishes and called the police.

344

CHAPTER EIGHTY-NINE

Karen

Karen didn't recognise Amy.

No make-up. Hair lank, messy.

'Sit.' Karen motioned for her to take the smaller of the sofas. 'I'll make us a coffee.'

'Not for me.' Her eyes were wide and scared.

What did she know?

'Okay. Say what you've come to say. You've clearly got something on your mind.'

Amy's attitude when Karen had tried to find out before about Saturday night had left a nasty after-effect. She wasn't sure whether she wanted to play Mrs Nice with her.

The crying – quick and hysterical – changed that.

'Amy?' Karen rushed over to her and put her arm around her shoulders. 'Whatever is the matter? Is it Dan? Maria? Sophie said you thought she was involved—'

'No.' The word firm between the sobs. 'It's not them.' Amy wiped her face and straightened.

'Okay, what then?'

'It's me, Karen.'

'It's you, what?'

'I'm the one. The one who drugged Sophie.'

Karen's arm retracted from Amy's shoulder. 'What? I don't understand.'

'I'm sorry, I'm so sorry.' Amy rocked back and forth, eyes wide, wet with tears.

Karen's chest cavity filled with pressure, a tightness, the pain radiating down her arm. Was she going to have a heart attack?

'Tell me everything.' She had to make sure she didn't lose it. If Amy ran out on her now, then she'd never hear the full story.

'Please believe me, I didn't know. I didn't know this would happen. He said it was only meant to frighten you.'

Karen lost her composure, jumped up from the sofa and stumbled. 'I don't think . . . I want to hear any . . . more.' Using the wall to keep her upright, Karen walked to the kitchen, got her paper bag and started breathing in it. Amy followed.

'I know you're going to hate me, everyone is, it's my fault. All of it's my fault.'

The re-breathing began to calm her. So, Amy thought this was all her fault. Karen thought it was hers. They needed to talk this through, and without the complication of Karen's panic attacks. *Get a grip.*

'When you say *he* only wanted to frighten me. Who is *he*?'

'My boyfriend. Or was my boyfriend until yesterday. Jonathan.'

'Where did you meet him?'

'Online, a dating site . . . the one you're on, actually.' She lowered her eyes.

'Oh.' Karen was taken aback. How could Amy be on the same site? How had she seen her, her profile picture was set as private? Not the right time to question it now. 'Right. Okay. What does he look like?'

Amy pulled her phone from her pocket, flicked through some pictures and held it up to Karen.

'That's Jay. The person who I now know is Jay.' Karen's stomach contracted, she looked away from the image. He'd played them both well.

'He told me . . . said you'd put his dad away. He opened up to me, cried, described how awful his life had been since. I felt so sorry for him. We talked for months, and I hurt for him, do you know what I mean?' She looked up, big eyes searching Karen's. She continued without a response, 'By the time he'd got to the point of telling me his plan, I'd bought into it, wanted to help him. Thought it was time for someone – you – to pay.' The tears started again.

'So you thought you'd make me pay by hurting Sophie?' Karen couldn't keep the anger from her voice.

'No. No, it wasn't like that. It was meant to be him taking a few photos.' She rubbed at her face, running her fingers through her hair, grabbing it, pulling at it. 'Sexual ones, to humiliate her, but to hurt *you*, he was going to pose with Sophie, make it look like he was willing to hurt her . . . it sounds so awful now—'

'Now? *Now*, Amy? Bloody hell, didn't it *then*?'

'He convinced me. Karen, I'm sorry. I thought Sophie would show you the photos, you'd be thrown into a panic, then Jonathan was going to message you, so you knew it was him, then he'd get some closure . . .'

'You put your best friend in danger, drugged her, knowing he was going to do all sorts to her . . . all because he wanted to get *closure*?'

'He said he loved me. I believed he did. He wasn't the usual type I go for, I'd got fed up of immature teenagers, pretty-boys who loved themselves more than me. I wanted someone older, who actually took a real interest in *me*. And Jonathan did. He bought me gifts, gave me his time – we often met up spontaneously, he'd just give me a ring and say he wanted me. It was such a rush. I didn't once question why he never took me back to his, there was no reason to mistrust him. I thought he was the one. So I wanted to be there for him, help him. I know Sophie's my best friend, I didn't think he'd hurt her. I mean, he didn't, did he? He only took photos.'

Karen couldn't speak, stunned into silence. Jay had worked a good one on her all right.

'He promised me it was only photos, that he wouldn't touch her, harm her in any way. I know it wasn't being a good friend, but I loved him, wanted to please him. I was so stupid, he took me in, I believed every word he told me.'

'What's different now? Why tell me all this?'

'He means to do so much more than he led me to believe. All this has blown up, got out of control. He killed Erin. He told me yesterday. Said he killed her because he could, because it would send a clearer message. To you. I've fucked up so badly.' Her face crumpled as she began to sob.

Karen ripped some kitchen roll off and handed it to Amy. 'You and me both, Amy. You and me both.'

'He had his own agenda all along, I was just someone he needed . . .' Her voice caught as another sob erupted. 'Someone he needed to help execute his plan, get Sophie to him. It took me too long to realise I meant nothing, really. He didn't love me at all, did he? I knew something was wrong, later, when Erin's body was found – knew it couldn't be a coincidence, however hard I tried to force that thought into my mind. He said he didn't do it, and I believed him at first, then alarm bells started. By then I knew I was in it too deep. I got scared. He told me I had to keep my mouth shut, or he'd shut it for me. Permanently. Said I was as accountable for Erin's death as he was.'

'What a mess.' Karen sighed. So unreal. How could this have happened? 'I don't understand how Erin got involved in all of this. You said you helped get Sophie to him, what about her?'

'He was getting something out of it . . . this is going to sound even worse . . . what was in it for me? I had this flash of an idea when he went on about taking photos – I suddenly thought it would be a good idea to get him to do the same to Erin.'

'Amy. Why?' Karen lifted her hands to her head, completely exasperated.

'She always copied me. Bought all the same clothes I did, shoes, accessories, everything. She annoyed the hell out of me. It got ridiculous. I couldn't breathe without her doing the same, the *exact* same as me. I asked her to stop, but she didn't get what my problem was and carried on anyway. It's so petty now. But at the time I wanted him to teach her a lesson. He was only meant to frighten her.'

Karen needed a break. Hearing this all in one go was too horrific, too painful. Her anxiety gathered momentum. She flicked the kettle on. 'I need coffee. Well,' she snorted, 'I need alcohol really, but coffee will have to suffice.'

'I'm sorry I came to you with this—'

'No. Don't keep saying that. I'm glad you came to me, Amy.'

While she made the coffee, Karen considered the situation. How would Sophie react when she learned of her best friend's involvement? The fact that she'd been purposely drugged by Amy? So far there was a dead girl, sexual images, stalking, threats of getting even, Bailey dead, and now a further revelation – that Amy had helped to orchestrate it all. Had she stopped helping Jay, or was this still part of his plan, her coming here and spilling everything? Could she trust her?

'How did you get Sophie and Erin to him?'

'He gave me Rohypnol to spike Sophie's drink. He said she needed to be out of it, otherwise she'd remember too much, tell you too early. He wanted some suffering first, before she let on to you. Then you were meant to work it out slowly from the clues he'd placed. When you figured out it was him, realised he'd had that power over you and could've hurt Sophie if he'd wanted, that was to be the end of it.' She laughed.

Saying things out loud had a habit of clarifying things, of making them sound as dreadfully ridiculous as they were. Karen'd had some experience of that lately.

'It was you who deserved to be punished, Karen, after what you did to his dad. You killed him. That's what he kept saying.'

'What?' Karen banged her coffee mug down on the worktop. 'What are you saying? I didn't kill him!'

'Jonathan told me the story over weeks. He said it was your fault that his dad was thrown back inside a hideous place and that he became depressed and lost the will to live.'

'So his dad killed himself?' The pieces came together with sudden clarity – the ultimate reason for the anger held within Jay's emails. The settling of a score could only mean one thing. An eye for an eye. The room stretched, Amy's voice was still audible, but it sounded muffled, a long way off.

'He manipulated me, I can see that now, but at the time he said if he got this out of the way, he would be in a better place and then we could have a real future. He told me we could get engaged, if I liked. When it was done.' Amy dropped her head in her hands. 'I'm going to go to prison for this, aren't I?'

Karen had no more energy. Her body, weakened by the morning's events, slouched. It was only midday. Sophie would be home in a few hours. How was she going to tell her? Amy was her best friend. Hearing this would devastate her, and Karen wasn't sure Sophie was strong enough to handle this now.

Karen pulled out the bar stools and told Amy to sit.

They had to come up with a solution to ensure the police caught Jay without her betrayal being discovered, or Amy being taken down with him. And to ensure Sophie didn't get into trouble for withholding evidence.

Karen sighed loudly.

Where did they start?

CHAPTER NINETY

DI Wade

'How are we doing? Sophie's phone signal bring up anything of interest?' Lindsay sidled up to where DS Mack was sitting and looked over his shoulder at the computer.

'Phone signal suggests she's at Stover Park, has been there for . . .' He glanced at his watch, 'the last fifteen minutes.'

'Meeting someone,' Lindsay said.

'Guess so. No live CCTV available though, so no way of knowing who, unless you want to take a car.'

'No, there's been nothing for the last week, probably nothing now. We'll swing by later, check their security tapes. Just keep an eye on her for now. Track her movements.' She straightened and walked to the whiteboard on the back wall of the incident room. Copies of the emails and the two pictures extracted from Sophie's mobile were pinned to the board, like an elephant in the room. They knew Sophie had failed to give them critical information. She'd clearly been afraid to tell them about the pictures, the fact that someone was sending her sexual images. Likely the man who'd killed Erin, although there wasn't anything to link the two at the moment, having still not found the primary scene. The emails themselves sounded as though they were from the killer, but could just be a hoax. It'd been impossible to tell the extent of Sophie's involvement, if any of her friends had connections to the killer, there was no solid evidence. They had to sit it out, watch and wait for someone to lead them to something concrete. Or to the killer himself.

Lindsay thought about Sophie's 'slip' of information when she and Mack had visited her at the college. She'd said 'That bastard stabbed her, strangled her.' Only no one outside of the investigation knew about the stabbing wounds. So how had Sophie known?

Their best shot at finding out was keeping her under surveillance, and they'd been doing that without raising her suspicion. Using a young girl for intel sat uncomfortably with Lindsay, particularly as Sophie had no idea of their intentions. But their observations of her movements hadn't yielded much. A meeting with Daniel Pearce, another meet-up at his house with the group from Saturday night, work, college. Nothing of importance.

Lindsay stared at one of the post-mortem pictures of Erin. It might not feel good, using Sophie in this way, but she could be a crucial part of the murder, a suspect even. She certainly knew more than she'd disclosed so far.

And sometimes the end justified the means.

CHAPTER NINETY-ONE

Karen

How could Karen judge Amy? Her own naïvety when it came to willingly divulging a shit-ton of information to Jay far outshone Amy's. And Amy was only nineteen. Not forty-seven, like her. Or a probation officer. *Bloody hell.* If she'd been so easily taken in by Jay's charm, Amy hadn't stood a chance. She couldn't be blamed. Would the police see it that way? She'd helped him, drugged a friend, aided a double kidnapping, withheld information. It didn't look good. Was the only reason he'd allowed her to leave so that, if it came to it, he could implicate her, blame Amy for everything?

Karen hadn't been able to protect Erin from the chain of events she herself had set in motion. She'd let her and Rachel down, was responsible for what had happened. But maybe she could rectify it, ensure no other lives were impacted because of her mistake. She could protect Sophie and Amy from the consequences of this. Protect each of their secrets.

'What do you want to do about this, Amy?'

'I'll have to tell the police, won't I?' Her voice flat, tears continuing their descent in a constant stream. 'It's my fault Erin's dead. They'll put me away, I'll go to prison for the rest of my life. Won't I? I'm as bad as him, everyone will hate me, and I'll be like that woman who knew her boyfriend killed those young girls, helped him hide it. Shit. *Shit*—'

'Calm down, Amy, come on, don't panic, shh . . .' She put her hand over Amy's. Her heart ached. All this pain and fear because of something she'd started seventeen years ago.

Karen played with the handle of the knife – the one she'd left on the breakfast bar after finding Bailey. The poor dog was still lying lifeless in the bath – how was she going to deal with him? His glassy, dead eyes flashed into her mind. She gripped the handle and turned it over. The sun caught the blade, sending a line of white light across the wall.

'No, Amy. I don't think you should go to the police. Maybe they'll never have to know you had a part in this.'

'*He'll* tell them. If they don't know already.'

'Let's think about it. The only evidence of your involvement is the fact you drugged Sophie, yes?'

'I guess. There's no CCTV, I know that much.'

'What about texts, emails?'

'Well, yeah, there are plenty of threads; none mentioning his plan though. Any specific discussion took place when we met up. I think.'

'Right. In that case, you probably can't be linked to the actual crime—'

'I used the Rohypnol in Erin's drink too.' A resignation in her voice.

'Okay. Well, the drug you gave would've left the bloodstream quickly; it wouldn't have shown in the post-mortem, I'm sure. That's why rapists use it. Nothing links you to the kidnap, or the murder.' Karen saw Amy visibly shudder at her words.

'But, Karen, didn't you hear me?' She jiggled up and down on the stool, waving her hands. '*He* is going to tell the police. If he gets caught, he'll take me down too. He told me so yesterday.'

'So, we have to ensure he can't.' Karen's thoughts calmed, the knowledge of what she had to do quashing the panic. 'It's apparently me who started him off on this deranged path of revenge. It should be me who finishes it.'

'How? How can you stop him if you can't go outside the house?' Hysteria crept into Amy's voice. 'You can't do anything, the police will have to. Don't worry about me.'

'There is something I can do. I have to act, Amy, because I'm pretty sure he's going to use Sophie to get to me.'

'Let's wait for Sophie to get home. She'll be back any time, won't she?'

'I texted her and said to come straight home, so yes. And she knows you're coming here?'

'Yeah, said I could come over at four.'

'Fine. We'll tell her where we're up to. Perhaps between the three of us, we can come up with a plan that'll mean none of us get put out to dry.'

But Karen knew she only had one option.

CHAPTER NINETY-TWO

'If you texted Sophie saying to come straight home, shouldn't she be here by now?' Amy checked the time on her phone. 'It's four thirty, Karen.'

'I'll ring.'

Straight to voicemail.

Karen jumped up, paced the kitchen. Sophie would have her mobile on by now; college finished an hour ago. There was never an issue with signal once she was outside of the college building. Not like Mike being on the moors, out of contact most of the time. Could Sophie have gone to see her dad? She dialled Mike, knowing it to be a waste of time. Voicemail, as she'd anticipated. She hoped he was all right, that he *had* gone to work as usual.

'Let's not panic.' Amy's tone displayed exactly that.

Amy's mobile rang. Her breathing visibly shallowed, quickening as she looked at the display.

Karen put her hand to her mouth. 'What? What is it?'

'It's him, Karen. What do I do?' Amy held the phone as if it were a ticking bomb.

'Answer. You have to find out what he wants.'

Karen held her breath. *Please don't have her.*

She accepted the call. 'Yes?' Amy's face blanched. 'Yes, I'm with her.' She thrust the phone at Karen. 'He wants you.'

A sharp pain hit Karen in the stomach. He had Sophie.

'If you want to save your precious daughter, I suggest you do as I tell you.'

Karen's surroundings melted away, a muteness swooped in, smothering her; all sounds other than his voice and her hammering heart ceased.

'Congratulations, Jay. Or Jonathan. Whatever your name is.'

'Thank you, Karen. I knew you'd be impressed. And it's Jason.'

She clenched her free hand and banged it repeatedly against her head. His voice, once the source of so many feelings of love and desire, now overwhelmed her with fear and repulsion. She listened as he instructed her to meet him at the old quarry off Bovey Heath. Alone. No police.

'If you contact the police, Karen, it's game over. I will kill her instantly.'

'I . . . I can't. I can't do it.'

'Yeah. Sophie said you had some pathetic *debilitating* condition. Get over it, Karen. You have to come here. To me.'

She couldn't drive herself. She'd never make it, she'd let Sophie down spectacularly. She'd have to get Amy to take her. She hesitated, couldn't speak to him, but a sudden plan was formulating in her head. He wanted her. Would he do anything to get her there?

'No, Jay. Not happening.' The words came out firmer, more steady than she felt.

'*What?* What did you just say?' Anger, shock.

Karen's hands shook. 'If you want me to come to you, I'll be the one to tell you where.'

Laughter erupted on the end of the line. 'I don't think you're in any position to give me instructions. I will kill her, you know that, don't you? I'll strangle the life from her, as I did that stupid friend of hers.'

358

Karen leant against the sink, staring out of the window at the darkening moors.

'I'm in the perfect position. I'll get back to you, Jay. *I'll* tell you where you need to be *with* Sophie. Wait by the phone.'

She hung up.

'What are you doing?' Amy flew at her with her hands raised. 'He'll kill her.'

Karen grabbed them, pulled Amy towards her and hugged her tightly.

'It'll be okay. He won't hurt her, yet.' She prayed she wasn't making a terrible mistake. 'Right, come on.' Karen pulled away and started towards the dining room and her laptop. 'We're going to arrange to meet him in an area as remote as possible on Dartmoor. You're driving, Amy.'

Her sudden confidence seemed to buoy Amy.

'Okay. Okay. So, what's your plan?'

CHAPTER NINETY-THREE

DI Wade

'Who's nearby? Send a squad car to Stover, will you? She's been there for over an hour,' Lindsay shouted above the buzz of the incident room.

'On it, Guv.'

They'd been working on a lead, Sophie's movements having been left to the other inquiry team in the meantime. DI Wade had finally got a hit from the techies. They'd already located the source of the emails sent to Sophie, although that had taken some time. The sender had been using multiple proxies to mask himself and that, in addition to the fact he'd been logging on in a public place, had meant a lot of running around. But they'd done it. The IP address led to a coffee shop in Torquay.

Now, they'd gone one better. Using the times the emails had been sent, matched with the footage from the cameras outside on the street, they'd come up with a couple of likely suspects. They'd immediately whittled it down, and with the E-FIT from the woman who'd reported a stalker following a female in Coleton – bingo. With some good detective work, they'd found him. And they'd been given an address.

Some digging had revealed a number of interesting facts. The last person registered on the electoral roll as living at that address was Andrew Watkins, now deceased. A small-time criminal, whose son, Jason, had been seventeen when Andrew was sent down for aggravated burglary. Three years later Andrew Watkins, out on bail, broke his conditions, and was recalled to prison. He later committed suicide.

And the person who recalled him was none other than Karen Finch. Sophie's mother, who, it turned out, herself had been the victim of an attack two years previously, at the hands of the Carey Park rapist. She'd been the lucky one.

'I want a team at Andrew Watkins' address. Now! See if Jason's still living at the flat there.'

'Guv.' The wary tone of DC Sewell found her ears. 'They've checked Sophie's last known location.'

Last known location? Didn't sound good. 'And?'

'No sign. Of her or her car.'

'How did we miss her leaving?' Lindsay strode to the table.

'They did find an iPhone at the scene,' DC Sewell offered.

'Bollocks. Right, let's get into the CCTV stream along that road. Find her.'

The room erupted into another frenzy of activity. A few minutes later, a shout.

'Got her vehicle, being driven along Bovey Straights half an hour ago, Guv.'

'Bovey Straights. Could be heading for Dartmoor. Going to see her dad? Someone get him on the line, see if she's with him. Okay, people, let's get a unit to the Watkins' place. And then we'll pay Karen Finch a little visit.'

CHAPTER NINETY-FOUR

Karen

She'd been breathing in and out of the bag for a good ten minutes.

'Come on, Karen, you'll be fine. We have to go.' Amy pulled at her arm, encouraging her towards the porch door.

'Wait.' The anxiety of getting out of the house coupled with the knowledge that a murderer had her daughter weren't exactly sympathetic to her condition.

'I'm assuming time isn't on our side here.'

'No. Right.' Karen put her head down, shut her eyes and felt her way out of the front door. 'Where's your car?'

'Along a bit. You might want to open your eyes.'

Karen didn't care for the condescending tone. Amy had no idea how difficult this was.

'You do have to navigate, you know that. You've chosen the location, you need to tell me where I'm going. That means looking, Karen.'

'Okay . . . okay. Don't lose it with me . . . it doesn't help.'

Karen locked her door once safely inside the vehicle. She put the torch and map down in the footwell. 'I'll look when we get closer. Just drive towards Bovey.'

Amy put the radio on. The banging bass filled the car. It felt appropriate, matched Karen's banging heart rate.

'I'm sorry . . . I've dragged you . . . into this, Amy.' Karen breathed in and out the paper bag. She'd need a new one after today.

'I didn't need much dragging. It's me who got involved with him.'

'He sought you out. Because of me. You didn't stand a chance.'

'Great to know I'm so gullible.'

'How do you think *I* feel?' She dropped the bag into her lap. 'A middle-aged woman falling for a man ten years younger . . . thinking he felt real feelings for me. I'm the gullible one.'

'He does love you though, Karen. He's doing this as some warped way of getting together with you. He wants you, despite also wanting to get his revenge. In his mind it all makes sense. It's obvious to me *now*; the way he acted when he spoke about you – he'd get all wound up one minute when he was talking about the past, and his dad, and then when he spoke about the future, and you, he always smiled. Looked happy.'

Karen grimaced. 'Funnily enough, that's of no comfort.'

They drove away in silence, only the music keeping her thoughts company. Dark thoughts. How were her dreams going to be once this was over?

How would it end?

Karen reached inside her bag and felt the coolness of the blade. Surely once Jay saw her, realised she'd come to him, he would let Sophie go. She was swapping herself for Sophie. He wanted her. The nagging feeling returned. *A score requires settling . . . We have to be on a level footing, you and I. For our future to work.* His words clear. Unambiguous.

They meant one thing. He was going to kill Sophie.

She couldn't allow it to happen. The knife gave only a little reassurance. She'd have to get close enough first. Put Sophie in danger, force his hand?

Maybe this wasn't such a good idea, thinking she could take him on alone. He'd said no police though. So she had no choice. She had to do it quickly. Do it right.

She had no qualms about killing him before he could harm Sophie. It was the right thing to do, it would sort this entire mess out. No way could he implicate Sophie or Amy, no way her stupidity would become known.

If she killed him.

Her hands shook. The fallout of her actions – recalling Drew, seeking out an affair, her infidelities – had impacted on her and everyone she loved.

If she carried out this plan, she'd be a murderer.

Could she live with *those* repercussions? Could her family?

'We're at the edge of Bovey. Which way, Karen?'

'Keep to this road, then take the second exit. Then we'll be on the road to Dartmoor.' Her mouth dried. 'Are you okay with this?'

Amy took her eyes off the road briefly and gave Karen a nod. She said nothing.

'When we get there, drive to the edge of the wood we found on the map. I'll walk from there, you stay in the car. Wait. Do not follow me, you get that?'

'Yes.' Her voice was only just audible above the radio.

Karen leant forward, switched it off. 'You don't mind, do you? I feel we need quiet.'

Amy inhaled deeply; Karen watched her knuckles whiten as she gripped the steering wheel tighter.

They'd reached the edge of the moor.

CHAPTER NINETY-FIVE

Sophie

Why had her mother told him to come here? A forest on the moor? Was she mental? Maybe it was to give Sophie an opportunity to make a run for it, to hide in the wood until it was safe. How was her mum getting here herself? The light was already fading; the deeper they went, the darker it'd get, any light being blocked by the tall trees. The usual stunning scenery of the moors, a place she loved to come to, now felt eerie, menacing – the trees moved in, enveloping her. Suffocating her.

He pulled at her arm, dragging her on; she stumbled over the uneven ground. Cried out.

'Shut up. Keep moving.'

His anger had been on the increase since the call from her mother back at the quarry. His contorted face, his shouts filling the empty room, his pacing, had all added to her own terror. He'd killed Erin. Surely she was next?

Now he moved quickly, too fast for her to keep up, her feet two paces behind her body. She wasn't tied. She'd watched as he filled a backpack with what he needed to restrain her when they reached the destination. A wave of nausea rippled through her. She'd not eaten, but suspected the sickness was due to fear, rather than hunger.

This couldn't end well.

CHAPTER NINETY-SIX

DI Wade

Michael Finch's Land Rover blocked the driveway, as if he'd driven madly and abandoned it in a rush. Lindsay shifted past it, Mack following close behind.

'Mr Finch, Detective Inspector Wade, Detective Sergeant Mack.' She flashed her badge as he answered the door. 'Can we come in?' She didn't wait for a response either way, stepping inside the porch as he stumbled back.

Michael Finch didn't look well. His bloodshot eyes were puffy, as though he'd been crying. His face was blotchy.

'Have we caught you at a bad time?'

'Not the best, it would seem.' He ushered them into the lounge. His manner was cold, off. He was cagey.

'We need to speak to you about Sophie, Mr Finch.'

He finally lifted his eyes to meet hers. 'Oh. Why?'

'Where's your wife?' Lindsay carried on, ignoring his question, and cast her eyes around the lounge, craning her neck to take in the dining area.

'I don't know. She wasn't here when I got home.' He slumped down on a sofa. 'It's not like her. She's agoraphobic, it takes a lot to make her leave this house. And I mean a lot.' His worry was evident.

'Can you think of a reason why Karen would head to the moors?' Lindsay wanted to test the waters, see how much he knew. His face, a blank, indicated that he knew little.

'Karen? No, and – I don't understand. What's happened?'

'Michael, your wife had contact with an Andrew Watkins, supervised him when she worked as a probation officer.'

'Right . . . and?'

'We've come from his residence. He's deceased, but his son, Jason Watkins, still resides there. Is that a name you recognise?'

'No. Doesn't mean anything to me.'

Lindsay observed his expression; he didn't appear to be lying. She carried on.

'He's a freelance web developer. Could you have used his services in the past, for the Dartmoor website perhaps?'

'Not that I'm aware, but I don't really have much to do with that side of the Trust.'

'On the premises, we seized a computer and photographs, all methodically placed and categorised, a bit OCD in fact.' She watched for any kind of reaction. He gave nothing. 'Photographs of Sophie. And Karen. It seems he's been watching them both for some time.' Now a look of shock.

'What kind of photos?' His face reddened as he shot up from the sofa. 'Why? How did he have them, from where?'

'Calm down, Michael,' Mack cut in, taking a step back. 'They're questions we want answers to as well. Currently though, we need to concentrate on finding Sophie and Karen. As you work on the moors, we were hoping you might be able to help.'

'Of course.' He turned abruptly, grabbed his ranger's jacket, and made for the door. He stopped. 'How do you know Sophie was going on to the moor?'

'CCTV picked her car up travelling along Bovey Straights,' Mack informed him, 'There's a team at a disused quarry along from there. They found a young man, Daniel Pearce, Sophie's friend, tied and gagged.'

'What the . . . are you serious?'

Mack looked to Lindsay, widening his eyes. He obviously wanted her to tell Michael the next part. Perhaps he felt she'd sound calmer, more sensitive.

'Daniel heard Jason bringing Sophie into the building.' She paused, allowing this to sink in. 'And then he heard a conversation take place. Between Jason and a female. We believe it to have been Karen. She agreed to meet Jason, told him to meet her on the moor. Daniel couldn't hear the exact location. Now, we've got teams out searching, and a helicopter, but no sightings as yet.' She stopped, Michael's pacing was too distracting. 'Mr Finch. Michael?'

'Yes, sorry, can't believe this, it's not happening.'

'We thought you might be able to give us a clearer picture of the moors, a starting point.'

'It's three hundred and sixty-eight square miles, Detective Inspector Wade.' His eyes – intense, frightened – bore into hers.

'Quite. It's vast. We could do with your help.'

Lindsay didn't need to say any more. Michael Finch was already out the door, heading for his Land Rover.

'You should come with us, Michael.' Mack called after him.

'No. My vehicle has everything I might need,' he shouted as he slammed the car door and started the engine.

Before either Lindsay or Mack could protest any further, the Land Rover screeched away from the driveway and sped off.

'Let's get a move on then, eh, Mack?' Lindsay ran to their car and jumped in the driver's side, Mack trailing.

'Guess you're driving then.' Mack said as he climbed in and clicked his seatbelt.

'I'm faster. We're going to need to keep up. I don't want to lose him on the moors too.'

CHAPTER NINETY-SEVEN

Karen

Karen stood by the car, hunched, both hands on the bonnet, her fingers tingling from the cold.

What am I doing, what am I doing?

The cover of trees should ensure no one could spot the car easily, and they'd driven as far off the track as possible. The branches cast a shadow on the windscreen; she couldn't make out Amy's face. Probably as well, her fear wouldn't be helpful.

Her legs refused to move, every muscle paralysed.

He'd be there. Waiting. She had to go.

All the things she should've done, the things she shouldn't – all swirled and mixed in her head. No room for regret now.

One foot in front of the other.

She hoped, having been here before, that the familiarity would offer some reduction in her anxiety level, bring it down to something possible to manage. It'd been such a long time, though; Mike had brought her here about four years ago, their anniversary. An attempt on both sides to inject some interest, try to remember the people they'd each fallen in love with.

Now, as she moved forwards, the guilt oozed from every pore of her body. She may have stopped the online contact with Jay in an effort to make things better with Mike, but she hadn't tried hard enough. Had given up. It was difficult, keeping their relationship alive, when all she did all day was cocoon herself. She had nothing to say to him. Their only topic of conversation was Sophie.

Karen stopped and lifted the mobile phone to her face. It was 17.30. There wasn't even a single bar of signal showing.

Mike might be home now. A pain gripped her, making her stop. Bailey. Mike returning home to find him dead, her missing. He'd be frantic. She hadn't considered leaving a note. He'd have no clue to her whereabouts. Her plan rested on her having the strength, the ability to kill Jay, get Sophie back to the car and Amy, and get home. The only people who knew their location were her and Amy. No one else would come and save them if it all went horribly wrong.

Suddenly she felt appallingly rash. Alone . . . small . . . and very stupid.

Too late to back out. She saw the bridge. Two figures to the side.

She pulled her coat tighter around her. The chill still found a way to penetrate it, finding some skin to bite. Her teeth clattered – because of the cold, or fear, she didn't know. Her legs continued to move her onwards, closer to her goal. All she wanted was for Sophie to be safe.

As she approached them, Karen could see Sophie more clearly. He was holding on to her, but she didn't look to be tied, as she'd expected. That was good. She was pale; a scared young girl, tiny against the backdrop of tall trees. Her little girl. A cramping pain gripped Karen's abdomen. She managed to give Sophie what she hoped was a confident smile. As for the man standing next to her, she felt nothing. After the months of closeness, intimate conversation, apparently exploring each other's souls, the desire and longing, she'd expected to *feel* something. But the figure in front of her was almost the opposite of the man she knew – slight, different colouring. He'd been a lie. This man was not the one she'd fallen in love with.

374

He was the man who had her daughter, who had threatened her.

The man she'd kill to make things right.

But was she any better than him? Wasn't that what he thought he was doing too?

'I knew you'd come, my Karen.' His smile, wide, smug.

His voice cut through her; she sucked in cold air between her teeth. 'You need to let Sophie go.'

The laugh burst from his mouth; it got trapped in the high branches, filtered through the trees, a malevolent echo. Her eyes shut tight.

Don't look at him. Keep breathing. Block out the sounds.

'No. Karen. I don't need to let her go. *You do.*' He had hold of Sophie's arm. As she squirmed, Karen made out bruised flesh. He was hurting her. She had to get closer.

'That's far enough. Stay there.' He pointed with his spare hand, indicating she should sit on the boulder.

She tried to keep her voice steady. 'Look, Jay. I know you hold me responsible for your dad's death, but you can't justify taking another's life because you blame me.'

'Oh, but I can . . .' He fiddled inside his jacket. 'See?'

Karen squinted; the light was fading rapidly, but the razor was unmistakable. A sliver of light snaked through the trees, reflecting off the tiny weapon – small, yet capable of taking Sophie's life with one smooth movement.

'Stay still!' he shouted.

Karen saw Sophie flinch as Jay tightened his grip around her middle. Her face ashen, her make-up ruined by tears. He stood behind her now, still a fair distance from Karen's reach.

'Don't fight it, it'll be quicker for you if you don't fight, Sophie.' He moved his hand around and held the razor to her throat. 'You need to go the same way as my dad, with the razor slicing through your windpipe, you gurgling and drowning in your own blood. Like he did.'

The sudden realisation hit her. She wasn't going to be able to stop him.

'Jay. No.' She jumped up, flinging herself forward. 'You want me, don't you? You want us to have a future? It won't happen if you hurt Sophie. I don't want you if you kill her. I'll hate you forever.' All the words flew out. She wasn't sure if they'd made any sense, but she was grasping desperately at any hope she might stall him.

Stall him, why? No one is coming.

'Stay back.' He took the razor away from Sophie and slashed it in the air towards Karen. 'Don't come any closer, Karen. Come on, don't ruin my moment.' He replaced his hand on her throat. 'It's me and you, Karen. All the way. You *will* want me, you may not think that now, but you will in time. I'll be all you have in the world, you'll need me as much as I need you.'

Her patience disappeared. 'You're delusional, Jay. I am not going to want you, or need you. Ever. You're wasting your time.'

'We'll see.'

Sophie's face darkened, like a veil had been pulled down over her. Her body shook, her eyes were pleading. Did she think Karen was going to screw up, get her killed?

Karen had to do something. Now.

She kept her eyes on him as she slid the knife from her bag.

He laughed. 'You can't use that on me.'

'No, you're right. I'll never be quick enough; you'll slit her throat before I've even taken a step.' Her voice lost its power. She wasn't getting Sophie out of this situation by killing Jay. She'd been full of bravado, thought she could take him on. Naïve, again.

There was only one way to save Sophie, to give her a chance to run, get away. He wanted to kill Sophie in a vain attempt to even the score, ensure they had a lasting bond because of the death of their loved ones. He wanted her.

She had to take herself out of the equation.

'Sophie.' She looked at her beautiful daughter and smiled. Hot tears fell. 'You know I love you. I want you to be safe . . .' Karen turned the knife on herself; put the tip to her stomach. 'RUN!'

Jay dropped the razor. 'No! What are you doing?' He left Sophie's side and ran, arms outstretched, towards Karen. She pushed the knife in, feeling a stinging pain as her skin popped and punctured. A deep, snagging agony followed as the blade slid through her gut. 'Nononono . . . Karen! What have you done, you stupid woman?'

He stood in front of her, his eyes wide, his hands grabbing at his hair.

Karen sank to her knees, searing pain taking her breath away as she pulled the knife back out. She looked up to Jay. His face was contorted, his mouth open wide in a scream.

'It could never have ended the way you wanted it to, Jay.' A warm flow of blood pulsated from her stomach. Karen dropped the knife and pressed her hands against the wound.

'You've ruined everything,' he shouted, and lunged for Karen.

An explosion. Blood splattered over her face.

Jay flew backwards, fell. A thud. A crunching of leaves.

Someone was screaming.

The treetops lowered, coming closer to her. Were they falling?

No, they weren't lowering to her, she was raising towards them. Weightless, floating.

A noise above her. Voices, disembodied, floated with her.

Mike.

Her body lifted. Pain burned. A warm, sticky mess covered her stomach.

'I've got you. I've got you.'

'Mike?' Her vision clouded. Her mouth, so dry. 'Sophie . . .'

'She's fine, Karen. So is Amy.'

'How did you . . . know where we were?'

'I didn't at first. But it's where we came together, it was as good a place to start as any.'

'I'm sorry.' The two words stretched out, distorted, like she was speaking in slow motion.

'I know. So am I.' He bent over her, kissed her forehead. Whispered in her ear. 'I know everything, Karen.'

The words seeped in. All this was for nothing. He knew anyway.

'How?' Her voice had lost its power; it was nothing more than a gentle sigh.

'Oh, Karen. I know you don't think I notice things. But I knew it wasn't right between us and I saw the change in you.' He brushed a tear from her cheek. 'I guessed your password, saw the messages from *him*.'

The disclosure made its way inside her dazed mind. So all the time he'd had his nose stuck in his iPad he was probably accessing her emails. None of that mattered now. Karen tried to lift her head. *Too heavy.*

'He's going . . .' *breathing difficult,* 'to tell the police . . . Sophie, and Amy, they're in trouble . . .' *Can't take a deep breath.*

'He's not telling anyone anything. Don't worry.'

'The noise . . . a shot? Police . . . killed him?' *Pain, can't breathe.*

'Not the police, no. They're just getting here now. I broke away from them at the last tor and got here first . . . I did it.'

'Oh, Mike . . . No.'

'I'm sorry for leaving you last night. I should've been with you.'

'Why . . . did you go?' *Are his arms around me? Can't feel him.*

'It all got too much, I thought I couldn't bear it. Knowing about you and him, that you would've left me if it hadn't been for your agoraphobia. I wanted out. I took my gun, was going to end it up here, on the moor. But I realised I could never leave Sophie. And no matter what, Karen, I wouldn't leave you.'

'My Mike. I'm so sorry. Now you will . . .' *Eyes heavy.*

'Karen, keep your eyes open.'

'. . . You will go . . . to prison.' *Head is so woozy.*

'Don't worry about me. Just you hold on, do you hear me?'

'Will the girls . . . Sophie, be okay?'

'I hope so. I wasn't allowing that scum to take my girls down with him. The secrets – everything – die with him.'

He's crying. Why's he crying?

'I don't . . . deserve you.' *Tired, need to sleep.*

'Stay with me, Karen. Open your eyes.'

'It's so cold.' *Toes so cold, numb, body is numb.*

Voices, many voices, rushing, shouting.

Oh, they're leaving now.

Silence.

I'm free . . .

CHAPTER NINETY-EIGHT

DI Wade

'You really couldn't have foreseen him having the gun. You can't beat yourself up over it.' Mack handed Lindsay a mug of steaming coffee.

'You reckon?' She took it, holding it in both hands, grateful for the warmth. Her body still hadn't recovered from the chill of the forest. 'It's not how this was meant to have ended, Mack. None of it.'

'No. Although we did catch the bad guy – the murdering bastard . . . well, technically Michael Finch did, but . . .'

'What a mess.' She rubbed a hand over her forehead. 'The bad guy might be dead, Mack, but at what cost to the Finches? I should have let you move in on Sophie Finch earlier – she should never have been taken like that. And I should've had an officer in Michael's vehicle with him. Him giving us the slip like that . . . He's going to go down for this.' Her mouth burned as she took too big a sip of coffee.

'I'm thinking he would've done it even if we'd been there, Boss. Really. You know what it's like, if someone is determined enough, they'll find a way.'

'I don't understand, though. Why?'

'I guess we'll find out, when he starts speaking.'

'If he does. Poor bloke is in shock . . .' Lindsay's voice trailed, her eyes drifting to look out the window. Not that she could see anything outside; her thoughts were the pictures against the blackness of the evening sky.

'Weird how it all came out at the last moment. All that running around we did, the suspicion, almost all of it misplaced.' Lindsay's attention returned to the room.

'I wouldn't say that. We followed the leads, that's all. And if certain people hadn't been holding information back, we might have saved some time. Maria Nickson was just afraid of ruining her new relationship as she'd recently escaped her abusive partner. We didn't have that information, or that she'd changed her name. Her behaviour fitted with someone with something to hide, and that's what we picked up on. If she'd told us the truth, we could've crossed her off our list.'

'I appreciate your use of "we", Mack, that's very gracious of you.'

'We were working together. It was *we.*'

Lindsay gave a weak smile.

'And Daniel Pearce?'

'Well, that was more me than you, Boss. I had him tagged as a strange one from the off, yet poor lad was merely an unwitting pawn in that psycho's poisonous game. Jason Watkins was a master manipulator, that's for sure.'

'Hmm. Yes.' Lindsay rubbed at her eyes.

'I'll leave you to it,' Mack said, 'I've got some paperwork to fill.' He put his hand on her shoulder, giving it a squeeze.

'Sure,' Lindsay placed her hand briefly on top of his. 'Yes, get cracking on it, Detective Sergeant Mack, I don't want you pulling another all-nighter. You look rough enough; some beauty sleep is long overdue.' She raised one eyebrow and smiled. 'Oh, and thanks, Mack. You did a great job on this case.'

Mack left, the door closing quietly behind him, leaving Lindsay alone.

She could've done more, she knew that. Questions would be asked as to how the outcome had been so devastating. They'd have to be faced. Erin Malone's parents would gain an element of closure. That had always been her goal, so that was the positive part.

But it was the negatives of this case that would stay with her for a long time.

Epilogue

The noise of the letterbox, a crashing against metal.

Loud. Like a gunshot.

She jumped, her hand flying to her chest.

Breathe in . . . and out. In . . . and out.

She crept to the window, pulling the edge of the curtain back an inch to peek outside. She blinked, the bright light stinging her eyes.

He was there again. The third time this week.

How long would he stay this time?

Had she locked all the doors, windows?

Get the bag, must get the bag.

She sat on the floor, her back against the sofa. She'd wait it out. She wasn't letting him in. He'd leave. He always did. Eventually.

The darkness of the room settled her. The shaking subsided. She was okay.

Alone. How she liked it.

Her mum had been right. You could only be safe indoors.

Leaving the house would kill you.

Acknowledgements

Huge thanks to my agent, Anne Williams, for seeing my potential and giving her expertise and guidance in shaping this novel and finding it a home. That home is with the wonderful team at Avon, who have all been so enthusiastic and delightful to work with. My special thanks to Natasha for championing it and for her insightful editing, and Ellie, whose hard work and passion – not to mention patience – has helped make this book one to be proud of.

I'd like to thank my friends, Tracey and Tara, whose belief I could do this made me believe too. Thanks also to my book club girls and early readers (too many to mention, but you know who you are) and my online writing group, Writers United – your critique and feedback was invaluable. Special thanks to Lydia Devadason and Libby Carpenter – you've both read this so many times now that you know it better than me. It's been one hell of a journey, and one I wouldn't have wanted to go on without you both. Your friendship has come to mean so very much to me. The writing community is amazing and I've been lucky enough to gain support and encouragement from a lot of authors. In particular, I want to extend my gratitude to Jane Isaac and Elizabeth Haynes.

I couldn't have done any of this without my family's support – I didn't make it easy. Danika – without you there'd have been no beginning; Louis – without your nagging voice forcing me to be brave, there'd have been no ending; Nathaniel – without your genuine interest in my writing and its progression there'd have been no middle; Doug – without your constant support I wouldn't have been able to write in the first place. I thank you all for your patience, for accepting that I'm not listening, for your forgiveness when I forget to pick you up – and for loving me regardless. And I want to thank my sister, Celia. It's been an incredibly tough few years. I couldn't have made it through without your love and support.

If you enjoyed *Saving Sophie*, turn the page to find out more about Sam Carrington and her writing in an author Q&A

Author Q&A

What was your inspiration for Saving Sophie?

The start of the novel was inspired by a real-life, personal incident. At the time, my thoughts and emotions were all over the place and although my experience ended well, I couldn't let go of the 'what if?' questions. It was these that I expanded on and the novel grew from there. As for the setting, I love living in Devon and I'm relatively close to the moors and the sea, so I wanted both of these to feature in the story.

What did you enjoy most about writing this novel?

I enjoyed developing the characters of Karen and Sophie. They became part of my life and I'd think about them even when I wasn't writing about them. It also brought my relationship with my own daughter into sharper focus and sparked a lot of interesting discussions!

What advice do you have for aspiring authors?

There's so much advice readily available for writers! I spent a lot of time online searching for tips and 'How To' books, and I attended some workshops which were really useful. Social media is also an amazing source of support that I would advise writers to tap in to, because writing can feel a lonely process at times, particularly when you're first starting out.

Joining a writing group can also be beneficial, as gaining feedback is invaluable. I would say, however, that you might receive a lot of differing advice, so in the end it's about learning what will work for you and what won't – I think there's an element of trial and error here!

One major piece of advice is DO NOT rush to submit your work to agents. It's so exciting to have finished a novel, so much so that it can be hard to hold back! But agents receive so many submission packages you don't want to give them an easy reason to reject yours. Make sure you read the individual agent's requirements, have a strong covering letter, a succinct synopsis to the length they ask, and make sure your opening chapters are polished, polished, polished! I DID send my work too early and received a number of rejections quite quickly. Then I was lucky enough to have my work edited by a newly qualified editor and afterwards I began getting requests for my full manuscript.

I'm also a big advocate of entering competitions. I entered my opening chapters of *Saving Sophie* (then titled *Portrayal*) in to the CWA Debut Dagger award and was longlisted. It was an amazing feeling to have my work recognised. Being placed in a competition validates you as a writer and gives a huge boost to your confidence. Even though my agent was already interested in my writing, I believe that being able to tell her I'd been longlisted was a factor in her decision to sign me.

Oh, and learn the art of patience – you'll need a lot of it (although I've yet to master this myself!).

Where do you write your novels?

I do change my writing area and I'm not sure I've found the perfect spot yet! I first started writing at my breakfast bar with a view to the moors, then due to a need for more space, I moved to the dining-room table. But my notes and books and general clutter became too much to move each time the family wanted to eat, so I now have my son's hand-me-down computer desk. This is currently in the lounge, mainly so I can also keep an eye on my border terriers! My dream is to eventually have a summer house that's all mine.

Can you describe a typical working day?

I try to get up between 6 and 7 a.m. and the first thing I need is coffee. Then I fire up the laptop and trawl through Facebook and Twitter while eating breakfast, replying to messages, tweeting and retweeting. I'm a bit of a sucker for social media and this is one area I need to curtail – it's easy to get stuck there and not start writing otherwise!

I'm an edit-as-you-go writer which means I don't always get a lot of words down. I might write a page then I'll go back over it. Sometimes I might even manage a whole chapter before reading back through it and tweaking. Although this makes writing a slower process, it does make editing quicker when the novel is complete.

I have a few coffee and snack breaks and I'll also stop writing around 2pm to take the dogs for a walk. Often my eldest son walks with me and we'll have some great discussions about what I'm writing and we brainstorm ideas and he helps me iron out plot problems.

I'll either carry on writing when home, or do other writing-related things, like blog posts or research. I don't tend to write in the evenings unless I'm nearing a deadline. Likewise, I don't generally write at the weekends, spending time with the family instead. So, I'm afraid I don't take heed of the 'write every day' advice!

Can you tell us a bit about your next novel?

My next novel focuses on forensic psychologist, Connie Summers. After she recommends a prisoner's release, he commits a serious offence which Connie feels responsible for, so she trades her role working with offenders for running her own counselling consultancy helping the victims of crime. One of her newest clients is Steph, a troubled young woman relocated by the Protected Persons Service, who is fearful for her and her son's life. When Connie begins to unpick these fears, she uncovers the tragic circumstances that led to the death of Steph's dad sixteen years ago. Meanwhile, DI Wade and DS Mack pay Connie a visit to tell her that an absconded prisoner has been murdered and his body dumped outside the prison gates. Initially, Connie thinks they are asking for her expert opinion and help in profiling the perpetrator. But then they tell her who the victim is, and that her name is written on the dead man's hand. Suddenly the past catches up, threatening to reveal Steph's true identity and ruin Connie's new career – possibly even her life.